A CALL TO ARMS

By the same author

Fred Archer: His Life and Times
Neck or Nothing: the Extraordinary Life and Times of
   Bob Sievier
The Cheltenham Gold Cup
The Sporting Empress: the Love Story of Elizabeth of
   Austria and Bay Middleton
Infamous Occasions: Racing Scandals down the Ages
The Sporting World of R. S. Surtees

Novels
Run for Cover
Stop at Nothing
Go for Broke
Grand National
Bellary Bay

A CALL TO ARMS

John Welcome

Hamish Hamilton
London

First published in Great Britain 1985
by Hamish Hamilton Ltd
Garden House 57–59 Long Acre London WC2E 9JZ

British Library Cataloguing in Publication Data
Welcome, John
    A call to arms.
    I. Title
    823'.914[F]   PR6073.E373

    ISBN 0–241–11435–7

Phototypeset by Input Typesetting Ltd, London
Printed in Great Britain by Edmundsbury Press
Bury St Edmunds

'Women and horses were born to make fools of men'
Old saying

AUTHOR'S NOTE

I wish to express my sincerest thanks to all my friends in Kenya for their help and hospitality while I was writing this book, but most especially to the late, great Syd Downey for his generous assistance unstintingly given, despite ill-health, with the chapters concerning Stephen Raymond's life and experiences as a white hunter in the bush and elsewhere.

J.W.

Part 1

KIT 1

CHAPTER I

As they landed over the second last bank in the County Kilderry Hunt Cup the two horses were so close together they almost touched. Stride for stride they raced for the final fence. It was a big, broad, double bank with a ditch on either side which had been left in its natural condition save that the growth on its top had been roughly cut and trimmed. Even when hunting it was a tough enough obstacle to face. Coming into it at racing pace it was little short of fearsome.

'Take a pull, Kit, for Christ's sake or we'll both break our necks,' the taller of the two riders called across.

'Go home and powder your nose!' was the shouted reply.

The first speaker had prudently steadied his horse for the jump. The other, laughing, kicked joyously into it. His mount met it just right and launched himself out into the far field without the semblance of a mistake. Having got first run he galloped strongly on to win by three lengths.

Kit Massiter was still laughing as he stripped the saddle from the winner. His brother, Hugo, his lips taut, slid to the ground in the second stall beside him. 'You bloody lunatic, you could have killed us both,' he said.

'I won, didn't I?' answered Kit. Still laughing he clapped his horse on the neck and walked into the tent, his saddle over his arm.

Two men who had watched the race from amongst the cars on the hill made their way down to the roped-off paddock. It was the older of the two who spoke. 'You know, Bob,' he said, 'three fences out Hugo's horse was galloping all over the other. You'd have said he couldn't be beat.' The man

9

walked with a slight limp, for he had left a leg in France in the War and, once a prominent Gentleman Rider, rode races no more.

Big Bob Ferris, the trainer, paused for a moment to watch the antics of a three-card man who had just relieved a baffled countryman of a ten shilling note and was persuading him to try his luck with another. 'You know what it is, Mr Murtagh, sir,' he said as they walked on. 'An' you know it better 'an I do. In racing it's the fire in the belly that counts.'

They had reached the tent by now and met Kit as he was leaving it.

'Well done, boy,' Desmond Murtagh said to him. 'Have you got your permit to ride under Rules yet?'

'Yes, sir, it came yesterday.'

'I've one in an amateur hurdle at Mallow in ten days time. You'd better ride him for me.'

'Gosh, sir, I'd love to – '

'Very well, come over and ride a school on him. I'll be in touch.'

Desmond Murtagh turned away to speak to a friend but Bob's eyes followed the boy as he walked away. 'The maker's name is on the blade,' he murmured almost to himself.

'What's that, Bob? I didn't quite catch it,' Desmond said, turning back to him.

'Nothing, sir, nothing,' Bob said hastily. 'Just thinking out loud. Silly thing to do. Getting old, I suppose, sir. Here's Lady Massiter now.' And just as well he *didn't* hear it, Bob thought to himself, though I wonder if he guesses, or if any of the gentry do and it's only the country people who know?

'Well, Babs,' Desmond said, greeting his daughter. 'That was very nice, wasn't it? Made sure of keeping it in the family. Is Andrew back?'

'No. He's due for dinner this evening. He'll be pleased. He always likes a winner. You're coming over later on, Bob, aren't you? I think he wants to go through the entries with you.'

'Yes, m'Lady, I'll be along after dinner. Pity it is the business that kept him in London and he missed this – '

'Well, you tell him about it, Bob, and how well Master Kit rode.'

Desmond laughed. 'Into the last as if it wasn't there,' he said.

'They're always talking about it,' Bob said slowly. 'But how few of them can do it?'

'I wish, though, he wasn't quite so reckless,' Babs put in. 'Look what he's like out hunting, and riding those awful screws anyone offers him – '

'Well, perhaps Bob will help to put some discretion into his dash – but not too much, eh, Bob,' her father said. And then, seeing Kit approaching them again, 'Well, young feller, what now?'

'Mr Russell has asked me to ride one of his in the next,' Kit said.

'Jimmy Russell,' Babs said in dismay as her son disappeared into the tent. 'Those brutes of his, they're half-broken and half-schooled, if that, and fed on turnips. Oh, dear – '

'Never mind,' her father said cheerfully. 'He's got to take the bad 'uns as well as the good 'uns if he's going to get on. Besides, when you're that age you've three spare necks in your pocket. By God,' he added inconsequentially, 'how I wish I were twenty years younger – '

Some hours later Babs Massiter sat facing her husband at the end of the long table in the dining room of Dunlay Castle. On either side of her were her two sons, Kit and Hugo, eighteen and seventeen respectively, one born within a year of the other, grown men now, and Kit, she realised with a little pang of horror, already eligible for military service with Hugo only a little way from it – if this terrible new war they were all forecasting was indeed about to burst upon them.

The boys had done them proud that afternoon – first and second in the Hunt Cup. Even Andrew had been pleased. He had opened champagne before dinner and filled the cup, and now the boys had been permitted to stay on for a second glass of port. But he might have been better pleased, she thought, if it had been Hugo who had won, not Kit.

In the flickering light of the candelabra that stood at intervals down the dark mahogany she looked again at her husband. The trim imperial was now tinged with grey but otherwise he had changed very little in the years she had known him and lived with him. She had married him at the end of the War, during the Allies' last push. It was when Stephen Raymond had been posted as missing from the RFC, when no news had come through those long sad weeks, and she, along with everyone else in the Bay, had come to believe he was dead.

Stephen had come back – back from the dead as she always thought of it – but too late to save her from this disastrous marriage, entered into when she hardly cared whether she lived or not, when she had seemed to be existing in a protracted nightmare of grief.

Her mind went back again over the years to that terrible time of the Troubles and Stephen's return to the family home, Bellary Court, which was now a burnt-out, blackened ruin with ivy climbing over its crumbling walls. She had never discovered if Andrew had had a hand in that burning, carried out, as was now believed, not by the boys on the run or the Flying Column or whatever they were but by the hated Auxiliaries, the officer *corps d'élite*, so-called, of the Black and Tans. If Andrew had had a hand in it his secret had been well kept. He had never once spoken of the burning to her nor, so far as she knew, to anyone else. That in itself was in some way suspicious, as if he were avoiding the matter, but then, even now, nearly twenty years later, people were still chary of openly discussing the events of those blood-stained years.

She had hated her husband then, hated him with a ferocity and intensity she scarcely knew she possessed. And yet, when what they were now calling the Anglo-Irish War or the War of Independence had passed into the Civil War, which was fought with a savagery far surpassing anything when the British were the enemy, she had come almost to admire him.

At a time when their friends were quitting the country left and right he had steadfastly refused to go. He had once told her, in a veiled threat when he had found that Stephen was still alive, that what he had he held. What was true of herself was also true of his other possessions, and of these Dunlay Castle, for which he had schemed, worked and, yes, swindled for, was the most precious. It was a symbol of his success and his establishment of himself as a personage.

12

As such he had determined to preserve it intact and, somehow he had done so. Having lived in the Bay for a mere ten years before the Troubles began he still ranked as a stranger, and he had not been a sympathetic landlord to the few tenants left him after the operation of the Land Acts, so the chances of his preserving his house and lands and even himself had at the outset appeared slim enough. Yet his nerve and his courage had seen him through. He had been shot at on his own avenue and again through his front door when, the servants having bolted, he had misguidedly gone to answer a call in the night. His cattle had been maimed and his workmen threatened. His horses, however, had been left alone. It was the horses and his sheer courage, she reckoned, which had saved him and his house and everyone in it. He had gone on racing his steeplechasers wherever he could and had played a leading part in keeping the hounds going.

Grig Gnowles, the then Master of the Kilderry Hounds, was another who had refused to leave. After his house had been burnt out he had taken up temporary quarters in the grooms' lodgings in his stableyard. Between him and Massiter a reluctant alliance had been formed with the object of saving the hunt. Because there was virtually no petrol, and motorcars had been either commandeered or immobilised, Andrew had hacked on to meets and back again, turned out always in full fig – top hat, white breeches and red coat, the hated colour of the oppressor, to all appearances oblivious of the threat of assassination which lurked behind every bank, outcrop of rock or hedgerow. Never once during that time had she seen him falter or shrink; his nerve remained unshaken to the end. So he had preserved his great house, earning the admiration of the few relics of the Ascendancy who had stuck it out like himself, and the right to go his own way granted by the men with the guns on either side.

Now, here he was, Sir Andrew Massiter, baronet, a pillar of society, a prominent owner of racehorses, Joint-Master of the Kilderry Foxhounds, and member of the Irish Turf Club and National Hunt Steeplechase Committee, the Governing Bodies of Irish racing. The baronetcy, she knew, had been a bitter disappointment. He had expected a peerage from Lloyd George for services rendered during the War and, after it, for

13

certain payments made. Instead he had been fobbed off by being made a mere baronet. 'Like any tin-pot Lord Mayor after a Royal visit,' she had once heard him exclaim in a rare moment of self-revelation. For herself she didn't care; she had her position in the Bay from her father and her family and wished for no more. She had never wanted a title nor bothered about it, such as it was when it come to her, and she despised the means by which it had been obtained.

Much of the reason for Andrew's having been granted only a baronetcy lay in his insistence in staying on in Ireland to preserve his house and his absence from the seat of power when payment and patronage were being made and granted. He had put his position in the Bay and his beloved Gothic monstrosity of a castle before everything else. From this sprang his determination to go on living in it, knowing as he did that, whatever chance residents had of preserving their houses when they were occupied, once empty they posed a threat to either side as a possible use for barracks or outpost and were an open invitation to arson. Her father, too, had stayed on untouched in his decrepit and decaying mansion, but then his roots went far deeper and stretched far farther back than Andrew's. Moreover she had a shrewd suspicion that her father had ridden with or against and gambled and dealt with several of the guerilla leaders, and that he knew them personally and in some inner recesses of his mind sympathised with at least some of their aims. Then, too, in their own way they liked him as a rogue and a sport, and his tenants had long since been bought out. All these things had helped to preserve what was left of his inheritance.

As she sipped her port her eyes went once more down the long table to her husband. He was lifting his glass to his lips and looking pensively at his eldest son, Christopher Murtagh Massiter, the heir to the baronetcy and to Dunlay Castle. Did he guess the truth about Kit's parentage? she asked herself for the thousandth time. If he did, never by a flicker of those strange tawny eyes of his did he betray that knowledge. Or was he, again she wondered as she had done over and over again, withholding it in the way he had, for use when he would judge it would hurt her most?

14

'Angels passing over, mum?' Kit said, noticing her silence and her abstracted look.

'I only hope they are angels,' his mother answered sombrely.

'Cheer up, mum,' Hugo said from the other side of the table. 'After all, we've something to celebrate, haven't we, even if Kit did do his best to break both our necks.'

'Don't be an ass, Hugo,' Kit said grinning.

'I've always heard,' Andrew pontificated from the head of the table, 'that riding into the last fence as if it wasn't there is all very well if you're full of running. In the deep or on a tired horse you should take a pull or you'll come down and lose the race. How were you going?' he said suddenly to Kit with a snap of his voice.

'We were both on the bit,' Kit answered. 'And that thing of Hugo's has the legs on me on the flat. I had to take a chance.'

'After all, that's what wins races,' Babs said.

'Sometimes it's what loses them,' her husband answered, looking from one to another of the boys. 'How did Westcott's horse run?' he asked.

Hugo laughed. 'It didn't,' he said. 'Or not as they wanted anyway. Third, beaten a distance by us both. He was making mistakes all the way round. He sent Dick Harbison down to ride it, too.'

'The dickens he did. The leading amateur. He must have fancied it then.'

'He did, or someone did,' Kit put in. 'They had a whopping bet on it.'

'And it wasn't Dick's money, he hasn't any left,' Hugo said. 'They say he wants the odds to fifty now before he gets up. Why were they allowed to run in the hunt race anyway?'

'They opened it this year. The committee said the entries were falling off. Any elected member of any hunt could run.'

'It must be pretty useful all the same,' Kit said. 'He's won two open races with it already somewhere up near Dublin. He just couldn't handle our banks. Dick said he never met one right.'

'Ridiculous bringing a Kildare horse down here,' Andrew pontificated again. 'There's nothing to jump in that country.

15

Shows how little he knows. He did it to try to wipe our eyes, of course. He's never forgotten his failure to get hold of the Lacken fishing and the fact that we didn't want him in the Bay. He won't be pleased when he finds my horses finished first and second. Ha!' Andrew took a satisfied sip at his port.

It was no secret that there was little love lost between Donal Westcott and Andrew Massiter. Both were self-made men, both possessed a driving ambition for position and power. Donal Westcott had made a fortune 'somewhere in the city', as the current phrase had it, and had returned to Ireland determined to leave his mark on a country he had left as a poor boy. The path to power as he conceived it lay in founding a stud and buying and racing horses on a grand scale. His racing empire extended to both flat and steeple-chasing. Cleverly chosen advisers had helped him, luck had favoured him and a couple of classic victories had soon come his way. These had led to his election to the governing bodies where his undoubted ability as an administrator had already secured him one term as a senior steward.

As was almost inevitable with two such characters, a personality clash with Andrew had followed, though no one knew its exact origin. Babs had once heard two members of the old régime discussing it outside the parade ring at Punchestown. Unaware of her presence one had said to the other, 'New money and newer money, they never mix,' and they both had laughed. There was something in that, she thought, for each would see in the other a threat to his own aspirations.

It was Westcott, as Andrew well knew, who had blocked his name from going forward to succeed him as a senior steward, so that when Westcott had tried to penetrate the fastnesses of the Bay by buying the Lacken fishing it was Andrew's money that had ousted him, for Andrew had stepped in and, with the concurrence of her father and the sporting members of the Bay, had bought it for himself. Now Westcott had clearly sent down his good point-to-point horse with the intention, as Andrew had said, of wiping their eyes and had had his own wiped instead. Two tricks to Andrew, Babs thought, reflecting as she did so that another thing which had not changed in her husband was his ability to

16

hate. It was not long since, she recalled, that he had returned from a combined business trip and safari in Kenya. At least that was what he said his Kenya visit had been, but she wondered if he had told the whole truth. When, long ago, he had said to her that what he had he held, he might have added that he never forgave and never forgot. And Stephen was in Kenya now.

She and Stephen had long since lost touch, but someone had brought back news of him, telling her he was a white hunter now and that they had seen him in the New Stanley looking bronzed and fit. Had Andrew's trip, she wondered, been inspired by that casual remark at a dinner table and had he been in some way able to threaten Stephen who seemed at last to have struggled to some sort of hard-won security? It was true that Andrew had business interests there, for at the height of the Troubles when it looked as if even he might be driven out, he had bought a farm at Molo and installed a manager to run it. But was that his only motive? Expense played no part with him when he was furthering his antagonisms. She looked again at him and saw that he was once more contemplating Kit, his eyes hooded now. She believed she had kept her secret well – but had she? A thin cold trickle of fear for things to come ran across her shoulders, and she shivered.

CHAPTER II

The boys were still arguing about the race as Babs' thoughts drifted on. She heard Hugo cough and put down his glass. He took a handkerchief from his sleeve and blew his nose.

'Cold coming on,' he said. 'Felt it all day. My throat's a bit sore, too. Early bed, I think.'

Babs concealed a smile. It was typical of Hugo to find some

way, even obliquely, of minimising or explaining his defeat. Like his father he thought everything out. Hugo's head was in charge of his heart and his eye was fixed firmly on the main chance. Even his last school report from Eton had said as much, indicating, in polite language, that he never missed anything that might lead to his own advancement. He, at least, had bred true to his sire. And there could be doubt about his parentage, for she could never forget the night he had been conceived.

At first during their marriage, despite the gap in their ages, Andrew had been an ardent and virile lover. Her responses had been mechanical, as part of what she had seen to be her duty, and she had tried to shut from her mind the ecstasies she had enjoyed with Stephen. Then, after the shootings at Bellary Court, its burning and birth of Kit some months later, she had asked for and been given her own bedroom. She had chosen one high up in the castle below and beside the tower, its tall mullioned windows commanding almost the whole majestic sweep of the Bay and its mountains. She had made it quite clear to Andrew that this was her own room, inviolate, into which her husband was not to enter unasked. Rather to her surprise he had agreed, which gave colour to her suspicion that somewhere deep down within him feelings of guilt were stirring for what had happened that night at Bellary Court. Or else, she told herself, her responses had proved too automatic and zombie-like to satisfy him. At any rate she had not asked for his presence and it had become her practice to retire early to bed after dinner to brood in summer over the shifting colours of sea and sky framed in the windows and in winter to read herself to sleep with a book. It seemed to her that she had carried her point and that her husband had acquiesced in the arrangement. It did not last long. She had, for once, sadly misjudged her man.

One evening when the colours had faded into dusk and she was reading by the light of a bedside lamp, the door of her room had been flung open. Andrew stood for a moment framed in the doorway. He was wearing a silk dressing gown, slashed and brocaded. He entered the room and pushed the door to behind him. Even now she could remember the click of the latch as it closed.

18

Their eyes met and they had stared at each other in silence for a moment. Then he crossed the room towards her, his fingers loosening the knot in the girdle of his gown. There was no mistaking his purpose.

She had fought him like a wild thing but his strength was too much for her. At length, exhausted, her struggles ceased. And then, something happened for which she was ever afterwards to hate herself. She had yielded to him, responded, and met his passion with her own. Later, spent and sated, he had held her tightly for a moment. Then he had laughed, the only utterance he had made during the encounter, a short, sharp laugh, like the bark of a fox she had thought when she remembered it.

Reaching down, he picked up the dressing gown he had thrown aside and, leaving the bed, had belted it about him. At the door he had turned to look at her once more. 'I hate you,' she had all but spat at him, her face distorted. 'Do that again and I'll kill myself.'

After he had gone she had lain, sobbing, her face pressed against the pillow, filled with self-loathing for the response the act of consummation had evoked from her. Then she had left the bed to sponge herself all over as if to clean away all recollection of it. When she returned and pulled the tousled sheets about her she found herself to her astonishment falling immediately into the deep slumber of the fulfilled and possessed.

From that union Hugo had been born. Andrew had never come back to her bed, nor had he attempted to do so. Soon she realised that when she had flung at him that threat of suicide she had fortuitously hit upon the one sanction that would deter him. Had she threatened to kill him he would have regarded it as a challenge which could not be overlooked, but he would never face even the possibility of a scandal such as would come were she to carry out her threat, a scandal which would undermine if not destroy the position in the Bay and elsewhere which he had won at such cost. And he knew enough of his wife to realise that, driven too hard, she might well do as she had said.

Looking at him once more across the lapse of years she wondered what she would have done had he returned. Had

19

he evinced the slightest shade of tenderness perhaps she might have accepted him. She felt sure he was as strong and virile now as he had been all those years ago, and somehow his courage, his ruthlessness, his single-mindedness, had compelled in her a sort of unwilling respect. She no longer felt for him the loathing she had done when she was younger and in a strange way she enjoyed his successes. And she was quite sure he was not celibate on his business trips to London and abroad.

As for herself, she was still young enough to feel the want of fulfilment, the stirrings and strivings of passion. Sometimes on long and lonely nights, especially during the languorous summer months when the heat seemed to seep up from the heather on the hills, the hay in the fields and the baking rocks along the shores of the Bay, she would lie awake with her whole body throbbing, incomplete and unfulfilled. If only, she thought for the thousandth time, Stephen had come back a month or so earlier before she had plunged or been plunged into this loveless marriage. Years ago there had been those few stolen and terribly dangerous meetings with Stephen in Dublin and elsewhere. All too vividly the events of that last night she had spent with him, more than ten years ago now, were etched in her mind.

They had met in a small hotel in Dublin, off Suffolk Street. Andrew was away on one of his business trips to London; so she had been able to leave Dunlay and the Bay on the excuse of a shopping expedition without its appearing anything out of the ordinary.

Always on these few stolen meetings they avoided the bigger, grander hotels that clustered round St Stephen's Green. The danger of being seen together by some friend or acquaintance or even recognised by someone they did not themselves know was far too great. It was a real fear, for their own section of the population seemed to grow smaller every day. Someone had once said to her that as far as they and those like them were concerned Ireland was one family and Dublin a village. It was a true statement and they both knew it, recognising the dangers it brought with it.

The risk of exposure was frightening and it terrified her. Even in these small hotels there was the ever-present chance of a servant come from the Bay or County Kilderry seeing them together and spreading the news around. For those reasons they avoided the public rooms where their clothes and their accents set them apart and drew attention to them, coming in late to the hotel and leaving early when few were stirring.

The furtiveness of it all served to increase the fears which built up in her to something in the nature of a revulsion for their relationship. Those fears, too, as she realised with approaching panic, were creating a barrier between them in their sexual embraces. Despite herself, fear made her less eager, less ardent and less capable of both giving and responding. But on that last occasion there had been an urgency about Stephen's short, secret message, something in it imploring, almost pleading that she come to him, which she felt she could not ignore.

Stephen had changed. That, too, she recognised whilst hating herself for doing so. The years had not treated him well since those heady days when he had fought and flown in France and had known a brief passing period of fame as the top scorer in a crack fighter squadron. Life had run wrong for him. His house had been burnt down, his lands had been appropriated by the Land Commission at a confiscatory price; she had married another. His involvement in the Nationalist cause, slight and involuntary though it had been, had seen him branded by his own as a traitor to his class.

Amongst his new associates he had fared little better. They distrusted him and fought shy of him because of his accent and his social assurance. To them he belonged to a race apart; whenever he opened his mouth his very voice represented to them everything they had fought to be rid of. Their leader, anxious to preserve the social and sporting graces he saw as embodied in the old Ascendancy, whilst at the same time stripping them of their power, had at first protected him. He had been useful then to advise on the niceties of dealing with the British, on forms of address and manner of approach, and he had been found jobs of more style than importance to help him supplement his dwindling income.

But now, it seemed, as he spoke to her and stared at her

with despair in his eyes, the last remnants of hope had run out on him.

'He sent for me,' he said savagely. 'Had me in as we used to say in racing. And do you know what he said – ' Stephen picked up the whisky bottle which stood on the cheap deal dressing table and poured a dark brown measure into the glass beside it. Then he stood, glass in hand, staring out of the window, reliving the scene.

When, in answer to the summons, he had entered the big office, it was empty save for the leader himself: the little man with the quiff, the wing collar and the dark suit, sitting behind the desk set at an angle across the room away from the windows. His subordinates, it was said, had insisted against his will – since no one doubted his physical courage or his moral determination – on his so positioning himself lest he present a target for a sniper's bullet. Memories of recent violence, execution and assassination were still fresh and would not die in the decades to come. You might have taken him, Stephen thought, for a clerk in some railway company perhaps, steadily working his way up to some minor position of trust. You might, that was, until you saw the steely resolution in his eyes and the lines which the strain of governing a tortured land had carved beside the lips under the clipped moustache. As was his way he had not wasted his words, nor had he attempted to soften the blow.

'You're young enough still to make another life,' he had said. 'There is no longer a future for you here nor for those like you. I am telling you now so that you may know in time. I can do no more for you. Public life – it's impossible in your case. You cannot enter the Dail. No constituency would dream of adopting you with your background. The Senate – there is room, a little room there for representatives of your class, but they have to be greater men with more behind them than you can command, men who can contribute to the future of the state – '

The catch-phrase common then in government circles, 'Willie dearly loves a lord', came to Stephen's mind as he stared into the cold eyes.

'I see,' he said. 'Titles or money – or both –'

The eyes did not so much as flicker. 'We are young yet as

22

a State,' the President said. 'Both these things can bring with them a third which you lack and which you have left out – influence.'

Stephen saw it then. The State, under this man's hand, had shown that it could survive. Money, rank and power were beginning to recognise the possibilities of its patronage – and his. The little help Stephen could give and had given was no longer required.

'I'm as Irish as you are,' Stephen said. 'My family have been here for five hundred years – '

'Too long,' the man across the desk said. 'They changed their faith. They acquired the instincts of the Ascendancy. And then you changed your coat yourself. As such you are suspect to both sides.'

'I didn't change it. It was forced on me. You must know that,' Stephen blurted out. 'And I tried to keep the middle way – '

The man with the quiff shook his head slowly. 'Perhaps, but that is not how it appears to the generality,' he said. 'What I suggest now is truly for your benefit. Start again. Try Kenya. You'll find many of your own kind there – '

'Misfits – ' Stephen said savagely.

The President sighed slightly and picked up his pen. He had already given up too much of his time to this man across the desk who had become a liability and showed signs of being a tiresome one. 'You would be wise to consider carefully what I have said,' he went on. 'One last service I can render. If you require assistance with your passage?'

'Thank you,' Stephen bit out as he rose to his feet. 'What you left me with when you took my land will pay for that – if I go.'

When he was half-way to the door the President spoke again. 'You fought a war for Empire,' he said, 'and that taints you, too. You and your kind would do well to remember that Mr de Valera and myself want the same thing – freedom from the shackles of imperialism. We only differ in the means of getting it.'

Stephen went down the great staircase of Leinster House in a blind rage. As he made his way towards the hall where once the Leinsters, the proudest family in the land, had received and held sway, he encountered one of the few deputies he knew and liked. Mikey O'Sullivan, one-time pantry boy at Bellary Court, leader of a famous Flying Column and Civil War hero, was now the owner of a stud farm, the elected representative of County Kilderry, prosperous, influential and a coming man in the new corridors of power. Together they went into the bar and Stephen, his wounds still raw from the interview, poured out his story of it.

'Faith, then, ye're lucky he didn't have ye shot,' Mikey said with a grin. 'The little man can be as hard as the hob of hell when he likes.' Mikey paused, took a deep breath and then went on slowly. 'But he's right, after all, when all's said and done. 'Tis sad but 'tis true there's no place for ye here. Ye're not a lord or a millionaire with money and a place to protect.'

'I see that now – and I hear he's making Westcott a senator.'

'And why wouldn't he make him a senator? He's got that big place and the stud and he's pouring money into it. He gives employment and he's the sort they want to encourage to stay on. Besides, that colt of his, Marrymore, that won the Middle Park, he's winter favourite for the Derby. It'd be a great thing for the country if a colt bred, owned and trained here won the Derby for us.'

'I don't think Marrymore will win the Derby,' Stephen said. 'There's sprinting blood on the dam's side. Who the hell is that jumped-up Westcott anyway? They don't like him in the Bay. He tried to buy the Lacken fishing and they wouldn't have him.'

''Twas Massiter stopped that, I hear. They've been at each other's throats for years. Anyway it would scarcely suit you to be a senator, would it?'

'You're right there, Mikey. I'm not cut out to be a legislator. Anyway it looks as though I won't be here for the Derby. Kenya, he said. That's where I should go – '

'Kenya, is it? That's where Mr Norris who had my place is. You could do worse. It's a great place to be, so they tell me.'

'Billy Norris? Is he there? I'd forgotten that. Alcohol, alti-

24

tude and adultery, that's what they say of it. And exile, they could add. That's what it'll be for me anyway. I never wanted to leave the Bay, and now I've got to leave Ireland too, it seems.'

'Is there news of the Bay?' Mikey said in the soft tones of those who loved it and were away from it.

'The Bay won't change,' Stephen said. 'And if I go I'll never see it again.'

'Sure if you make your fortune out there coffee farming or whatever they do there, can't ye come back? Glory be to God, Master Stephen,' Mikey said, suddenly relapsing into the old ways and the old idiom. 'It's a queer country, that's what it is. Who'd have thought the likes of me would be sittin' here tellin' the likes of you what to do?'

'It's a queer country all right,' Stephen said bitterly, finishing his drink and putting down his glass. 'And getting more so all the time, for us, anyway. No Mikey, I feel it in my bones. I'll never see the Bay again.'

He repeated those words to Babs when he had finished telling her all that had happened. Then, after staring out the window for a moment while the sounds of the street below came up to them, he had turned to her. 'Come with me,' he said.

A long silence fell between them. She rose from where she was sitting on the bed and walked around the room, picking things up and putting them down. She avoided meeting his eye. Then, very slowly, 'I can't,' she said quietly.

'Why not,' he said equally quietly. 'You hate Massiter. You've always hated him. We should have cut and run years ago.'

'That's it, perhaps. Too much time has passed. We're older. Too many things have happened. There are the boys. I can't leave them.'

'Bring them with you.'

'He'd get them back.'

'Bring Kit then. We can start again, out there, the three of us.'

Suddenly he swung round and faced her. 'He's my son,' he blazed at her. 'And you know it.' He took her by the

25

shoulders and shook her. 'I have a right to him, and by God, I'll get him – '

She put up her hands and freed his from her. 'No, Stephen,' she said, shaking her head. 'I can't take him. It would ruin his life.'

'What about our lives?'

'Our lives are wrecked already. The War did that to us.'

'The bloody War. I should never have gone. I should have stayed at home and ridden Bob's horses for him like he said all those years ago. Or died in France along with Haynes and Hank and the best of them. Haven't I the right to something?' He went on bitterly. 'Haven't I the right to my own son? What if I go to Massiter and tell him straight that he didn't father Kit? What if I claim him?'

'He'd never admit it. He'd never let him go. He'd fight you through every Court in the land and he'd win. He always wins. Besides, Stephen – ' she looked at him directly now. 'You're not going to do that. You know what it would do to the boy. He's happy where he is, in the Bay with his horses, his dogs and his riding, like you were long ago. He's going to be a good rider, Stephen. Bob says he's a natural. You're too decent to do it.'

'Decency doesn't seem to have got me very far. Maybe it's time I tried something else. . . .'

'I suppose it hasn't,' Babs said looking down at the flash of diamonds on her finger that was Andrew's engagement ring. 'Except that you can live with yourself.'

'I don't find myself very good company just now.'

'Stephen, if you have to go, do you have to go so far? Couldn't you go to England? What about that friend of yours in the Squadron, in the War, wouldn't he help?'

'England? Do you think anyone in England would look at me twice with my record in Irish politics and the turn-coat tag that's been put on me? As for Clare de Vaux, I haven't heard of him for years. Besides he should be about to inherit a title about now if the old boy dies, which he's due to do – he must be about a hundred. And a deputy-lieutenancy with it, I shouldn't wonder. He wouldn't touch me with a forty-foot pole. Anyway, the little man and Mikey, they're both right. If I go it's far better I clear completely out. Look at me, Babs. Are you saying no to me?'

She forced herself to meet his eyes. 'Stephen,' she said. 'Listen and please try to understand. We both know our lives have been wrecked. Let's at least try to make it all right for the boy, give him security, happiness, the things we missed because of that wretched War, and what came after it. I can only do that by staying at the Bay.' There was something else but she would not hurt him more by saying it. The furtiveness of their meetings had curbed her passion. A little of the longing to be with him had faded and died. She now knew she loved her son more than she loved his father, and that much of her former love for Stephen had been sublimated on to Kit. She wanted above all things to stay and watch the boy grow into manhood in the peace and security her war-torn generation had never known. Their youth had been lived against the tempo and thunder of the guns in France and the ever-present probability of death or mutilation. She would never leave her son, nor would she snatch him away into exile in some faraway place. She would stay with him and watch over him.

'You don't love me,' Stephen said, turning away from her.

'I've always loved you, Stephen, and I always will,' she told him, wondering as she said it how much of it was a lie; and she had spent the night weeping in his arms. That had been nearly ten years ago. Often afterwards she pondered on whether she had made the wrong decision. Almost to her surprise she found the longing for Stephen after he had left coming back to her with redoubled force, especially when Kit was at school and she realised that she was losing him to the passing years, that he would and must make his own choices and his own way in the world. More and more she found herself coming back to that photograph of Stephen she kept in a locked drawer. There he was in the old high-collared RFC tunic, the wings on his chest and the purple and white ribbon of the MC beneath them. The fore-and-aft forage cap was set slightly aslant on his head and he was laughing at the camera. That was they way she would remember him. It had been taken in Paris, she recalled, when they were snatching a few hours from the dance with death that was being

27

played out up the line and of which the rumble of the guns was a constant reminder. Those furtive meetings in squalid hotels, his raging against fate were forgotten; the scrawled signature, *Stephen with love*, and the laughing boy was the way she would think of him. He had written once, from a place called Naivasha, where he said he would remain if he could because it reminded him of the Bay. Fear of discovery, fear for her son, had stayed her hand from answering, and now, she reminded herself, Kit was all she had.

CHAPTER III

The entrance of Atkins, the English butler, at that moment, shook Babs out of her reverie. 'Mr Ferris is here, sir,' he said to Andrew, coughing slightly and deferentially in the way he had. 'I've put him in the billiard room.'

'Thank you, Atkins.' Andrew finished his port and rose to his feet.

The boys were not permitted to attend these conferences, so Hugo again expressed his intention of going to bed early to look after his cold and Kit said he would go to the yard to make sure his point-to-pointer had eaten up all right. Babs followed her husband down the passage to the billiard room.

Bob Ferris was waiting for them, sitting by the fire with a glass in his hand. He rose to his feet as they entered. 'Ah, Bob,' Massiter said. 'They've got you something, I see. Well, you had a good day, today.'

'Couldn't have been better, sir. And Master Kit, he rode a great race.'

'So I'm told. A little reckless, perhaps?'

'You don't win races without a drop of dash, sir.'

'Hm, well, perhaps. Now, about these entries, Bob.' Massiter crossed to a tray of drinks on a side table and poured himself a whisky and soda. 'Fill your glass, Bob,' he said, 'and we'll discuss them.'

The trainer poured himself a good four fingers of whisky and returned to his seat. 'Here's a health and good luck to you, sir,' he said, raising his glass. 'And to m'Lady too. And many more winners.' He drank, put the glass down and reached into an inside pocket. 'I've brought the entries with me,' he went on, taking out a sheet of paper. 'Now, sir, Matchbox is in at Mallow and I think you ought to let him run. He's well in himself and should go well. I can get Jerry O'Connor to ride him.'

'It's a three-mile handicap chase, isn't it? He has ten-seven in it, I recall. But, I wonder, would it be too far for him?'

Once again Babs was struck by the way in which her husband could carry details of all his many activities in his head and switch from one to another at will without making any mistakes.

'He'll get the trip all right, sir,' Bob said. 'And Mr Westcott has one in it,' he added slyly. 'He'll just about start favourite at the weights and you should beat him.'

'Very well, then, let him go,' Andrew said with a snap.

'And at Malloran Park the day after tomorrow,' Bob went on, looking down at the paper he held in his hand. 'We've that big, young horse, Thunderhead, in the bumper. It's his first time out. Will you be there yourself, sir?'

'I'm afraid not, Bob. There's a fishery meeting in the morning and I have to see my solicitor in Kilderry in the afternoon. In any event first time out you'll be doing very little with him. You'll see he's not knocked about?'

'I'll do that, sir. I was wondering if you'd let Master Kit ride him. He has a nice pair of hands. It'd be good experience for them both.'

'Kit? Surely not, Bob, on a young horse. He's much too impetuous.'

'Only when he needs be, sir. If you ask me he has a head on his shoulders. He'll do what I tell him, I'll be bound. As I say, sir, it'll do them both good.'

'That's true, I suppose. But I should have thought Master Hugo better suited to this horse.'

'He can't,' Babs put in. 'He's fishing the home beat at

29

Derryquin Lodge with young Roughty on Saturday, so he tells me. That is,' she added drily, 'if his cold is better.'

Her husband looked at her in astonishment. 'The home beat?' he said. 'Hugo? How did this come about?' Then he turned back to the trainer. 'Very well then, Bob, Master Kit rides, but take care he doesn't do anything foolish. I don't want that big horse ruined – '

'No fear of that, sir. I'll look after them both.'

When the trainer had left Andrew poured himself another whisky, then, fingering his imperial, he turned back to Babs. 'Now, what is all this about Hugo and the home beat at the Lodge?' he said. 'It's most extraordinary. That beat was always kept strictly for family friends. Are you sure of this?'

'Hugo is. Charles Roughty asked him.'

'Roughty? Where does he come into this?'

'Hugo met him out hunting. Picked him up and caught his horse for him as a matter of fact.'

'Hunting? But Derryquin will have nothing to do with the Hounds. This gets more extraordinary every minute.'

'It does, I know. It's nice for Hugo though, Andrew, isn't it? Aren't you pleased?'

'That depends. Would you mind telling me how it all came about?'

Lord Derryquin had once been the grandee of the Bay, his Irish lands then stretching to over ten thousand acres. Those estates, acquired from a buccaneering Tudor ancestor who had stolen and grabbed them from the natives, finally enlarging them by a convenient marriage into the old nobility, had all gone now, having been either sold to the tenants or expropriated. All that remained was the fishing on the rivers and lakes of the lower Bay and the snipe and woodcock shooting on the bogs and woods about the Lodge.

The Lodge itself had been burnt down in the Troubles and Lord Derryquin, a ponderous and slow-moving man who had served for a short time as Foreign Secretary in the twenties until, as one unkind back-bencher put it, 'he was so stupid even Baldwin noticed it,' had refused to set foot in Ireland again. The loyalists who remained in the country he regarded as objects of contempt, branding them as 'horse-coping half-rebels, the lot of them'. He detested horses, hunting and racing and anything to do with them, having been known to boom through his heavy moustache after his third glass of port anathemas against 'racing swine', an expression he had picked up in his youth during a brief period as ADC to the Viceroy of India.

His younger son, Charles Roughty (pronounced 'Rooty') did not, however, take after him or share his opinions. He was, in fact, a throwback to the roistering Irish aristocracy into which his forebear and founding father had married. Now in his first year at Oxford he was a wild and winning young man who craved action and excitement. Somehow he had recently persuaded his father to make over to him what remained of the Irish estates. Fishing and shooting he found, on the whole, slow. Fox-hunting, on the other hand, satisfied at least some of his craving for excitement and action. He had built himself a flat in the yard of the ruined lodge and there, unbeknown to his father, he stabled a couple of horses which he hunted with the Kilderry Hounds.

Roughty's horsemanship did not match his enthusiasm. The day before, with hounds running hard, a mistake at a narrow bank had sent him sailing over his horse's head. 'Seeing that brute he bought off McCrea galloping away and going spare, what could I do but catch him for him,' Hugo had told his mother when recounting the incident. Babs had smiled to herself, for she very much doubted if Hugo would have caught the horse and brought it back had its previous owner been riding it. 'I had to put him up, too,' Hugo went on. 'The horse was going round in circles and he was hopping about on one leg with the other in the stirrup. Couldn't get on. Damn comic. Anyway he was so delighted he offered me a day on the home beat.'

Babs now repeated the story as she had heard it to Andrew.

'I suppose it's all right,' Andrew said doubtfully. 'But you know how jealously Derryquin preserved that water. It was about the only interest he took in this country.'

'Of course it's all right, Andrew, why wouldn't it be?'

'I hope Derryquin himself knows about it, that's all.'

'Does it matter if he doesn't? Surely a day's fishing – '

'Derryquin is a fool and they kicked him out of the Cabinet

pretty quick. But he still has a number of directorships in the city. I come across him occasionally. I wouldn't care at this moment to run foul of him. And I happen to know from some thing he let slip at the Beefsteak he's not too happy about the way that boy of his is going.'

'But if Charles Roughty asked Hugo he could scarcely refuse, could he?'

'There's that, I suppose,' Andrew said doubtfully. 'But no stranger has ever been allowed to fish that water before to my knowledge. However, as you say, the damage if damage it is is done now.' With that Andrew put down his glass. At the door, he turned to her. 'I don't want anything to happen that might hurt Hugo,' he said looking directly at her.

CHAPTER IV

It had been Bab's intention to accompany Kit to Malloran Park and to see him ride his first race under Rules, but early on that Saturday morning Mrs Garvey, the housekeeper, came to her. 'If it pleases you, m'Lady,' she said to her. 'That Bridie O'Leary is complaining something terrible of a pain in her stomach. And,' she added with the relish of her kind, 'she's vomiting up everything she has in her, saving your presence, m'Lady. 'Tis a bleedin' ulster, I'll be bound.'

'It's scarcely that,' Babs said, for she thought it far more likely to be an unwanted pregnancy, the all too frequent fate of these girls. Whatever it was she would have to summon the doctor and stay to learn his diagnosis, and her plans for racing would have to be abandoned.

So it was that Kit was packed off with his crash helmet, his saddle and weight-cloth to travel by himself with Bob Ferris to the meeting.

Big Bob Ferris belonged to a generation brought up on

horses who regarded motor-cars with deep suspicion, a total lack of understanding and, although they did not care to admit it even to themselves, a slight secret fear. His car, one of the new model Ford As, wore a battered appearance, its mudguards and bodywork being dented and scratched from encounters with gateposts, garage doors and other obstacles. Nothing about it ever worked as it should, it was slow to start, its steering was erratic and its brakes almost invariably faulty. Bob drove it sitting up stiff and erect, gripping the wheel firmly with both hands and staring fixedly out through the windscreen. During the drive he scarcely opened his lips save to swear at an occasional stray bullock or wandering donkey which they encountered, and he removed a hand from the wheel only to shake his fist at anyone or anything he held to be impeding his right of free passage.

It was fortunate for him and those like him that in 1939 motor cars on Irish roads were still something of a rarity and their possession something bordering on luxury. This morning, on the one occasion that they met an oncoming car while passing a walking countryman, disaster nearly overtook them.

'Those as walk the roads must look after themselves,' Bob muttered as his swerve caused the countryman to leap for the ditch. 'Is he all right, now, Master Kit?' he asked a moment later as the old car lurched from pot-hole to pot-hole and he straightened her with some difficulty on to her course.

'He's on his feet anyway,' Kit answered looking back and seeing an angry man picking up his hat and shaking his stick at them.

'The divil mend these things 'twas he who designed them for sure,' Bob observed as they proceeded on their way along the narrow, twisting country roads.

The softness of spring was touching the countryside everywhere and the yellow fire of gorse was commencing to light its flames across it. They had left the heather and mountains of the Bay behind them and were running through the lush farming lowlands of County Kilderry. Soon they would begin to climb again to another range of blue hills that lay hazy on the horizon beyond the stretch of superb hunting country that swept up to them. As they ran through a straggling village which topped a rise, Kit looked about him and thought how much he loved all this countryside from the rocks and rivers, lakes and mountains, the scenic grandeur of sea and sky that was the Bay to the galloping grass they were now traversing with its patchwork of fields and banks, almost every one of which at one time or another he had ridden over. It was not a bad place to spend your days, his mother had said to him once as they hacked home from hunting. That was one of the understatements of all time, Kit thought as yet another twist of the road enabled him to catch a glimpse of the tall purple peaks which guarded the entrance to the Bay.

Bob's attention to his driving, which became even more fiercely concentrated after the countryman's dive for the ditch, precluded further conversation and Kit's thoughts turned to the race he was to ride. He supposed Bob would give him instructions some time but he was not unduly concerned. Never much given to worry, on this occasion he felt he had little need to. He had ridden the horse at home; he was, as they said, a big baby and a lazy one. He would have no trouble holding him. Nothing would be expected of him; it would be all too easy really. He sat back in his seat and allowed himself the pleasure of drinking in the changing colours of the countryside and dreaming of the time when he would be the leading amateur. He was beginning to imagine the scene – his being led into the winner's enclosure at Punchestown after winning the Conyngham Cup, as Desmond Murtagh his grandfather had done years ago – when they passed through the gates of Malloran Park. Beside him Bob breathed what seemed like a sigh of relief and then muttered a curse as the footbrake failed to come on. Hauling on the handbrake he brought the car to a shuddering stand-still only a foot away from the elegant back of some wealthy and important owner's glittering Daimler.

As he heaved himself from his seat the trainer appeared suddenly to remember that this was to be Kit's first ride on the racecourse proper and that he had better say something to him about it. 'Now then, Master Kit,' he said. 'Not frightened, are you?'

'Not much,' Kit said with a grin.

'That's fine for ye, then. But remember what the Sir said.

Don't be doin' anythin' hasty. This fellow is only a baby and he's not to be knocked about. I got you the ride and don't you be gettin' me into any trouble now.'

'I'll be as good as gold, Bob, I promise you.'

'I hope you will, then,' Bob said doubtfully, looking at his laughing eyes. 'Remember now, Master Kit, and never forget it, fire in the belly is all very well, but sometimes in this game and in every other, too, I do be thinkin', you want to damp it down a bit. Keep quiet and sit still and ye shouldn't have any trouble for he's a big lazy bugger. D'ye know about goin' through the scales. 'Tis much the same as a point-to-point – '

'Yes, Bob, I'll manage.'

'Get changed and weighed out in good time so as I can have the saddle. I've a runner in the one before it. I'll see ye in the weigh room.'

The Malloran Park Maiden Plate, confined to amateur riders, and colloquially known as a 'bumper' because of this, was run over a distance of two miles and 160 yards and was the last race on the card. The amateurs' dressing room was a corrugated iron shack with benches down two of its walls and wooden clothes pegs above them. It was bare of furnishings save for a kitchen table, two rickety chairs and an antiquated army-issue washstand which stood in one corner. Having looked around him and left his gear with the valet Kit went out to walk the course.

There had been a drying wind and the turf was firm and springy. 'Good chasing ground,' he heard someone behind him say. 'Couldn't ask for much better.' That should suit the big horse on his first outing, Kit thought, and make him less likely to injure himself than on heavy or holding going.

Malloran Park racecourse lay in a bowl of blue hills. The track itself was set on a slope and laid out in the shape of a large oval. There was a fairly steep fall of ground to the final bend, part of this fall being concealed behind a plantation of firs. From this last bend the track sloped upwards again to the stands and the finish. The two-mile start was at the bottom of the incline.

When Kit went to change he found that the only other occupants of the room besides the valet and himself were

Dick Harbison, the reigning amateur champion, and one other older, saturnine-looking man whom Harbison addressed as 'Captain'. Already the days of segregating amateurs and professionals into different rooms were passing, since many amateurs were drifting into the professionals' room where there was more comfort and company and better service. Once in they stayed there.

Kit knew Harbison slightly from having ridden against him in point-to-points and when the saturnine captain left they chatted together, exchanging the names of their mounts and gossip of hunting and point-to-pointing. Harbison, as was to be expected, was riding the favourite. Together they walked across to the weigh room. As they went Kit almost collided with a tall girl dressed in tweeds who was the centre of a little group of men. He had a glimpse of a striking face, a shade too long for beauty, a short upper lip and a pair of very direct grey-blue eyes.

'Two lengths and it should have been ten,' she was saying to a man beside her. 'If that silly bitch hadn't hit me for six at the last – oh, hullo, Dick – ' she broke off the conversation on catching sight of Harbison. 'Another winner, I suppose?'

'I'll tell you that in about twenty minutes,' Harbison said.

'Who is that girl?' Kit asked him.

'Carlow Concannon. Didn't you know? No, I suppose not. You people down there in the Bay never know anyone but yourselves.' Harbison laughed. 'They used to live here and left in the twenties,' he went on. 'Her mother died recently and she and her father have come back. She's about the best they've got in ladies' point-to-points in England. Now she's here she can ride in open races against us – and if you're upsides with her at the last, my boy, look out!'

Kit looked at her again. She was laughing at something the man beside her had said. Her features seemed to print themselves on his memory, and then he had something else to think about.

Passing the number-board he saw his name MR C. MASSITER, drawn in untidy chalk lettering, appearing on it for the first time. It gave him a small stab of pleasure. At the same time a fixed determination came to him to get 'out of the chalk' and see his name in permanent paint on one of those boards, worn and battered from much use like that of the man beside him who passed it by without a glance. At least now he was making a start; he was on the racecourse getting somewhere in his resolve to be an amateur rider, and there was Desmond's promise of a ride in a hurdle next week, too. Sometime, some day, he told himself, he'd top the list.

The scales presented no difficulty. He made the weight, handed the saddle to Bob and, feeling rather as he had done as a new boy at school, stood with the other riders waiting to be called out. Once in the ring he went straight to where Bob was standing with another trainer. Touching him on the arm Bob led him aside. 'Seven runners,' he said. 'It's cut up a bit. And that thing of Captain Smailes is useless like all of his. Can't think why he does it. He'll be last ten lengths. He always is. Now remember, Master Kit, like I said, don't go tryin' to beat the others out of sight on this big fellow. I've said it to ye before and I'll say it again, he's not to be knocked about. If he takes to it he might just run into a place but I think this lot'll go too fast for him first time out. Anyway they say Harbison is past the post already – '

A bell rang. The lad leading Thunderhead turned him in and they walked towards him. Bob stripped the sheet off him and pulled up the girths. Then his hand was underneath Kit's leg, whisking him into the saddle.

'Good luck,' he said. 'And remember now, Master Kit, no bloomin' fireworks!'

With these words ringing in his ears Kit joined the others circling the ring. He was immediately behind the saturnine captain who was riding a good hunting length on a herring-gutted bay.

Kit had ridden the big horse at home and knew that Bob was right when he said he was lazy. But here, on the race-course, the moment he got on his back he gave him quite a different feel than on the home gallops. He had woken up; he was on his toes. Head up, he played with his bit, danced about and looked around him like a conqueror.

Going out on the track it was the same. Thunderhead put his head down and caught hold of his bit, nearly cannoning into the saturnine captain in the process and earning Kit a blistering string of curses. Every trace of laziness had

37

vanished; it was as if the sights and sounds, the excitement of seeing the crowd and the whole atmosphere of the race-course had woken something within him and he had suddenly realised that this was what he had been bred and trained for. Immediately his hooves touched the turf he was off. The feel of the horse in the paddock had given Kit some warning and it was lucky that it had. He could hold him, he thought – but only just. The fact that the ground sloped away from the stands gave the big horse's gallop all the more impetus. For a few seconds Kit knew he was in peril of losing control and making a fool of himself in his first ride in public. Swearing under his breath and wondering what Bob in the stands was thinking he managed to catch the stride and anchor the big horse, but it was a near thing and he knew it. Pulling up at the start, panting and out of breath, he began to fear for what was in store for him.

'Takes a hold, does he?' Harbison said, looking him over. 'Big strong devil he is, too. Nice horse though. One of your father's?'

'Yes. He doesn't do this at home. It takes you all your time to wake him up.'

'Some of them are like that. You'll want to watch him coming down the hill.'

Behind them the saturnine captain was looking balefully at Kit and muttering dark things about 'Snotty-nosed young pups who can't keep their horses straight.' Then the starter was calling the roll. In a minute or two they were lining up. 'Come on then!' the starter called and they were off.

In three strides the big horse pulled himself and Kit to the front. Passing the stands he was five lengths clear of his field. Do what he could Kit could only just hold him. Down the hill for the first time Thunderhead, stretching his gallop and thoroughly enjoying himself on the firm, springing turf increased his lead with his rider little more than a passenger.

Round the bend past the stands the order remained the same and then, near the top of the hill, the others began to close on him. But each time Thunderhead heard the thud of hooves coming at him he pulled out something more. He was still a good three lengths clear as they began the drop down the hill. 'God Almighty,' Kit thought as he took yet another pull with his aching arms. 'I could win this and then what will they do to me?' Bobs' instructions were ringing in his ears. They'd never believe him if he won. They'd say he was showing off, that he'd lost his head and made the big horse fly. Certainly his father would, and Bob, too, more than likely after the lectures he'd given him.

Then, down the hill, the big horse suddenly began to run out of steam. Thankfully, Kit took a pull and hauled him back. Behind the trees he thought he had him anchored, and round the bottom bend there were four horses in front of him. He heaved a sigh of relief. But the respite had only served to give Thunderhead a breather. The moment he met the rising ground he began to run on again. As he did so Kit realised something else: his own strength was giving out. He had thought that he was fit from riding work and point-to-points. But work on the home gallops and point-to-pointing with its intervals for jumping had not prepared him for this trial of strength over an extended two miles on the strongest horse he had ever sat on. Every muscle ached and shrieked at him. His legs felt like putty and his arms appeared to be about to part from their sockets.

The saturnine captain had long since fallen back into the far distance. The horse beside him was labouring. Now they were pounding up the hill. Thunderhead seemed bent on glory even if his rider wasn't. Everything else forgotten, Kit was concentrating on holding him, on not allowing them to say he'd knocked him about. He was alongside the second horse whose rider was hard at work. The winning post was coming closer; suddenly Kit realised what he was doing and how it must appear to the watchers on the stands. There was nothing for it. He sat down and loosed the big horse's head. He failed to catch Harbison on the favourite by a fast fading neck.

At the unsaddling stalls Bob was standing, a worried look on his face. He gave the horse a perfunctory pat on the neck as Kit slid to the ground. 'I couldn't hold him,' Kit said to him under his breath as he undid the girths.

'Ye made a damn good try by the look of it,' Bob said grimly. 'Get weighed-in now. But there'll be more about this, I be thinkin'.'

Dick Harbison was already in the dressing room when Kit returned to it. He looked at Kit quizzically and then laughed. 'For this relief much thanks,' he said. 'They had a monkey on mine. How much of it do you want or did they put it on for you themselves? Seems you may need it. I fear, young feller me lad, you've been and gone and done it.'

'Oh Lord,' Kit said miserably. 'I suppose it did look awful.'

'So I'm told by those who saw it. I only heard you breathing down my neck. Let this be a lesson to you, my lad, and never to be forgotten. If you must stop a horse do it in the country or behind the trees, not in front of the stewards' stand.'

'I tried to – no, dammit, I didn't mean to stop him. They told me not to knock him about – '

'And he took off with you. I know what it's like,' Harbison went on more sympathetically. 'It could happen to a bishop, not that, I suppose, it very often does.'

'Will they have me in?'

'I wouldn't care to lay odds against it. They'll be blind if they don't. And this lot aren't. And Westcott's in the chair.'

'Westcott!' Kit echoed dismally, feeling his bowels begin to churn. 'Oh my God, that's torn it, torn it good and proper.'

He sat down heavily on the wooden bench. 'I thought he was a senior steward and couldn't act here.'

'He's between terms at the moment so he can act locally. And this, let me remind you, is his home course. And he and your father aren't exactly bosom chums, are they?'

'That's right, go on, rub it in,' Kit said, some of his true spirit coming back. 'What the hell was I to do with Bob telling me to give him an easy ride and then finding you couldn't stop the bloody horse with a traction engine!'

'I should get changed as quick as you can,' the other said, more kindly. 'It's bad enough as it is without keeping them hanging about after the last. Ah, as I thought, here comes the executioner!'

40

CHAPTER V

An official was standing in the doorway. 'Mr Massiter?' he said. 'The stewards want to see you.'

'Just a minute,' Kit said, pulling on his tie.

'Never been in before, even in a point-to-point?' Harbison asked him.

'This is the first time and I hope it's the last,' Kit said, tugging at a refractory knot.

'It won't be, but never mind. Take a tip from an old hand. Play the idiot boy. Sing dumb. Say as little as you can. Let the trainer do the talking. Westcott will sound off at you. He always does. He doesn't really know anything but he loves to hear his own voice. Whatever he says and however bloody silly it is don't put him right. If you do he'll crucify you.'

'I won't know what to say anyway – '

'The trainer – it's Bob Ferris, isn't it? He's had plenty of time ever since he watched your antics out there to think up some bloody good lies.'

'I hope so.'

'Don't take it to heart, for Christ's sake. Happens to us all. Like I said, could come to a bishop. And good luck.'

'I'll need it. After this I've got to face my father.'

Outside the door of the stewards' room Bob was waiting, his normally good-humoured face set and anxious. 'It's Mr Westcott,' he whispered to Kit out of the side of his mouth. 'Take care, now, Master Kit.'

The official opened the door and beckoned them in. 'Mr Massiter and Mr Ferris, sir,' he said.

The door closed behind them and they stood together before a beige-covered table at which three men were sitting. Donal Westcott, as chairman, was the centre of the three; he was flanked by a local dignitary, and a tall man with a long, humorous face wearing a regimental tie. Of little less than medium height Westcott had all the bristling air of power and ferocity cultivated by some small men. When he spoke it was in a sharp, rasping voice. Wasting no time on the preliminaries he barked out: 'We are enquiring into the running and riding of the horse Thunderhead in the last race. What were your instructions, Ferris?'

That was the very question Bob had been dreading. As Harbison had told Kit all his thoughts since watching that finish had been concentrated on hatching up some explanation for the inevitable enquiry he knew must follow. Bob's thoughts, however, did not move very fast, nor was he fluent in giving expression to them. He had failed to come up with an even remotely convincing reason for the running of the horse and he knew it, nor was he equipped to put into persuasive words such explanation as he had. 'He'd shown us nothing at home, sir,' he said. 'In fact he's a lazy b— blighter at home and its hard to get him to show anything at all. I couldn't believe my eyes, sir, the way he ran. It's his first time out – we couldn't know – '

'You're not answering my question, Ferris,' Westcott snapped. 'What did you tell the boy to do?'

Bob was in a terrible quandary. If he told the stewards he had said to Kit, 'Win if you can,' the all-embracing let-out for a trainer in such a situation, he was likely to get Kit into serious trouble. Apart from his own affection for the boy and his understanding of the predicament he had been in, there were his own interests to consider. If dire consequences came to Kit from anything he said Andrew Massiter was going to be far from pleased. And Massiter when displeased had a way of taking out his wrath on the object of his displeasure. Bob had five of Andrew's horses in his stable now; he was his best owner. It would go hard with him, especially at this time when there was so little money about, were he to lose them. He began to flounder even more than before. 'I thought the best he could do was to run into a place, sir. I told Mr Massiter, that. I'd no idea he'd run as he did. He's a big sheep at home, sir – It's his first time – I couldn't know – ' His voice tailed off and he looked helplessly into space above the chairman's head.

'Then you don't know your job,' Westcott barked. 'Totally inadequate instructions, especially to an inexperienced rider. Now, boy,' he turned to Kit. 'How many rides in public have you had?'

'This was my first, sir.'

'It may be your last for some time.' He looked again at Bob. 'What do you mean, Ferris, putting an ignorant and inexperienced boy up on a horse like this?'

'He's a good rider, sir,' Bob said sturdily. 'He's won five point-to-points. Mr Murtagh, sir, is putting him up on one of his in a hurdle next week.'

'If Mr Murtagh is fool enough to let him ride one of his it's no concern of mine.' All the same, Kit, watching him, thought he blinked a bit at the mention of Desmond's name, for Desmond, in his own way, was now a power in the world of National Hunt Racing. 'As for you, boy, how do you explain your riding?'

'I thought he'd need waking up, sir. Instead I couldn't hold him. I – I think I must have lost my head – '

'That's no explanation.'

'But, sir – '

'Don't answer me back, boy. Wait till you're spoken to. It was one of the most disgraceful exhibitions I've ever witnessed on a racecourse.'

The man with the humorous face looked up. 'How many point-to-point winners did your trainer say you'd ridden?' he asked. 'Five wasn't it?'

'Yes, sir.'

'Out of how many rides? You're not very old, are you?'

'No, sir,' Kit mentally tried to count up his rides. 'Twenty, sir, I think.'

'Never been taken off with like this before?'

'No, sir, never.'

'I saw him going down. He looked like a handful. Oh, and one other thing, did Mr Ferris, your trainer, tell you not to knock him about?'

Kit swallowed. He had been dreading this question and all that it implied. 'I – er – I think I was too excited to – '

'I see, well perhaps we won't press you too far,' the tall man said. He turned and whispered something in Westcott's ear. The chairman nodded.

'Wait outside,' he snapped.

As they were leaving the room the tall man looked at Kit again. 'Mr Murtagh is your grandfather, isn't he?' he said.

'Yes, sir,' Kit answered.

'Well, you're bred right to ride anyway,' the tall man said and they left the room.

The weigh room was empty save for a man sweeping the floor who looked at them curiously and then went on with his task.

They sat on a bench and waited. 'What do you think they'll do to us, Bob?' Kit asked.

'God knows, Master Kit. That Westcott, he could do anything. And he'd no call to go on the way he did. Tellin' me I wasn't fit to hold a licence and I've held one for nigh on forty years. It's a good job I mentioned your grandfather's name. I think he's a bit frightened of him.'

'The other man seemed decent enough.'

'Colonel Swenson? He's not a bad old stick. But that Westcott – '

The hands of the clock on the wall crawled slowly on and still no call came for them to return. The wait seemed interminable. 'They're taking their time, damn them,' Bob said.

'Will they send us on?'

'Up before the senior stewards? Your first ride? They shouldn't. I dunno, though, that Westcott might. But then your grandfather will give him tally whack and tandem if he does. I dunno what they'll do, Master Kit. But what is it at all that's keepin' 'em?'

At length the door opened and they were called in again.

Donal Westcott favoured them both with an angry stare. Then he surveyed them individually, looking them up and down in silence. He's doing this on purpose, damn him, to frighten us, Kit thought. What's more, he's succeeding, the brute. After letting the silence linger on while he fingered the papers in front of him the chairman cleared his throat and pronounced judgment. 'We have considered this case at some length,' he said. 'The stewards take an extremely serious view of it, especially where you, Ferris, are concerned. You gave totally inadequate instructions to an inexperienced rider and you used the racecourse as a training ground. Your clean record is the only reason we are not sending you on to the senior stewards of the National Hunt Committee. You are fined twenty pounds and severely cautioned as to the future running of your horses. Is that clear?'

'Yes, sir, thank you, sir,' Bob said, and Kit thought he heard him give a sigh of relief.

'As for you, boy,' Westcott continued, turning to Kit. 'The only reason you are not going forward is your inexperience and, I may add, the intervention of Colonel Swenson. You are fined five pounds and given the most severe caution as to your future riding. I warn you, too, if there is any repetition of your conduct you will go forward to the senior stewards. Don't let me ever see either of you here again. You may go.'

Outside Bob took a huge bandana handkerchief from his breast pocket and mopped his brow. 'And this is only the beginnin' of it,' he said. 'The Sir isn't going to like this. I don't know what he'll do or say to me. Master Kit, I've got to have a drink. Come on now.'

The bar underneath the stands was still packed. Bob fought his way through the throng and came back with a large whisky for himself and a mineral for Kit. He was in the act of handing the glass to Kit when a figure, pushed by the press of the crowd, knocked his arm and spilt most of the contents on the floor. 'Christ, I'm sorry,' a voice said: 'Damn these people anyway.' Looking up, Kit saw that it was Carlow Concannon, the girl he had seen outside the dressing room. Standing beside her was Dick Harbison.

'Hallo, there,' Harbison said. 'Come out of it alive, have you, or in shattered fragments? What did they do to you?'

'Fined a fiver,' Kit said. 'Bob got twenty quid taken off him. He told us we were bloody lucky not to get sent on. . . .'

'Westcott took it, I suppose? Sounds like him.'

'It was Westcott all right.'

'That bastard,' Miss Concannon said succinctly.

'Now, then,' Harbison said. 'Such aspersions on our worthy chairman – '

'If you ask me,' Miss Concannon went on, 'he's the biggest shit in racing.'

'That's putting the jumps pretty high,' Harbison said with a grin.

'Gave me a lecture after the Kildare ladies' race,' Miss

45

Concannon said. 'Told me I'd crossed some silly bitch who tried to come up on my inside.'

'And you didn't, of course?'

'She'd no bloody business to be where she was. Afterwards I found she was his niece.' She turned to Kit. 'Let me give you another drink. I should think you need one after being in before Westcott. They say there are good bastards and bad bastards. I know where he'd go in my book.'

Bob had gulped down his drink and was giving Miss Concannon a look in which astonishment and open disapproval were equally mixed, for it was long before the time, especially in Ireland, when feminine acquaintance with four-letter words was openly acknowledged. 'We'd better be going, Master Kit,' he said. 'We've a long drive before us.' When they were outside the door of the bar he turned to Kit again. 'That young lady should buy some mouthwash,' he said primly.

'But, Bob, she offered me a drink. And I thought she seemed rather fun – '

'That's enough now, that's enough. Haven't we sufficient trouble on our hands without you getting mixed up with the likes of her? Miss Concannon,' he added darkly. 'I've heard of her. A divil to ride, they say. They say other things, too. D'ye know what it is, Master Kit, an' heed what I'm tellin' ye, those sort o' hard goin' women, they're like hardy race mares, they're bad 'uns to breed from!'

By this time they had arrived at the car and he began to rummage in his pockets for his keys. 'I hope this ould yoke will start,' he said as he opened the door. Start, however, she did with several protesting bangs and splutters and they set off on their return journey to the Bay.

Neither Bob nor Kit could know of a conversation that was taking place between the pair they had left behind them in the bar. 'Well,' Dick Harbison said. 'You're a nice one, aren't you? All this talk about bastards – '

'What do you mean?'

'Didn't you know? No, come to think of it, you wouldn't since you've only just come back. Young Kit, they say he's not Massiter's son at all.'

'Jesus! I did say the wrong thing, didn't I? Who's the sire?'

'Some chap who was in the Flying Corps in the war. He had a walk out with Massiter's missus during the Troubles or so the story goes. His place was burnt down and he got mixed up with Cosgrave's lot during and after the civil war and people wouldn't have much to do with him. Then he went off to Kenya. I don't know any more, no one does know the real truth of it all and if they do they're not telling. They're a cliquey lot in the Bay.'

'There's another brother, isn't there?'

'Yes, and quite a different kettle of fish. Smooth as be damned. Rides nicely but hasn't got the guts of this one. Have another drink and are you coming back with me?'

'Perhaps,' she said. 'We'll see.' Their eyes met before he moved away to the bar.

In the village on the crest of the hill which they had passed through on their way to the races Bob slowed the car to a stop. 'I've no matches for me pipe,' he said. 'I'll just drop in here now and get some. Keep the car going, Master Kit. There's no knowin' she'd ever start again if she stops. I won't be more 'an a minute.' He disappeared through the open doorway of a shop which, Kit saw, bore on its headboard the inscription: *Licensed to sell beer wine and spirits.*

Smiling inwardly to himself Kit decided that Bob was either drowning his sorrows or preparing himself for the coming interview with his father. He hoped that his old friend would be coherent enough to carry the interview off. If only they had been up before anyone but Westcott! They had delivered themselves straight into the hands of the man his father disliked more than any other in racing, and that he would be furious was an understatement. What he would do about it was another matter. But perhaps he would decide to take it out on Westcott and not on them. Kit's natural resilience made him almost believe this might be the case. Comforting himself with that his thoughts turned to the girl he had seen before the race and in the bar after it – Carlow Concannon.

Already everything about her had begun to haunt him – that almost angular, striking face, those grey-blue eyes with a hint of laughter in them and the brown hair with its auburn

47

tints. There was, too, about her a sort of damn your eyes attitude in everything she did, even in the way she stood, that conjured up an excitement in him and made him long to meet her again. He turned over in his mind ways in which he could contrive such a meeting. The point-to-points weren't over. Perhaps she'd come down to ride in Kilderry, or maybe she'd be at Thurles where he was to ride that one of Desmond's, if Desmond, that was to say, would put him up after this. But somehow he didn't think his grandfather would be influenced by Westcott's strictures. Desmond would laugh like hell and tell him to do it again but not so obviously the next time.

Bob's reappearance, bringing with him a strong aroma of freshly consumed whisky, interrupted his thoughts. It occurred to Kit that the passage home might be even more perilous than the outward one with several large doubles under Bob's belt. But the whisky, in fact, seemed to have had the effect of concentrating Bob's thoughts and his reflexes, for he drove more steadily than when he was sober. It had, however, loosened his tongue. 'That big bugger,' he said. 'I never thought he'd do that to me. Horses, Master Kit, horses, all they do to you is to make fools of you. Like women, an' like women ye never know 'em till ye've tried 'em.'

'He'll win next time out, Bob.'

'He'd better, or else we'll be in again. Though I'm thinking you won't be ridin' him when he does. What's the Sir goin' to say to us at all at all, I wonder? He won't be pleased.'

'That way of putting it, Bob, is not putting the jumps very high as Dick Harbison said in the bar.'

'Be the holy, 'tis not. 'Tis a bad business altogether that's what it is.'

Then they were passing through the ornate battlemented gateway of the castle and making their way up the long avenue with its trim iron railings. Along by the private harbour the car seemed to be going ever more slowly, as though Bob was hoping for something or anything to occur to prevent or postpone the coming interview.

Dusk had fallen and the great bulk of the castle loomed up against the darkening sky like some huge cliff jutting out from the side of the hill. Slowing the car to a crawl Bob looked up at it. 'This will be all yours some day, Master Kit,' he said.

'I suppose so,' Kit answered. He had never given much thought to his inheritance. Now, gazing up at the sham machicolations, the Gothic towers, the crockets and finials, he wondered if he wanted it. It was too big and grand and formal for him.

'Aye, and the title too,' Bob went on. 'Sir Christopher Massiter, bart. That'll be a turn up for the books for there's some as'd soon see ye didn't have it, I'm thinkin'.' Then he coughed as if the realisation that he had said more than he should had caught up with him. His foot pressed down on the accelerator and he set the car going past the mouth of the harbour, round the bend and through the cutting that had been hacked out of the solid rock by countless poorly paid peasants so as to give a grander approach to the castle. In a moment or two they were pulling up on the gravel sweep before the tall arched doorway.

Getting out of the car Kit led the way through the line of bogus cloisters to a side door which gave on to a flagged passage. They passed the gun room and came to the billiard room where Hugo was idly knocking the balls about.

'Hullo, you two,' Hugo said. 'How'd it go?'

'Not too good,' Kit said. 'How about you?'

'Four fish,' Hugo answered. 'Two twelve pounders, a fifteen and a twenty-pounder.'

'Golly,' Kit said. 'That's a bit of all right, isn't it? What about Roughty?'

'None,' Hugo said laconically. 'He fishes almost as badly as he rides!'

The door opened and Babs came in. 'Now,' she said, 'tell me all about it. How did he run? I'm dying to know everything. Goodness, you both look very glum. Is it Thunderhead? Is he hurt?'

'It's not the horse m'Lady,' Bob said to her. 'I'm afraid we got into a bit of trouble.'

'Trouble? What sort of trouble?'

'The stewards had us in, m'Lady.'

'The stewards? I don't understand. Who was acting?'

'Colonel Swenson, another gentleman and – Mr Westcott.'

'Donal! Oh, dear!' Babs sat down on one of the padded benches. 'But what on earth happened?'

49

'Well, m'Lady,' Bob began when they heard steps outside in the passage.

'Here's the Sir now,' Hugo said. He had left the table and, leaning on his cue, was listening intently to all that was going on. 'You'd better tell him,' he added, and it seemed to Kit that there was a note of quiet satisfaction in his voice. After all he had had a successful day in the best of company while Kit's had ended in trouble if not disgrace. This more than made up for the point-to-point. 'I don't think he's going to be amused.' He leant over the table and casually potted the black.

Andrew came in and surveyed the little group. 'You're very late,' he said to Bob and Kit. 'I was wondering what kept you. How did the horse run, Bob?'

'I'm afraid he ran a bit too well,' Bob blurted out.

'Too well?' Andrew frowned. 'I don't understand. What do you mean?'

'He's goin' to be a good 'un, no question of that. He gave me the surprise of me life, sir. But, well, the long and the short of it is – ' Bob took a long breath and the whole story came out with a rush.

Oh Lord, Kit thought, watching him. He's not doing this at all well. He's making it appear worse than it is if that's possible.

Andrew listened, a deepening frown cutting furrows across his forehead and his lips tightening in the way they had when he was becoming more and more coldly angry. 'Donal Westcott,' he repeated when Bob had finished. 'Westcott. Tell me again what he said, Bob.'

The trainer repeated word for word as best he could the objurgations, warnings and cautions given them. Andrew's frown deepened further. 'I see,' he said. 'And this or the gist of it will appear in the *Calendar*.'

'I'm afraid it will, sir.'

All of them knew to what Andrew was referring. A record of penalties, warnings and fines handed out by the stewards appeared each week in *The Racing Calendar*, for all the sporting world to see. Such a notice affecting his son and his trainer would be a reflection on himself and a terrible blow to his pride, especially when it had been handed out by Westcott.

He turned on Kit, his strange tawny eyes blazing with an emotion Kit did not then recognise: he only knew it frightened him. Later he was to recall it and know it for what it was – pure hatred. 'I knew it was a mistake allowing you to ride,' he said, biting out his words. 'I might have guessed something like this would happen. Have you no sense at all, you stupid boy?'

Before Kit could answer Bob intervened. 'It wasn't the lad's fault, sir,' he said. 'It's me that's to blame. I told him to take the horse quietly and on no account to knock him about. It was my instructions that was wrong, sir. That big horse, he fooled us all.'

'That may be but it's no excuse. If the boy had a head on his shoulders at all, the way the race was run so you tell me, he'd have let him go.'

'And what would we have said to him then, sir, after all we had told him?'

'That's quite enough, Bob. Now you two boys cut along and change. You'll be late for dinner otherwise.'

'What are you going to do?' Babs asked him when the others had gone.

'I'll ring Roger Swenson after dinner and find out just what did go on at that enquiry. Then I'll make up my mind.' He turned abruptly and left the room.

Dinner that night was eaten in almost complete silence, save for the one effort Babs made to lighten the atmosphere by describing how Bridie O'Leary's illness had been diagnosed as an acute appendix and she had been removed with all speed to the local hospital.

'I shall have to see the girl tomorrow,' Babs said, 'and bring her something. These people are hopelessly improvident and I believe the food in that hospital is terrible. She's over the operation all right. They never tell you much in these places but they did say that when I rang up to enquire.'

Silence then fell on the table once more. It was broken only by Andrew saying to Kit as they rose. 'I'll see you in the library after church tomorrow.'

'Yes, sir,' Kit answered and then endeavoured to divert his thoughts from that interview by concentrating them on Miss Carlow Concannon.

51

'I wonder just what the Sir has in store for you,' Hugo said to him when the two boys were together in the billiard room after dinner. 'You are a bit of an ass, you know. Why didn't you loose that young horse's head and let him go?'

'I'd like to know what you'd have done,' Kit responded hotly. 'What did they expect after lecturing me about being reckless and God only knows what rot?' All the same he had a sneaking feeling that in a similar situation Hugo would somehow have managed better, for he had a way of turning things, however bad they seemed on the surface, to his own advantage. Although he was a year younger he always appeared the older, possibly because, Kit thought then, he had never really seemed to be young at all. And he knew all about everyone and everything that went on, for as well as being both observant and enquiring he listened in silence to adults' conversations and stored away in his mind all that he heard while Kit was daydreaming about horses and hounds and jumping fences and winning races and where he would next run his two point-to-pointers. 'Hugo,' he went on, 'did you ever hear of a girl called Carlow Concannon?'

'Of course,' Hugo said in his patronising way. 'The Concannons left during the Troubles. Mother's dead. She lives with her father. Kilkenny or somewhere. She's a nailer to ride. He's a bit of a bounder, they say. Trained under permit in England and made things too hot for him. That's one of the reasons they're back. They're nothing much, you know, the Concannons. They're not in Burke's Landed Gentry.'

'Neither are we, if it comes to that,' Kit said.

'The 1912 edition,' Hugo said loftily, 'gave a lot of offence by putting in the wrong people and leaving out others.'

'Including us and the Concannons, I suppose?'

'We're different. The Sir had only just come back from South America then and bought this place. The Concannons wouldn't have made it anyway. They're people of very little account. Hatters or millers or something.'

'I don't give a tinker's curse about Burke's Landed Gentry or millers or hatters. She seemed damn good value to me and you should have seen old Bob's face at her language.'

'Where'd you meet her?'

'In the bar. She was with Dick Harbison. She was bloody nice about the enquiry. She doesn't think much of Westcott.'

'Who does? But he's a clever swine to have got all that power. That's why the Sir doesn't like him. And he's dropped you into it all right.'

'Yes,' Kit said gloomily. 'I wonder what the Sir will do to me tomorrow.'

'No one knows what the Sir will do. That's why he always wins. Come on, I'll play you fifty up.'

Hugo won without much effort and the two boys went to bed, Kit to dream of taking Miss Carlow Concannon on at the last fence and laughing about it afterwards. The dream turned suddenly into nightmare, in which his father, those strange eyes of his blazing fire, was pointing a finger at him, accusing him of some nameless sin and warning him off – what? He wasn't sure because the dream then became blurred. He woke sweating and shaking for the first time in his life to be lulled again into a dreamless sleep by the early sun streaming in through the windows and beyond the soft peace of sea, sky and mountain that was the Bay.

CHAPTER VI

Attendance at Sunday morning service for those few Protestants left in South West Ireland in the late nineteen thirties was both a ritual and an obligation. It was a coming together of the clans, a proclamation of identity and an advertisement of their segregation from those amongst whom they lived. Not to be a churchgoer was to let down one's class in some ways almost worse than that most heinous of all crimes – that of changing one's religion and becoming a Roman Catholic. The very fact of their numbers being so few made attendance all the more essential for it served to emphasise to those others

53

that for some at least the old ties still held, the old Ireland of the Ascendancy still existed in mind if not in fact. The King was still prayed for along with the Bishops and clergy; the real rulers of the state in which they lived were left to their own church, to their own devices and in the minds of most of the congregation, to the devil.

At Dunlay Castle this Sunday observance was all but a parade. The family assembled on the flags of the great hall, the boys in their best suits, Andrew, too, formal in dark grey with the currently fashionable Anthony Eden Homburg in his hand, Babs in tweeds. Prayer and hymn books for each were laid out on a refectory table by the entrance. Taking these, they made their way to where the Rolls was waiting on the gravel. Inside the boys perched on the rumble seats facing their parents. Andrew picked up the speaking tube to the chauffeur and they moved off at the stately pace appropriate to the churchgoer. A few miles of curving road along the shores of the Bay brought them to the town of Bellary and the little church with its square tower built by the second Lord Derryquin on an eminence overlooking the town so that those of his own religion could be seen to be publicly proclaiming their faith and its observance before an alien population.

Inside the church the most striking feature was the faded regimental colour of the South Western Horse which hung above the chancel. It should have been laid up in Christ Church Cathedral in Dublin along with those of the other Irish Regiments disbanded at the treaty of 1921 but the South Western Horse was the Bay's very own regiment. Its surviving members, along with the entire protestant population of the Bay, had fought long and hard to keep it where they felt it belonged and at length, aided by the influence of one of the new senators drawn from their own class, they had succeeded. Now it hung there, fly-stained and worn, swaying gently in every draught, a tattered and all but forgotten memorial to past glories, as were the marble plaques that covered much of the wall space. Most of these, too, were of a military nature, testimonials to the martial spirit of the Ascendancy. Carved reproductions of regimental badges, crossed flags and lances, hussar busbies, tents, scrolls and even faithfully reproduced artillery pieces proliferated.

54

The seating of the congregation was graduated from front to back in descending order of rank and importance commencing with the high-sided, gated pew of the Derryquin family that faced the chancel. Brass plates set into the mahogany displayed the names of the owners of each pew. Though by far the richest family in the Bay – and still slightly suspect because of it – the Massiters were placed about half-way down the church. It mattered not that the pews in front of them were empty and would remain so, their owners having died out or been burnt out or just simply departed, for the names inscribed on those brass plates, though tarnished and unpolished now, kept them inviolate. There was in any event little competition for the empty places as there had been in the heyday of the Ascendancy, for the congregation was shrinking year by year.

The church itself was decaying like the society it served. Between the memorials the few bare places on the walls showed large areas of damp, the paint on the windows was peeling, the harmonium wheezed and groaned; in the porch was an appeal for funds to repair the roof.

The parson gave the impression of being nearly as old as his church. His sermons, read unashamedly from a book in a high quavering voice, droned on and interminably on. Usually during them Kit occupied his time learning by heart and repeating to himself the inscriptions on the memorials. But today such brave records of imperial derring-do as Captain Sir James Sinclair Jarvis dying valiantly for his country at Isandwhla or Surgeon-Lieutenant Michael Somerton giving up his life at Barrackpore tending the victims of a cholera epidemic failed to hold his attention or divert his thoughts from the coming interview with his father.

At length the preacher droned out the welcome words: 'And now to God the father, God the Son and God the Holy Ghost.' The congregation with an almost audible sigh of relief rose to their feet to join in the final hymn and place their offerings on the collection plate.

Outside the church, the service over, the families split up into little groups to discuss the topics then occupying their minds and thoughts, most of them concerned with sport or the weather and its effect on farming and their crops. Leaving those he was with Desmond Murtagh came swinging up, his horseman's swagger accentuated by his artificial leg, to where the Massiters were standing. Taking Kit by the arm he drew him apart. 'Can't hear most of what that fool of a rector is saying and what I can hear I don't understand,' he said. 'Well, young feller, seems you've got yourself into a spot of trouble.'

'I'm afraid so, sir.'

'I shouldn't worry. Can't remember the number of times I was in. As for Westcott – did he shout at you?'

'He did a bit, sir.'

'Thought so. Thinks he knows it all, but he doesn't, you know. Never ridden himself. No business carrying on like that for a first ride in public. I'll tell him so, too, and in no uncertain fashion next time I see him. Good job we kept him out of the Bay. Anyway you'll ride Deerstalker for me next week. Mind you don't stop him, boy!'

Kit grinned. He and his grandfather had much the same attitude to life. 'I'll try not to, sir.'

'Has your father said anything to you about yesterday?'

'Not yet, I'm to see him now, after church, in the library.'

'Keepin' you in suspense, is he? Well, that's his way. Good luck.'

In the Rolls the Sunday papers – the *Sunday Times*, the *Observer* and the *Sunday Despatch* were folded on the seat beside the chauffeur. The *Irish Times* did not produce a Sunday edition and despite the fact that there were two other Irish Sunday papers no member of the Bay's protestant population would have thought of reading them or introducing them to their houses except perhaps to the servants' hall.

Back at the castle Andrew put the papers under his arm and walked towards the library. Increasingly apprehensive, Kit followed him. No word, not even Andrew's usual comment on the length and prosiness of the sermon, had been spoken on the return journey in the car. His father, his lips set, had stared straight in front of him; Babs, nervously fingering the prayer book in her lap, had looked out of the window beside her watching the clouds gathering over the high peaks at the entrance to the Bay. They would close

56

in soon, Kit thought, and the rain would come. Whatever happened it was going to be a gloomy afternoon.

His father was in his chair behind the big desk when Kit entered the library. That, in itself, was a bad sign for it meant that he was sitting in judgment.

Kit had nourished a very slight hope that Colonel Swenson might have put in a word for him which would have led to some softening in Andrew's attitude. But one glance at his father's face was enough to dispel that hope. He was not told to sit down – another bad sign – and he did not dare to take a chair without being asked. His father stared at him in silence for a few seconds before he spoke. 'I hope there's no necessity for me to stress the stupidity of what you have done,' he began. 'You've made a fool of yourself, you've made a fool of me and you've brought my name publicly into disrepute. Worse still, you have given Mr Westcott the opportunity of taking it out on me and indeed on all the Bay. Do you realise that had it not been for Colonel Swenson you would have been sent on to the senior stewards? They're a weak lot this term and Mr Westcott has considerable influence with them. They could well have withdrawn your licence to ride. I don't find that prospect a pretty one and I intend to take good care that it does not occur again. Do you understand?'

'Yes, sir,' Kit said swallowing and wondering what was coming next.

'I'm sending you away, right away – '

Cripes! Kit thought, Australia! No, it couldn't be – but Andrew was going on:

'You've always said that you wanted to make your life with horses. Very well, you'll have your chance. You will go to Angus Robarts as a learner. And I warn you I shall instruct him to treat you as he would any new lad in the stable. He may lick some sense into you.'

Kit swallowed again. It meant leaving his beloved Bay and missing all the point-to-point rides he had lined up. Angus Robarts, too, who had trained a couple of jumpers in England for the Sir a year or so back was a tough nut, he knew that. But it might have been far worse. At least he'd be in a racing stable and not compelled to go jackarooing in Australia. He'd be in for a rough time, he knew that by the gleam in the Sir's eyes, but he thought he could take it. That there was no use in appealing for mercy or a second chance, one look at the Sir's set face told him. Anyway, young as he was, he had his pride; he would not beg. 'When am I to go?' he asked.

'You will catch the mail boat on Wednesday.'

'That means I can't ride Deerstalker on Saturday.'

'You don't seriously think I'd allow you to ride in public again until you have learnt a modicum of responsibility – if ever you do. One thing – there can be no question of your earning money as I suppose you realise. If you do you can never ride as an amateur. I won't have that for a son of this house. You won't starve. I shall open an account for you in England and fifty pounds a month will be paid into it. I consider I'm being generous.'

'Thank you, sir.'

'Now pay attention. I'm giving you a second chance. You've made a fool of yourself; far worse, you've made a fool of me. If it ever happens again you may expect nothing further from me. Do you understand?'

'Yes, sir.'

'That is all then. You may go.'

After he had left, Andrew, his lips still set, sat for a moment or two staring out across the Bay. The rain which has been threatening all the morning was sweeping in a squall across its surface, and clouds were creeping down from the peaks to the foothills. Suddenly, in the way it had, the squall passed and the clouds parted. A shaft of sunlight shot through the rift, directly illuminating the bluff above Bellary where the charred and roofless ruin of Bellary Court could just be seen above the trees that had sprung up around it. Andrew stared at it for a moment and then looked away for it was a reminder of things past which he still did not care to have recalled to him. Then he shrugged, picked up the *Observer* and began to turn its pages. As he did so the door opened and Babs came in. 'What have you done with him?' she asked.

'Hasn't he told you?' Andrew answered. 'I expected him to run to you for sympathy.'

'I haven't seen him. He's gone down to the yard to look at the horses, Hugo says. I'm asking you again, Andrew. What have you done with him?'

'I'm sending him away. He will go to Angus Robarts as a learner.'

'When is he to go?'

'He can cross on the mail boat on Wednesday. I've sent Robarts a wire.'

'So soon. How do you know Robarts will take him?'

'I've mentioned the matter to him before. You may recall the boy has always said he wants to make his life with horses. I consider I'm treating him very well.'

Their eyes met. There was much that Babs could say but she dared not say it. Andrew wanted to be rid of Kit; she guessed that now, and this incident had played into his hand. As always he had planned in advance and once the opportunity came he was ready to take advantage of it.

'It's harsh,' she said. 'Sending him away at a moment's notice and just for one thing. Bob said it wasn't his fault. You know yourself how these things can happen – horses – ' Babs gave a little gesture with her hands.

'Harsh? He is lucky I didn't take sterner measures. He is being given his chance to do what he has always said he wanted.'

'Angus Robarts is a brute,' Babs said.

'He may well instil some sense of responsibility into him. Do you realise that Roger told me Westcott would have sent them both on but for him? What do you think of that? A son bearing my name – ' he looked her full in the face as he spoke – 'sent on to the senior stewards after his first ride. It is quite intolerable. Something has to be seen to be done. As for Westcott, I shan't forget him, either, but he can wait.'

Babs sighed again. She, too, knew that further argument was useless. 'This means Kit can't ride Deerstalker on Saturday,' she said.

'Of course. You don't imagine I'd permit it after the other deplorable performance. Hugo will ride if Desmond agrees, as I'm sure he will.'

Babs looked down and her eyes caught the headlines of the paper Andrew had opened. NEW PEACE DRIVE. A WAVE OF HOPE, she read. TENSION EASED IN PRAGUE. 'Is there going to be a war, Andrew?' she asked.

'Certainly not. Hitler doesn't want war. He's bluffing. He's in enough financial trouble as it is. I was reading an article in the *Observer* about his difficulties when you came in. He has no oil. His tanks are made of cardboard. He can't fight a war even if he wanted to.'

'But did you read that speech of Churchill's? And Anthony Eden, he's been saying – '

'Churchill!' Andrew exclaimed contemptuously. 'He's an irresponsible hothead. An adventurer. Surely you remember the Dardanelles? Chamberlain won't have him in his cabinet at any price and he's quite right. Pay no heed to him. And as for the gang he has around him – jitterbugs every one of them. Eden – he's too damn good-looking and Duff Cooper – another swashbuckler. There will be no war, I assure you.'

'I hope you're right. If it did come, the boys, they'd have to go, wouldn't they?'

'Oh, yes. We've given a guarantee to Poland; we'd be in it.'

'Why we have to fight wars to save these foreigners I never could understand. It was the same the last time and that seems only yesterday.'

'We have to abide by our commitments. But I assure you it won't happen.'

It occurred to neither of them that they were citizens of an independent sovereign state which owed no allegiance to the country whose policies they were discussing as their own.

'Well, you're usually right, Andrew,' Babs said. 'You know about these things. I only hope you haven't made a mistake this time.'

The door closed behind Babs. Andrew stretched out a hand, picked up the *Observer*, and seated himself before the fire that glowed in the coals behind the club fender. He was not quite as convinced as he had seemed to be when he reassured Babs that there would be no war, but the present policy of those commercial interests with which he was connected dictated that any sign of 'jitters' should be suppressed. Besides, he and his friends rather agreed with Babs; they saw no reason why England should pull middle European chestnuts out of the fire for them. But if by chance there was a war, by sending Kit to England he had moved him one step nearer to it.

CHAPTER VII

Angus Robarts was a big, florid, rough-tongued Scotsman who had married money and a house. The house was Hetherington Grange, a Queen Anne gem, medium-sized by the standards of the day, set in its own park and surrounded by its own thousand acres on the edge of the Sussex downs. The money belonged to his wife, Beatrice, the sole and only daughter of a Victorian railway magnate who had made his pile and set himself up as a country gentleman and owner of racehorses.

Beatrice Robarts was a small woman with delicate hands and feet. Her ash blonde hair was worn coiled in tight curls round her head not a strand of which had ever been seen to be out of place. No one in racing had ever quite made out why she had married Angus, but the answer in fact was not far to seek. Her air of fragility belied her true character. Behind those delicate features lay a restless disposition, a will of iron and a compulsive desire to interfere in the lives of those about her.

Angus had been struggling when she married him but she had divined that behind the rough manner lay a flair for picking out the promise in the big horses then fashionable in steeplechasing and exploiting it when he got them. Moving into the Grange he had set up his stables there and his few owners had followed him. With her money behind him he had bought them good horses, and other winners began to flow in, amongst them victories in two Grand Nationals. With the winners came more and better owners sedulously cultivated and cosseted by her. Her Sunday morning champagne receptions became famous as did her presence on the racecourse. She was everywhere, brisk, knowledgeable, demanding and interfering. Jockeys dreaded her sharp comments, stewards and handicappers blanched at her approach. Someone christened her Mrs Meddler and the name stuck. She was the power behind the stable and she knew it.

But the marriage was childless, and she had never quite

succeeded in smoothing the rough edges from her husband. The years of covering up for his uncouthness, of repairing rows between him and his better owners whom he had offended by some gaffe or other had had their effect on even her tough spirit. By the time Kit arrived at the Grange she had become disenchanted both with her marriage and her way of life. She had bought a house in Brook Street. Her thoughts were turning more and more towards London and the louche edges of café and literary society to which her money had gained her entrance, and she was no longer devoting all her energies towards furthering her husband's career.

This was one of the reasons for the stable's decline. The other was that Angus could really only train one type of horse, the big, tough chaser with which he had made his name and which was becoming harder and harder to find. Always on the look-out for what he called 'hardy' horses he had scouts in Ireland spotting for him; but even these, when he got them, he consistently over-worked and over-galloped. He had always been a hard master of men and horses and he could not or would not change. Nor would he realise that already a lighter-framed horse was coming into steeplechasing from the flat. He spurned these recruits and would not have them in the stable. All these things combined to make former owners drift away and new ones fight shy of him. With Beatrice's knowledge of racing and ability to handle people she might have done much to arrest this decline had she put her mind to it, but she could no longer find it in her to take the trouble. She still presided over the Sunday morning gatherings but without the sparkle which had done much to lighten her husband's lowering presence; lack of success had done nothing to sweeten Angus' temper. Kit, although he did not know it, was being pitched straight into an unhappy atmosphere.

A taciturn chauffeur in an Austin shooting brake met him at Wyborough station and drove him to the Grange whose pillared entrance gates and double lodges were on the outskirts of the village. Turning into an immaculately swept yard the chauffeur pulled up by a small building set apart from the rest with stone steps leading up to it. 'The Guv'nor's office,' he said nodding towards it. 'He'll see you now – in there.'

Going up the steps Kit found himself in a narrow passage with a door on either side. Both were closed and there was no indication of what lay beyond them. Choosing one at random he knocked once. In response a gruff shout from its farther side told him to enter. He opened the door and stepped inside.

He was in a small room panelled in pitch pine. Most of the floor space was taken up by a large desk. Sitting behind the desk was a burly red-faced man whom he knew must be Angus Robarts. On the wall behind him were two montage pictures of his Grand National victories. Shelves bearing bound volumes of *The Racing Calendar* and *The Bloodstock Breeder's Review* filled the rest of the wall space.

The trainer looked up as Kit came in and he found himself staring into a pair of angry green eyes set rather too close together. 'So you're young Massiter, are you?' was his greeting.

'Yes, sir,' Kit said.

'Very well. Your father has sent you here as a learner. Now get one thing clear. I won't have useless hands about the place. You'll be treated as one of the lads. No favours – understand?'

'Yes, sir,' Kit repeated. There didn't seem to be much else to say.

'And another thing,' Angus went on, his voice becoming more and more angry as he progressed. It was characteristic of him, as Kit was later to find out, that he always seemed to be working himself into a passion: 'Never forget who is the master here.' He tapped his chest. 'I am. I won't have any questions and I won't have any queries. You'll do as I say. Some of you young fellows from Eton and Harrow think you can come it across the likes of us because we were brought up rough. Not here you can't. One smart-alec word out of you and I'll kick you out so quick you won't know what hit the seat of your pants. Can you ride?'

Kit remembered in time the warning Bob Ferris had given him before he left. 'Now listen to me, Master Kit,' he had said. 'Don't let on to them that you've ridden work or ridden races or they'll think you're putting on airs and they'll crucify you. Play foolish and stay quiet. Them English stables is tough places and that Angus Robarts, he's one of the worst.'

'A little,' Kit said.

'A little, hey? Well, we'll soon find out. The first lot goes out at half past seven. See you're there in good time. There are lodgings for you in the village. Brooks will take you down.'

The interview was obviously over. Kit turned to go. As he reached the door: 'Have you a bicycle?' came in a bellow from behind him.

'No, sir, I'm afraid I haven't.'

'Get one, then. We're a mile from the village. Lateness is slackness. Be on time.'

The lodgings in the village consisted of a bare room with a narrow iron bed and a deal dressing table, the use of a bathroom, three meals a day and the shared occupancy with the family of the dining room and the little parlour that looked out on to the street. Mrs Hardy, the landlady, a hard faced woman with iron grey hair drawn back in a bun, led him up bare board stairs to his room.

'Another of them,' he heard her say to her husband, a worker on the estate, who had just come in, as she bustled into the kitchen to prepare the evening meal. 'I wonder how long he'll last.'

But she unearthed from somewhere a rusty bicycle and on this Kit set out the following morning for his first day in stables.

Angus Robards was standing in the yard dressed in a dark brown hacking jacket, breeches and leggings, holding a Long Tom whip in his hand. The lads were standing by their boxes about to bring out their horses. Kit had arrived just in time. He was soon to learn that when Angus mentioned a time he meant ten minutes earlier. It was one of his methods of torment. 'Firecracker is in there,' he barked at Kit, lifting a finger to indicate a box. 'Get him out.'

Someone had already tacked the horse up, Kit saw. It had only been done, he guessed, lest his ignorance and inefficiency should make the string late. Firecracker was a big horse, coal black all over save for a star on his forehead. Kit went to his head and led him out into the yard.

The other members of the string had left their boxes by now and the lads were mounted. They were turning in the saddles looking at him, and Kit could sense an air of expectancy. 'Get up,' Angus barked at him.

Putting his hands on the horse's withers Kit vaulted towards the saddle. He never got there. No sooner was his leg across Firecracker's back than there was a crack like a rifle shot behind him. Firecracker went straight up into the air. His head went down and his quarters came up as he spun round to face the noise. Kit was catapulted forward. He hit the hard raked ground and rolled over. All the breath was knocked out of him and he felt as if he had been assaulted with a sledgehammer.

'Get up,' a voice snarled at him. 'What the hell do you think you're doing lying about there? You're not hurt. Get up.'

Kit was hurt; but he had had falls before and he reckoned nothing was broken and not much wrong beyond a few bruises and some gravel rash. One of the lads had caught Firecracker and he scrambled back into the saddle. 'Are you all right?' the lad said to him under his breath. 'He always does that, the bloody old bastard,' he went on looking over his shoulder to where the trainer, his back towards them, was mounting his hack. 'Your fellow will be all right now. It's the noise 'e 'ates.'

The string filed out of the yard, Kit bringing up the rear – fortunately for him since his arm and side were now hurting quite considerably. Firecracker was amongst the group only set to canter that morning. He had gone quietly enough on the laneway leading to the hundred acre field where the gallops were, only trying to play up once when a bird burst out of a hedgerow, but this time Kit had been ready for him.

Cantering, too, was something he had often done at Bob's and although Firecracker took a nice steady hold he had no difficulty in keeping to his designated place.

The riding part of his life at the Grange, as everyone called it, came easily enough to Kit. The work in the stable was another matter. Always before there had been grooms at Dunlay to do the heavy menial work with the horses. Now

65

he had to be initiated into the mysteries of 'setting fair' and 'doing over'. But because he was young and strong and healthy it did not take him long to fit into the stable routine and the general scheme of things. Since he had some experience riding out for Bob Ferris and being about his stable it was only a short time too, before he realised that there was something seriously wrong at the Grange.

There weren't any winners; that was the first and most important thing. When winners are scarce in a stable discontent is almost always present and Angus was having a bad season even by his recent standards. But this was only a symptom; the real trouble lay far deeper. Morale was bad. Everybody was at odds with each other and the Guv'nor was at odds with everybody. The head lad, Wilson, disapproved of his employer's harsh training methods and took little pains to conceal the fact. 'This is where he loses all his races,' he said to Kit a few days after his arrival as they filed on to the hundred acres. And it seemed to Kit, watching Angus' training methods as the days passed, that he was right. The horses were galloped too much, too far and too often.

In particular he thought that this applied to Firecracker, the horse that had unshipped him the first day and who was now in his charge. Firecracker was one of the modern type of jumpers that had come in from the flat. He was a far lighter-framed horse than Angus liked to train, but he had to keep him for he was the property of Lord Marchester, one of the longest standing and more important of his owners. From stable gossip Kit learned that 'the Lord' as he was known in the stable was old and ill and his horses were now supervised by a nephew called Clare de Vaux, his heir, whose interests lay elsewhere and who cared nothing for them but carried them on out of loyalty to his uncle. He also learnt that Marchester and through him, his nephew, were about the only people whom Angus either respected or feared for Marchester had been not only a leading GR in his day but also a National Hunt Steward and a pillar of the National Hunt Committee. He was too old and ill now to come near the stables, and perhaps for Angus' sake it was just as well, for his knowledgeable eyes would soon have perceived that things were far from right. Firecracker, as it happened, had

66

been bought by de Vaux in some sort of deal or exchange in which, so Wilson told Kit whom he was making into a kind of confidant, "'E didn't know what 'e was doin' but 'e done it an' we've got 'im.'

The lads themselves were paid a pittance, but their living accommodation which had been arranged by Beatrice when she took an interest in such things was reasonable enough. They slept in a dormitory over one of the range of boxes which was clean and airy and they had ample locker space for their belongings if they had any. There was a communal dining-cum-recreation room and the food was plentiful, also due to Beatrice's influence. It was during the days that they suffered torture, subjected to a constant barrage of abuse from their employer which was sometimes accompanied by the laying across their shoulders of the Long Tom he always carried with him. One of those who suffered most was Cayley, the lad who had spoken to Kit on his first day when he had ridden Firecracker. He was a gangling boy of about sixteen who could never do things quite right. It was Cayley who had been told off to initiate Kit into the mysteries of getting his horse's box and the horse himself ready for inspection and of tacking up in just the way Angus wanted.

Although Cayley could show Kit how it should be done he could never quite master these things himself. His boxes always contrived to look untidy, his horses never shone from his strapping however hard he worked at it and there were frequently mistakes in his tack which Angus' eyes instantly spotted. Then the yard would resound with roars of 'You useless, idle little bastard, Cayley', and the Long Tom would be mercilessly laid on.

The end result of all this was that Cayley was terrified. The more frightened he became the more mistakes he made and the more he was persecuted. Kit, who picked things up quickly, did what he could to help but it was not much use for Angus' eagle eye missed nothing and any overt act of assistance would bring down a roar of 'Leave him alone, damn you, boy. Let the little bastard do it himself.'

'Why do you stick it?' Kit asked him one evening, finding the lad in tears in one of the boxes.

'I 'as to,' was the reply. 'It's this or the dole and I 'as a sick mother in the village an' 'e knows it the old fucker. Look – ' bending down he pulled his jersey over his head. Across his puny shoulders were a series of raw, red weals. 'That's what 'e done to me with that fuckin' Long Tom,' Cayley said with a wail and a sniff. "E said me throat lash was an 'ole too tight an' it wasn't, damn 'im. An' now d'you know what 'e says 'e's goin' to do to me?'

'No. What?' Kit said, wondering what was coming next.

"E says 'e's goin' to give me Moonstruck to do now Bill Denton has gone sick.'

Moonstruck was well named. He was potentially a high-class steeplechaser but he was unpredictable in stable or out of it. One day he would be as quiet as an old sheep, the next virtually untouchable and lashing out at everything. One day he would school like the most brilliant of park fencers; the next he would take everything by the roots. Bill Denton was the only lad in the place who could get on with him. By a combination of strength and cunning he had achieved something like a working partnership with him. But he had gone down with 'flu. It had been a matter of speculation in the stable who would get the unenviable task of standing in for him. It seemed that Cayley had drawn the short straw.

Bicycling back to his lodgings that evening Kit tried to think of some way in which he could help Cayley, but could find none. For the first time in his life he had been brought face to face with the brutal fact of the prison built about those unprotected by money or privilege. Virtually the whole village depended on Angus for employment. These were the hungry thirties and he alone stood between them and the dole. If Cayley went there were plenty of others waiting to take his place. One of the worst aspects of the whole thing to Kit's mind was that Cayley, as he had soon seen, could ride. He had gentle hands and if he was left alone horses went for him. He was probably too nervous and highly-strung ever to make a jockey but there was some sort of talent there which Angus was systematically ruining. Nevertheless, Angus too must have sensed something in Cayley, for even he would not have given him Moonstruck just to torture him. Maybe, Kit thought, if he did well with him, Angus would lay off him for a bit.

In any event when he arrived back at the village there was something waiting for him which put Cayley and his troubles out of his mind. After stowing the bicycle away in the shed at the back he came in through the kitchen where Mrs Hardy was doing her washing. 'Message for you,' she said with a sniff. 'She sent it down. It's on the table inside.'

An envelope was lying on the coloured cloth of the parlour table. Picking it up Kit opened it and took out a sheet of thick, heavily deckled and embossed writing paper. It bore an invitation which was in the nature of a command to present himself at the Grange for pre-luncheon drinks on Sunday morning. Beatrice Robarts had decided it was time she looked over her husband's new pupil.

CHAPTER VIII

Beatrice's Sunday mornings were still fashionable even though the fortunes of the stable were declining. Kit had to thread his way through a clutter of expensive motor cars parked on the gravel sweep before entering the drawing room which was thronged with people whom he didn't know and who were mostly much older than himself.

It was a beautiful room, long and graceful with three tall windows looking out towards the Downs. It had been done over for Beatrice all in white by Syrie Maugham and this suited both the perfection of its lines and the cool elegance of the hostess herself.

Standing by the Adam fireplace, a martini glass in her hand, and a rope of pearls at her throat she surveyed Kit with the air of offhand insolence she adopted towards first acquaintances, especially those whom she thought likely to be of little use or interest to her. 'So,' she said. 'You're the new pupil, are you. Straight from Ireland, I hear. Where were you at school?'

'Er – Eton,' Kit said.

'Were you, indeed.' Her eyes betrayed a flicker of interest. 'That's a change from the last one, anyway. I think he came from a polytechnic, whatever that may be.' Her glance lingered for a second on his suit and shirt and Kit realised that she was deciding they, at least, passed muster. 'Drinks over there,' she said, gesturing vaguely towards a corner of the room, her eyes already dismissing him and looking over his shoulder at another newcomer. 'Well, Clare,' Kit heard her greeting him. 'Quite a stranger, aren't you?' We don't often see you saying ha, ha, amongst the horses – or have I got my Biblical quotations wrong?'

Kit moved away. Near him Angus was standing in the middle of a little group, his accustomed savage expression on his face. He was listening or pretending to listen to owners' chatter which he answered with monosyllabic grunts interspersed with long pulls at a very brown whisky. 'You'll run him at Sandown, then,' Kit heard one owner, greatly daring, enquire. Angus' face grew even darker at this presumption.

'Sandown!' he spluttered, and took another deeper pull on his whisky. This seemed to inspire him into giving a longer reply than his usual grunt. 'Sandown? I was a damn fool to put him in. He's bloody useless. A seller at Market Rasen. That's his mark.' Then, catching sight of Kit, he turned on him. 'Hey, you,' he all but shouted. 'Don't stand about there idle. Help Curtis with the drinks.'

The drinks were laid out on a long table covered with a white cloth. There was, as always in racing parties, an abundance of champagne. As well there were pitchers of martini, gin-and-lime, "gimlet" they called it then, whisky for those few who wanted it at lunchtime and bottles of the new-fangled tonic water which was just coming into fashion as a mixer. Curtis, the butler, was arranging glasses on a tray. 'Roped you in, has he?' he hissed between his teeth as Kit came up. 'Cheap labour inside and out, that's 'im.' And then, addressing a smart lady who had drifted along beside them, 'Yes, madam – a glass of champagne?'

Kit took a tray of glasses and began to circulate the room

70

with it. The company appeared to have separated into two groups, one of which stood at the far end of the room discussing London doings, café society gossip and the stock market and those nearer the drink table of which Angus was the centre, who were talking racing.

Beatrice was standing by one of the windows with the man who had come in after Kit. As he proffered the tray the man turned and reached out a hand for a glass. Their eyes met and the hand was suddenly arrested in mid-air. The other man stood poised, staring at Kit for a long uncomfortable moment. 'Good God,' he said, and then repeated it, 'Good God.' Then, murmuring an apology, he took the glass and turned back to his hostess.

Moving on to another group Kit wondered what could be the reason for the little scene. In the brief instant of the encounter he had noticed that Beatrice's companion was blind in one eye and that there was a patch of scar tissue below the left cheek bone.

When he was out of earshot Beatrice, having followed him with her eyes, said quietly: 'Good heavens, Clare, what is it? You look as if you had seen a ghost.'

The other paused before replying. His eyes, too, followed Kit across the room. 'I wonder,' he said quietly. 'I rather think I may have done. Who is that boy?'

'He's Angus' new pupil. Irish. Name of Massiter. Does that convey anything to you?'

'No. Irish, is he? Where's he from?'

'A place called Bellary in County Kilderry. Don't ask me where that is. Somewhere in the bogs, I suppose.'

'Kilderry? Bellary? Good God.'

'What *is* it, Clare?'

'Just that everything about him reminds me of someone I once knew. A very dear friend. In the war. Our old war. I wonder – '

After the guests had gone and the last Lagonda, the last Alvis Speed Twenty, the last Rolls-Bentley had purred off down the drive Beatrice poured herself a final martini and, sipping it, picked up the *Sunday Express*. Then, while Curtis and a parlour-maid cleared away the glasses, she settled down before the blazing log fire to wait for lunch. Turning to Valentine Castlerosse's gossip column, 'The Londoner's Log', and finding no mention there of any friends or acquaintances, she put the paper aside and allowed her thoughts to run on the strange incident of Clare de Vaux and her husband's new learner in the stable.

Like most of her set Beatrice thrived on gossip and liked it better when it was tinged with mystery. Clare de Vaux, as she was aware, knew nothing of horses and cared less. He managed them in a desultory way as best he could out of kindness to the old man with whom he lived, and who was, although Clare would never admit it, taking an unconscionable time a-dying – about ten years at the last count.

All his life, Clare had told her, he had hated the bloody things. It was because of them and his indifferent horsemanship that, he had explained, in 'our old war' he had left his cavalry regiment and joined the RFC. But Clare had seemed almost stunned by that glimpse he had got of Kit. What could be the connection, she wondered? Getting to her feet she went into the library and fetched down the current edition of *Who's Who*. A glance at the entry under 'Massiter' told her little more than that he had acquired a baronetcy in 1921, had two sons, was Joint-Master of the Kilderry Foxhounds, a member of the Irish Turf Club and National Hunt Steeplechase Committee. His seat was Dunlay Castle, Bellary, County Kilderry and his club the Carlton. There was nothing in the entry to link him with Clare in any way.

Then, reading it again, she recalled that the mention of Bellary and Kilderry had struck some sort of chord in Clare's recollection. Loving mystery and intrigue as she did, she could not leave the matter alone. Over lunch she worried at it in her mind and afterwards, when they were having their coffee, she brought it up with Angus. 'Clare looked as if he had seen a ghost,' she said as she finished.

Angus grunted. 'It may be nothing to do with the boy at all,' he said. 'It might have been that old wound of his. Gives him hell now and then, I know.'

'He was in the RAF, wasn't he?'

'The Flying Corps they called it then. Yes, did damn well,

too. Commanded a fighter squadron and a good one before he was shot down.'

'I'm sure there is something there. It was the way he looked. He couldn't be his own son, could he?'

'Good God, of course not. He was married once, just after the war. Wife and child killed in a car smash. Don't talk rubbish, woman.'

At that moment Curtis came in to say Angus was wanted on the telephone. When he came back he was frowning. 'The plot thickens,' he said heavily. 'There must be something there whatever it is.'

'Why? What happened?'

'That was Clare. He wanted to know if the boy could ride. When I said he could, a bit, he wanted me to put him up on Firecracker at Fontwell next Saturday.'

'There is a connection then. It must be from the Irish angle. Clare recognised the place whatever it's called, Bellary, when I told him that's where he came from. He repeated it and the name of that County in the bog. Incidentally the boy was at Eton. Did you know that?'

'I knew it. It's no recommendation to me. So far as I'm concerned he's carrying overweight.'

'I can imagine. Are you going to put him up?'

'Of course not. It's an amateur hurdle. I've asked young Harbison to ride him.'

'Dick Harbison, I thought he was in Ireland.'

'He was. He's come over here to see if he can get into this new war that's coming.'

'I thought any of the young who think about it at all are trying to get out of it – taking to the hills or getting into something safe early on like searchlights or ack-ack. That's the talk in London anyway.'

'I daresay it is in the circles you mix with. They're not all like that, thank God. Harbison did part of a short service commission in the RAF. I don't know why or how he got out. Too deep in with the books probably. Anyway he's over here now trying to get back in. He'll probably manage it. If he flies as well as he rides the Huns had better look out.'

'Has he brought his lady love with him?'

73

'The Concannon girl? She's about too, or so I'm told. Ireland was too slow for her.'

'What will you do about Clare and young Massiter?'

'Nothing. He can travel with the horses. It'll save me sending a lad and Clare can have another look at him if that's what he wants.'

Beatrice picked up the paper again. 'Do you know,' she said. 'I rather think I'll go racing myself on Saturday.'

CHAPTER IX

Carlow Concannon was standing by the rails of the parade ring at Fontwell when Kit caught sight of her. She was wearing a long, white, belted mackintosh; on her head was a tweed hat with a regimental badge at its crown. She looked cool, collected and ready to damn anyone's eyes at a moment's notice. Kit thought that never in his life had he seen anything so attractive. Greatly daring, he approached her. 'Hullo,' he said shyly.

Her insolent grey-blue eyes looked him up and down and for a moment he thought he was about to be damned and dismissed. Then, suddenly, she smiled. 'Well I never,' she said. 'If it isn't Mr Massiter of Malloran Park. Westcott's friend from the stewards' room. What the devil are you doing here?'

'I'm with Angus Robarts as a learner.'

'Learner? You won't learn much there except how not to do it. Dick rides one for him in the third.'

'I know.'

'Any chance?'

'Not an earthly,' Kit said. He knew very well that he had no right at all to say it since he had an idea that Angus fancied Firecracker a bit but he was carried away by the fact that he had this exciting girl all to himself and, if he had to confess it, the desire to impress. Moreover what he had said about Firecracker's chances were accurate and he knew it for he had ridden him in his winding-up gallop. Angus had sent him down with two others to do a mile and three quarters.

'Come along all the way,' he had said. They had done just that and the end of the gallop on the hundred acres was against the collar. When they pulled up, steaming, Angus was still not satisfied. 'Go back and do it again,' he said.

'See what I mean,' the head lad had whispered to Kit as they hacked back. 'That'll fix him, you'll find.'

'That's worth knowing, anyway. Thanks,' she said, glancing down at her card. 'What will win it then? Merrie Monarch, perhaps. Toby Revere rides. If he's an amateur Dick's an apprentice. Hullo, here's Mrs Meddler. What brings her here? I thought she'd gone out of racing.'

Beatrice Robarts had been eyeing them both from a little distance. Now she began to walk towards them. 'What are you doing coffee-housing about?' she said to Kit as she came up. 'You were sent here to work.' When he had disappeared in the direction of the stables she turned to Carlow. 'Now then,' she said. 'What do you know about that young man?'

'Not much,' was the reply. 'I only met him once. He'd been given a bollocking by Donal Westcott in the stewards' room at Malloran Park.'

Beatrice was momentarily distracted from her main purpose. 'Westcott,' she said. 'He owns Irish racing, doesn't he?'

'He thinks he does. I'm not sure he's right.'

'What sort of trouble was young Massiter in?'

'Nothing much. It was his first ride in public, Dick said it could have happened to a bishop but Westcott went to town on it. There's some sort of family feud between Westcott and his father – if he is his father.'

Beatrice's eyes snapped. She was on to something now and determined to pursue it. 'Not his father? What do you mean?'

Carlow regarded her coolly. She rather regretted having allowed this piece of gossip to slip out. 'I really don't know,' she said. 'He comes from a place called Bellary Bay in County Kilderry. I've never been there but it's supposed to be a sort

75

of world of its own. Ask Dick. He knows more about it than I do. I want to look at these horses. Toby Revere rides Triplex. He'll be favourite.'

'Toby? He's back again, is he? I saw him when I came in, wearing the buttons on his blazer of the last regiment he'd been kicked out of. He'll stop it if it suits him. Anyway he has a bit too many miles on his speedometer now, hasn't he?'

'Maybe. He can still ride rings around most of these bumpers – except Dick of course.'

When the time came for Firecracker's race Beatrice stood by the rails intently watching the little group about him. Kit had been given the task of leading Firecracker around. She saw Clare recognise him as he brought the horse in, smile and speak to him. Then, as they left the ring, she noticed Clare touch Kit on the arm as he was gathering and folding the rug and exchange further words with him. Clare was obviously more interested in the boy than the horse, but this was not surprising since Clare almost openly proclaimed his indifference to the performances of his uncle's runners. In fact, Beatrice guessed, it was only because of Kit's presence that he was there at all.

It was just as well that he was unconcerned about the outcome of Firecracker's race for the horse ran listlessly and finished well back, Toby Revere's mount having duly obliged and cantered in by five lengths.

'He tired,' was Dick's laconic comment as he dismounted and then, catching sight of Kit: 'Hullo, what brings you here? Not warned off yet, are you?'

'I'm with Mr Robarts,' Kit said. 'My father thought I'd be better out of Ireland after that business at Malloran Park.'

'Getting you out from under Westcott's eye, eh? No love lost between 'em, is there? Anyway, see you again somewhere, racing. We'll have a laugh.' He put the saddle over his arm and walked towards the weighing room.

Clare had watched the race in silence and listened to the exchange between trainee and rider without comment. Beatrice had been correct in thinking that what happened to Firecracker affected him very little though he would have to make some sort of report to his uncle, he supposed, if the old

76

man was well enough to receive it. The boy, Kit Massiter, interested him far more. Everything about him reminded him of Stephen Raymond, his closest friend from the war days. He and Stephen had shared the perils of the skies of France when neither knew if the next day or the next hour or minute for that matter, would be their last, though Stephen's skills in the air far exceeded his. Wartime friendships fade quickly, but he had always blamed himself for his failure to keep up with Stephen. He had heard of the burning of his house and something of the vicissitudes of his career after it. Dredging in his memory he thought he recalled a Massiter who was a friend of Lloyd George and who had come with him once to inspect the squadron. There was a girl from home, too, that Stephen had sometimes mentioned. But it was all twenty and more years ago.

Clare shook himself mentally and came back to earth to find himself standing in the little group around the horse. 'I'd like to take this young man off and give him a drink,' he said.

Even from the heir of Lord Marchester and his horses Angus was not prepared to have his routine interrupted or any of his workforce directed away from his allotted task. 'Only after he's cooled off the horse,' he growled. 'He's here to learn, and learn he damn well will.'

'And you can wait, Clare,' Beatrice said in her waspish way. 'I don't see you having much interest in the rest of the sports.' She watched Kit lead the horse away and then went on, 'He got into trouble in Ireland, and was in before Donal Westcott. That's why his father banished him and sent him to us. Though there's more than a bit of an if, it seems, whether he is his father.'

'What the devil do you mean?' Angus demanded.

'I've been talking to the Concannon girl. Ask the boy-friend Dick Harbison, if you want to know more. She says he has the whole story.' Beatrice looked slyly at Clare and ran her tongue over her lips in the way she had when savouring some tasty piece of malice.

'That'll do now,' Angus said. Turning to Clare he declared in his uncompromising way: 'That damn horse, Clare. He's useless. Get rid of him.'

77

'I daresay. I'll tell m'uncle. And tell the boy I'll be in the members' bar when he's free.'

Kit found Clare sitting at a table with a bottle of champagne in front of him. 'The only thing I can drink nowadays,' he said. 'That and whisky and they don't mix. Care for a glass?' Without waiting for an answer he filled a tumbler almost to the brim and pushed it across the table to Kit. 'Never drink out of those saucers on stems they give you for it,' he said. 'They're only for tarts. Tankards or tumblers are the things for the Boy. You come from Bellary Bay, they tell me. A great friend of mine from the war lived there then. Stephen Raymond – ever heard of him?'

'The Raymonds lived across the Bay from us,' Kit said. 'They were burnt out in the Troubles. I think I've heard my mother mention your friend. He went to Kenya afterwards, didn't he?'

'You never knew him?'

'Oh no, sir. He must have gone when I was very young.'

'I did hear he'd taken himself off to Kenya. He was a fine pilot. Best shot in the squadron.' Clare began to search in his waistcoat pockets. 'Where did I put the damned thing? Ah, I have it. Here it is.' He produced an eyeglass and screwed it into his good eye. 'Used to wear it for show – swank, you know, when I was young. Since the Huns got my other one I need it, dammit.'

Kit realised he was being studied intently. He could not understand the interest this rather formidable-looking man with the ravaged face was taking in him. It was a strange sort of world he'd been thrown into, he told himself. One minute he was being cursed crooked like the most ignorant and inefficient stable lad, the next he was drinking champagne with an earl's nephew. And all of them seemed to want to know more about him than he knew himself.

Clare took a sip from his glass. 'You're a learner with Angus, I gather,' he said. 'That's a sort of unpaid dogsbody, isn't it? What are you going to do later on?'

'I don't know. Something with horses in it I hope.'

'There's going to be a war any minute now. Ever think of flying?'

78

'No sir, I hadn't.'

'You can ride, I'm told. You're the sort of chap the RAF is looking for. There won't be any horses in this war. And it's closer than most people guess. Wishful thinkers all of them. There'll be no racing then. Think about it. Angus knows where to find me. He sends me the bills.'

After Kit had gone back to his duties Clare sat on. The remainder of the programme meant nothing to him and he had no intention of watching it. As he sipped from his glass his thoughts ran back over the years. Because of his injuries he could no longer fly, but the Flying Corps had made him. Up to then he had been a failure, laughed at in the regiment for his indifferent horsemanship, despised and openly derided by his colonel, a famous GR. But he had not failed as a flyer. He had got his Flight and later commanded a Squadron, though he knew and was grateful for the fact that much of his initial success, indeed his survival, he owed to Stephen, before Stephen's own career had foundered through no fault of his own. After the armistice and his demobilisation he had maintained his interest in the peacetime RAF. His record and his social position had enabled him to keep in touch with certain senior officers and those not so senior, whom time-servers and yes-men had passed by in the race for promotion. From discussions he had had with the latter he had come to believe that the Service had gone soft—not in the quality of its personnel but in the thinking behind its direction. There was too much emphasis on drill in the air, 'square bashing in the sky' he had heard it called, and on spit and polish on the ground. The RAF was, he believed, being trained for peace not war. 'The best flying club in the world' someone said of it, no doubt correctly, but this was no preparation for a shooting war. It was a little like the pre-1914 Navy which felt that the firing of its guns might tarnish its paintwork.

Clare now felt as sure as he could be that this boy was either Stephen's son or closely connected with him. He cared for neither Angus Robarts whom he regarded as a roughneck, nor his wife whom he thought to be a scheming little bitch and he thought the boy would do no good there. The only way he could help him was by getting him into the Service

79

with a head start. If the war came he would have to serve anyway and Clare's instinct told him he was of the stuff from which fighter pilots are made. In return, too, he just might, if there was time, learn from him something of the current RAF thinking on fighter tactics as taught to those who would have to employ them. That is to say if there was any such thinking for insofar as fighter tactics existed at all they seemed to Clare and his fellows to smack of the Hendon Air Display more than war in the air.

Clare sighed and sipped again, his thoughts once more on Kit. Massiter, he repeated to himself, surely he knew something about him? Had Stephen mentioned him or was it more recent whatever it was? The memory proved as elusive as before. Then he looked up to see Dick Harbison and Carlow Concannon entering the bar. Lifting a finger he beckoned them over. 'This horse of m'uncle's you rode,' he said to Dick when he had filled their glasses. 'I suppose he's no good. How did you find him?'

'He gave me a nice ride,' Dick said cautiously. 'But he didn't quite get the trip. Perhaps a shorter distance would suit him better.'

Despite his lack of interest in racing Clare had been around long enough to realise he was not going to learn anything here. He was therefore surprised when Carlow spoke up. 'Angus always over-cooks his horses,' she said. 'Your fellow Firecracker has been galloped off his legs. I'll swear that's his trouble. A summer's rest and a change of air, that's what he needs. If you'll sell I might have a customer.'

Clare raised his eyeglass and regarded her through his good eye. 'Well, fancy,' he said. 'I'll tell m'uncle. You seem to be well-informed, young lady.'

'I collared Kit Massiter a few minutes ago. He told me your horse could jump and go a bit. Anyone could tell you the rest.'

'How well do you know that boy?'

'Not as well as Dick. He's ridden with him.'

'Is he any good?'

'He's a natural,' Dick said. 'If he gets his chances he'll go to the top. That is, if he doesn't smash himself up by pushing on too hard.'

80

'I see. He bears a strong resemblance to a great friend of mine I flew with in the war. He used to ride races too. In fact he won one for the squadron at a cavalry meeting. Upset them a bit.'

'I say, sir – flying,' Dick put in quickly. 'There's going to be a war, isn't there? I did a bit of a short service commission a while back. I want to get in again if I can. Is there any chance, do you think? Do you know anyone likely to help?'

'I know plenty of people.' Clare took a thin black notebook from his pocket and slid a gold pencil from its side. 'Give me a few particulars. Name and address? And what did you fly?'

'Bulldogs and then Furies at the end.'

'Fighters. Mm.' Clare suddenly looked up and stared at him. 'Why did you leave?'

Dick concealed a grin. 'Too many race-meetings,' he said. 'My CO didn't care for it.'

'That's not altogether surprising.' Clare closed the notebook with a snap. 'I'll make a few enquiries. I may be able to do something.'

When he had gone Carlow looked at her companion. 'You seem damned anxious to get yourself killed,' she said.

Dick grinned. 'You heard what he said,' he told her. 'There's going to be a war. When it comes I want to be where I was before – flying fighters. They're like racehorses. Bombers – you might as well be driving a bloody bus. The best chance I have is to get in now. And by the way, who is this customer you have for that bad brute I rode today, Firecracker or whatever he's called? It wouldn't be yourself, would it?'

'Perhaps,' she said. 'Or my father might have a job for him. They'll throw him out and he'll come cheap. He'll pick up a seller or two. Care to take a leg in him?'

'Not bloody likely. Let's have another bottle. Thanks to what young Master Massiter told you I had a fiver on Toby in our race.'

'Master Massiter seems to be attracting a lot of attention in certain quarters one way or another. What is this dragon of a father of his anyway?'

'Who is his father is more the question. Come on. Let's have that bottle.'

They were starting on it when Toby Revere came into the bar.

'Share of the spoils, Toby,' Dick greeted him. 'I had a small touch on yours.'

'Thanks. Don't mind if I do. That thing of Angus' any good, Dick?'

'No. Useless.'

'Galloped off his legs at home, I suppose. It's a question whether he runs them before they break down or they break down before he runs them. I hear you're trying to get back into the Air Force.'

'Yes. There's a war coming. No racing then. What about you?'

'Me?' Revere gave one of his wolfish grins. 'No war for me. I'm off to Kenya. Been there before, y'know. Went out to win the Kenya Grand National. Got done at the last.'

'That's not like you, Toby,' Carlow said. 'Whoever did you must be a bit more than useful.'

'Oh well, can't win 'em all. Got to know a lot of the chaps when I was out there. Rode for a chap called Winthrop and stayed on a bit. Winthrop says he'll look after me whenever I want to come out again. Happy Valley, old boy. That's the life. That's the place for me if there's a war on. Cheers.'

Driving home alone, Clare turned over the events of the afternoon in his mind. Firecracker would have to go, he supposed, but his thoughts did not linger long on the horse. Harbison looked the right type to get back into the RAF if his confidential reports were not too appalling. 'Too many race-meetings.' Clare smiled to himself. That could cover a multitude of sins, but the old RFC at least had never worried too much about a man's extra-regimental activities provided he could fly and fight. And then there was young Massiter. He must be Stephen's son. He wondered how much that little bitch Beatrice knew or Stephen himself in Kenya for that matter. Massiter – what *had* he heard of him? Ah, he had it now. Some Irish racing chap who had come to see his uncle had mentioned him as being a ruthless bastard in sport and business. He had kicked the boy out for some trifling racing offence. If Massiter had guessed the parentage as he surely had then the future looked black for Kit. He still felt he owed Stephen something and he wondered how he could help his son. As it happened, the opportunity was to come sooner than he thought.

CHAPTER X

After that day at Fontwell it seemed to Kit that things in the stable so far as he was concerned took a turn for the worse. He was at a loss to understand the reason unless it sprang from his continued efforts to help Cayley. Moonstruck, as Cayley had expected and dreaded, was proving a handful and, to add to his troubles, Angus was giving special attention to him, watching his every movement and damning him during most of them. There was little Kit could do to help, for any plea for mercy from him on Cayley's behalf would only cause more trouble. In any event he was constantly being harried himself.

On many evenings when he should have been free he was despatched to the secretary's office on the pretext of being taught about entries, declarations and accounts. 'You can damn well lend a hand when you're there,' Angus bellowed. 'I suppose they taught you how to read and write at that damned school of yours. And don't mess up the declarations or I'll have your guts for garters.' Then, too, there were invariable criticisms about the state of the yard outside his and Cayley's boxes and they would be put to crawling on their hands and knees searching for wayward pieces of straw or chaff. Frequently he was sent on his bicycle on menial and often meaningless errands to the village and then damned on his return for leaving something undone in the yard. On racing days Angus would capitalise on his unpaid presence by sending him off to do a lad's work with the horses. This was in many ways a relief since it got him out of the yard and brought him into the atmosphere of racing. He enjoyed hearing the gossip and exchanging crack with the lads from other stables, feeling all the rustle, bustle and tension of the racecourse about him and sharing its excitements. It gave him an opportunity, too, of seeing more of Dick and Carlow. Dick had brought his reputation with him from Ireland and was riding more and more and wherever he went, it seemed, Carlow went too. They appeared inseparable but that did not prevent Kit from worshipping from afar and sometimes from much nearer when he would watch Dick's races with her and exchange knowing comments on the running and riding. Both of them were always friendly towards him, hailing him when they met, standing him drinks when they won, and one way or another treating him as a sort of junior member of the partnership they formed. Once he was able to give them a long-priced winner passed on to him by the lad who had come with it, and on another occasion put them on to one of Angus' few runners that had a chance and did, for once, come up.

Beatrice, however, had discovered a renewed interest in racing. When the stable had a runner she was usually present and her sharp little eyes missed nothing. Left to himself Angus would probably have been too busy or preoccupied to notice how his pupil was employing his few spare minutes on the racecourse but Beatrice did and took care to enlighten him. 'Master Who,' (which was how she had taken to referring to Kit) 'seems very taken with the Concannon girl,' she said one night at dinner and went on to dwell on what she had seen.

Which was why, when Kit came to tack up Firecracker next morning, he was greeted by one of Angus' louder roars. 'What are you doing hanging about with that pair of rips?' he bellowed. 'You were sent here to learn, not to cast sheep's eyes at a jockey's mattress. The likes of you won't get much of a bounce out of her, my lad!'

He was standing straddle-legged, the Long Tom in his hand. His words echoed and boomed around the yard. From the other lads busy about their boxes came concealed sniggers and sly grins. Kit found himself flushing. All his resentments over his recent treatment began to surface inside him. There was a stable bucket at his feet. He was tempted to take it up and hurl it at Angus' head. Instead he turned and went into Firecracker's box. But he was in a mood of black rebellion when a few minutes later he led the horse out to join the string.

Beside him he saw that Cayley on Moonstruck was white and shaking. 'This fuckin' devil,' he said to Kit between teeth chattering with fright. ''E's in one of 'is moods. An' we're schoolin' today. 'E'll kill me. I swear 'e will.'

Kit looked at Moonstruck. His ears were back, his eyes were rolling and there was a lot of bloodshot white showing. Everything about him spelt trouble, and Kit did not envy Cayley his ride. 'He'll be fine when we get there,' he said with a conviction he did not feel. 'Take him steady and you'll be all right.'

The schooling ground at the Grange was laid out in the park not far from the stables which gave horses little time to settle down. The moment they moved off Moonstruck immediately began to hand out further danger signals. He was kicking and bucking and sidling and had nearly unshipped Cayley twice by the time they turned onto the grass. 'Can't you keep that bugger quiet?' Angus shouted at him. He had driven down in the shooting brake and was waiting for them, Long Tom still in his hand. 'You three,' he shouted stabbing a finger at Moonstruck, Kit and another rider. 'Come up over those fences. A steady canter. Stick that bloody Moonstruck in the middle.'

Moonstruck answered these instructions by giving a hearty buck which all but sent Cayley flying. 'Sit tight, can't you, you useless little bastard,' roared Angus. 'You need bloody glue on your arse. Stop frigging about and get on with it. We haven't all day.'

The schooling fences were laid out in a series of rows. There was a line of those of full size for the experienced horses, a separate open ditch, and four smaller but solid fences for beginners. It was to these that Kit and the others trotted. They pulled up, turned into line and set off.

Moonstruck took hold of his bit, put his head down and jumped into a gallop. 'A nice steady canter, my God,' Kit thought and decided that there was nothing to do but bring

85

Firecracker upsides of him. When they reached the first Moonstruck stuck in his toes, swerved and tried to run out. Finding this impossible with a horse on either side he scrambled over the fence ending up at a standstill on the far side with Cayley round his neck. There was an apoplectic scream from Angus followed by roars of abuse and they were sent back to start again.

'Christ a'Mighty, what's 'e goin' to do next,' Cayley moaned as they set off.

What Moonstruck did was to jump the fence perfectly. The second he took by the roots but remained on his feet. He hit the top of the third hard but still stood up; the fourth and last he met all wrong, managed to put in a short one, bucked over and then pulled himself up, snorting and looking wildly about him. Cayley had been out of the saddle more than he had been in it during the whole performance but by some miracle had remained on top.

Angus strode over to them. 'You weak, cowardly little bastard, Cayley,' he shouted at him. 'You're bloody terrified, that's all that's wrong. Take him over those three. That'll teach him and you. You two go with him.' He pointed with the Long Tom at the line of full-sized fences.

'The man's mad,' Kit said in a voice quite loud enough for Angus to hear. He was still raging inside and the treatment of Cayley had done nothing to cool his temper. He was not worried about himself for Firecracker had proved a safe enough conveyance. He looked at Cayley. He was even paler than before if that were possible; his hands were shaking as he caught hold of the reins.

'Oh, Gawd,' was all he could bring himself to say.

Angus stationed himself about five yards from the fence, the Long Tom at the ready. Moonstruck had settled down a little and they came into the fence at a reasonably steady pace. All might have been well had it not been for Angus and the Long Tom. At their approach he raised it. Moonstruck's rolling eye caught sight of it. He swerved and cannoned into Firecracker. The Long Tom came swirling round his hocks. He charged the fence blindly, hit it low down, smashed the guard rail and turned over with a crash.

Kit was too preoccupied with his own troubles caused by

Firecracker's swerve to see exactly what had happened. When he and Firecracker arrived somehow on the far side of the fence Moonstruck was getting to his feet and Cayley was lying prostrate beside him.

Kit jumped down and ran over to the boy. He was breathing, so he was still alive. That was something. But his face was a ghastly colour, his eyes were closed and there was blood coming from his mouth. Kneeling down beside him Kit stretched out a hand for his pulse.

'What the hell are you doing? Get back on your horse,' came a roar almost in his ears.

Kit got to his feet to find himself staring into Angus' angry eyes. Long Tom still in his hand, he was standing only a few feet away.

'He's badly hurt. Can't you see?' Kit said.

'Rubbish. There's damn all wrong with him. Leave him there. He's of no account. Let him rot.'

All the frustrations and resentments of the past weeks suddenly came to a head inside Kit and then boiled over. 'If he's useless it's your fault,' he shouted back. 'You've damned him and blasted him and fucked him and blinded him every minute since he's been here. He's badly hurt. Get a doctor and if you won't I will.' He began to turn towards his horse.

'Just a minute.' Angus' voice had become ominously quiet but his eyes were blazing. Unbeknownst to each other they had drawn a little apart from the group now gathered about Cayley. Behind them Wilson was bending over the injured boy. 'No one speaks to me like that,' Angus went on. Here or anywhere else. Get off the schooling ground – on your feet.'

'Excuse me, sir, I think he's coming round.' Wilson's voice broke in.

Cayley was trying to sit up. He got groggily to his feet, staggered and would have fallen if Wilson had not caught him. He looked glassily at them and put his hand to his forehead. 'Bit of a bang on his head, sir, and he cut his tongue on his teeth when he fell,' Wilson said.

Angus turned back to Kit. 'I'll see you in my office,' he said.

CHAPTER XI

The shooting brake was drawn up at the office steps when Kit got there. Angus was seated behind the desk turning over papers. After a moment or two he looked up. 'You're finished here,' he said directly. 'If there's anything of yours about pack it up. You've twenty minutes to get out of the place.'

Kit stared into the angry eyes. 'I'd be lying if I said I was sorry – for anything,' he said.

'Understand – once you're out of here you'll never come back.'

'I wouldn't even if I was on my knees.'

Angus continued to glare at him. Then the anger died slowly from his eyes. 'You've got guts between your ribs and your arse, anyway,' he said. 'Not like that worthless thrash Cayley.' And then, 'You don't like me, do you?'

'That's right. I don't.'

'Nor my methods, either, I'm thinking.'

'My mother told me you were a butcher. Anything I've seen here proves it.'

'Your mother – eh.' Kit thought he caught some strange emphasis behind the words before Angus went on. 'Now, you listen to me, I was told by your father to give you hardship and to stand no nonsense. Those were my instructions and they're no bad ones either. Men and horses you've got to find whether they'll stand work.' He swung round in his chair and faced the two montage pictures of his Grand National winners. 'See them – ' he pointed a finger at the pictures. 'Look at the rear ends of 'em. They're the type to jump Aintree. You could never get to the bottom of 'em. They were real steeplechasers in those days, not like the rubbish from the flat we're getting now. Aye, and the men, they were men not mock-ups too. He swung back to face Kit again. 'I wanted to see what you were made of and I've found out. But you can't stay here. You've got to go.' Surprisingly, he reached down, opened a drawer and took out a bottle of whisky and two glasses. Pouring a generous measure into each he pushed one across the desk towards Kit. 'Try that,' he said. And then, after taking a pull at his own drink, he went on, 'I'll tell you something. I've no one to come after me. You've got the root of the thing in you wherever you got it from. Your father doesn't want you back. He as good as told me so. If what happened today hadn't happened I was thinking of taking you on as an assistant.' His voice became rough again. 'You've had your chance and you've mucked it. Now, get out.'

As he closed the door behind him Kit's last glimpse of his master was of him pouring another large measure into his glass.

Wilson was waiting for him in the yard. 'You're for the off, then,' he said.

'Yes,' Kit answered. 'What else did you expect? How is Cayley?'

'He's okay. Bit of concussion. He'll be all right.'

'What about a doctor?'

'He's been. I told herself up at the house. She's not the worst if you get the right side of her. And she's the only one who can handle him.' He nodded his head towards the office door. 'She phoned straight away and old Murray from the village came up. Told him to lie quiet for a day or two.'

'Will the guv'nor let him?'

'Once she knows about it he will. The poor little bugger, he was shit scared and when he came down he was half-shamming. The guv'nor knew that.'

'I should have guessed. But he looked awful – '

Wilson grinned. 'You Irish, you're terribly hasty,' he said. 'But you're lucky. You've got a home to go back to. Not like us. Only the dole for us.'

'That's just it. I haven't. My father kicked me out. From here on in I'm on my own.'

'Cor! You are in a mess, ain't you? Him inside there won't be much help to you either. Best o'luck, chum.'

Back in his lodgings Kit sat on his bed in the bare little room contemplating a grim future. His father had warned him and Angus had repeated that he would not be welcomed back at Dunlay. To make matters worse he had been in the wrong as things had turned out and Angus was sure to point this out in the report that he was probably even now writing to the Sir. It was, too, more than likely that his father would cut off his allowance. He had spent little since his arrival at the Grange, so money was not for the moment a problem but that bank balance would not last forever and what was he to do then? It was just possible he could get a job in stables though jobs were not easy to come by and if he did he would forfeit all right ever to ride as an amateur again. He knew he had neither the experience, the strength, nor the skill to turn professional even if they would give him a licence, which he doubted.

In one respect at least Kit had been born lucky, in that he had inherited much of his mother's sanguine and resilient spirit and he lacked the ultimate self-doubt that made Stephen so vulnerable. But on this occasion even he was cast down. He walked the little room turning over and over the few alternatives that faced him and none of them offered any hope at all so far as he could see. Of one thing he was certain; he was not going to go running back to his father. He remembered the grim look on Andrew's face when he had dismissed him and his minatory warning still rang in his ears: 'If you get into any further trouble you can expect no help from me.' That scene in the library was still vivid in his mind along with his father's cold fury over his being up before Westcott. But was there something else behind his father's punishment of him? There were the strange remarks that Bob had let drop after consuming all that whisky on the way back from Malloran Park which he had never bothered really to think about until now. His father, too, had always favoured Hugo but, happy with his horses and his own affairs he had never given this more than a few moments' thought, when he considered it at all, to be because Hugo was the clever one, Hugo knew all the answers, Hugo was sophisticated and worldly and had grown up before his time and all these things would appeal to Andrew. But now Kit began to wonder if there was not more behind it all, though what it was he could not guess. There was something, though. What about the interest this strange man with the strange name was taking in him, and Beatrice too, for that matter?

He went back to his bed and putting his head on his hands,

let his mind return to childhood and the years between. There was nothing of profit to be found there, except, he reminded himself, that if there was favouritism his mother had appeared to favour him. He shook himself. Look on the bright side, he told himself. After all, he did have those few quid in the bank; he wasn't on the breadline yet and maybe Dick and Carlow could help in some way. They would be sympathetic and it would be fun to see them again and have a laugh. And, at least, too, he was out from under Angus' bellowing and bully-ragging. He was turning over the pages of his bank book to see the extent of his credit when there was a knock on the door. Opening it he found Mrs Hardy on the threshold.

'There's someone downstairs to see you,' she said with her usual disapproving air. 'I've put him in the parlour.'

Kit frowned. Bad news travels fast, he knew. But who the devil could this be? Going to the window he pulled back the lace curtain. A black Rolls-Bentley coupé was drawn up outside the door in the street below and two small boys were gazing admiringly at the Lalique mascot. He went downstairs and opened the parlour door.

Clare de Vaux was standing by the table in the centre of the room.

Part 2

STEPHEN 1

CHAPTER XII

Stephen Raymond sat in the men's bar of the Muthaiga Club in Nairobi drinking whisky and contemplating failure. The bar was empty save for one other occupant sitting by the fire in the alcove reading the *Tatler*. The Munnings prints on the walls brought back memories of other days to Stephen and made his bad mood worse. He pushed his empty glass across the counter and ordered another double.

When Stephen had come to Kenya ten years ago he had been lonely and lost. The clammy heat of Mombasa had made him feel sick and the long slow train journey to Nairobi had done nothing to lighten the black depression which had sat upon him for most of the voyage. The train had been thronged with people all of whom appeared to know each other and none of whom knew him. They stared at him with the arrogance of members of an enclosed society summing up a newcomer or ignored him altogether while they bandied about gossip between themselves of how the altitude had at last got to old Johnny Durrance at Nanyuki and Mabel Endersley had run off with Dickie McEwan, and the Eames's at Eldoret had finally given up and sold out to some perfectly ghastly people from, can you believe it, Birmingham? He felt like an outsider, a position to which he was becoming more and more accustomed; nor did he much take to the manners and appearance of those about him with their hearty voices and brick-red faces though he told himself he was being unfair and that heat, loneliness and something approaching despair were clouding his judgment.

The sight of Billy Norris, to whom he had written before

coming out, standing on the platform at Nairobi with his cheery greeting did something to lift his spirits. Billy had borne him off to the Club, had signed him in, and there, in this very bar, over pink gins, they had started to talk and to swap memories.

'I'm damned if I know what I'm going to do,' Stephen had said. 'I could buy a farm, I suppose. I'm told the banks are pretty free and easy here and that land is cheap. Trouble is I know damn all about farming. I suppose I could learn.'

'You could,' his friend had said. 'But it's a heart-breaking and a back-breaking business. Often and often I thought I couldn't stick it out. But I'd nowhere else to go. When those IRA bastards burnt us out we lost everything – house, furniture, plate, every stick and stone.'

'It wasn't the IRA burnt me out,' Stephen said. 'It was the Auxiliaries, the bloody Black and Tans.'

Billy Norris did not seem to hear him. He was back in the black, bitter night when the raiders came with masks over their faces, petrol cans and guns in their hands, hauled them out of their beds and set fire to their house. 'The only things we salvaged,' he went on, 'were a silver sugar bowl and a writing desk. I've got them still. We never did them any harm. We were good landlords. Why did they do it?'

'Land hunger,' Stephen said, as they settled themselves at a table in the L-shaped dining-room popularly supposed to have been built that way so that one party to a marriage could not observe another's strayings. 'They thought they had been dispossessed, and a lot of them had. You're lucky it's not likely to happen here.'

'Isn't it? I don't know. I wouldn't say this to anyone but you and I'd be damned unpopular if anyone heard me. But you and I, we've both been through it. Ever hear of a chap called Meinertzhagen?'

'Can't say I have.'

'He was out here at the very beginning seconded from his regiment in India to the KAR. Arrogant bugger by all accounts. But he could see a thing or two and he wasn't afraid to speak his mind. He went about prophesying doom right up to the Governor. Said that the whole policy of claiming the White Highlands for ourselves alone was madness, that we were building a tinder barrel to sit on and that it would blow our bottoms off sooner or later.'

'I can see he might not have been greatly loved.'

'He even told it to Delamere and that didn't exactly go down like an oyster, as you can imagine. In the end they got rid of him under some sort of a cloud and his name's not mentioned here in the best circles. But he may have been right for all that. Look what happened at home.'

'My father always said we were there by conquest or on sufferance. He wasn't too popular either for saying it and my mother told him he was mad and that we'd be there for ever.'

'It's the same here, only more so. They think they're safe, that it's white man's country and will stay that way. It's Delamere's creed and they follow it blindly. Trouble is they've never lived through it like we have. Would you have believed when you went to the war that you and I would be dispossessed and driven out, sitting her in the heat waited on by wogs and eating our hearts out for a bloody country we can't go back to and doesn't want us? And sweating on the next coffee crop, what's more.'

'And who would believe that my pantry boy would be living in your place and running the country? But is there land hunger here?'

'Of course there is. The Kukes think they've been driven out and their land grabbed by a lot of white interlopers. It isn't all true. In fact bloody little of it is true. Without us the land would still be unclaimed waste, but they think it is and there's a grain of truth in it. And there are those all too ready to tell them we tricked them out of the White Highlands, most of them agitators educated by us, what's more. Mission schoolboys, they're the worst of the bloody lot. Anyway to hell with it; it'll probably last our time. Do you really want to buy a farm?'

'Not much, but what else is there?'

'You used to ride a bit, didn't you? I seem to remember your winning a bumper or two for Bob Ferris before you went to the war.'

'That's right. And after the Troubles had died down I looked after Billy Wilmot's horses for a while. Then he gave up and cleared out.'

'I've got a job for you then, I think. Job Hannaford farms at Naivasha. The farming is only a side-line and not much of one at that. He's been training his own horses and few for others since the war and making a fair go of it. A couple of weeks ago he was ringing a young one and something went wrong, I don't know just what. But he ended up with a twisted ankle and an injured shoulder. He's chairbound, cursing like hell and in need of someone to supervise the string.'

'Doesn't he have an assistant?'

'He kicked the last one out. Some useless little bugger from a family at home who was foisted on him. I mentioned you to him. He'll give you a try. You should get some time after game, too, if you want it. He's a hell of a hunter, Job. Does it the hard way and thrives on it.'

'What's the rest of the establishment?'

'If you mean has he a wife, he hasn't. She got tired of playing second fiddle to the horses and the game and went off to live with Simon Harling on the Coast. If he likes you and you like him you'll be there as long as you care to stay.'

'Sounds better than pushing a plough. When do I see him?'

'As soon as you can make it.'

It was a day or so later, when he had kitted himself out with what Norris told him were the necessities, that a Buick with a box body met Stephen at Naivasha station. They drove for a mile or so along the rough road by the lake shore before turning into a track between a line of jacaranda and flame trees. The track twisted and turned as the Buick bounced over ruts and holes in the red earth before eventually coming out on an open space in front of a long, low, stone-built house. A verandah ran the length of the house with bougainvillaea climbing all over it and a dining porch which was built out at one end. Stephen got down from the Buick and paused to look about him. Below him was the lake lying blue and placid in the sun, all around were the purple hills, the mass of a mountain at one end and another behind and above him. In some strange way it all reminded him of the Bay. The air was so clear it could have come through a filter. He took a deep breath of it. I think I'm going to like this place, he said to himself.

Turning again towards the house he made out a figure sitting in the shadowed depths of the verandah. On a table beside him was a jug and a glass. 'Come up here and let me have a look at you,' a friendly voice called. 'I'm spanseled goddammit, with this blasted ankle.'

Stephen mounted the steps and crossed to the table. He found himself looking into a pair of merry grey eyes set in a small, red, round face, wrinkled in places like the skin of an apple. 'You walk like a horseman, anyway,' Job Hannaford said. 'And you've a pair of hands on you, too, I see. Sit down. Have a beer. Boy!' he called half-turning in his chair.

An African in a spotless white kanzu materialised as if from nowhere, placed a fresh jug of beer on the table and disappeared as silently as he had come.

Stephen sipped the strong beer while Job Hannaford looked him over in silence for a few moments. Then he said: 'I've twelve horses out there eating their heads off. The syces are all right just so far and no farther as you'll find out. They can do a horse over and muck out and that's about all. As for riding work – how fit are you?'

'Not very. I've just come off the boat. But it'll come back. It shouldn't take long.'

'These boys can ride work because I've taught 'em. But they're like children. You've got to watch 'em all the time. They lose their heads in a minute. And for two pins they'll ride a match flat out when they're supposed to be doing a steady canter.'

'You'd better know straight away,' Stephen said. 'That as far as the farm goes I know nothing about farming.'

His host looked at him, the corners of his eyes creasing up in a smile, a characteristic Stephen would come to know well. 'Who does?' he said. 'We farm here by guess and by God. Anyway it's ranching country. As far as farming goes all I want you to do is to keep an eye on my wogs while I'm out of action. It's the horses that matter. Now come and have a look at them.' He set down the glass with a thump and shouted again. Once more the boy materialised and Hannaford issued a string of instructions in Swahili.

In a few moments another boy appeared pulling a contraption which resembled a home-made rickshaw. 'Absolutely my

99

own patent,' Hannaford said with a grin, pointing to it. Can't manage a crutch and my shoulder as well.' More orders and instructions in Swahili followed and he was helped down the steps. Once settled on the seat, with the cushions arranged to his satisfaction behind him, they set off, the boy between the shafts and Stephen walking beside them.

The horses were in a row of boxes some distance from the main house and the cluster of rondavels in which the staff lived. Immediately Stephen sensed that the syces seemed happy and contented as they stood by their charges. Whatever faults his predecessor had had they had not interfered with the morale of the stable. Their teeth glistened in smiles as Hannaford introduced the new bwana Raymond to them.

By the quality of the horses Stephen was not so impressed. To his eyes, accustomed as they were to stock reared on good Irish grass, they appeared to lack both scope and class. Hannaford, whose sharp eyes, as Stephen was later to find out, missed little, guessed something of the thoughts passing through his mind as he followed his appraising glances. 'Not quite what you're used to – eh?' he said. 'Not what you'd see at Newmarket, or the Curragh for that matter – that's what you're thinking – eh?'

'Well – ' Stephen said cautiously.

Hannaford chuckled. 'It's natural enough,' he said. 'These are by English stallions out of country-bred mares. I'll tell you the breeding and other things later. It's a good job I've got 'em in my head. That useless bugger I had before you kept nothing up-to-date. What you need in a horse here is toughness. They've got to stand up to the climate and about a thousand diseases no one knows about and that you won't find in Mr Hayes' veterinary book. Now – best wine to the last, they say. What do you think of this fellow? Pioneer, we call him.'

Pioneer was a strong, compact bay gelding. Standing into him Stephen thought him only a little over sixteen hands. But he looked as if he could jump and he looked a racehorse. When the syce led him out Stephen liked him even better, for he stood over a lot of ground and had strength written over him. 'I can see why you think so much of him,' he said slowly. 'What are you going to do with him?'

100

Hannaford gave his infectious chuckle. 'I'm going to win the Kenya Grand National with him,' he said. 'And if you're worth a damn you're going to ride him for me.'

CHAPTER XIII

It did not take Stephen long to fit into his new way of life, and as the days passed one into another he found himself liking it more and more. The hurt that Ireland had inflicted on him was still there together with the longing to see his son and the constant nagging speculation as to where he was and what was happening to him. But the hard, physical work in the cool, clear air of the Rift Valley prevented his dwelling too much on these things.

He lived in a rondavel set a little apart from the others. It was primitive enough by European standards. There was an earthen floor with a worn rug on it, a camp bed, a rough dressing table and a wash stand with a pewter basin and ewer. Just after first light every morning, he shaved and dressed. The he would walk to the stables watching the mist curl off the blue waters of the lake, and the outlines of the Narok escarpment taking shape beyond its farther shores. Above the farm was the towering peak of Kinangop purple in the dawn, and away to the west the mysterious bulk of Longonot with its extinct crater and the lava beds on its slopes.

Every day he rode out, getting fitter and harder all the time. Sometimes the morning's work would be enlivened by the presence of spectators not to be found on gallops at home, and Stephen on occasion found himself hurtling towards a herd or zebra or passing giraffe lined up beside the gallop who regarded the horses and riders placidly out of their mournful eyes. Accustomed to these incursions the horses took little notice of them and soon Stephen came to accept the presence of straying game as part of the landscape, while Job chaffed him with comparisons with the Curragh. More and more as he lived with him and worked for him, Stephen found his affection growing for this merry little man with the quiet manner, friendly nature and sharp eyes.

The morning's work done they would breakfast together on the porch overlooking the lake. The silent boys would have ready for them plates of mango followed by bacon and eggs and sausages, scones hot and steaming from the pan, thick honey from the farm, all washed down with draughts of strong coffee. Breakfast over there was morning stables, then getting the second lot out if there was a second lot followed by lunch and then riding round the farm which was really only a matter of putting in an appearance to 'keep the wogs up to their work'. After that evening stables, a hot bath, a change into pyjamas and whisky with Job before a roaring log fire in the long living room behind the verandah, listening sometimes to the crackling wireless, dinner and an early bed.

Like most settlers of the time Job led a lonely life. He had, too, Stephen guessed, become more and more withdrawn into himself and his horses since his wife, of whom he never spoke, had left him.

Someone, Stephen guessed it must have been the absent wife, had filled the house with books, many of which had been left behind, but Job's own reading was confined to the East African Standard and the MFH edition of the works of Surtees which he kept beside his bed, knew almost by heart and from which he delighted to quote. Borrowing them Stephen remembered past enchantments and greatly to Job's delight quoted back at him.

During those long evenings they talked, mostly about the horses, their entries and their chances, seldom about themselves. As Stephen was to find out, amongst settlers at that time, provided you had someone to vouch for you at the Muthaiga Club, on the racetrack, or in the bush, you were accepted for what you were and what you could do.

The White Highlands of Kenya were a place apart and those who made their lives there a race apart. They were a place for a fresh start if you wanted it. But you had to work;

there was no room for weaklings mental or physical; either you survived or you got out. The visiting American journalist's smart wisecrack, 'A place in the sun for shady people', was bitterly resented by the great majority of the settlers as was the presence in their midst of those who gave credence to it, rich layabouts, many of them titled, the 'Happy Valley' lot, most of whom had run away from their creditors, their responsibilities or both to seek a lotus land that existed only in their own fantasies. You found these propping up a bar in the Muthaiga Club or swopping wives in the grandiose mansions they built on their estates but never wringing a livelihood from the unwilling soil, riding a finish in a steeplechase or facing a charging buffalo on safari.

As for the Africans themselves Stephen found little difficulty in dealing with them. In many respects they reminded him of the country people in Ireland he had known in his childhood and left behind him, especially the Kikuyu. They were feckless, clever, charming, cunning and often exasperating. Those whom Job employed and had trained could handle horses with sympathy though as Job had warned him even the simplest of the higher skills such as putting on a bandage was beyond most of them. But, living with the Africans and watching them, Stephen began to wonder if they would always be as contented with their lot as these seemed to be. There was a latent bright-eyed intelligence in many of them which, should anyone take the trouble to educate and cultivate it, might well make them aspire to better their lot and, in addition, cast critical or envious eyes on their masters, the whites.

Stephen's experience of the upsurge of nationalism in his own country made him quicker to perceive this than the vast majority of his race who never could and never would accept that a change might be coming. His conversation with Billy Norris had also remained in his mind.

As it happened there was one amongst the workforce who personified his embryo doubts and fears, a bright-eyed mission-educated boy called Kidogo who clearly considered that he was being employed below his station and capabilities. Articulate and resentful, he specialised in his attitude towards his masters in what Stephen remembered from his army days

103

as being known as dumb insolence. Just his presence amongst them was sufficient to cause ripples of discontent, slight but still apparent, to spread amongst the other boys. It was Stephen's predecessor, 'the useless bugger', who had engaged him during the time Job had been completely incapacitated. He didn't last long. Despite his disability Job had him spotted as a trouble-maker pretty quickly and had him out of the place the moment he was certain of it. He departed spitting defiance and saying he would have no difficulty in getting a clerk's job in Nairobi.

'And the trouble is,' Job said that evening over their whiskies, 'maybe he won't get one. Then like as not he'll fall into the hands of worse agitators than himself. It's these bloody mission schools with their half-cracked ideas of education that are behind it all. If I had my way I'd run the lot of them out of the country.'

'But,' Stephen said. 'I suppose we have to educate them, haven't we? Isn't that one of the reasons for colonising? And if we don't perhaps someone else will.'

'Education!' Job snorted. 'What do the wogs want with education? Look at those fellows outside. They're happy and contented, aren't they?'

'They seem to be, but how long will they stay that way?'

'Forever and a day. They've full bellies, a horse to ride and a woman to sleep with. What more could a man want?'

'Land, I suppose,' Stephen said. 'We took their land, didn't we? Sooner or later they'll want it back.'

'Rubbish!' Job exploded. 'Agitator's balls! Who've you been talking to? This is our land. We made it. There wasn't a blade of grass for stock to eat or a strip of broken earth for a crop to grow until we came here. The Kukes never did a day's work in their lives until we made 'em. This is white man's country and that's how it's going to stay. And don't you forget it.'

'I was only thinking of what happened at home. We thought we were safe – '

'Maybe. It won't happen here.'

'I hope you're right.' Stephen realised he was being unwise in talking as he did but all the bitterness against the fate that had driven him here to this lonely land was suddenly welling up inside him. 'I hope you'll never be burnt out, blown up or shot at,' he said. 'We reckoned we were there for a thousand years. We lived like you do – once.'

'You didn't keep 'em *there*.' Job put a broad, spatulated thumb on to the table beside him and pressed it down, grinding a few crumbs of biscuit beneath it. 'That's where they belong and that's where they'll stay.'

'Will they? Did you ever hear of a man called Meinertzhagen?'

'That blinking bounder! That's who you've been hearing about, is it? Pushed out of his own regiment and came here telling everyone their business before he'd been in the place five minutes. A damn trouble-maker, that's what he was. You forget about him, young feller. This is our country and we're here to stay.'

Stephen sighed. 'I expect you're right,' he said. 'We've lost a country. You've won one.'

Job looked at him, a kindly glint in his grey eyes. 'I think I know how you feel,' he said quietly. 'Or some of it anyhow. Now, let's have some more of this whisky and look at these entries.'

For, of course, they raced. It was the whole reason for their existence. On racing mornings the horses and the boys would be packed into box wagons at the station and off they would go to Thompson's Falls, Limuru, Nakuru or Nanyuki and there they would meet their fellows and run their races, and gamble and often drink and talk far into the night in the local club.

Stephen soon found that he had done more race-riding than most of those pitted against him, whose only experience was, as Job put it, 'to bounce about in a few point-to-points'. But a certain Captain Adrian Sprott had reached a far higher standard than that. He ran a stable at Limuru and between him and Job there existed at these up-country meetings a rivalry often friendly but sometimes, when they clashed, bitter enough to make feelings run high. 'That cut 'em down captain and his quods,' was how, after Jorrocks, Job described Sprott and his stable, muttering too that his rank had probably been earned in the Horse Marines. But wherever he and his captaincy came from there was no denying that Sprott could ride: 'like a demon', Job reluctantly admitted. He was in the business to make money and he did not care for his schemes to be upset. Stephen was soon to be the means of thwarting one of them.

At Nanyuki and Thompson's Falls the last race on the card was known as the 'Kwaheri', Swahili for 'farewell'. Its conditions specified that it was open only to horses which had run but not won at the meeting. Sprott was accustomed shamelessly to exploit these by bringing a flock of horses to each meeting and stopping those to be kept for the last in which he would run two or three, carefully disguising from everyone but himself which he was backing. As often as not he put up his wife, a lady of almost as formidable talents as himself, in these races, so as further to complicate the issue for punters and bystanders.

'Now watch 'em both,' Job cautioned as he put Stephen up for the first time to ride a Kwaheri against them at Thompson's Falls. 'He's as hot as hell's last issue and she's a match for him!'

A furlong from home Stephen was lying fourth. A settler who was 'bouncing about' was in the lead, with Sprott second and his wife third. Stephen did not know which to take on, Sprott or his wife. He thought it was probably Sprott's mount which was off that afternoon as the other horse seemed to be dropping back. Not realising that Stephen was outside him and close enough to hear and in any event probably profoundly contemptuous of Stephen's abilities of which he had as yet seen little, Sprott half-turned in the saddle. 'Come on Mabel for Christ's sake. What the hell do you think you are doing!' he called to his wife.

Mabel came on and, disregarding Sprott who up to this had seemed to be going the better of the two, Stephen did the same. He collared her on the line and won, cleverly, by half a length.

Job was delighted. 'Well done, boy,' he said as he led Stephen in. 'And we'll do the same to him at Nakuru in the National, you'll see.' Sprott, however, was not so pleased and he and his wife directed deadly glances at Stephen as they watched him unsaddling. Job was even more overjoyed when Stephen told him how he had detected and defeated Sprott's little plan for winning the Kwaheri. 'Maybe that will teach him a lesson,' he said chuckling. 'He's always up to something or other. And better and better it was Gervase Winthrop, one of the Happy Valley lot, who owned the one you beat.'

Job was still chuckling over the story that night in Barry's Hotel and, very late, long after Stephen had gone to bed, he could not help retelling it. When Job had had his measure of drink or a little more he became loquacious, and the story therefore, lost nothing in the telling. As he finished he added expansively: 'And I'll beat him in the Grand National, too. I've the best horse in Kenya and the best man to ride him.' If he had left it there no harm would have been done though the story of the race was to spread far and wide through the White Highlands. But Job's tongue on these occasions was accustomed to run away with him and he now went on to make a remark which, though he could not know it, was to have a considerable influence on Stephen's future in the colony. 'Though he does have some damned odd ideas about what is going to happen to us all,' he said.

'What's that?' someone in the audience asked.

'Thinks we'll have to hand over everything to the wogs,' Job said, and then, turning to the bartender. 'Same again all round, Ahmet.'

'Good God. One of those. What the hell are you doing with him, Job?'

Realising too late that he had mentioned the unmentionable Job said hastily, 'Told him it was all tommy rot of course. You see he – '

Before he could continue another voice cut in. 'If that's what he thinks you'd better tell him to get out before he's put out – feet first.' And to this there was a general murmur of assent.

'Said it happened to him in Ireland,' Job said, seeking now desperately to repair the damage his unthinking remark had caused. 'He's Irish, you see.'

'Oh well, the Irish, they're all mad,' the first speaker said.

But Captain Sprott, who had just come in with his owner, Gervase Winthrop, heard the passage and remembered it—as did Winthrop.

107

CHAPTER XIV

Soon all Stephen's and Job's energies were directed towards
getting Pioneer ready for the Grand National at Nakuru. He
came on steadily and both Stephen and Job were pleased
with his progress. Job's ankle was mending quickly. Within
a week he had discarded the rickshaw for a stick and after a
few days more even that was left behind. He never mentioned
the injury to his shoulder for he was not the complaining sort
but Stephen sensed that it was still bothering him and once
or twice when bending down or turning quickly he thought
he saw a spasm of pain cross the other's features.

One morning, after work, in which Pioneer had gone
particularly well, Stephen came to breakfast to find Job
frowning over a day old copy of the *East African Standard*. At
Stephen's approach he looked up. 'What do you know about
someone called Toby Revere?' he said.

Stephen gave a short laugh. 'Too much,' he answered.
'Everyone in racing knows him. He's too hot to handle. Why?'

'He's staying with Gervase Winthrop at Gilgil for the
Grand National meeting. He's to ride one of his in the race.'

Stephen whistled. 'The devil he is,' he said. 'What's he
been up to at home, I wonder, that he's come out here?'

'Pretty useful GR ain't he?'

'The living best. But he couldn't lie straight in bed, as they
say in Ireland. He'd rather lose a race going straight if he
couldn't win it going crook. He started, you know, in India,
in the Deccan Horse. He was too hot even for them and they
fired him out. In the end some of his pals had to smuggle
him out of the country in a piano case.'

'The Drunken Horse – I've heard of 'em. If they couldn't
hold him he must be pretty hot. A nice pair of fine natural
blackguards, as Mr Surtees says, him and Sprott. You'll have
to watch it, lad.'

'What'll he ride?'

'Constant Hero, I imagine. That's that big horse you beat
in the Kwaheri. I want to win this race. It's the first time
I've had a real good 'un in it.'

108

'I know that.'

'By the looks of things it's not going to be easy with the two of them up to their tricks. Sprott didn't like being beaten in that Kwaheri. Why the hell,' Job added, 'haven't that Happy Valley lot got the guts to ride their own horses?'

'It's not going to be easy.' Those words ran through Stephen's mind as he stood in the paddock at Nakuru waiting to be put up on Pioneer. For, in fact, they were more accurate than Job himself knew. In Stephen's opinion Pioneer, while useful enough, was not as good as Job thought. Always the optimist, Job's geese were invariably swans, his horses a few pounds better than they actually were. Moreover Pioneer was a difficult ride, because he had to be held up for just one run. He was strong and brave but he had that kink in him and Stephen felt sure that Sprott would know of it. Job's intentions and the ways of his horses were seldom secret.

Job himself, standing beside him, was as near to being nervous as he ever permitted himself to be. 'Now remember,' he hissed to Stephen as he put him up. 'Don't come too soon. And don't come too late either, or you'll lose it.'

Bloody lucid instructions, Stephen thought to himself as he rode out on to the course for the parade.

It was a great occasion in the sporting and social life of the colony. The ladies were in their best finery, some of it bearing the scent of moth-balls having been dug out of cabin trunks long put by, the men in terai hats and white duck suits. The Governor himself had come down to grace the meeting and a portion of the stand had been set apart for him, his lady, his daughters and his ADCs. The great Lord Delamere, he of the flowing locks and unpredictable temper, was there, too, with his wife and son. Champagne corks popped, beer and whisky flowed in abundance, the sun blazed down.

As they walked their horses round at the start Stephen saw Revere running his eye over Pioneer. Revere nodded to him. 'Seen you somewhere before, haven't I?' he said. 'Not much like Aintree in March, is it?'

The Kenya Grand National distance was about two and a half miles which entailed two circuits of the course. On the first the runners jumped two fences in front of the stands, the water and an open ditch, on the second they switched to an inner track, the last fence being a plain one.

All went well with Stephen and Pioneer the first time round. The gallop was a steady one. Pioneer was measuring his fences and jumping perfectly. Revere was not having such a happy ride. Twice the big horse blundered and Stephen heard him curse. At the second last Stephen was lying third with Captain Sprott ahead on the inside and another runner, obviously beaten and dropping back, between them. As they left it Stephen heard a crash and spared a moment to hope that it was Constant Hero blundering again or even falling. Nothing untoward had happened so far, and he began to think that for once Sprott and Revere were playing it straight. He was starting to plan where he should unleash his run when he heard the rattle of hooves on his left and Revere on Constant Hero ranged alongside him.

They matched strides for a moment or two before Revere, who was niggling at Constant Hero, went a length up. Then he began to drift across on top of Stephen. At the same time Sprott left the rails. The gap between him and Constant Hero was closing in front of Pioneer. Far from playing it straight Revere and Sprott had planned their move well. Knowing that Pioneer had only one run in him they were shutting him in so that he could not make it. If Stephen pulled out now to come round Revere he had lost the race. 'Damn them,' he thought, 'they're not going to get away with this.'

The last fence was almost on top of them. Stephen had only a second in which to make up his mind. He sat down and drove Pioneer into the narrowing gap between the two leaders. Pioneer answered the challenge and lengthened his stride. But the gap had closed. The three horses took off together in a tangled, unbalanced bunch. Together they smashed into the top of the fence which disintegrated with a crash of birch and flying twigs. Stephen had a glimpse of another horse cart-wheeling beside him. But Pioneer, too, despite his strength, could not survive the impact. He dived into the ground and Stephen went with him. The smack of the iron hard turf went through every bone in his body. For a moment he blacked out and lay where he fell. Then his head cleared and he got groggily to his feet. Captain Sprott was leaning against the rails holding what appeared to be a broken arm. He was gazing at Stephen with malevolence and cursing fluently.

Between them Pioneer was lying, his neck at an unmistakable angle. It was broken. Job's best horse was dead. Stephen had lost the race and killed his friend's horse. As the full realisation came to him another wave of blackness engulfed him and he passed out again.

Stephen was out of circulation for two days and was still very shaky when he pulled himself from his bed, left the rondavel and walked across to the main house for breakfast. Although he believed Job knew racing well enough to understand what had caused that last fence fall he was bitterly sorry for the outcome and to some extent uncertain of his reception.

Job was spreading honey on a scone when he walked on to the steps to the dining porch. Steadying himself with a hand on the back of one of the carved chippendale chairs Stephen gazed across the blueness of the lake framed beneath the deep green of the Mau forest. Then he took a deep breath and turned to his employer. 'I lost your race and I killed your horse,' he said.

Job munched his scone and poured himself more coffee. Then he looked up at Stephen. 'When I was a young feller,' he said, 'we lived in the Shires. We hadn't much money and I used to ride the young ones for Marty O'Brien the dealer – ever heard of him?'

'Of course. He used to come to Bob Ferris's when I was at the Bay.'

'My father, who didn't much care about my hunting and thought I should go into a bank or become a solicitor or an accountant or something bloody like that, went to Marty and asked him what'd happen if I killed one of his valuable young horses, because he hadn't the money to pay for it. D'you know what Marty said?'

'No,' Stephen said. 'Though I might be able to make a fair guess.'

" 'Tell him to bring back the saddle and bridle. That's all I want.' That's what Marty said. Does that answer your question?'

'I hoped you'd say that,' Stephen said, pulling out the chair. 'But – '

'But me no buts. And if it's any other consolation to you I'd have done the same thing myself. Sit down, lad, and don't be standing there looking woebegone. Have some breakfast. Worse things happen at sea.'

A boy brought Stephen some mango. He picked up a fork. 'They did me properly,' he said. 'If I'd pulled out we were beat anyway. How did it look from the stands?'

'Not too good, if you want the truth. Those who don't know racing were bellyaching a bit and the Governor and his ladies, they weren't best pleased. Not that that matters. He's a stupid old woman who doesn't know a horse from a hen. But that Mabel Sprott, that madam, she should have known better, tried to make what capital she could out of it. She was going round howling about foul riding and demanding an enquiry.'

'Foul riding where Revere's concerned, that's pretty rich,' Stephen said.

Job chuckled again. 'The trouble was,' he said, 'they won with the wrong horse. It was Sprott who was to win and collect and they hadn't a bob on Revere. And Sprott broke his arm which'll keep him out of mischief for a bit.'

'What happened about the enquiry?'

'There wasn't one. Dickie Ormerod who was the senior steward on the day said he wasn't going to be bullied by Mabel Sprott, the Governor or anyone else. He used to ride a bit himself and wasn't too careful where he went. He'd been drinking champagne all day and had his eye on one of the Jackson girls from Nakuru. That might have helped, too.'

'Christ, Job, I'm sorry about it all. If you want me to go – '

'Go? To hell with that. You and I get on fine. Forget about it; everyone else will have in a fortnight.'

'I hope so,' Stephen said.

As often happens in racing, when one trouble strikes, others follow. Within the next three weeks a colt they were getting ready for Nairobi Race Week broke down and would be out for a year at least; another contracted the dreaded horse sickness and was dead in two days; a third cut into a tendon in a gallop chiefly due, Stephen believed, to the syce's carelessness in letting him sprawl before pulling him up.

Job took these setbacks philosophically, far more so than Stephen, who had not yet lost his remorse and self-accusation over the killing of Pioneer. This was made worse by the belief being borne in on him that failure was destined forever to dog his footsteps. He had lost Babs, forfeited the right to call his son his own, failed in his futile attempt to carve out some sort of career in the new Ireland that was struggling to establish itself as a nation, and now here, in Kenya, brought himself into disrepute on the racecourse. He told himself that he was staring out of a black past into a bleak future. He also reminded himself that that way of thought was an indulgence in self-pity and self-pity was a step on the way to self-destruction. Nevertheless, he could not get rid of the premonition which had haunted him for some time that fate, in the words of an author whose book he had pulled from Job's shelves to read before sleep came to him, was waiting for him round the corner with a piece of lead piping. It was in this dark mood that he walked across one evening to the main house after supervising the treatment and banadaging of the cut tendon.

Job was sitting by the fire, whisky glasses and decanter on the table in front of him. Beside them was a double barrelled gun which looked at first sight like an ordinary twelve-bore shotgun. When Stephen had settled himself comfortably in his chair, Job said to him: 'Can you shoot?'

'I used to at home, when I was young,' Stephen answered. And then, he never quite knew why, (though, thinking back, he decided that it was the black mood of failure that was upon him which made him mention his one brief period of success), he added, 'I did a bit in the war, too.'

'The war? Shooting? My war was out here. I thought yours was all bombs and mud and artillery. Sniper, were you?'

'I wasn't in the trenches. I was in the RFC.'

'Flying Corps – were you then? How many Huns did you shoot down?'

The old, inevitable question they all asked, Stephen thought. But, even so, it brought memories back. 'Eighteen I think,' he said slowly.

113

'Eighteen! How old were you? You're not that old now.'

'I was eighteen. One for every year. That's what Lloyd George said when he came to have a look at us. Good Lord, it all seems so long ago. Another life – '

'Eighteen – ' Job said again, looking at him speculatively. 'That makes you, what d'ye call it, an ace, doesn't it?'

'Maybe. We didn't go in for those sorts of names between ourselves. I was top scorer in the squadron for a bit. But I was never in the same class as the real aces if you care to call them that. My first major, now, he was one of the greats. He had forty-six and they couldn't find anyone good enough to shoot him down. They got him in the end, from the ground when he was trying to help a new man home.'

'You'll be telling me soon the bloody plane flew itself and the guns went off of their own accord.'

'Well, don't put too much pass on it. It's a lot of luck and anyway, as I said, I was never really on the top.'

Job leant forward and refilled his glass. 'You know,' he said, 'you quiet buggers, you're the ones that surprise you. When you came here first I wondered if you had enough blood in your guts to drive one into the last. When I saw you taking on those two blackguards at Nakuru who were trying to do you I knew you had and what you've just told me confirms it. Eighteen, by God. See that gun there? Pick it up.'

Stephen reached out and grasped it by the stock. When he came to lift it it almost pulled him from the chair. 'Good Lord,' he said. 'What is this? A cannon?'

'It's a Rigby .470. We use it for bigger game. We may need it where we're going.'

'Going? What about Nairobi Race Week? What about the horses?'

'We've nothing for Nairobi. What we've got left are bloody useless. Those new bomas will hold them. We'll throw the buggers out.'

'Won't you miss the fun? I'm told – '

'I'm getting too old for these jollifications. Get yourself packed up, Stephen, lad. We're going on safari.'

CHAPTER XV

There were no frills about Job's safaris. He liked to do things the hard way, which was how he had done them when he was young, and he saw no reason to change. Packed into the box body of the Buick were two tents, some spare provisions and medical stores, Kamau, the gun-bearer who doubled as tracker, and Muchai the supernumerary and general dogs-body. Last to be loaded was the most important item of all, the armoury. This consisted of the big Rigby .470 for heavy game, a Winchester .458 magazine rifle which Job maintained in proper hands could stop anything, and a .250 Savage, a particular favourite of his which he told Stephen was the most accurate rifle for light game ever made.

Although Job was genuine in his desire to go on safari there was another motive behind his decision. He had played down to Stephen the effect that the last fence smash-up had had on the minds of many of the onlookers, especially those without a knowledge of racing and what went on in a race. He knew that what had happened or rather what those people outside racing thought had happened had done Stephen no good in the small enclosed circle that made up settler society in the colony. Gervase Winthrop might be a waster but he dined at Government House; Adrian Sprott, too, whatever was thought of some of his activities, ran an established stable. Stephen on the other hand, was a newcomer, unknown and already somewhat suspect from those remarks of his which Job had repeated that night in Barry's Hotel and for which he was still kicking himself. The Governor, Job had been told, had been heard to utter pronouncements about the dangers of steeplechasing to horse and man and how they were increased by rough riding. The Governor was an old woman who had never been on a horse in his life, but that would not reduce the effect of his pontifications on those about him. Job sincerely hoped that his own rash repetition of what Stephen had said had not been carried back to Government House, though he feared it might have been. He was well aware of the tightly linked social intelligence which quietly identified settlers' attitudes and filed them for future reference. Meiner-tzhagen, after all, though it was true he had been far more outspoken and indiscreet than Stephen, had been shipped home under a cloud that had never quite been dispersed, for his demands for an explanation had never been met.

Altogether Job had decided that it would do Stephen, for whom he had conceived a genuine liking, no harm at all to be taken out of circulation for a month or two. Also he had plans for his own future and for Stephen's which were coming to fruition in his crafty old head.

So it was that two days later, with Stephen at the wheel, the Buick trundled and bounced down the long avenue between the flame trees and made for the plains.

As was the custom with a newcomer on safari, after zeroing in the rifles, Job 'shot in' Stephen on light game. Using the Savage, Stephen without much difficulty brought down the hartebeest and impala presented to him.

'All very well,' Job said that night, looking directly at Stephen as they sipped their whiskies before a blazing log fire. 'But a man can shoot well enough to be a good calm shot until it comes to the big five: lion, elephant, rhino, buffalo and leopard. They're what separate the men from the boys. You're about ready to try. We'll start looking for buffalo tomorrow.'

'Buffalo?' Stephen said. 'Any reason for picking on him?'

'He's the big daddy of them all. He's a rum 'un the old buffalo and no mistake. He's as mean as hell, the old buff. He'll rip you in pieces in a minute and trample on what's left and it takes a man to stand up to him. He never gives up and half the time when you think you've killed him he's still got a kick left in him that'll kill you. I admire the old buffalo for he never knows when he's beat. Like old John Jorrocks and the fox it's not that I don't love the fox best but I love the 'ounds more. And in this case we're the 'ounds.'

'So he's the most dangerous of them all, is he?' Stephen said.

'The most dangerous of them all is the one that gets you,' Job said with a short laugh. And on that note they turned in.

But there was to be no buffalo on that safari. It was late when they came back to the camp after a fruitless day's tracking. Tired out, Stephen had his bath, changed into a fresh shirt and shorts and walked over to where the drinks were laid out on a table under a thorn tree. He was pouring himself a stiff whisky when Job left his tent and came across to join him. Sitting down heavily in his chair he reached out a hand for the bottle. 'My brother is very ill,' he said. 'I've just got a message. It's his second heart attack. We'll have to cut this trip short. I must get back. Sorry, lad, you won't have your chance at the big stuff this time.'

It never ceased to be a marvel to Stephen how messages got through to those in the depths of the bush in the days before wireless, but somehow they did. The Africans, it seemed, had a wireless of their own; runners made use of it and sooner or later found anyone, however far from ordinary communications they might be.

Job's brother, he explained, farmed beyond Nanyuki. He was a bachelor; there was no one else in the world near to him. Job knew he had no alternative but to return and could only hope he would arrive in time.

They broke camp next morning and set off on their journey home. Job was anxious and worried and there was no question of their stopping to look for game, but as they went they continued to shoot for the pot. Earlier Stephen had marvelled at Job's quickness and the accuracy of his shooting. But now he noticed that once or twice the speed of his lift and swing faltered. He had seen, too, as he shot, that twinge of pain which he had noticed before. When it crossed Job's features he would sometimes instinctively put his hand up to his shoulder. Stephen guessed that the injury he had sustained when the young horse had dragged him was still troubling him, but when he mentioned it Job only shrugged and said it was nothing. By this time Stephen himself had never been fitter in his life. He was baked by the sun, lashed by rain, torn by thorns and tough grass and as hard as nails. He was also loving every minute of it.

It was when they were making their way across the Mara that the rains caught them, coming down in long slanting spears that pelted into the ground. The rough track they were following ran down to a drift which Job had said was fordable but by the time they reached it the brown water was surging and pouring past them in spate. Only a glance was needed to tell them it was far too deep and strong even to contemplate putting the Buick into it. There was nothing for it but to pitch camp and wait for the waters to subside.

Going to sleep that night the rattle of the rain on the canvas above his head was in Stephen's ears, but when he woke next morning the deluge had ceased as quickly as it had come, the sun was shining and the sparkle was back in the thin clear air. As he left the tent he saw Job talking to two tribesmen a little distance away. They were Masai, tall, self-assured, leaning on their spears with the casual arrogance that was their nature. In the background was a circular, mud-walled Masai village which the rain had obscured from their view the night before.

In a minute or two Job left the tribesmen and walked back to the tents.

'What is it?' Stephen asked.

'A lion,' Job answered. 'He's been raiding their stock. They went after him themselves and wounded him. We'll have to get him.'

'Where is he?'

'That's what we'll have to find out,' Job said grimly. 'They think he's holed up in that bush behind the boma.' Job waved a hand in the direction of the village. Turning he went into the tent and came out holding the big Rigby. As he broke it and slid the two heavy, steel-jacketed bullets into the breech he looked at Stephen, hesitated and then said, 'This may be a bit hairy. It might be better if I went in alone.'

'I hardly think that's a very good idea,' Stephen said.

'I thought you might say that. Very well. Get the Winchester and check the action.' After he had seen Stephen load the magazine and work the bolt he went on: 'When we go in keep on my right and a bit behind – and watch it. Since he's wounded he'll probably growl a warning. It'll give us a second or two to position ourselves before he comes. And if he comes he'll come out fast. On the other hand he may be dead in there.'

'But you don't think so.'

'Not from what they said, I don't. Come on, let's get moving. Kamau!' he called to the tracker.

There was a burst of Swahili between Job and the tracker which Stephen didn't understand and then they were all piling into the Buick. Stephen started the engine, they swung away from the camp and bumped across the hard ground, the long grass swirling at their wheels. The two Masai were waiting at the edge of a clump of thicker, higher grass. Beyond was a mass of tangled thorn trees and scrub leading up to a pile of rock.

Kamau quested about for a moment, almost, Stephen thought, like a hound on a scent. Then he straightened, pointed and said something to Job.

'He's in there all right,' Job said, 'and alive I'll lay my bottom dollar. And damn dangerous.'

The whole village now appeared to have turned out to see the sport and was ranged in a semi-circle behind them.

As they advanced into the bush Stephen kept Job in the corner of his eye. He was walking slowly, tensely, his eyes quartering the thicker undergrowth in front of them. Stephen found himself imitating him, putting one foot forward with deliberation before following it with another. He was reminded of Kipling's lines which he couldn't remember properly, of no one wanting to face them and every beggar must and moving off to do so 'uncommon stiff and slow'. He also remembered Job's remark an evening or so back that the most dangerous animal was the one that got you. Then he pushed these thoughts to the back of his mind. Concentrate, he said to himself as he had said so often before in moments of danger. Concentrate, for Christ's sake.

A few minutes passed which seemed like hours and then they were nearing the thick, green, almost impenetrable bush at the foot of the rocks. If he's here at all we must be close to him, Stephen thought. Everything in him was tightened in anticipation, all about him was blurred save for himself, Job and the small area of bush before them which stood out starkly in the harsh light. They both paused to search it with their eyes.

Then the growl came, low and menacing, from above them and to their right. A second later the scene erupted.

There was a blood-curdling grunt almost, it seemed, only a few feet away. A roar like thunder followed and a tawny, murderous streak of animal ferocity shot out of the bush straight at Job.

Stephen had a glimpse of the great open jaws and furled, arched mane, the ground-devouring, crouching run. He saw Job swing the big rifle – and fail to get it up. In that split second he knew what had happened. Job's injured shoulder had rebelled and locked. Then the Winchester was against his own shoulder. He was shooting and working the bolt with the same cold concentration that had come to him long ago when an enemy machine was in his sights. The first of the solid, killing bullets took the lion behind the point of his shoulder, the second tore into the base of his skull and dropped him dead five yards from Job's feet.

Job stared at the twitching body of the great beast for a moment. Then he turned an ashen face to Stephen. 'My shoulder,' he said. 'It jammed. Thanks, lad.'

'I don't know if I hit him where I should.'

'You hit him well enough.' Job's lips twisted into a wry grin. 'I reckon you'll do.'

'Maybe that makes up for Pioneer,' Stephen said.

Then, suddenly, the villagers were all about them laughing and cheering. Kamau, too, materialised and stood looking down at the dead lion. 'Bwana Raymond use the big rifle now,' he said looking at Job, his teeth showing in a grin.

'So be it,' Job said slowly. 'And now, as Mr Jorrocks said, "Vere's the brandy?"'

It was whisky which they opened when they got back to the tent. 'Well,' Job said. 'Everyone wants to get a lion and you've got a good one. You'd better keep his skin for a hearthrug if you ever have a hearth to put it on.' He downed one whisky quickly and poured himself another. 'Now, Stephen lad,' he went on. 'I'm going to tell you something I hadn't intended to until we got back. I wanted to see how you shaped up. After the lion I reckon you'll do for what I'm suggesting. But first things first. I'm selling up.'

'But – '

'Wait a bit. Let me finish. My brother's got seventy thousand acres up at Nanyuki. In his state of health even if he

120

recovers from this attack he can't run it all alone. He's been asking me for some time to come into partnership with him and help look after it. I'd made up my mind before we left. It's all the more urgent now.'

'What about the horses?'

'They'll have to go. I'm getting too old for them anyway. Besides, he has a pack of hounds up there. Hunts warthogs with half-bred Alsatians and Dobermanns. What would old Jorrocks say?'

" 'Dash my vig," I expect,' Stephen answered.

Job chuckled again and poured himself more whisky. It had, as was usual with him, loosened his tongue. 'Now, then, Stephen lad,' he went on. 'Don't think I'm turning you out. I've come to like you in the few months we've had together and I've thought about what I could do for you. You can handle horses and ride 'em too but you haven't the capital to set up a stable. Anyway, I dunno, racing here isn't all that much after what you've been and seen and done at home – that's right, isn't it?'

'Well – '

'You don't have to say it. I know.' What Job knew too but did not say was that in the tiny world of Kenya the tag of 'the fellow who killed Job's good horse' would stick to Stephen for some time and that Adrian Sprott and Gervase Winthrop were unlikely to let it die. Job looked at Stephen speculatively and took another sip of his whisky. 'Now, then,' he said slowly, 'what about going for a hunter professionally? You'd have to start at the bottom. It's a rough life but, I dunno, I think you've got it in you.'

Stephen stared at him for a moment. Then he put down his glass and laughed outright. 'You cunning old bugger,' he said. 'You had this in mind all along. That's why you took me out. That's why you were so anxious to try me on buffalo. I wouldn't put it past you to have wounded one yourself to see how I'd stand up to his charge.'

Job looked shocked. 'No one does that or would ever dream of it,' he said. 'As you will learn there's a hunter's code ten times as strict as anything in racing. It's founded on three things – respect for the animal, preservation of it and yourself which means a quick clean kill, and commonsense. And commonsense means no unnecessary risks so don't think I faked that shoulder-locking this afternoon. Anyone who cheats with big game ends up in the right place for him – a box.'

'Sorry,' Stephen said quietly. 'I shouldn't have said that. I'm beginning to understand.'

'I can give you a chit to Hayes and Franklin in Nairobi. They're the best of the firms that run safaris. Both are old friends and I've hunted with them both, though Bert Franklin is mostly behind a desk now. They'll give you a trial on my say so. Mind you they'll put you through the hoop to try you out. Probably as a start you'll be driving one of the lorries. Don't go off with romantic ideas of fancy floosies queueing up for you to roger 'em. More likely you'll be sent off to shoot for the pot and have to trudge miles in the heat to do it. Maybe you'll spend your time at first pulling lorries out of swamps or searching for camp sites and then getting sworn at to hell for picking a wrong one, but if you're what I think, you'll stick it and soon enough you'll come to find there's no life like it. Nothing at all.'

Stephen bent to throw more logs on the fire. 'Not even steeplechasing?' he said with a wry grin.

'Not even that. Not even getting one just right at the open ditch; not even sitting with a double handful at the last. But since you mention it there's one thing they have in common. If you ride races and go on riding 'em sooner or later you'll take a fall that hurts and if you go after big game sooner or later one of 'em will sort you out – probably the buffalo, that mean old bugger that thinks and damn nearly talks and is always going to outsmart you when you least expect it.'

'Are you trying to put me off?'

'Nothing can do that once it's in your blood. But there are two sides to every picture. That's one thing I've learnt from life.' Job stared into the fire. 'Keep your mouth shut and your eyes and ears open. You'll learn a lot from listening to the old hands talking round the fire at night. Some of it will be tales strictly for clients' consumption but you'll soon spot those.' He sighed. 'How I wish I were starting it all again,' he said. 'Ah well, you can't put the clock back.'

They were both silent then. Stephen sat, holding his glass,

looking out at the bright, clear African night. The stars were coming out to sprinkle the sky in their hundreds; the noises of the bush which he was just beginning to differentiate and identify were all about them. The primitiveness of the continent encompassed the little encampment. Save for the creatures of the bush who prowled in the darkness and disturbed it, they were alone in the vastness of Africa, with nothing to protect them but their own skills and hardihood.

All of this struck a chord with Stephen. In a strange way it recalled to him his days as a fighter pilot when in that tiny box of wood and canvas called a Sopwith Camel he had been alone against the elements and the enemy and had survived. Suddenly he knew that here, isolated in the bush, he felt more at peace, more at one with himself than he had done for years. He was being offered a new challenge to make a new life. It was his chance to rid himself of the black dog of failure that seemed destined to follow him everywhere. He took a deep breath and used the same words he had spoken to Billy Norris those months ago in the Muthaiga Club. 'I'll give it a go,' he said.

'Good lad. I thought you would. You can have the guns at a valuation, if you want 'em. Except the Winchester. Keep that for free to remind you of that lion back there. I reckon you've earned it. I shan't be needing any of them any more with this shoulder of mine. And one other thing – always carry your own gun. I know some of 'em don't but you can lose precious seconds that make all the difference.'

Stephen laughed. 'Bob Ferris said a trainer was no good unless he carried his own saddles.'

'It's the same way of thinking. Now we'll drink on it – where's that whisky?'

CHAPTER XVI

Just as Job has said, Stephen commenced his apprenticeship driving a lorry on one of the big safaris. From this he progressed to being taken out by an experienced hunter. At this stage he was on trial, his every attitude and action watched and summed up, for if he was to be entrusted with taking clients out himself, one mistake, one weakness of resolve or loss of nerve could cost a life. As Job had advised he kept his mouth shut and his ears open, listening to the talk round the fire at night when whisky and adrenalin had loosened tongues.

In his search for knowledge of the animals he would be up against he obtained the skulls of both elephant and buffalo and cracked them open to examine their strengths and weaknesses. He found and measured the four inches of thin frontal bone between the elephant's tusks, the only place for a killing shot to go when he charged, as sooner or later he would, and Stephen would find himself standing up to him. In contrast the buffalo had a heavy carapace of bone that protected his brain from even the solid shot fired from the big Rigby or other rifles like it. The actual space occupied by the brain itself surprised Stephen by its smallness. Remarking on this to one of the older hunters he had received the reply: 'That may be, but never forget, small as it is it works, and it's wicked. And,' the older man had gone on to say, 'remember, too, that when you're facing him he'll come at you just about as fast as a racehorse moves – what's that, thirty-five or forty miles an hour, isn't it? And, my boy, the end of a buffalo's charge is later than a man might wish.'

Before he was passed as fit to take out clients, Stephen had faced that charge and killed his buffalo, though the power and weight and courage of the great animal had carried him dying almost to his feet to prove the truth of the old hunter's saying. But by then Stephen had killed more lion, seen an elephant come crashing down to his gun and stared from a hide into the frightening yellow eyes of a leopard, whose predatory intensity he found with a sudden shock reminded him of Andrew Massiter and brought his past crowding back to him.

By this time he had learnt, too, that besides chaperoning the client to the kill the white hunter had to be many other things – administrator of a team of twelve or more very different human beings, maintainer of machinery to keep the hunting vehicles moving, procurer of licenses and keeper of records, and above all entertainer, to see that the clients never became bored in the intervals of hunting, a sort of raconteur, professional host, handmaiden and goodfellow rolled into one. That was a part of the job he disliked, for many of the clients were wealthy thrill-seekers whom he despised. They were the type that you brought to the target by the exercise of hard-won skills and who then put you into danger by foolishness, stupidity or just plain cowardice. The women who tagged along with them were mostly worse than the men, rich bitches bored and hungry for sensation. Some of them came to his bed and when they did, he took them and forgot them, or tried to. One thing he was short of in his lonely life was sex and this was the one thing most of them were good at. 'Better by night than by day,' as one hunter put it and their sensual skills would often return to haunt and torment him.

By and large many of the big safaris set up for the rich seemed to Stephen to be artificial and meretricious. He avoided them when he could, and if he had to take them out preferred to act as second to another hunter.

He was happiest when he could hunt on his own, alone save for a tracker and a couple of boys. One of the first things he had done when he knew he was going to make this his life was to search out Job's tracker, Kamau. 'Still carrying own gun, Bwana Raymond,' Kamau had said with his wide grin. Thereafter he became Stephen's friend, companion and right hand man. Whenever he went into the bush Kamau went too. Always something of a loner, as the years went by Stephen found himself withdrawing more and more into himself and caring less and less for the company of his fellows. The few belongings he had were packed into two tin trunks stored in the Norfolk Hotel. When he was not on safari he spent much of his time there, sleeping, reading or sometimes drinking alone in one of the cottages. These were only intervals for, as Job had prophesied, he always longed to get back again, preferably to the Tana river country where he had come to love those limitless miles, stretching away under the bright hard sky to the sea in one direction and the Somali border in the other. There was something about this vast expanse, studded with acacia trees, with the wide, green slow-moving river winding through it past its dongas and sandy inlets where game came to lie up or to drink, that drew him back again and again. He never quite knew why. Perhaps it was its very loneliness, its sense of emptiness of all traces of humanity that appealed to his solitary spirit.

But there were some clients whom it was a pleasure to take out. At first it seemed that the Americans, Harvey and Betty Lang, a youngish couple who were on a world-wide sporting tour which would include fox-hunting in Ireland, would prove one of these. Both were quiet, unaffected and anxious to learn. When they found out that Stephen was Irish and had raced and ridden to hounds they plied him with questions about the country and the sport, and what had brought him to Kenya. Stephen found himself talking freely to them, telling them of the Bay and the Troubles and the loss of his house.

Betty, a tall girl with corn blonde hair and high, firm breasts under her bush shirt, was, Stephen thought, the stronger character of the two. She was straightforward and fun to be with, and as the days went by Stephen found his liking for her increasing. When they went shooting guinea fowl or francolin for their table there was a fluid grace of movement about her as she swung the sixteen-bore that had come in their armoury along with the heavier guns and the cameras which woke something in Stephen. She was a better shot at wildfowl than Harvey, so much so that when they went out with the shotguns Harvey would often not accompany them but stayed in the camp writing letters or posting up his diary.

Stephen hated women who talked too much or too foolishly, who asked stupid questions or thought they knew it all. Betty did none of these things and tramped through the heat and the bush without complaint, contriving somehow at the same time to look as if she had just stepped straight off Fifth Avenue. He found himself looking forward more and more to those days they were together, for they had discovered, too, a shared sense of humour. Altogether it was a comradeship heightened by the knowledge of sexual attraction such as he had not known for years. All in all, Stephen told himself, she was just plain nice. And then he knew he was allowing his thoughts to dwell on her too long and too much.

There was something else, too, that soon gave him cause for thought. Although on the surface all seemed well between Harvey and Betty he began to sense an indefinable tension which was disturbing their relationship. It showed in little things: Betty's eyes were always watchful and when she thought Stephen was not looking a frown would cause a furrow to appear between them as they followed every movement Harvey made.

Harvey, too, at times, would fall into long, abstracted silences. These, few at first, became more frequent. Then he would sit brooding over something and when he spoke, easy and pleasant as his conversation always was, the words might almost have come from an automaton. Then, or so it seemed to Stephen, there was emptiness or hollowness in him as if he had lost something he could not find. In themselves these were small things. They might mean anything or nothing and Stephen might well not have noticed them at all had not his instincts been honed to observe the ways of clients, to make mental notes of their reactions and behaviour for reference and use if and when a time of testing arrived. He came to realise, too, that Harvey, though he would not mention it, had not cared much for Betty's performing better with the shotgun than he had and that this was one of the reasons he stayed behind in camp on those shooting days.

Because of those signs and because Harvey at the outset had frankly admitted his inexperience with a rifle – 'only a shotgun, I'm afraid. Quail in Carolina, high pheasants in Oxfordshire, grouse in Scotland, and not much good with it either, and that's about it,' he had said – Stephen brought him along more carefully than usual.

But there was nothing wrong with his shooting. He dealt with light game cleanly and steadily and made no mistake with his lion. It had not been a difficult kill. They had found the lion in the long grass and got close to him so that he presented an easy target. Still Stephen had known clients to get over-excited and over-hasty at the sight of their first lion but when he said, 'Bust him – now', Harvey had shot and shot again and the lion had keeled over dead.

But that night, over drinks, the brooding was back. Harvey sat playing with his glass, staring into the night.

'Well, Harvey,' Betty said. 'You got your lion. A clean kill. You can't do better than that, can you, Stephen?' She turned towards Stephen as she spoke and there was a look of pleading in her eyes as if she was beseeching him to say how well her husband had done.

'Too true,' Stephen said. 'Everyone wants a lion. You've got a good one. And you hit him right. No mucking about. No going in after a wounded one. That I would not have liked.'

'You set him up for me,' Harvey said dully. 'You and that tracker chap.'

'We didn't shoot him for you,' Stephen said.

'I half wish you had.'

Stephen sighed. What was the man getting at? What the hell did he want? He should have been over the moon after his first lion properly killed. He had a mental note to keep an especially watchful eye on him. Harvey didn't seem the type to create a situation just for the hell of it like some of them did, but you never knew. 'Look,' he said. 'We're not here for heroics. We're here to see you safe. The best safari is the one where the hunter never has to fire his gun.'

Harvey looked up and suddenly gave Stephen his slow, pleasant smile. 'I know it,' he said. 'I'm talking like what you British call a b.f. Sorry, Stephen. Forget it, please.'

Betty got to her feet. 'It's time to turn in,' she said abruptly.

'You do,' Harvey said. 'I guess I'll stay on a bit. Don't you wait, either, Stephen. I like sitting here listening to all these noises.'

But things did not improve over the succeeding days. In fact, Stephen thought, the tension between them became more apparent. And then Harvey developed the dreaded 'buck fever'.

They were in the Tana river country and, working with the wind, Stephen had brought him to a small group of gerenuk. One, a buck, was a little apart, grazing. He was a simple side shot, for they had come silently and the distance was a bare thirty yards. 'There you are,' Stephen whispered. 'Take him.' Then he waited for the report of the rifle. When none came he looked back to see Harvey's gun weaving uncontrollably on his shoulder.

There was a look of dumb bewilderment on Harvey's face as he tried desperately to steady the rifle. All his efforts were useless and, at length accepting this, he finally lowered it to the ground without attempting to fire. There was a terrible hurt in his eyes as he turned to Stephen. 'Jeez, Stephen,' he said. 'I've got the shakes. I couldn't hit City Hall. What is it?'

'Buck fever,' Stephen answered. 'It happens to us all at one time or another. Had it myself. Not to worry. It'll pass.'

'But why, Stephen, why?' He seemed in anguish. There was more than normal reaction here.

'You're trying too hard,' Stephen said. 'I don't know if you play games. I don't but I'm told its like 'pressing' in golf or tennis. Relax. You'll get over it.'

'Will I? It doesn't look like it to me.' He picked up the Winchester again. Once more it swung out of control as he raised it to his shoulder. 'Get over it – huh,' he said. 'How?'

'We can try one cure,' Stephen said. He shouted for Kamau and in a minute or two was handed the forked stick that would serve as a rest for Harvey's rifle. 'Now,' he said. 'We'll get you something easy to bring your confidence back.'

They found an impala not far away. It was another simple shot. Stephen pushed the stick into the ground and placed the rifle in the fork. 'Take your time,' he said. 'He's all yours. Wallop him.'

But, even with the rest, Harvey's rifle wandered. This time he did press the trigger but the bullet took the impala in the quarter instead of the heart. He gave one buck, seemed to fold up behind and then began to drag himself away. Stephen looked at Harvey. He was shaking. 'Over-trying doesn't do this,' he said wretchedly. Raising his own rifle Stephen brought the impala down. They trudged disconsolately back to camp.

It was not a cheery evening. Harvey drank more whisky

than he was accustomed to and went early to bed. Next morning he did not appear at breakfast. 'He has a stomach upset,' Betty said briefly. Her eyes were red-rimmed as if she had been crying. Something was badly wrong between them, whatever it was. Stephen saw her teeth close over her lower lip as if to stop it quivering. Then she lifted her hand to her forehead to brush back her hair. It was a simple unconscious gesture done with that easy grace he had come to know well. Too well, he told himself. All she did, the way she moved and spoke, was doing things to him. He wanted to help and did not know how to set about it. He wanted more than that, too, and thought she knew it. He was experienced enough now to know, too, that she was not indifferent to him. If he were to make a move things might happen very quickly between them.

The recollection of the last woman he had had came suddenly back to him. She had been a bitch, one of the 'travelling harlots' as he mentally dubbed them, but she'd been all woman just the same. She'd known what she'd been about in bed and her skills had made him want more of it. With an effort he pushed those thoughts away and came back to the present and its problems. He was running a safari; Harvey was his client; it was his job to find out what was wrong and to rectify it if he could. 'Is it what happened yesterday?' he asked. 'Did he tell you?'

'Oh yes, sure he told me,' she answered. 'Buck fever, that's what you call it, isn't it? Does it matter?'

'Not as much as he seems to think. He'll get over it.'

'It matters to him.'

'Would it do any good to talk about it?'

'No. Not now anyway. He said would you and I go out with the shotguns. At least I'd be able to hit something if he couldn't. That's what he said. Damn you men, always wanting to prove something to yourselves. Come on. Let's go.' She got up and walked to the tent where the guns were kept locked to a rack.

But their shooting that day was not a success. Betty was unlike her usual calm and confident self; she was abstracted, out of sorts and silent. Birds, too, were few and far between and those that got up she mostly missed. Harvey was still in his tent when they returned and he did not appear at the evening meal.

'How is he?' Stephen asked.

'Better,' she said. 'He'll be about tomorrow.' And then, looking directly at him and meeting his eyes she added defiantly, 'It must have been change of diet, or overdoing things, or the heat – ' Her voice tailed off. She looked away. She was lying and both of them knew it.

'Are you sure,' Stephen said, 'it wouldn't do you good to talk about it?'

'No. Yes. That is I'm not sure. Oh, hell – ' She turned away, got up and walked to the tent.

Stephen sat on, a puzzled man. He liked them both and was close to liking Betty too much. That was only part of the problem, and in a way a minor one. Whatever was between them was on the point of ruining what should have been a good and happy safari and he did not have the least notion of how to deal with it or what to do next. Perhaps, he thought, the toughs and the tarts were the easiest in the end. At least you knew where you were with them. White hunters were supposed to know all the answers. Well, he hadn't any to this one.

He must have remained there for the best part of an hour looking at the stars, sipping a weak whisky and thinking, when there was the sound of a soft footstep beside him. Looking up he saw Betty standing by the table. All sorts of possible crises shot across his mind. 'What is it?' he said. 'Is Harvey worse?'

'Harvey's taken two sleeping pills. He's out for the count. Is there any whisky in that bottle?'

'Quite a lot – still.'

'Pour me a stiff one, will you, Stephen?'

She pulled up one of the folding chairs and sat down. Cupping the glass in her hands she put her elbows on the table and stared across it at Stephen. Their eyes met and Stephen could read in hers as plainly as if she had written it that she knew he wanted her and that that want was returned.

'You said would it do any good to talk,' she said slowly. 'Well, it's come to that. I've got to, I guess. I can't keep bottling it up any longer even though I feel I'm betraying

131

him. You've sensed there's something wrong between us. I've seen that the way you've looked sometimes. You'd better know what it is. Maybe you can help. It's our only chance, I guess – '

'Try me, anyway.'

The words came pouring from her with the sudden flow of release. 'It's eating his heart out and this goddam buck fever has been the last straw. He's impotent. He can't get it up. Or only once in a long, long while. He's tearing himself to pieces over it – '

'The poor devil,' Stephen said. 'Now I think I begin to understand.'

'He's been to doctors and psychiatrists,' she went on, the words tumbling over each other. 'It was those – the head-shrinkers – who suggested this trip. They told him there was a theory the air in Kenya was sexually stimulating or something. He began to think it might work. He was shooting so well, you said so too. And now this buck fever's come to ruin everything. Oh God, Stephen, you can't believe the premium American men put on their virility.'

'Not only Americans,' Stephen said. 'How can I help, or can I?'

'Would I be sitting here telling you all this if I didn't think you could? He's decided to give up, to cut the safari short. He says he's finished, that it's no use going on. If he does, it's the end. He's lost and he'll never find himself. You've got to persuade him to go on.'

'I can try. It may not be easy the way he is.'

'I'll start on him when he wakes. He likes you and he respects you. If you throw your weight in I think we might just swing it. But this buck fever, can it be cured?'

'It may be gone by tomorrow. Just let's hope.'

'You see,' she went on. 'If he could do something really well on his own, just once even, that might work. The shrinks all say it's partly, what do they call it – an inherent insufficiency. If he could get reassurance inside himself he could be all right. That lion now, he's persuaded himself it was all a nothing, that you and Kamau nursemaided him, that it was all too easy.'

'It was a quick, clean kill. They don't all do that, believe

132

me. Some of them, when they see a lion close to, go into a jelly or miss him or wing him. He didn't.'

'But it wasn't a very good lion, was it?'

'As lions go it wasn't a record and it wasn't in its first youth, but – '

'He's got hyper-sensitivity about himself and whatever he does he has to find a flaw in it. And he reads things that aren't there into everything. That's a symptom, too, they say. It's tragic. He's a man, you know, behind it all.'

'I never doubted it. But what about you? What's it doing to you?'

'Can't you guess? Do you think I don't want it? Especially here – I don't know, in the heat, the emptiness, the aloneness, the whole feeling of life teeming about you. Perhaps it's true what they say about Kenya – you'll never know what it's like lying beside him night after night, longing for it and him half-crying because he can't – '

She stood up suddenly and Stephen found himself on his feet facing her, their eyes locked. She pushed her hair back with that gesture he knew so well. The air was vibrant between them. 'Don't touch me, Stephen,' she said breath-lessly. 'Or I'll explode – don't – '

'He'll never know – ' Stephen found the words coming out involuntarily, as if they had spoken themselves, driven out by his need for her.

'Oh yes, he will. Haven't I told you he senses things? It would kill him. Don't think I don't want to. I don't even know if I love him any more, but I know I can't do it to him. Just tell me this, Stephen – would I be only one of your one-night lays?'

'You know you wouldn't.'

'Well, thanks for that and, for that matter, for everything.' She turned towards the tent. 'No, don't you dare come nearer. Dear God, is this what Africa does to people?'

133

CHAPTER XVII

When Stephen crossed to the breakfast table spread under the thorn tree next morning Harvey was already there. He was looking pale and ill, drank coffee and ate little. 'Took two sleeping tablets last night,' he explained to Stephen. 'They always leave me with a hangover. Look, Stephen, I hate to say it but I think we'd better call it all off. It won't make any difference to the fees of course. I just – well – I seem to have made a hash of it – '

'Nonsense, Harvey. You've done damn well. Far better than most of the clients I take out. You mustn't say that. Not even think it.'

'I do say it. I've decided it's time to call crack. That's what racing people say, isn't it?'

'Some of them. But not you, Harvey. You're all right man. I've seen you shoot. You don't have to worry about a thing.'

'It's this buck fever – '

'Forget that. Like I said, everyone's had it. Theodore Roosevelt – there's one for you. Your own fighting President. He had it, or so I'm told—he was a bit before my time. All the greats talk about it – Karamoja Bell, Percival, Selous – ' Stephen was improvising now and he spared a moment to hope that in whatever Valhalla these mighty hunters were they would not think the worse of him for it – 'it didn't stop them. You're not going to let it stop you, are you?'

'I don't know – you make it all sound convincing. But then you're not suffering from it.'

'But I have.' Stephen could feel Betty's eyes on him, imploring him to persist. 'You can't quit now, Harvey. Besides, what does Betty say?'

'She wants me to go on too,' Harvey said, half-sulkily. Then, more like his old self, he smiled. 'Is this a conspiracy?' he said.

'Call it that, if you like,' Stephen said. 'But it isn't, or not a criminal one anyway. Seriously, Harvey, you'll kick yourself forever if you pack it in now. And there's another thing. Speaking for myself, as you know, none of us wants to lose a

134

client. Cutting short a safari is almost as bad if not worse. What'll they be saying about me in the pubs and bars around Nairobi and the Muthaiga Club and points west if we all come trooping home after a few weeks with our tails between our legs and nothing to show?'

Harvey stared into his coffee cup. 'That figures, I suppose,' he said. 'But what about this damn buck fever?'

'That'll be all right, you'll find,' Stephen said. 'Have a rest day today and we'll start again tomorrow.'

Harvey took a deep breath. 'Very well,' he said. 'To use your own expression, Stephen,' he said. 'I'll give it a go.'

That evening Kamau brought news of an elephant. From what he said Stephen thought it likely that the next day's tracking would be long, hard and exhausting. It was decided to leave Betty behind in the camp, and he and Harvey set out at first light in one of the hunting vehicles. For the first time Harvey took with him the Bell and Howell cameras as well as the guns.

When they got down from the car to begin tracking in earnest Harvey drew Stephen aside. 'Say, Stephen, wait a minute,' he said. 'There's something I want to say to you.'

'Let's go into the shade first,' Stephen said. Wondering what was coming he led the way to where a baobab tree was spreading its great branches. A fallen log made a rough seat. Taking out his cigarette case he offered one to Harvey. It took Harvey a little longer than usual to light up, then, avoiding Stephen's eye and drawing on the cigarette, he said, 'I suppose you'll despise me forever for telling you this but, well, look, it's this way, well, the fact is, I don't like killing things. There it is, it's out now. Now you know – '

'I don't despise you,' Stephen said. 'Get that out of your mind straight away. I think perhaps you've got it wrong about chaps like us – white hunters. The popular idea is that we're butchers with a blood lust or some such rot. We're not. We're conservators in a way. You must have noticed that when we shot light game we shot for the pot only, for ourselves and the boys to eat, to keep the show on the road. When we kill bigger game it's a matter of, if you like, honour to kill cleanly and well. When you shot that lion – '

'I hated doing it – '

'You did all right. But the point is, he wasn't in his first youth. Sooner or later, and probably sooner, some of the younger ones would have got him. Sometimes we kill off the older ones to spare them something worse, sometimes we cull because we have to, and sometimes, of course, it's a case of kill or be killed. And I'll tell you something else, too.'

'What's that?'

'I don't much like killing an elephant even when I have to. He's so damn big and primeval and, I think, vulnerable with all that size, though God knows he can be wicked enough when he wants to. Now, the buffalo, he's different. He's a warrior; he's built for battle and he knows it. He'll take you on any time, any place, on ground of his choosing or yours and when he does – look out! I haven't much compunction about the buffalo. I know if I don't get him he'll find a way to get me. I like the old buffalo and I admire him, but I'll kill him just the same.'

Harvey gave a short laugh. 'Every man kills the thing he loves,' he said.

'What's that mean?'

'It's a line of poetry by a man called Oscar Wilde.'

'I rode a horse called Oscar Wilde once. Useless bugger he was.'

'Some would say the same about his namesake. Since I've said so much I'll say more. You must think me a right sonofabitch to have come out here on safari after what I've told you. Well, I'll tell you the reason we came out here – '

'Don't if you don't want to.'

Harvey threw away his cigarette. 'I'd been overworking, over-trying at various things,' he said. 'I've a pretty full life back in the States. It got me down in the end. My nerves went to pieces. That sounds silly out here now, but that's how it was. Betty persuaded me to go to a psychiatrist – a shrink – and it was he who suggested this trip.'

'Did you tell him you didn't care about killing?'

'I kept that back. Foolish of me, I suppose. But Betty was all for coming. Our marriage, well, let's just say it had hit a bad patch. I've never told Betty either. So she doesn't know. I thought it would finally convince her I was all washed up.

I thought it would make her despise me all the more because as it was, well, that bit doesn't matter. She's so good at everything, you see. She can knock birds out of the sky like nobody's business – far better than I ever can. Say, listen, am I the most God-awful client you've ever taken out?'

'Far from it. Look, I'll say it again. Killing comes second in this business; it's the skills that count.'

'I think I see that now. I'm going to come to that point in a minute. In fact I'll come to it now. That's why I brought the cameras along. Would you think less of me if from here on in I used them instead of the gun?'

'I'll think all the more of you,' Stephen said. 'For my money it's a damn sight more dangerous getting close in with a camera than it is with a gun. Besides you're in good company. The Prince of Wales, when he was here a few years back, preferred a camera to a gun, and Finch-Hatton, who I suppose was the top-notcher amongst us all, had become convinced of it too before he was killed flying – not hunting let it be said if it worries you.'

'It doesn't. You can't guess, Stephen, how glad I am to have got that off my chest. You won't mention it to Betty, will you? She thinks you're only one step underneath the Almighty – if that.'

'I wouldn't dream of it. You know it's a damn funny thing, but we poor devils often find ourselves acting as sort of confessors. It's something to do with the isolation, I've often thought, the sense of being right out of civilisation, almost on another planet. The air and the altitude may have something to do with it, too.' And I wonder, he told himself, how much the Roman Catholics hold back when they're in that curtained box stating their sins. He had never expected Harvey to tell him the whole truth and he admired him for the way he had handled it. He was fighting his own devils and doing pretty well. 'Go get the cameras and we'll set out,' he said, and fancied he saw more of a spring in Harvey's steps than had been there before as he watched him walk to the lorry.

When Stephen stood up he found Kamau beside him. The tracker had located the elephant's spoor. It was one worth following, he said, for this was no cow that they had in front of them but a bull and a big one. They assembled into a little party and went on through the bush, Kamau questing before them all the time, now upright, now bent almost double picking up those slight tell-tale indications known to him alone, that any white man, however experienced, would have missed. Soon they had confirmation that his information had been accurate and his interpretation of the signs and symbols correct, for an immense pile of ordure that was the elephant's droppings confronted them.

'Get that smell?' Stephen said to Harvey. 'Once got, never forgotten. It's said to be as good as a tonic if you're a true elephant hunter.'

Harvey wrinkled his nose. 'I can take it or leave it,' he said. 'What's next?'

Stephen beckoned to Kamau who advanced to the pile and prodded it with his big toe, testing its consistency. 'He can tell by that how long he's gone and how far we are from him,' he explained to Harvey.

They pressed on through the heat and the thick bush. On and on they went, mile after mile, Kamau giving little clucking noises and gesticulations as he picked up the spoor. Stephen directed sidelong glances at Harvey to see how he was sticking it. He appeared to be taking it well and showing no signs of faltering, though sweat was pouring from under his bush hat. At length they came to the country of the sand dunes south of the river, and then the huge footprints began to stand out stark and clear in the sand. 'Getting nearer,' Stephen said to Harvey.

The next great pile of droppings was damp and steaming. Looking at it Kamau and Stephen held a consultation. When they had finished Stephen turned to Harvey. 'Unless we're very much mistaken,' he said, '*tembo* – that's our friend the elephant – may be over the next ridge. What's the range of that thing?' He nodded towards the camera.

'About twenty yards, but I'd like to get nearer.'

'Does it make much noise?'

'A slight sort of whirr.'

'Tembo can't see very well but his hearing's about ten times better than yours or mine or Kamau's for that matter. He can sense and smell to make up for that loss of sight, but his hearing's the thing he relies on most. Can you adjust the noise at all?'

'No, I can't.'

'Well, just bear it in mind when we get close and it starts to whirr as you call it. He may not like it. I'm going on now with Kamau to see if we can spot him.'

Their feet sinking through the soft powdery sand, together they climbed to the top of the dune and peered cautiously over it. Below them was a water hole with a stunted palm on its far side. In the shade of the palm was the elephant. At the moment he was relaxing, idle, silent and unmenacing. As often as he had hunted them the sheer size of these vast survivors from another age always took Stephen's breath away. While they watched he swished his trunk lazily at a branch which came crashing down. He stamped one of his great feet on it and then returned to his rest and relaxation. Stephen and Kamau turned and slid down the slope.

Back on level sand they discussed in hushed whispers the best methods of approach. Not far from where the elephant stood Stephen had noticed a cleft in the dunes which, if they could find a way into it under cover, should bring them out very near him, provided he did not move and nothing happened to disturb him. Stephen sent Kamau off to reconnoitre its entrance. Then he beckoned Harvey up to him. 'He's in there,' he said quietly. 'Kamau's gone to find a way of getting up to him.'

In a minute or two Kamau returned and confirmed that they could enter the cleft from dead ground, that the wind was right and with care and luck they should be able to get very close.

'Mind where you put your feet,' Stephen whispered to Harvey. 'A rattle of a stone or a touch on a twig can send him flying – either away from us or at us.'

At the slowest of paces, step by step, they inched up the narrow defile. When they came to where it debouched on to the water hole and the sand became firm under their feet, they paused. The elephant was still there, standing broadside on, massive, huge, primeval in all his bulk and, for the moment anyway, undisturbed. They were so close they could pick out each wrinkle on his leathery skin; his tusks gleamed in the sunlight, the great ears were laid back peacefully against his shoulders. He hadn't scented them; he was still taking his ease.

'What a shot,' Stephen could not help thinking to himself as he mentally put the weight of the tusks at about sixty or seventy pounds – a fair trophy. One was slightly crooked and shorter than the other, probably as the result of a fight. He lifted a finger and beckoned Harvey up to him. Standing rigid at his first sight of the huge beast so close to him Harvey breathed, 'God Almighty but he's *big*.'

'Most people say that, seeing him for the first time,' Stephen whispered back. 'Go ahead. Shoot.'

Harvey put the camera to his eye and began to turn the handle. As he had said, a faint whirring noise came from it. Stephen balanced himself on the balls of his feet, adjusting his stance on the sand, the safety off the big Rigby, every faculty alert and concentrated. These were the minutes of greatest risk. They were well within charging distance. Even the slight noise of the camera might disturb the big bull.

It did.

All of a sudden the elephant threw up his head; the huge ears flickered, his trunk quested this way and that. He had not yet seen them but he sensed something strange was near him, something that could hold menace for him. He began to move. At first his lumbering footsteps took him away out of danger to himself and to them. Then either a slight shift in the wind brought their scent to him or that sixth sense of his told him where they were. With a neatness and delicacy of movement that would have been incredible in one of his bulk if Stephen had not often seen it before, he spun round. Unerringly he came straight for where they were standing. The speed of his progress, too, was deceptive. It was not yet a charge but it might become one at any moment.

'Get out, run,' Stephen said out of the corner of his mouth to Harvey. 'I'll cover you.'

'Not on your life,' was the answer. 'I'm staying here and I'm getting this on film. Oh, boy!'

The elephant came on and the camera continued to whir. Stephen mentally measured the decreasing distance between them, working out how late he could leave his shot and

140

concentrating on that centre spot of the line drawn between the ears. 'Shoot at the third wrinkle on the trunk,' the old hunters said, and that was where his killing shot would have to go. But all the time there was the thought in his mind that the last thing he wanted to do was to kill this huge beast whose harmless midday rest they had disturbed.

The thud of the great feet came nearer and nearer, but he hadn't charged – yet. He might just be only investigating these uncouth strangers who had invaded his resting place. But the time was only seconds away from when Stephen would either have to shoot or persuade him by other means to go away. He picked out a boulder some twelve yards from where they stood as the point of no return. Until the elephant reached that there was a chance of stopping him. He decided to take that chance. 'Cut the camera now!' he said to Harvey. 'That's an order!'

There was click and the whirring ceased. The elephant paused in his approach, his trunk swaying from side to side. 'Shoo!' Stephen shouted waving his arms. 'Go home, you silly old bugger! Go away! Bugger off! Be gone.'

The elephant lowered his trunk and looked at them. At this distance Stephen could see his little eyes quite clearly, surveying them, deciding whether to charge or let them go. His huge bulk seemed to fill the landscape. But there was no gut-rending screech that preceded the charge, when the ears were spread, the huge head was up. Stephen began to think that his tactic was succeeding. 'Get away with you!' he shouted. 'Get the hell out of here or I'll do you in!'

For a space of seconds the two stood facing each other. Suddenly the elephant made up his mind. He turned round, shuffled off and disappeared over the sands of the far ridge.

Beside him Stephen heard Harvey's breath come out in a long hiss. 'That's the hairiest half-minute I've ever had,' he said. 'What'd you do to him, Stephen, mesmerise him?'

'Called his bluff,' Stephen said shortly. 'Sometimes it works, sometimes it doesn't. But I'd have nailed him anyway if I'd had to.'

'I sure hope so. Mind if we sit down now and have a cigarette? My knees feel sort of shaky.'

Stephen passed him his case. When they had lighted up

141

Harvey went on, 'I got the pictures. They should be quite something.'

'You got something else,' Stephen said quietly. 'I think you got yourself. You stuck it out. You didn't move when I told you to bugger off. Those pictures must be damn near unique.'

Back in camp, after their baths, over whisky and their supper of soup and stewed guinea fowl, they retailed their adventures to Betty. When coffee came up Harvey produced a bottle of brandy from somewhere and the reliving of the day's doings took place once more.

'Well now,' Harvey said, sipping his drink. 'Ireland and fox-hunting next stop. You've been so good to us, Stephen, anything we can do for you there?'

Because he liked them both so much and felt he knew them so well, Stephen found himself saying: 'Bellary Bay, that's where we used to live. You remember I told you how we were burnt out? You'll probably get there and if you do there's a family called Massiter living there. The eldest boy, Kit he's called, could you find out what he's doing and where he is? I've rather lost touch.'

'Godson or something?' Harvey said lightly.

'That's it. Something like that,' Stephen said gravely.

Then Harvey was back reviewing the day once more. Before Stephen's eyes, as their talk went on and Betty listened, rapt, he could see his self-confidence come surging back. Soon he was looking at his wife in the contemplative, hungry, lingering way that is an unmistakable prelude to sex. What with isolation, alcohol, and the discarding of inhibition that comes from danger successfully survived the whole area surrounding the table became suffused with an aura of sexual excitement. Betty was caught up in it; her eyes were bright with anticipation as she looked from Harvey to Stephen and shifted to and fro on the camp chair. Soon Harvey yawned and stretched. 'Well,' he said. 'It's been a long day – ' Together he and Betty walked to their tent.

Not it was Stephen's turn to sit alone with the bottle. Two nights ago when she had been sharing her secrets with him he could have taken Betty himself, he knew, for her renunciation had only hung by a hair and would have snapped at his

142

touch. He had wanted her then and he wanted her now. She was outgoing, self-possessed and there was a wilful streak of steel somewhere in her, he guessed, whereas the Babs he had loved so long ago had been soft, willing and compliant. But Betty's calm competence drew her to him as did her body and he wanted it – all of it. He could imagine her firm breasts tightening under his hands and her body arching against his. But it was for Harvey those things were happening – five yards away.

Memories of those stolen times with Babs came crowding back to him, combined with thoughts of Kit and speculation of what he was doing now and what was happening to him. He reached for the bottle. 'Well, Dr Raymond, you've made your cure, now cure yourself,' he said to the night and the brilliant stars.

The bottle was empty when he went to bed.

CHAPTER XVIII

Some two months later Stephen came back from safari, checked his gear into the Norfolk, dined and drank and on his way back to his cottage collected his mail from the desk. It was only a sort of ritual gesture for there was seldom if ever anything of interest in it. Babs had long since ceased to write, and there had never been any love lost between him and his elder sister now married to some smart hunting chap in Leicestershire – living the life she had always wanted and anxious to forget her 'drifting useless brother' as he had once heard her describing him. Job, as he put it himself, was a poor hand with the pen and their association nowadays was limited to a few boozy evenings when they happened to be in town together. The little pile of envelopes therefore usually contained only circulars and bills and not many of them since he lived frugally. To his surprise that evening he found one bearing an Irish stamp and addressed to him in a bold feminine hand.

Slitting open the envelope he saw the embossed heading: *Barronstown, Kilrue, Co. Tipperary.* A line had been drawn through this and beside it was written: *As from the Shelbourne Hotel (our base).* Turning the pages over he came to the signature and smiled as he read: *Betty (Lang, in case you've forgotten me with all those loose ladies about in the bush.)*

Pouring himself a whisky, Stephen threw off his clothes, climbed into pyjamas and picked up the first page.

Dearest Stephen [he read]
Everyone out here has been terribly kind, almost too kind, the entertaining is quite something. There are hordes of servants everywhere and it seems to cost nothing to live. We had a day with the United in Cork. Jiminie crickets it was frightening over those tall stone-faced banks. Harvey has ruined two hats already and the pub after nearly ruined both our constitutions. Harvey says Cork ought to be spelt Corks.

The letter ran on in an account of their doings and then Stephen came to the final page:

We haven't got down to the Bay yet but someone from there was hunting yesterday. I think his name was Murtagh or something. He lost a leg flying in the war and still rides like a dream. He was thrilled when we told him we'd seen you and sent you all sorts of messages. So you see you're not forgotten. I asked him about Kit Massiter like you said that evening – remember? He said he was fine. Riding the legs off everything he could get hold of, he said. A chip off the old block he told me particularly to tell you – whatever that may mean! And a funny thing happened last night at dinner. Our host here is a man called Westcott. I'm not sure I like him much. He's a bit sort of what my mother would call purse-proud but he's a big wheel in racing here apparently. Anyway Harvey sat next to him over the port. Harvey has drunk so much port since we came here he says he's becoming a two-bottle man and is planning to bring back a pipe – what's that? – with us to the States. Anyway he told Westcott that your name had come up between him and Murtagh and how you had taken us on safari and that we'd become friendly and how sad you were about losing your house and weren't the Black and Tans the worst thing the English had done since Cromwell? Harvey said Westcott then gave him a sort of odd look and said: 'Oh, but it wasn't all the work of the Black and Tans, there was someone else behind it.' Harvey wanted to find out more but he couldn't because some racing pal of Westcott's butted into the conversation and claimed his attention. Harvey says conversations over the port are always pretty haywire and that dirty stories are clean out of fashion. He's dead disappointed he can't bring back some for the locker room. Harvey is quite *himself* still. I wanted to tell you this about what Westcott said as I know how you loved your house. We both remember so well what came into your voice when you talked of it and the Bay. I often think of you, you're too nice to be so lonely. With love, dearest Stephen, and I'll always remember that night we never had.

Stephen put down the letter and stared at the wall. Then he picked up the last pages and read them again. What did Westcott's remark mean? His mind went back to that terrible night which was etched indelibly into his memory, when he had seen his house go up in flames and he had faced death at the hands of Conway, the half-crazed Auxiliary leader.

He was still staring at the letter when the knock came to the door. He sat on, motionless, transported by what he had read back to the time when the 'knock in the night' was something to be feared and dreaded. It came again, soft and with something stealthy about it – not the peremptory summons of the armed intruder that his memories had brought back to him, nor was it the deferential tap of a servant. He got up and crossed to the door. When he opened it a figure stepped in and closed it quickly behind him. As the man stood for a moment blinking in the light, Stephen stared at him in unbelieving astonishment. 'Mikey!' he said.

'Mikey O'Sullivan. What in the name of all the powers are you doing here?'

Mikey O'Sullivan, one time pantry boy, one time guerilla leader, now member of Dail Eireann, stud farm proprietor and bloodstock owner, coughed slightly before he spoke. 'Sure, I could hardly leave the country without seein' ye, could I now,' he said in the soft lilting brogue of the Bay which brought more memories crowding back.

'It's good to see you, anyway, Mikey,' Stephen said. 'It's like a breath of old times. How are they in the Bay? How is Lady Massiter as I suppose I must call her now?'

'Sure she doesn't change. Always the same with everyone, the old darlin'.''

'And the boys?'

Mikey gave him a quick look from under his eyes. 'The elder one, Master Kit they call him,' he said. 'He's a divil to ride though they do be sayin' he and his father don't hit it off like. He's the sort though ye'd be proud to own if ye take my meanin'. He's been winning point-to-points this year or so back. The other one, Master Hugo, he's a connivin' sort of lad, a bit like his old man. Things is bad in the old country though. They're slaughtering calves, and farms is goin' for nothing if ye can sell 'em, which mostly ye can't. And what about yerself?'

'I manage. It's a lonely sort of life. I think of the Bay a lot.'

'Don't we all when we're away from it. But ye're a great man here now or so I hear. Sure didn't I tell ye ye would be that time we talked in Leinster House? A white hunter, whatever the divil that is.'

'It's a sort of professional huntsman, only the fox is bigger and can kill you. But again, Mikey, what are you up to out here?'

Mikey seemed reluctant to answer. 'Ye wouldn't have a drop of the craytur, would ye?' he said.

Stephen nodded to the side table. 'Help yourself. It's Scotch I'm afraid.'

''Twill do.' Mikey poured himself three fingers, added a dash of water and sat down. 'I'm here,' he said slowly, 'on

146

the invitation – ' He checked himself. "Tis what ye might call a fact-finding mission that I'm on.'

'And just what facts are you supposed to be finding?'

'Well now, we're a quare country at home, sure you know it yourself, none better, and maybe we haven't done too well with it since we got it but we're the first to have won our freedom. Now, d'ye see, there are others after it. The Indians, they sent a delegation to Willie T. when he was in power to find out how we done it.' Mikey paused to scratch his ear. 'There are things stirring here,' he said.

Stephen stared at him. 'I have a feeling that a lot of people might call this fact-finding mission of yours mischief-making or something a good deal stronger,' he said.

'That's as maybe,' Mikey said, sipping his drink. 'But what happened at home is goin' to happen all over the world that's painted red. They can't hold on to it forever.'

'You may well be right but why come to me? I've had my war. I've had the Troubles. I've a sort of niche here now. All I want is to be left in peace.'

'I came for old times' sake, for I wanted to see ye again. But to be honest I want something else. And I came at night because I thought it mightn't do ye any good to be seen talkin' to me. Ye see, there's this fellow now living in London called Kenyatta. Did ye ever hear of him?'

'No.'

'Well, ye will, I'd be thinkin'. He's as black as your hat but he's what they call mission-educated. He has brains to burn that one.'

'Mission-educated is not exactly a recommendation to the powers that be out here.'

'I dunno about that but he says sooner or later they'll have to listen to him. He's from a tribe they call the Kikuyu, is it, and he says they've been dispossessed by the British just like Cromwell did to us. He's been all over Europe talkin' to them that's oppressed and finding out about fighters for freedom. He came over to us just like the Indians did to ask about how we threw off the yoke. In the heel of the hunt we suggested someone come out to talk to people here and find out how we could help. The Government agreed and sent me off all expenses paid.'

147

'And have you talked to people?'

'I've talked to the blacks.'

'We call them Africans but never mind.'

'Africans then. It's the ould country all over again. Sure can't I see the land hunger jumpin' out of their eyes. They're sufferin' what we suffered – confiscation, eviction, to hell or Connaught. The British swept them out of the Highlands and grabbed the best for themselves.'

'All right, Mikey. I've heard it before and I'm not sure I want to hear it again. A man called Meinertzhagen has been preaching this or something like it for years. Ever hear of him?'

'I've met him,' Mikey said surprisingly. 'I talked to him in London before I sailed. He showed me his diaries and I copied some of them out.' He reached into a pocket and pulled out a notebook. 'Listen to this,' he said. ' "If a white settlement really takes hold in this country it is bound to be at the expense of the Kikuyu who own the best land and I foresee trouble," and,' said Mikey, reading on, ' "the Kikuyu are ripe for trouble and when they get educated and medicine men are replaced by political agitators there will be a general rising," and, if you want any more: "I cannot see millions of educated Africans submitting tamely to white domination. It is an African country and they will demand domination and then blood will be spilt." Them words were written in 1902 – what do you think of that?'

'I think,' Stephen said, 'that you'd better be careful when and where you quote that gentleman. He's not exactly a household word in the colony.'

'Aye. That's it. And that's why I've come to you. I went to the whites, the landlords, the settlers and I can't get near them. All I've been able to meet are a few useless guerriers in the administration. It's the others I want to know about. They hang out in that club with the queer name that they wouldn't let me into if the Pope of Rome introduced me.'

'The Muthaiga. I see what you mean. I don't think that sponsor would carry much weight there.'

'Do they know what's going on under their feet? That there are young fellahs that's been educated and are ready to be roused like that Meinert what-d'ye-call-him said. And if

148

they're roused they'll fight for their freedom – *uhuru*, they call it. What'll the whites do about it then? You've lived with them, you're one of them – '

'Not quite. I'm Irish for a start, though I suppose you and yours, Mikey, would say I'm only half-Irish if that. But to them I'm Irish and that makes me slightly suspect or I think it does, perhaps because it was said at home that I'd betrayed my class getting mixed up with your lot. But because I've seen it at first hand I think there's a lot in what Meinertzhagen says. Though I'm told he said it too loudly.'

'Aye. He struck me as a know-all sort of old sod.'

'Since you've asked me I'll tell you what I think about the settlers. They don't give a damn. And they're a tough lot. Whatever Meinertzhagen and your Kenya pal in London say, you've got to remember they built the place, they didn't get it handed to them on a plate like the Cromwellians in Ireland. They won it and made it through their own sweat and tears and tragedy in many cases. Having got it they say they're going to keep it for their children and their children's children and no one is going to take it away from them. And they mean it. Make no mistake, and believe me they know how to.'

'What'll they do if the home government sells them out? They're a lot of old women at Westminster now. That Chamberlain is only a clucking old hen. Dev can twist him round his little finger.'

'I daresay but I still think they'll fight. They don't think much of the old women at Westminster either. And it'll be a bloody business. The settlers will win the first battle anyway and the last will be the hell of a long way away.'

'That ould fool of a feller in Westminster is goin' to walk Britain into a war. Wars change things awful fast. Britain may get beat. There's plenty at home and here who hopes she does.'

'They won't find Mr Hitler a pleasant alternative, believe me. They may be backing the wrong horse. Talking of horses, Mikey, how are they going for you?'

'Rotten. If you breed a good 'un you can't sell him. You can't get a bet and the prize money isn't worth running for. Though they do say Westcott is tryin' to do something about the stakes. He thinks he runs racin' now, whether or no he's a steward.'

'Westcott – that reminds me – ' Stephen picked up Betty's letter from the table. 'Listen to this,' he said and read out the passage containing Westcott's remarks to Harvey over the port. 'What do you make of that?' he said. 'What does it mean?'

For the first time Mikey failed to meet his eyes. He looked down at the floor and it seemed to Stephen that he almost scuffled his feet. 'Come on, Mikey,' he said. 'Why are you not saying anything? You knew all that went on at the Bay. Dammit, man, you saved my life that night. I've money in the bank now. Should I go home and find out?'

Mikey looked up. 'Them times is past,' he said. 'The things that happened then is best forgotten.'

'How can you say that? Isn't the whole of Irish politics now based on what happened in the Troubles?'

'Not on what happened in the Black and Tan war. We were all together then. It's what happened after the split, the Civil War, that's what we're still fighting these days.'

'Maybe, but Westcott must know something. He says it's no secret. If it isn't then you know what it is.'

'Westcott's a divil. He wants power. Power in racing, for he's not going to get it anywhere else, him being a protestant and a sort of West Briton and all and Dev never ratified him for the Senate when he got in. He doesn't like them that stand in his way.'

'You're still not answering my question. If there was someone else behind those bloody Black and Tans or Auxiliaries or whatever those cut-throats were called that night they burnt my house, who was it?'

Mikey stood up. 'If I knew,' he said, 'I wouldn't tell you. As I said, them days is dead and gone, for the likes of ye anyway. Ye have your life here. 'Tis no use rakin' over the embers. 'Twill do no one no good. Leave it alone, Stephen Raymond. 'Twill only bring hurt and trouble to ye and perhaps to those ye love.' He turned to go. ''Twas a pleasure meetin' you again, and the best of luck to ye here. Bedad I'm thinkin' 'tis nearly as quare a country as our own.' He opened the door and, before Stephen could say anything, was gone into the night.

Stephen was not left long to brood over what Betty had written and why Mikey had refused to speak out. That Mikey knew something if not all of what lay behind the burning of Bellary Court he was convinced, but very soon he had other more immediate things to occupy his thoughts. A day later he received a summons to present himself at the offices of Hayes and Franklin.

'Sorry to send you out again so soon, Stephen,' Bert Franklin said, getting up from behind his desk. 'But McAllister got sorted out by a rhino last week and Ronnie Baines is in bed with malaria. By the way, the Langs that you took out, how were they? I never asked.'

'Fine. Nice couple.'

'The reason I ask now is that she's written a letter from Ireland thanking us and all the rest of it and damn near drooling over you – ' He raised an eyebrow.

Stephen laughed. 'No need for that look,' he said. 'Nothing happened or at least lots did but not what you're thinking.'

'Know who he is?'

'No. I can't recall I asked.'

'His mother's a Boston Brahmin – know what that is?'

'I don't, but does it matter?'

'I'll tell you anyway. They're the upper-upper crust of New England society, the sort that talk only to Lodges and the Lodges talk only to God. He's the heir to one of the biggest of the older American fortunes and he's a six-goal polo player.'

'My hat! He had a small go of buck fever and I asked him if he played games! He didn't tell me. That's the sort of chap he was. Said he was over-trying. He was, too.'

'It's a word I don't know but it seems a good one. There was something about not shooting an elephant?'

'Harvey preferred the camera to the gun. He didn't much care for killing, he said. We tracked down an elephant near the Tana. He came at us and Harvey got some good pictures. There was no point in shooting him. I bluffed him out of charging.'

151

Franklin gave him an odd look. 'You're a rum devil sometimes, Stephen,' he said. 'Always doing things your own way.'

'Who doesn't in our game? This new client now – man,
woman, child or all three?'

'Man, and there'll be no reluctance to kill where he's
concerned. He's a fire-eater by all accounts. Name: Anthony
Royle. The Honourable Anthony Royle. Nephew of the
Governor and His Excellency's blue-eyed boy or so I'm told.'

'Anything else?'

'Don't ask *him* if he plays games, it mightn't go down so
well. He's a cricketer. Captain of Warwickshire and in the
running to captain England against the Aussies next year if
Mr Hitler allows us to have a next year. He's been out before.'

'Who took him out?'

'Neil Colley. He's in Tanganyika now. They didn't get
anything big. Luck ran against him. He wants a buffalo.'

'I'll do what I can for him.'

'He's at Government House. Go and collect him, and for
Christ's sake bring him back alive.'

CHAPTER XIX

The Honourable Anthony Royle was a fair-haired English
type, freckled across the forehead and nose, sturdily built
and broad in the shoulder as befitted one who had scored a
thousand runs, most of them in double quick time in the last
three seasons of county cricket. He had brought with him
an impressive armoury ranging from a double Holland and
Holland .500 to a pair of Purdey shotguns.

Having been out before, he was a little inclined to be
patronising, making no secret that the one prize he wanted
on this trip was a buffalo and that he did not much care for
Stephen's insistence on shooting him in on lighter game. 'It's

just,' Stephen explained to him quietly, 'that we have to get used to each other's ways. No two hunters are exactly alike in their methods. You were with Neil Colley last time, weren't you?'

'Yes, and I think I should tell you that I asked for him again, but I gather he's in Tanganyika. We got along together.'

'I'm sure we will too,' Stephen said, though there was something about Royle that raised his hackles a little. Was he a touch over-confident? Did he protest his nerve and ability rather too much, and did these things spell danger? His next words served further to awaken Stephen's slight doubts about him.

'Well, then,' he said. 'What are we hanging about here for? Haven't we done enough of that? Can't we press on after the bigger stuff? I want that buffalo.'

'You're very different from the last client I took out,' Stephen said. 'He didn't want to shoot anything except with a camera.' And then, because Royle's whole attitude of aggression was needling him, he added: 'In many ways I agree with him. As I told him, killing isn't everything in hunting. You know,' he went on, slowly, 'it's an old saying that there are three stages in a hunter's life – if he lives. One: he thinks he knows it all and actually knows nothing. Two: he realises he knows nothing and begins to learn. Three: he realises he'll never know it all but if he's lucky he has learnt enough to keep himself and, if he's a professional, his clients, alive.'

Royle looked at him sharply as if he were about to make some biting answer and then changed his mind. 'Good advice, I suppose,' he said half-sulkily. 'Maybe it could go for cricketers, especially cricket captains, too.'

That conversation seemed to bring about a sort of mutual understanding between them, and after it they worked well enough together. Despite his fair pigmentation Royle stood up well to the heat and appeared unaffected by it. He was fit, too, and covering anything up to twenty miles a day saw him no more than normally tired. His drinking was sparing and controlled; he shot accurately at light game and swung the Purdeys with authority and skill at wildfowl. Stephen forgot his earlier doubts and decided it was shaping into a successful and trouble-free safari; and though he could never bring himself to like the client he told himself this was nothing new and that he didn't have to.

They trekked on towards the Tana River country that Stephen knew so well. When they reached it they set their camp at the river's edge under one of the great trees of the Rivereine Forest. No sooner had Stephen supervised the erection of the tents, the placing of the lavatories and all the other necessary chores than one of the boys came to him with the news that the engine of a hunting vehicle was giving trouble. He would have to diagnose it himself and see to its repair. This was likely to take some time. Accordingly he decreed a rest day for the morrow. Rest days, however, were not something favoured by Royle. Bursting with energy and confidence, he suggested that he and Kamau should go out alone. Royle's suggestions were usually couched in the manner of a demand. All along he had made it clear that it was he who was used to exercising authority and that he did not much care for submitting to it. Now he said that he had heard Stephen mention that meat for the boys was running a bit short, so, he suggested, he and Kamau would go and get some.

Stephen hesitated. He always slightly resented Royle's peremptory manner but there seemed no real reason why he should not agree. To date Royle had done nothing wrong and Kamau was both experienced and responsible. After thinking it over for a few minutes he decided to let them go, cautioning them that on no account were they to go after bigger game or anything likely to bring them into danger.

Late that evening they returned with their bag of an oryx for themselves and a grevy zebra for the boys. That would please them, Royle made a point of saying before he went off to his bath. Kamau's eyes followed him into his tent. He made no move to go but turned to Stephen as soon as he saw the fly of the tent close behind Royle. 'He is not steady, bwana,' he said.

'What do you mean?' Stephen asked him. Gradually, in a mixture of Swahili and English, the story came out. While they were searching for zebra Kamau had come upon the

154

spoor of a buffalo. Kneeling to examine it, he had found it fresh. Remembering Royle's thrusting tactics and his expressed anxiety to get a buffalo, he had expected exhortations to press on after it and to disregard Stephen's cautions. So sure had he been of this that he had been turning over in his mind ways and means of dissuading him. 'He may be about, bwana,' he had said, 'and we have only the light rifles.' To his astonishment Royle had seemed only too anxious to agree. There followed a burst of Swahili which Stephen could only translate to himself by understanding that Royle had 'spooked' at the thought of the buffalo lurking in the bush about them. Moreover, Kamau had added, Royle had not shot as well as he was accustomed to after that encounter. 'He is not steady, bwana,' Kamau said again. 'I know it. I can feel it.'

That, Stephen knew, was as far as Kamau would or could go. Kamau did not reason: he sensed. It was his instincts, not his brain, which made the signals, and in Stephen's experience those instincts were rarely wrong. Yet all that had happened to date pointed the other way. Royle had been relaxed and competent with lighter game. He had so far given no indication of nerves; indeed he had been if anything too thrusting and over-eager to get to grips with the big stuff. But could he, perhaps, be over-compensating, trying to prove something to himself? Stephen had known this to happen, and he knew, too, none better, the old oft-repeated white hunter's covenant first told him by Job that a client could be a good calm shot with small game and do something foolish when it came to elephant or buffalo. And, he reminded himself once more, Kamau, his friend and companion for years, was rarely wrong. As if divining his thoughts Kamau spoke again. 'He is not steady, bwana,' he repeated. 'Mbogo is there, a big bull. We find him tomorrow. Be careful, bwana.'

'Kamau tells me you found buffalo spoor,' Stephen said to Royle that night over supper. 'He'll be there, a big bull. We'll go after him at first light tomorrow.'

'Good.' Royle leaned back in his chair. 'I've heard a lot about buffalo one way or another. He's the toughest trophy of them all, or so I've been told. That's why I want him.

155

You've said yourself every hunter has different opinions and different ways. Now you tell me about him.'

Royle's eyes gleamed in the lamplight; everything about him indicated eager anticipation. But, for the hundredth time Stephen told himself you never knew with clients. One way or another, though, there was no point in playing danger down. If Royle was going to be frightened he had better know what he was facing. " 'Mbogo", the Africans call him,' he said. 'He's a wicked and wily old bugger. His brain is about the size of a pea but he doesn't need it, for he's got something else – an instinct for killing is what I call it. He's bred to fight and he's bred to kill and when he's hurt he wants to kill. That's why no one can afford a loose shot. He can turn like a polo pony and charge when you least expect it. And when he charges he can carry as much shot as'd sink a battleship and still keep coming. So here's how you'll kill him.' Stephen picked up a stick and began to draw a diagram in the dust. 'We'll bring you up to him broadside on,' he said. 'And that's the place where you'll hit him.' He placed the stick behind the shoulder. 'If you do you'll kill him cleanly and well. When he goes down we'll give him time and then we'll put a couple more into him for insurance. Dead buffalo have killed more people than maybe – got it?'

Royle was leaning forward, staring at the diagram. 'Absolutely,' he said.

'If you miss killing him – ' Stephen began.

'I'm hardly likely to do that,' Royle said.

'I daresay, but just listen for a moment. He may charge straight away. If he does you've got a frontal shot. It's the most difficult of all.'

'Why?'

'He'll come at you like a big, black express train and at much the same speed. You've got about six seconds if you're lucky to kill him dead and there's only one place to do it.'

'And where's that?'

'He's got a helmet of bone two inches thick and six inches wide over his brain that can make anything bounce off it including the solids that big Holland and Holland of yours can throw at him. He charges with his nose stretched forward so you shoot him just above its bridge – slap into his brain.'

156

'I seem to have heard most of this before, but go on.'

'Even if you do hit him where it hurts most it may not stop his charge. He never knows when he's beat, old *mbogo*. And another thing – when he's in the bush he'll come at you when you least expect him. He has a dozen tricks in his locker and every one of them is connected with killing. It's never happened to me but I've heard often enough that he's even been known to set up an ambush by circling round and coming at you from behind. Oh yes, my friend, old *mbogo*, he takes a bit of catching and when you've caught up with him he takes a bit and more than a bit of killing.'

'Well,' Royle said. 'Here's to tomorrow, that's what I came out for.'

They breakfasted together before first light. 'Sleep well?' Stephen asked Royle.

'Like a top,' was the answer as Royle reached for the coffee pot with a steady hand. There was no sign of nerves or jumpiness that Stephen could see, and his doubts and fears began to dissipate with the morning mists. For once, he told himself, Kamau must be wrong. 'Good,' he said. 'We'll check the armament and then set off.'

Together they crossed to the tent where the guns were slotted into racks. Royle took the Holland and Holland and handed it to his gun-bearer. Stephen put the big Rigby he had taken over from Job in the crook of his arm, smiling at Kamau as he did so, for the 'carrying his own gun' was a sort of private joke between them exchanged at the beginning of each hunt.

Dawn was breaking through the forest trees and tracing colours from the vegetation along the river banks as they left the camp. When they had been working through the bush for about an hour Kamau suddenly gave an exclamation. He pointed in front of him and then knelt down. Stephen's eyes followed the tracker's finger. There it was, in the dust, that firm footprint half-way between that of a horse and a cow, the sight of which never failed to set his pulse beating faster. It signified that *mbogo* was about and wherever he was, being what he was, he would be ready, wicked and waiting.

Kamau straightened up and spoke to Stephen in short, sharp bursts of Swahili.

'What's he say?' Royle asked.

'It's a bull, a big one, probably the one you picked up yesterday. He thinks he may not have gone far. The spoor is fresh.' Stephen looked at Royle. 'It seems as if you're going to get what you've been waiting for,' he said.

With Kamau leading, picking up and following spoor and signs that were invisible even to Stephen with all his experience, they made their way on through the heat. Presently they came to a clearing in the bush where an acacia tree grew. Here Kamau quested about and then came back to Stephen. They both looked at the tree. Stephen nodded and Kamau went up it like a cat. In a few minutes he was back, standing beside Stephen and talking softly to him.

'He's here all right,' Stephen said to Royle. 'Lying up in a donga about a mile away. We'll wait a bit. Round mid-day he begins to become sleepy. Takes his nap. Makes it easier for us to get up to him. So, let's relax and have a smoke.' He took out his case and held it out to Royle. Was it his imagination or did Royle's fingers shake a little as he extracted the cigarette? Certainly he appeared to be a bit itchy.

'Can't we get on?' he said. 'What's the point in waiting?'

'Doing it the right way, that's the point,' Stephen said. 'And here's how we'll do it. First we'll work the wind all the way along the donga. Show him, Kamau.'

The tracker bent down and picked up a handful of the sandy soil. Lifting it he allowed it gently to trickle through his fingers. The slight breeze took the particles of sand and drifted them away.

'That's how we'll know where to position ourselves to windward of him,' Stephen said. 'You'll keep just behind and to one side of me. We'll get as near as we can. Twenty-five yards if possible. Under fifty anyway. And don't shoot until I tell you to wallop him. Got it?'

'I suppose so,' Royle said sulkily. 'But you said yourself that I could shoot. Why can't I take him when I'm ready without all this nursemaiding?'

'Because if you wound him we're in trouble and the nearer you are the more likely you are to kill him clean.'

'Fellow at home told me he killed one stone dead first shot at seventy-five yards.'

158

'Beginner's luck. I wonder what his hunter said to him. Get as close as you can and then ten feet closer. That's the way to kill buffalo.'

'You're full of these old saws.'

'They're what keep you alive.'

'Can he charge when you're as close as that?'

'He can charge at any time or on any leg for that matter. Mostly when you least expect it, the old devil. But usually he won't unless he's been wounded or hurt somehow before. That's when he's really dangerous. Now I'll just have a recce myself.'

Taking the field glasses Stephen climbed the tree. 'He's still there,' he said when he came down. 'Sunning himself. Now then,' he went on, turning to Royle. 'Where do you get him when I tell you to let go?'

'Behind the shoulder. Low down, less than a third of the way up.'

'Good man. You won't have any problem. In a little while you'll have got your buffalo and he's a good one, believe me. Soft-nose are best for a broadside shot. Got 'em in? Okay, let's go.'

Throwing away their cigarettes they started off again once more with Kamau in the lead. As they neared the donga the tracker paused every few yards to let the sand run through his fingers. In silence, yard by yard, they worked the wind. Stephen could feel the adrenalin beginning to flow as it always did when he approached a buffalo. Every sense was sharpened; everything about him stood out clear and sharp harsh in the strong light.

A thick screen of bush along the bank of the donga conceaaled the buffalo from them. Nevertheless, Stephen thought, you could almost feel the menace emanating from him. He was *mbogo*, the great bull, the king of them all. A lion was a puppy compared to a Cape buffalo in all his pride.

They came in from the river side, Stephen was a few paces ahead of the others, moving step by step, every nerve taut. You never knew what would happen next when hunting buffalo; that was his challenge, his endless fascination. He could have changed his position; he might somehow have winded them and be waiting for them, ready to come crashing

159

out of the bush with his relentless charge which would give them about six seconds to stop him – if they could.

Stephen hefted the big Rigby in his hands, felt in his cartridge loops to make sure the re-loads were there and ready. Then he parted the fronds in front of him.

The buffalo had not moved. A great old bull, he stood there, alone, resting, driven no doubt from the herd by some younger champion anxious to take over his wives, and angry and resentful about what had happened to him. The big, dark head moved slowly from side to side, as if sensing a threat but not knowing where it would come from. There was, Stephen could see, a tremendous stretch of horn. He looked magnificent. You gallant old bugger, Stephen breathed to himself. But if we don't get you your own young ones will when you try to return to the herd. He gazed again at the width between the horns. If he clobbers this one he'll have something to talk about in the Long Room at Lords, he thought. And he should. It's a perfect broadside shot. We'll have to get nearer though. This must be all of seventy yards. He surveyed the ground, deciding on his angle of approach. Having made up his mind he began to turn to Royle.

At that moment there was the roar of a rifle almost in his ear. It was followed by the sonk and thud of a bullet hitting flesh. The buffalo gave an angry roar, threw up his head and plunged into the bush. A series of crashings and bangings followed. Then silence.

'Jesus Christ,' Stephen said quietly. He got to his feet and looked at Royle, who stared defiantly back.

'What was the point in hanging about?' he said. 'I could see him quite clearly. I hit him, didn't I?'

'You hit him,' Stephen said with quiet contempt. 'Round about the loins so far as I could judge.'

Royle passed his tongue over his lips. 'Well – er – what happens next?' he said.

Stephen swallowed his fury. You did not lose your temper with the client, however badly he behaved. You tried to put right what he had done wrong. But this was going to be a nasty one. Royle had touched up the buffalo just enough to make him killing angry, and the pain would only sharpen his wits. 'He's in there,' he said. 'In that thick bush, wounded,

160

sore and eager to take it out on someone – that's us. We've got to go in and get him.' Kamau and Stephen looked at each other in silent understanding. Kamau shook his head slowly as if to say, 'I was right, bwana.'

The unspoken words behind Stephen's and Kamau's attitudes penetrated even Royle's self-conceit. 'Look,' he said. 'It all seemed so simple. There he was in front of me and that fellow told me he had killed one at that distance – '

'That fellow, whoever he was,' Stephen said, 'was either a fool or a liar or probably both.' Opening the Rigby he slid two hard-nosed bullets into the breech. 'Come on, Kamau. *Twende!*'

'I'm coming too,' Royle said.

'That's your privilege,' Stephen said tersely. 'But this time do as I say. Keep behind me and keep your eyes and your ears open.'

It took them only a few minutes to find where the buffalo had entered the bush. Immediately Kamau picked up the spoor and followed it. At first there were specks of blood about, but these became fewer as they went on. The bush was high and thick and they had to push their way through it. No view, Stephen thought, no angle of fire. Everything was stacked in the buffalo's favour. He could be lying in wait almost on top of them and they would not know it. All they had was Kamau's sixth sense. That might give them just enough warning.

The eternal, scorching heat pressed down on them as they penetrated further and further into the bush. If Stephen's nerves were stretched before, they were singing now. Every step was laden with threat. Where the hell was that buffalo? They had been progressing in this fashion for about ten minutes, with Kamau questing in front of them, when all of a sudden he paused. A little behind and to the right Royle, anxious to see what was happening, had closed up. Kamau was clearly puzzled. He stared at the soil in front of him, a frown furrowing his usually cheerful features. After a moment or two he bent down to peer along the ground. Then he straightened and, every movement demanding silence, turned as if in slow motion towards Stephen. When he came to face

161

him his eyes suddenly dilated with horror and he shouted, pointing over Stephen's shoulder.

There was a tremendous crash behind them followed by the thud of hooves. Stephen swung round, the big Rigby coming automatically up to his shoulder.

Seeming to fill the whole landscape, trampling the thick bush in his charge, the buffalo came at them, head high, rampant, determined on killing. It went through Stephen's mind in a flash that it had happened and that they were true, those old tales of ambush. The wily old bugger had doubled back and caught them wrong-footed.

But conscious thought had no place here. Reflex, training, instinct and experience took over. The Rigby was zeroing in for a brain shot. Stephen's forefinger closed for the first pull. Then, without warning, the rifle was all but knocked out of his hands. Someone cannoned into him and sent him spinning. It was Royle and he was running.

Stephen felt the recoil of the Rigby as he was thrown off balance and after that everything became blurred. For the big bull had located his chief enemy; he had him down and was on top of him. A great horn was slicing through his leg from ankle to thigh. Soon the hooves would be mangling what was left of him. This, then, he thought, is how it all ends, finished off by a buffalo. And all because of a little Government House pet who thought he knew everything and then ran away.

The black, spadelike head loomed over him. There was blood on the nostrils. Maybe I nailed him before he got me, Stephen thought, with a clarity that surprised him. Pain had not yet come and it all seemed to be happening to someone else.

Suddenly there was the report of a gun almost in his face. Through a mist he saw Kamau with the rifle Royle had thrown away in his hands, its barrel resting on the base of the buffalo's neck. Then the second barrel went off and the back of the great bull's head disintegrated. More blood poured from the open, distended nostrils. The buffalo gave a convulsive heave and rolled sideways off him – dead.

The last thing Stephen heard was Kamau saying, 'It was you who killed him, all same, one shot, bwana,' and then his swearing softly in Swahili as he struggled to draw Stephen free. After that unconsciousness came.

CHAPTER XX

When Stephen came out of hospital he went straight to his usual cottage in the Norfolk. As he collected his mail and messages he sensed, or thought he did, a coolness towards him and a slight turning of the shoulder by those whom he met. It did not cause him much concern; he had always kept to himself and he had been out of circulation for some time. Next day, still limping a little, he made his way to the office of Hayes and Franklin.

'Going a bit short still, are you?' Bert Franklin greeted him. 'You were lucky that Jenny Carlin had her Avian on the airstrip at Garissa. She flew you back.'

'I know. Kamau patched me up and got me there in one of the hunting cars. I was semi-delirious and pretty well out from loss of blood. It was he who pulled me through. What about that little bastard, Royle?'

Above them the fan revolved in the heat. From below the noises of the street came clearly up to them. Franklin reached over and pushed a sandalwood box across the table. 'Have a smoke,' he said. Dropping the match in to the ashtray and stirring it with his finger, he went on, 'Look, Stephen, you're not going to like this but I've got to say it. There are some pretty unpleasant stories going about.'

Stephen stared at him. The cold looks in the hotel the night before came back to him. They were taking on more significance now. 'Such as?' he said.

'I'll give it to you straight. Such as Royle says you ran away.'

Stephen sat up. 'Why, the little shit,' he said. 'It was he

who buggered off and so bloody fast he nearly knocked me down. If he hadn't I wouldn't be walking like this. As it was he nearly got me killed. Run away! Jesus! Do you believe it?'

'No. But a lot of people do.'

'Have you talked to Kamau?'

'Yes. I've talked to Kamau. I've heard what he has to say. He bears you out all the way. But who's going to take the word of an African against that of a white man – and one from Government House, what's more?'

'You'd better tell me the whole story.'

'Very well. This is it, so far as I can gather. Royle came back to Government House, a bit shaken as you can imagine. One of the first people he met was a guest of the Governor. He has a farm out here, out Molo way. He's a rich chap, Master of Hounds and God knows what from your part of the country. Said he knew you. A Sir Andrew Massiter.'

'Good God,' Stephen said. 'Andrew Massiter. I think I begin to see. Go on.'

Franklin drew on his cigarette and blew out a cloud of smoke. 'Well,' he said. 'It seems Massiter asked Royle how he had got on, and Royle said he'd had this nasty do. Massiter wanted to know who his hunter was, and when Royle mentioned your name, he said something to the effect that he wouldn't care to go hunting with you, that you'd been court-martialled for cowardice in the RFC.' The two men's eyes met across the table. 'Were you?' Franklin asked quietly.

'Yes. It's a long story. I was framed. The verdict was an honourable acquittal, and there are damn few of those, let me tell you.' Stephen's temper, always slow, was beginning to burn. Were Massiter and his past to haunt him forever? 'Listen,' he said. 'Before I was shot down I'd clobbered eighteen enemy aircraft. Christ Almighty, Bert, we've known each other for years. You can't think – '

Franklin held up his hand. 'Take it steady,' he said. 'I've done some checking. I got hold of a chap in Wilson Airways who was in the Flying Corps. He was in your squadron for a bit, it seems. Said you were one of the cracks or aces or whatever they were called. Said he didn't believe a word of it. Has Massiter got anything personal against you?'

'He may have.' Stephen bit back the words: 'I slept with

his wife and fathered his first-born,' which came unbidden to the edge of his lips.

'I see. He seems to have seen his chance to injure you and to have taken it.'

'He would. He doesn't miss many tricks.'

'Whether Royle intended from the first to spin his yarn or whether what Massiter said put it into his head, I don't know, but here's what he told the Governor – '

'Let's have it. I'd like to get my hands on him.'

'You won't. He's safely on a boat back to England and the cricket season – and with that buffalo head if it interests you, a trophy for Mr Rowland Ward.'

'Good God. He's lower than a snake's belly and that's even lower than I thought.'

'He could hardly do other than claim it after the story he spun. Here's how it is – he said that all along you seemed strangely reluctant to let him go after buffalo and were determined to keep him to lighter game. And he brought up that business of your refusing to shoot an elephant when you were with the Langs which apparently you told him. It made him convinced you were losing your nerve.'

'Jesus!'

'When you did get on to the spoor of a buffalo you were damn slow about following it up and he had to push you on. Then through your incompetence – he wasn't very precise about this but they don't know anything up at Government House so it doesn't matter and he got away with it – the bull charged. You panicked, threw away your rifle and legged it. The buffalo caught you and he, splendid chap, had to shoot him off you. Boy's Own Paper stuff. Goes down very well when retailed by His Excellency at Government House dinner parties.'

'Did you see him?'

'Oh, yes, I saw him. After I'd talked to Kamau and that Flying Corps chap. Very cocky he was, too. I threw him out of the office and told him he'd never come on safari again with me or anyone else. And that hasn't done me any good with Government House, though I don't know just how he explained it away to them. And, Stephen, I'm afraid that's not all.'

165

'What's next on the menu?'

'They've dragged up that business about foul riding in the National years ago and killing Job's horse, or the Governor has. And someone on his staff has reminded him there was chat about your saying the Africans were the real owners of the land, and that what had happened to Ireland would happen here. Worst of all, some wild Irish MP who has been here sowing dissension, or so they say, was seen recently leaving your cottage at the Norfolk late at night after a long visit.'

'Mikey O'Sullivan. He was our pantry boy when he was a kid at the Bay. Surely he had every right to come to see an old friend?'

'Government House don't know he has that connection, or if they do they're not saying. Anyway they've treated him as an undesirable and pushed him quietly out. Before he went he was hobnobbing with one Kidogo, a leader of the Kikuyu youth movement. Know who he is?'

'No. And the way things are going I don't much care.'

'It's another stick to beat you with, I'm sorry to say. He was employed by Job for a bit when you were there before Job kicked him out. Some of the tongues that are wagging are now saying that you must have infected him with your what-d'ye-call-'em – liberal notions.'

'Kidogo! I remember him now. Mission-educated little brute. Job sent him off spitting defiance. So he's a subversive, is he? Job won't be surprised. It's a lie, of course. I never had anything to do with him, though I suppose I was sorry for him getting the push. Now, after that catalogue, there's not much more to say is there?'

'No. But, Stephen, well, I don't know how to say this. I believe every word you and Kamau have told me. But this is an unforgiving business – '

'You mean I'm all washed up as a hunter?'

'Hardly as bad as that. But why not go off on a safari on your own? These things get forgotten. I believe you, Stephen, but you see how it is – '

'You may believe me but I don't believe you. I see how it is, all right.' Stephen spoke through his teeth. He got up,

166

walked to the door, closed it very carefully behind him and went down to the street.

Ten minutes later he was in the Muthaiga Club drinking whisky and contemplating failure.

Was life always to do this to him? Was fate forever to be waiting round the corner with a piece of lead piping? Worst of all, he told himself, now he was lost, far more lost than he had ever been when he was alone at sixteen thousand feet in the friendless Flanders skies or isolated in the trackless bush. He had tried everything he could, and failure had followed him. What the hell was he going to do now?

While these thoughts were whirling through his head he became conscious of the fact that someone had come in and was leaning on the bar beside him. A little later he realised that the man, whoever he was, was conducting a sort of semi-incoherent monologue into his drink. Shortly afterwards he stiffened on his seat, for it became clear that the monologue was being directed at him.

'Bloody Irish,' the man was saying as he raised his glass to his lips. 'Bloody Irish. Only good for shooting policemen in the back. White niggers, that's what they are. Look what that bugger did to young Royle. Shouldn't be let into a decent club – '

All Stephen's pent-up frustrations gathered into a ball in his brain. A cold mist of fury danced in front of his eyes. He slid from his seat. 'I gather you're referring to me,' he said. 'I don't much care for your manners, your remarks, or for you either, for that matter.' Then he hit him. As his fist went up it welled through his mind that though he had killed men in the air and animals on the ground this was the first time in his life he had hit a man in anger. Behind the punch was the weight of an arm strengthened and toughened by years of carrying and swinging the big Rigby. His fist connected where it was intended to – on the side of the other's jaw. He staggered backwards, rocked on his heels and went over with a crash.

The man who had been reading in the alcove stood up and crossed to them, the opened copy of the *Tatler* still in his

167

hand. 'I heard what he said,' he told Stephen. 'That sort of *canaille* – Good God, it's Gervase Winthrop!'

At that moment a boy appeared in the doorway. He surveyed the scene with frightened eyes and then looked at Stephen. 'You're wanted on the telephone, bwana,' he said.

Part 3

KIT 2

CHAPTER XXI

Kit and Clare de Vaux had stared at each other in silence across the table in Mrs Hart's stuffy little parlour. Then, 'You've run into a spot of bother, I hear,' Clare said to him quietly.

Kit swallowed. 'I've been kicked out,' he said.

'So I gather. What are you going to do about it? Go home?'

'No,' Kit said. 'My father and I – well, I don't think he'll be glad to have me back. Not after this anyway.'

Clare's lips twitched. 'From what I hear,' he said, 'you spoke out of turn to Angus.'

'I suppose I did a bit.'

'He's not accustomed to that.'

Looking at the boy in front of him, Clare's mind went back twenty years to Stephen standing up to Conway, their brutal and bullying squadron commander in the old RFC. What's bred in the bone, he thought to himself. Born rebels, both of them. 'I once knew someone else who would have done much the same,' he said.

What did that mean and how had he heard about it all anyway, Kit wondered. Clare's next remark enlightened him in part. 'Mrs Robarts phoned me,' he said.

Beatrice's call to Clare had come after Angus had exploded in wrath over two enormous pre-lunch pink gins and poured out the whole story to her. Clare's interest in Kit still intrigued and to some extent mystified her, and, as ever, she was reluctant to leave things alone. The moment Angus had stumped off to his office after lunch she had gone to the telephone and put the call through to Clare. 'Your young Master who has got himself into a peck of trouble,' she said.

'Oh, and why?'

'It's quite a story. There's a lad of no account here called Cayley, who's a sort of pal of his apparently. Cayley is scared out of his wits and you know what Angus is. As soon as he sees a lame dog he wants to kick it. He put him up schooling on that bad brute Moonstruck, and of course he dropped him. Cayley lay for dead. Massiter who thought he *was* dead or thereabouts let fly at Angus. You can imagine what happened – '

'Just about.'

'They had a rare old set-to. I rather wish I'd been there to see it. But the end result is that Master Who is out bag and baggage if he has any. Massiter *père* won't have him back, so Angus says.'

'What'll he do?'

'Starve I expect,' Beatrice said and replaced the receiver. Having done so she looked at it, patted it and then chuckled, satisfied she had started something, the unravelling of which she would watch with interest. Clare, she was sure, knew or had guessed far more of Kit's real parentage than he had revealed to her.

Her instinct had not played her false. Frowning, Clare put down the telephone. He was in the room that he used as a study. On one wall were momentoes of the war, photographs of squadron groups, a black cross from a shot-down Albatross, a wrecked propeller hanging where another might hang a college oar, a photograph of two young men in front of a Camel fighter, one with his arm thrown round the shoulders of the other. Clare picked it up and stared at it for a moment. It was not imagination, he told himself, though perhaps it was more in the similarity of attitude than features that the likeness lay. But Stephen Raymond had shot Huns off his tail more times than he cared to remember. And twenty years ago Stephen Raymond had been about this boy's age. He pressed a bell and told the footman who answered it to have the Rolls-Bentley sent round. Half an hour later he was standing in Mrs Hardy's front parlour.

'You've never flown, you told me,' he said without preamble.

'No, Sir. I've never been up in an aeroplane.'

'Hm. Well, we can soon put that right. Anyway I want some advice about these damned horses. You'd better come back with me. You can take a look at the young ones, too. You've probably guessed, if Angus hasn't already told you, I don't know a hock from a spavin.'

So, his mind in a whirl, Kit was born off in the Rolls-Bentley to the vast square neo-Tudor block that was Brackley Place, seat of the Earl of Marchester, where Clare lived and waited for the kindly, dotty old Earl to hand him on his inheritance. They dined that night in the private dining room of Clare's apartments in the great house. There was one guest, a small, spare, bristling red-headed Welshman who was introduced as Squadron Leader Dai Evans. He had been in Clare's squadron in the latter stages of the war and had emerged as one of its leading scorers. The talk across the table was all of flying and the coming war.

'Never flown, have you,' the squadron leader said to Kit. 'Don't know what you're missing. Best thing in life you can do that isn't horizontal. Know what I mean? Right, aren't I, eh, Clare? Nothing to touch it?'

'Well, he mightn't agree. He's ridden a bit,' Clare said mildly.

'Races, has he? That's the sort of chap we're looking for. Get in now before the rush comes. Learn your job properly and then you'll be ready to clobber 'em. That's the thing in air fighting! Get in close and clobber the buggers!'

'That's if they're ever allowed to get in close,' Clare said. 'This new theory is all wrong. They say there'll never be another dog-fight. It'll be fighters versus bombers only. Fighters will attack the bombers line astern, one, two, three. What will the other fighters be doing, I wonder?'

'It's all balls. Trouble is fellers laying down tactics now never sat behind the guns themselves.'

'What we learnt, we learnt the hard way last time,' Clare said. 'They seem to have forgotten it.'

' "Always above, seldom on the level and never underneath," Mick Mannock's doctrine. I told 'em and kept tellin'

173

'em but they wouldn't listen. Vics of three, they said. That's the way we do it now. That's what the book says – '

'You told them too loud and too often, Dai. That's why you never made more than Squadron Leader.'

It all seemed to Kit a far cry from his home in the Bay, bounded by blue mountains, where life was lived at a casual pace and death in the skies something not even remotely to be imagined and, for that matter, a far cry too from the small enclosed world of a racing stable which he had just left, where nothing mattered save the next winner – if there was one. 'Is there really going to be a war?' he asked.

'War? Of course there is,' Evans said. 'Wish I was twenty years younger and I'd be in the thick of it. You, young feller want to fly? Of course you do. I can see it in your eye. Come to Marston airfield tomorrow at three o'clock and I'll take you up.'

It was a challenge and Kit had never turned his back on a challenge yet. Besides, this talk of flying and fighting had excited him. It never occurred to him that he was being indoctrinated, and not very subtly at that. 'I'd love to,' he said.

Kit's thoughts were still in ferment when he went to sleep that night, and even more so when he woke next morning, not very sure where he was, to find a manservant placing a tray with tea and biscuits on his bedside table and asking him: 'Which suit will you wear today, sir?'

At breakfast Clare told him he thought he ought to write to his family to explain what had happened and who he was with and that he would find writing paper in the library. Angus, he knew, would have already written to his father. Angus would be believed, and anything he said to the contrary would only make matters worse. He thought, however, that his mother should know his side of the story and he wrote it to her in full. She at least, would understand. Then he thought of Hugo. He, lucky devil, had come in for his rides at home and had won on one of them. But the coronet on the writing paper would be sure to impress him. He pulled a sheet towards him and began: *Hullo, old chap. Here I am at the moated grange* – when a sound behind him made him turn round.

174

A stocky, square-shouldered man was standing a few feet away, regarding him steadily from under a pair of bushy, startlingly white eyebrows. He was turned out as if to take part in a smart Edwardian shoot. His bird's eye-blue stock had a diamond pin thrust through it, his knickerbocker suit was heather mixture and tailored to perfection, fawn spats covered his highly polished brogues. His voice when he spoke was pitched a shade higher than modern cadence. 'Ha, hum,' he said. 'So you're the refugee from Robarts my nephew told me about, are you? Thought I'd have a word with you. That nephew of mine knows nothing about horses and cares less. They won't let me go and see mine run now. Tell me it's too much for me or some such rubbish. You know my horses, boy?'

'Yes, sir. I remember them well.'

'Well now, what d'ye think of them?'

Kit drew a deep breath and looked at the Earl. The old man looked back at him from a pair of blue eyes veined with age but suddenly bright with intelligence. 'I used to ride them myself, you know,' he said. 'Things were different then.'

Kit drew another breath. But he was never one to be overwhelmed by his company or to be slow to express his opinions. 'There isn't a decent one amongst them, sir,' he said. 'They say there's a war coming,' and he never knew quite what made him add: 'They'd be better in a tin feeding soldiers.'

The Earl blinked. He bent his old head forward and looked hard at Kit. Then he suddenly chuckled. 'You're a remarkably forthright young man,' he said. 'Ho, ho, "Better in a tin feeding soldiers", that's good, that's very good! And what do you think of my trainer?'

This question did make Kit hesitate. He owned no loyalty to Angus and disliked him personally. His private opinion was that Angus couldn't train creeper to climb up a wall but there is a freemasonry amongst those who make their living from horses. He might well be able to damage Angus irretrievably with the Earl but he wouldn't. He tried to choose his words with care. 'I think he's better with chasers than hurdlers,' he said. 'Big strong ones. Those are what he does best with.'

'And he's damned hard on them, too. All right, boy. I know what you're thinking. Now I'll tell you something else, boy. Tell an owner his best friend is sleeping with his wife but never tell him his horse is no good – that is unless he knows it already! Still, I like a young feller who speaks his mind. No use for these mealy-mouthed creepin' jesuses you get nowadays. Now then. Time for me mornin' sustainer.' He toddled over to the brocaded bell-pull and gave it a hearty tug. In a moment or two a footman came in bearing a salver on which was a small cut-glass decanter, a glass and a jug of water. 'Pour it out, Wilkins, pour it out,' the Earl commanded. When a substantial measure had been mixed he raised it to his lips and drained it in two swallows. 'Once more, Wilkins,' he said setting the glass down with a bang. When the second draught had followed the first the Earl made a grimace. 'Can't think where that nephew of mine gets his whisky from,' he said. 'His grocer, I suppose. Knows as much about whisky as he does about horses. All he thinks about is those damned aeroplanes. Still, better than nothing. Elixir of life. Brandy and soda it used to be in my young days. B and S we called it then.' He peered again at Kit. 'Taken rather a fancy to you, young feller,' he said. 'I'll give yer another tip. Ever take a gel out to dinner? Chorus gel? Never?'

Kit shook his head.

'Bless my soul.' The old boy stared at him as if he was a species he had never seen before. 'Then this is what you'll do – give her clear soup, a wing of chicken, a pêche melba, and – that don't matter much but this does – a bottle of sweet champagne. The only trouble is, you'll have to drink some of the filthy stuff yourself. Still it should serve. *Bon souper, bon gîte et le reste*, as the Frenchies say.' The old eyes suddenly clouded over. 'It's all so long ago,' he murmured. 'Romano's. The Roman. Abington Baird, that blackguard, Lily Langtry, Bob Sievier, knew 'em all. Rode against the best – ' He began to hum a long-forgotten tune and tottered off.

Kit had just finished his letter to Hugo when the door opened again and Clare came in. 'My uncle's been with you, I gather,' he said smiling.

'Yes, he asked about his horses.'

176

'And you told him. You seem to have made quite a hit. Did he have his drink?'

'He did and didn't enjoy it much.'

'He thinks it's whisky. It's not. It's cold tea. He'd kill himself otherwise, poor old boy. He's eighty-nine. He's served in two wars and he'll see another if he lives a couple more months. He was second in the National back in ninety-six and always says he should have won it but some wild Irishman nearly knocked him over at the last. He was one of the best shots in England up to a few years ago. On his good days he can still knock high pheasants out of the sky you and I couldn't even see.'

'I liked him.'

'If he hadn't liked you I doubt if even I could have kept you. I hadn't intended letting him loose on you unattended but he's as slippery as an eel when he wants to be and he knows every twist and turn of the old place. Now, a glass of champagne and then we can get along to the airfield. We can lunch there.'

It was a Tiger Moth in which the squadron leader effected Stephen's introduction to flying that afternoon. Having seen him strapped in, he taxied out and took off cross wind in a climbing turn. Peering over the side Kit savoured the sensation of swoop and speed as he watched the chequerboard of fields, roads and houses diminishing beneath him. 'Like to try yourself,' came down the headphones, as the aircraft levelled off. 'Right. Feet on the rudder bar. That's in front of you. Hand on the joystick. Gently. Think it's a young horse. Stroke it. Hold her straight and level. Watch that bubble in the tube. Keep it in the middle. That's the ticket. Steady as you go.'

It seemed rather fun to Kit. After a few minutes Evans said to him, 'All right. Not bad at all. I've got her. Not likely to be airsick, I imagine. Well, then, I'll throw her about a bit.'

Almost immediately the Moth and Kit's stomach appeared to try to turn themselves inside out. Evans looped, rolled, spun, stall-turned, looped again and half-rolled off the top. Flying straight and level once more he said into the tube, 'You've got her again. Watch the bubble.'

It was racing backwards and forwards across the container. Much like my head, Kit thought, as he fought with his own dizziness and began to stroke the stick. His stomach and the bubble steadied at much the same time. When they did the realisation came to him that at no period had he felt airsick and that he had enjoyed the sensation of being thrown all over the sky. In fact he wished he had been doing it himself and began to wonder how long it would take him to learn. Then he concentrated once more on the bubble in front of him.

'Not bad, not bad at all for a first shot,' came down the earphones. 'We'll come in now. I've got her.'

Even to Kit in his ignorance, the landing, when it came, seemed a singularly heavy one. The wheels hit the ground with a bang that jarred the whole fuselage.

'So you still haven't learnt,' Clare greeted Evans when they joined him on the tarmac. 'How many SEs did you write off on landing?'

'Nearly as many as the Huns I shot down. Remember what we used to say? Any landing you can walk away from is a good landing.' Evans took Clare's arm and they moved a little distance from where Kit was pulling off his helmet and looking appreciatively at the Moth. 'It's a bit early to say,' he said. 'But he looks good. He's under age. I suppose you'll have to get his father's consent?'

'Somehow I don't think there'll be any difficulty about that,' Clare answered sombrely.

CHAPTER XXII

The letter from Angus detailing Kit's sins and Kit's letter to his mother arrived by the same post at Dunlay Castle, deliveries being dictated by the whim of the Bellary postmistress and the state of the postman's bicycle.

178

Andrew found his on the long table in the hall when he came into the house for lunch. Taking it with him to the library for his pre-lunch glass of sherry, he slit it open and began to read.

As each unsparing sentence Angus had dictated to his secretary came home to Andrew, his brow furrowed further and further in anger. He said nothing during lunch lest the servants should hear, but once the meal was finished he summoned Babs to the library. 'You see what your son has done now,' he said, handing her the letter.

Babs turned over the sheets in silence and then stared at her husband where he stood by the window, his lips compressed into a thin line. 'But, Andrew,' she said, 'you haven't heard Kit's side of the story. I always said Angus was a brute.'

'That's enough. I warned him when he was leaving that if he got into any further trouble he could expect neither mercy nor help from me. I am washing my hands of him. I regard myself as havine been very generous to him. That's at an end. As from now I intend to discontinue his allowance.'

'What will happen to him?'

'That is something he must solve for himself.'

'You can't do this, Andrew.'

'Indeed I can and I shall.'

She knew that it was useless to argue with him and that in fact argument might only serve to make things worse. Her own post was in her sitting room and she had not been there before lunch. In it she found Kit's letter. Having read it and re-read it she remembered Clare de Vaux, his friendship with Stephen in the old RFC and his devotion to flying and the Service. Turning these matters over in her mind she began to fear even more for Kit. There was only one person now, she thought, with whom she could take counsel, and that was her father. Sending for her car, she drove the little Morris Minor along the roads that bordered the Bay to the old rambling house where her father still lived and which had once, in happier times, been her home.

Desmond Murtagh was supervising the ringing of a young horse when she arrived. 'Nice looker, isn't he?' he greeted

179

her. 'Moves well, too. What brings you here, my dear, at this time of day?'

'It's Kit,' she blurted out immediately.

'Oh, and what has he been up to now?'

'He's had some almighty row with Angus. I knew no good could come from his going there. Angus has chucked him out. And Andrew says – oh, dear – ' Babs groped for her handkerchief.

'We'd better go inside,' her father said. 'All right, Larry,' he called to the man at the end of the rope who was listening attentively and pretending not to. 'Carry on. Another ten minutes should do it.'

Desmond evicted sundry dogs from the chairs in the shabby well-lived-in morning room of the old house, selected a pipe from a rack near the fireplace, hitched his artificial leg into a comfortable position and sat down. 'It's the wrong time of day,' he said. 'But you look as if you could do with a drink.'

'No, thanks. I'm worried sick about what will happen to Kit,' she said. 'Andrew says he's had his last chance. He's going to cut him off. Now, Clare de Vaux, of all people, do you remember him, has turned up and taken him in. He's written me about it. Here, read it – ' She took Kit's letter from her handbag and gave it to her father.

Taking a pair of half-glasses from a shelf beside him and swearing at the necessity of having to use them, Desmond perched them on the end of his nose and then read the letter slowly through. 'Of course I remember de Vaux,' he said when he had finished. 'Though I had forgotten about his money and his aristocratic connections. He had the squadron after Stephen was shot down. It looks as though Kit has fallen on his feet.'

'Fallen on his feet! Can't you see what he says about flying? They'll have him in the RAF next. Flying! Look what it did to us last time – ruined Stephen's life and your leg – do we have to go through it all again? Oh, Dads, is there going to be a war?'

Her father took off the glasses and looked at her. 'I don't know whether there is or not,' he said. 'We're too far away here to judge. I can only say it looks that way.'

'Will the boys have to go? Why should they? Haven't we

180

all done enough and given enough? And we're supposed to be some sort of different nation now, aren't we?'

Desmond got up from his chair and limped across to the window. There he looked down the long sloping lawn to where the sun was dappling the waters of the Bay and striking colours from the mountains beyond. 'We're Irish in England and English in Ireland and that's the long and the short of it,' he said. 'The boys have been educated in England and once that happens they are English for all outward purposes anyway. Like the RCs the old boy network can fetch you back by the twitching of a thread.'

'What are you trying to tell me?'

'If they feel they must go, my dearest girl, you can't stop them.'

'I can try.'

'You'll lose them more surely than ever if you do. Look, Hugo goes up to Oxford next term, doesn't he?'

'Yes. Andrew insisted. You know how he is. It was the right thing to do, the right place to go – '

'They used to say you went up to Oxford to acquire that effortless assumption of superiority but Hugo, I think,' Desmond said with a smile, 'has that already. If there is a war all his friends will be going. You wouldn't want him to bolt back here, would you?'

'Maybe I would. At least he'd be safe. But it's not Hugo so much. I have a feeling about Hugo that whatever happens he'll come through.'

'And I'm sure,' her father said gravely, 'that he'll make certain it is in one of the best regiments.'

'I wish you wouldn't make fun of me, Dads. You never take anything seriously. It's Kit I'm scared out of my wits about. You know how reckless he is. If Andrew throws him out, and he will, for when he says he'll do something he never retracts, then he can't come back here.'

'Not to Dunlay, anyway. I see that.'

'Joining the Air Force would be just another adventure to him. And it isn't like that. I know. I remember Stephen in Paris the last time, the nightmares, the nerves, the dread of facing out over the lines again – oh, God, I shouldn't be telling you this.'

'I knew,' Desmond said quietly. 'I was there too, you must remember. I know, I knew, all about you and Stephen and, I must say it, about Kit, too. I know just what he means to you. But, and now my dear I am deadly serious – ' he crossed the room and took her hand—'this war, if it comes, will be, I don't know, a sort of crusade. You brought up those boys not to be afraid of anything and to stand on their own feet and fight their own battles. You know you did and you were right. None of us contemplated another war when they were growing up. It was unthinkable. Now, perhaps, it's on top of us. You can't change them now. It's too late. You wouldn't want them, Kit especially, to turn against you for trying, would you?'

'What you are saying is that if I interfere I may lose them altogether? And – and I've already lost Stephen?'

'That's about it, my dear.'

Babs took out her handkerchief and dabbed her eyes again. 'Damn Hitler and men and wars,' she said. 'The Germans have sons too. Why can't women run the world? We'd do it a damn sight better. Now, I think I will have that drink.'

Only half-convinced by her father's arguments Babs drove back to Dunlay. But, half-convinced, she hesitated to write her doubts and fears to Kit. Having hesitated she was lost, for while she was still pondering what course to take as she tossed in her bed on sleepless summer nights, a buff envelope addressed to Andrew arrived at Dunlay. It contained a formal request that he should permit his son Christopher Murtagh Massiter to be accepted as a pupil pilot by the Air Ministry.

Andrew signified his consent in two brief lines. Having sealed the envelope and left it for posting, he informed Babs of what he had done. 'It's quite the wisest thing,' he said. 'And we ought to be grateful to de Vaux for arranging it. What else was there for him? He'll be able to live on his pay. I'm told they can in the Air Force. It's unlike the Army.'

'If he lives,' Babs said bitterly. 'Every time they go up they take their lives in their hands.'

'The choice was his,' Andrew said coldly. 'It's been made. Now I have to tell you that I'm flying out to Kenya shortly. I shall use their new Imperial Airways service to save time.

182

I'm not entirely happy about how things are at the farm and I want to plan its future.'

'Its future – does that mean you've changed your mind about a war coming?'

'Partly. I don't like the situation. Chamberlain has been extremely foolish in giving this guarantee to Poland and introducing conscription. He's playing into the hands of the warmongers, Churchill, Eden and company. It's all insanity. No one wants a war. Least of all with Germany, who is our best bulwark against communism. I never dreamt Chamberlain could be so stupid.'

'But aren't the Germans doing dreadful things? Dads says if this war comes it will be a sort of crusade.'

'Crusade? Crusade? What the devil does he mean by that? It's the communists we should be fighting. They want to take everything we've got.'

Babs sighed. 'Is anything ever worth a war?' she said. 'Look what happened the last time. To think we've got to go through it all again. And now Kit, too, in the Air Force.'

Her husband's eyes held neither mercy nor pity for her. 'War is an extension of business interests by other means,' he said. 'One must protect what one has. And if we should be foolish enough to fight Hitler it should be a short war. He has no oil nor the means of getting it. His equipment, I believe, is second-class. 'Our fellow in Germany, Henderson, a first-class chap, who is friendly with those in power there reports, I'm told, that they don't want a war, that they're not ready for it. It's all a gigantic bluff. Many of his tanks are only mock-ups. The French Army is the best in the world. It and our Navy will bring him to his knees in a few months.'

'And how many mothers' sons will die, however short it is?'

'There is little point at this juncture in indulging in sentimentality. It may never happen. But one must take every precaution to secure oneself in case it does. To return to our own affairs it seems to me that the problem of the boy and what to do with him has been solved very neatly, thanks to the assistance of that de Vaux fellow.'

She turned aside to avoid the sudden flare of hatred that flashed across his tawny eyes.

183

CHAPTER XXIII

For Kit the chance and the choice had come to him out of the blue and he had grasped it eagerly. Between Angus and his father he felt he was all washed up in racing. Flying both excited and fascinated him. There was something of the thrill of race-riding about it, combined with the attraction of mastering a new element and adventuring into the unknown. Already he had been up again with Dai Evans several times and had been initiated into the mysteries of effect of controls, flying straight and level and rate one turns. When Clare put it to him that the RAF offered him a chance of the next best thing to a life with horses, it seemed a wonderful opportunity and he had answered, 'Yes, if they'll have me,' without a moment's hesitation.

'No trouble about that. I'll look after it,' Clare had said. 'Besides,' he had added slyly, 'if there isn't a war there will be time off for race-riding. That is, if you can get anyone to put you up.'

'What's that? What's that?' The old Earl had suddenly materialised beside them in the way he had and had picked up the end of their conversation.

'I was telling him, sir,' Clare said patiently, 'that if he joins the RAF he should have time off to ride races provided he could get anyone to put him up.'

'Don't know about that. Funny service, the RAF. Always struck me as officers pretending to be gentlemen, not like my regiment where we were gentlemen pretending to be officers. No chargers. Only those damn stinkin' aeroplanes you're so fond of. Tell ye what I'll do, boy. I'll put you up. Taken a sort of fancy to you. You'll ride one of mine. Where we runnin' next, Clare?'

'Damned if I know.'

'Well then, ring Robarts and find out.'

Angus' temper had not improved in the interval since Kit's departure. If he had to confess it he would have had to admit that deep down he had a sneaking regard for Kit, but the

184

manner of his leaving and the words they had exchanged still rankled. The loss of a paying pupil, too, had made itself felt, for things generally were running against him. It had been a wretched season and now it was dying. There was little left to hope for before it finally expired at the end of June since most of the horses for which he had had any expectations were either out at grass already or being roughed off. There was one, however, for whom he had hopes, though not very strong ones, that he might just pick up one of the last of the hunter chases. The opposition at this stage of the season would not be great and the stable badly needed a winner. He had asked Dick Harbison to take the ride but Dick, who was now back in the RAF, had excused himself on the grounds that he did not know if he could get away. Angus, remembering his own soldiering days, thought the excuse a flimsy one and that Dick did not think the horse good enough. This did not sweeten his temper and he was considering whom he should try to get hold of instead when Clare's call came through.

'Playfellow in a hunter chase at Stratford,' Clare said when Angus had answered his query. 'That's very satisfactory. You see Lord Marchester wants young Massiter to have the ride.'

The full impact of what Clare had said did not sink into Angus for a moment. When it did, his reaction, as Clare had expected, was choleric. 'What! That brat! Are you mad!' he shouted down the telephone.

'I'm quite sane, thank you,' Clare said coldly. 'Those are Lord Marchester's instructions which he has asked me to convey to you.'

Angus' first impulse was to tell Clare he could take himself, Lord Marchester and all his horses to hell and gone and out of the yard in twenty-four hours. The words were forming on his lips when warning bells sounded in his brain and somehow he choked them back. The Earl was one of his oldest and best patrons; he was, too, still an influential name in racing. The loss of prestige which would follow the removal of his horses would be something in the nature of a disaster. More important than that, his bills were paid on the dot and without query, and Angus was at that moment living in dread of the figures his accountant was going to come up with at the end of the season.

With a great effort he controlled himself, growing almost purple in the face with fury as he did so. 'Very well, if that's what you want,' he said, and then his rage impelled him to add, 'Perhaps you'd be good enough to tell Lord Marchester that he might have had a chance of winning this race. He has none now.' With that he slammed down the receiver and sat glowering at it.

Although they had drifted apart, Angus still on occasion used Beatrice as a sort of safety valve to whom he could pour out his woes and rant at over a drink. But Beatrice was in Brook Street, no doubt entertaining her fancy friends as he put it to himself, and with the season waning her Sunday mornings were dropping off, so he did not know when she would return. There was no one therefore in whom he could confide or blow off the head of steam which was boiling within him. Opening the drawer of his desk he took out the whisky bottle and poured himself a stiff measure. When he had drunk it, as was his custom in moments of stress, he turned in his chair to contemplate the montage picture of his Grand National winners which hung on the wall behind him.

Those had been his great days. Giving himself another drink and raising the glass to his lips, he wondered what had gone wrong. He could not bring himself to admit that the fault lay with him, that times were changing and that he had refused to adapt. It was the horses, he told himself, that weren't right, not his methods. But the stark fact remained that the stable was woefully short of winners. Once more his thoughts came back to Playfellow and the instructions he had just received. He would have to tell Wilson he was putting young Massiter up. The whole yard would know about it and he could imagine the sniggers behind his back when the news went around that he was being made to give the ride to the pupil he had just unceremoniously kicked out. Morale was low enough in the yard as things were and this would only make it worse. Emboldened by his two drinks, his hand was reaching out for the telephone to tell Clare and Lord Marchester and the whole bloody lot of them to go to hell when once more the voice of caution stayed him. Things *were* bad.

It was only Beatrice's money, he knew, that was keeping the place going at all, and what would she say if he lost his best owner? He had a sudden longing for her to be back again, for life to be as it once had been when she looked after owners, managed his moods and pretty well ran the stable too, for that matter. But she wasn't there; he couldn't ask her what to do. His hand reached for the bottle again, looked at it and then, deciding he was resorting too much to its comfort, rammed the cork firmly back into its neck.

Beatrice for her part had no intention of going to Stratford until she opened *Sporting Life* as she breakfasted in bed on the morning of the race and saw 'Mr C. M. Massiter' against Playfellow's name as his probable rider. What on earth was going on, she wondered? Had some miracle occurred to reinstate Kit, or was it a mistake? Picking up the telephone beside her bed, she rang Angus. His reply to her enquiry left her in no doubt that it was not, at any rate, a mistake. 'It's that bloody Clare de Vaux who's behind it, damn him,' were his final words after his initial explosion. 'I'm beginning to wish I'd never seen him or old Marchester or their damned horses.'

'I don't know about that,' Beatrice said sweetly. 'Think of all those nice cheques. As a matter of fact I do believe I'll go to Stratford myself.'

'Do if you like. I'm damned if I will,' was Angus' reply.

Telling her maid to put out a tweed costume and, because she disliked racecourse food, the cook to provide a luncheon hamper, Beatrice studied the runners again. Dick Harbison, she saw, was down to ride the favourite, Joyful Days. That wouldn't improve Angus' temper, she thought, as she was sure he would have wanted to get him if he could. She didn't think much of Playfellow's chances but it would be interesting to see what happened. She chuckled to herself as she pinned a diamond brooch to her lapel and then went out to her car.

Kit, too, had looked up the form. The opposition appeared weak enough with the exception of Dick's mount which had the numbers 132 opposite his name. Playfellow he remembered as a plodder and a pretty moderate one at that, a judgment which was confirmed by the travelling head lad who was in charge of the declarations and saddling since

Angus had refused to come. 'He'll get you round all right,' he said. 'But he'll take the hell of a long time doing it.'

Beatrice was standing in the parade ring when he entered it with the other riders. Crossing to her, he raised his whip to the brim of his cap in salute and smiled at her.

'Well now, Master Who,' she greeted him, 'this is a bit of a turn up for the books, isn't it, riding one of our horses? I suppose you think you'll win it and score off the stable. Is that Clare's idea?'

'No,' Kit said. 'It's no one's idea. The old man got me the ride. And if you want to know I don't think much of it. He's so slow he couldn't catch himself up, and it'll be a miracle if we run into a place.'

'How to get on in racing without really trying,' she said tartly. 'Just go on saying those kind words to all your owners.'

Kit grinned suddenly, and for the first time she noticed it was a very infectious grin. 'After all, you asked me, didn't you,' he said and walked to where the lad was leading the horse in.

Beatrice found she was standing next to Carlow Concannon as they watched the riders mounting. 'Where *did* that young man spring from? she said. 'I suppose Dick will win this.'

'They're backing him like it if that means anything,' Carlow said. 'And he thinks he will.'

Kit thought so too. There were only four other runners and the pace initially was slow. This suited Playfellow, who was able to keep with them, and his jumping, as the travelling head lad had said, was bold, safe and accurate. The open ditch claimed a faller and as they turned into the second circuit Kit could see Dick on the favourite going quietly within himself and giving the impression he could go on and take his race whenever he wanted. Kit was in no such happy position, for with the pace improving he was kicking and scrubbing to hold his pace.

The bad old bugger doesn't even stay, he muttered to himself. But to his surprise Playfellow did not weaken or drop out as they came down the back straight. He plodded on at the one pace and suddenly it seemed to Kit that those in front were beginning to come back to him. There were three of them with Dick going easily and tracking the two leaders.

And then, at the second last, the whole aspect of the race changed.

One of the leaders blundered badly and was almost down. Dick's horse, which had up to now never put a foot wrong, perhaps unsighted by the blunder, took the fence by the roots and turned over.

Good God, I'm going to be placed, Kit thought and kicked and kicked again.

Round the final bend he caught and passed the horse that had made the mistake. The error had put paid to his chances for he was under pressure and not responding. At the last, to his astonishment, he found he was closing the leader though it still seemed a hopeless chase. Then, suddenly a gap appeared between the leader and the rails. There was room enough, or just about anyway, Kit thought. He rammed Playfellow up along the rails. Whatever shortcomings he had, Playfellow had never been known to turn his head at anything. As if he realised the challenge he went through the opening and threw his best jump of the day. The tired leader had wandered and Playfellow landed a clear length ahead.

Kit sat down and kicked for dear life. The game old horse seemed to realise that for once he was there with a chance. He responded as he had never done before. The post came just in time. They won by a short head.

'So Angus has a winner at last,' Beatrice said as she watched him dismount. 'I do hope he's pleased. I thought you told me this fellow was useless?'

Kit paused with the saddle over his arm. 'That's right, I did,' he said. 'And I still think so. That was a stinking race and we had all the luck that was going. If Dick had stood up he'd have won a street. That old devil will never win another race.'

'I'll tell Angus his jockey's considered opinion. He'll be pleased, I'm sure.'

'He'll still be a fair hunter, though,' Kit added with a grin.

'Well, well, well,' Beatrice murmured as she watched him make his way towards the weighing room. There's more to you than meets the eye, my lad, she said to herself as she made her way out of the parade ring.

The first person Kit met after he had changed was Carlow

Concannon. 'Cheeky little bugger, aren't you, pinching the inside,' she said to him. 'If Dick had been there he'd have had you over the rails.'

'And you would too if it'd been a point-to-point,' Kit said. 'Anyway he wasn't there, was he?'

'No, and just as of this minute he's licking his wounds and examining the hole in his pocket. Mrs Meddler wants us all to have a drink with her. To celebrate your win, I suppose. Angus won't know whether to laugh or cry.'

'He doesn't do much of either or didn't when I was there. But I wonder what he'll say – '

'A winner's a winner when all's said and done. But I wouldn't bank on his putting you up again. Now let's get that drink.'

Beatrice was waiting for them with an opened bottle of champagne before her. 'Pour it, will you,' she said to Dick, and then, turning to Kit: 'And just what plans have you for your future? You wouldn't be taking over from Clare as the old man's racing manager by any chance? Where is Clare by the way?'

'He's in London on business,' Kit said. 'I think he's gone to the Air Ministry. I'm waiting to be called up for the RAF.'

'So you'll be in it too,' Dick said, looking at him. 'I'm back, you know, thanks chiefly to Major de Vaux. I'm on a conversion course at Uppington now.'

'Another bloody fool wanting to get himself killed,' Carlow said looking at Kit.

'At least he's not running away back to the bog like some,' Beatrice said. 'The Wild Geese homing, I've heard them called.'

'No. I'm not doing that,' Kit said.

'Well then, if you're at a loose end on leave you know where I am – 14A Upper Brook Street. There'll always be a drink and a sandwich if nothing else. You, too, of course, Dick. Finish the champagne. I must go and break the news to Angus that he's had a winner ridden by that up-and-coming gentleman rider, Mr C. Massiter.' She gave a little laugh and began pulling on her gloves. 'Don't forget,' she went on, tapping Kit lightly on the cheek as they stood up to allow her to leave. '14A Upper Brook Street.'

190

'The only thing she didn't say,' Carlow said tartly as they watched her thread her way through the thronged bar, 'was, "Come up and see me sometime".'

When Kit arrived back at the Towers that evening a familiar buff envelope was waiting for him. It enclosed a railway warrant and told him to report forthwith to Halling Airport in Northamptonshire for pupil-pilot training.

CHAPTER XXIV

Clare had returned from London the evening after Stratford to find Kit and his uncle in close confabulation in the library reliving every yard of the race. His uncle was drinking draughts of cold tea from the decanter, pressing Kit to share it and chuckling gleefully. 'Got the inside, did you,' he chortled. 'Te he, te he, done the same meself. Takin' a chance they say. They used to tell us we couldn't do it unless we had a stone in hand. Balls, balloons, air balloons, my boy. Takin' chances wins races. Have some more of this whisky – No? Perhaps you're right. Filthy stuff it is. Ah, Clare, back, are you? You must do something about this grog. Tell you what, my boy, we'll have a cigar, cigar, a small cigar. Wilkins! Where the devil is that man? Pull that bell, my boy.'

Clare left them to it, deciding that he would talk with Kit later. When he entered his own room the telephone bell was ringing. It was Beatrice.

'Your protégé won a race for us today,' she said. 'So the stable's had a winner at last. That's quite a remarkable young man. Going flying now, so he tells me. I shall follow his future with interest. There's one thing, though, that I might mention.'

'And what would that be?'

'The boy should go far, that is,' her throaty chuckle came

down the line, 'unless he tells his grandmother in the shape of his CO how to suck eggs or, to use the language of the stable, my dear Clare, to put it where the monkey put the nuts which, from what I saw of him today, he's quite likely to do.'

Clare laughed as he put down the phone. Sometimes Beatrice amused him; sometimes she annoyed him. But she was no fool and there was sense in what she said.

Clare was far from friendless in the corridors of power, and he had been to see the Air Minstry about a job for himself when the war came, but he had also taken the opportunity to make certain enquiries about Andrew Massiter. In the bar in White's he had run into an Irish owner of his acquaintance. 'Massiter?' the Irishman had said in answer to his query. 'Of course I know him. Wants to run Irish racing. He and Westcott are forever squabbling over who does run it.'

'Where does the money come from?'

'Damned if I know, but there's a hell of a lot of it. He's in Kenya now, they tell me, looking after his property there. Setting up a funk-hole if things go wrong, I shouldn't wonder. Always hedges his bets, Massiter. If you want to find out more about him try someone in the City. They'll know.'

Clare's merchant bankers did know – something. Plenty of money, they said, originally made in South America and shrewdly got out before the Argentine government clamped down on its export, well-managed, rock solid and far-flung with interests in Rhodesia, South Africa, Canada and Kenya. More sinister, perhaps, its owner was said to be flirting with fascism and in touch with the pro-German elements in London society.

Kit would be well out of that ménage, Clare thought as he opened his evening paper in the first-class carriage from Paddington. Whatever slight doubts or pangs of conscience he had had in taking over Kit's life had been blown away by the information he had received.

When Kit came into the room he told him to sit down. 'Have a proper drink,' he said. 'Your posting's arrived, I gather.'

'Yes. I'm to report to Halling Airfield forthwith. I suppose that means tomorrow.'

192

'It's come through quickly. They're beginning to wake up.'
Clare looked at the boy sitting opposite to him and was struck
again by the resemblance to Stephen. Clare had commanded
a squadron on the Western Front when he himself had been
only in his early twenties, so that he had had experience of
dealing with high-spirited young men. Subservience to their
seniors did not rank high in their list of attributes as he well
knew. To use a horsey metaphor, to get the best out of them
you had to ride them on the snaffle and pretty sensitively at
that. Beatrice's warning, therefore, had struck a responsive
chord. He did not want Kit to throw away the chance he had
got for him by talking or acting out of turn. A muted note of
caution would, he thought, suit the occasion and he felt that
behind it all Kit was sensible enough to accept it.

'You'll need a base,' he said. 'And there'll always be a
room for you here when you want it. But a word in your ear.
You're joining a peacetime service. There'll be all sorts of
regimental restrictions which you'll hate and want to kick at.
But they're there and they've been there for a long time and
they'll stay there after you and I have gone. We had a saying
in my day: don't take on the Army, it always wins. Do you
see what I'm getting at?'

Kit gave one of his infectious grins. 'Yes, sir – just,' he
said.

'And another thing,' Clare went on, smiling. 'About a
hundred years ago when I was a snotty-nosed subaltern in a
cavalry regiment – they kicked me out because I couldn't sit
on a horse – we had a saying too – 'stand behind a gun, in
front of a horse and a long way from your senior officers'. If
you bear those two things in mind you won't go too far wrong.
Now, what about that drink? It's not every day you join a
Service. Here's to happy landings – and many of them.'

CHAPTER XXV

Next morning, as Kit was making his way to the car which was to take him to the station, he met the old Earl roaming the house in the way he did. 'Off again, are you?' he said. 'Going flying or some such damn fool thing like that. Always the same. As soon as I find someone who can talk to me about my horses he goes away. Here boy, here's something to help take that gel out to dinner and don't forget what I told you!' He reached over and pushed an envelope into the side pocket of Kit's jacket.

In the car when he opened it Kit found inside ten crisp, glossy, five-pound notes.

Kit was lucky. As Dai Evans had advised, he had got in in time, for it took a minimum of ten months to train a fighter pilot. His early entry saw that he got that training, so that when the test of battle came he was equipped as best he could be by the standards of the time to face it, unlike many of the later war-time intake who were thrown into the holocaust with a bare fortnight's 'advanced training'. He was lucky, too, in that under the pupil-pilot training scheme flying took precedence over everything; and Kit found that he loved flying. The sense of being at one with the aircraft had something in it of riding a well-schooled horse or having a young one suddenly come right as it yielded to hand and leg. Then, too, once he had graduated to aerobatics there was the thrill of throwing the aircraft round the sky and the satisfaction of performing each evolution with the precision the drill book and the instructor's patter demanded. All through the course he waited impatiently to get into the air and fretted when bad weather curtailed flying. So caught up in this new life was he that he even found himself paying attention to the lecturers on airmanship, theory of flight, rudimentary navigation and suchlike. Having listened to Clare and Evans, the one thing in life he now wanted was to be passed out as a fighter pilot. For the first time he had a real goal to aim at and he was determined to achieve it. His dream of becoming a leading amateur rider was, he now saw, only a dream; but here was something which gave purpose to all he did. Because of his obvious promise in the air he was soon marked out for one of the higher classifications as a pilot. In the mess he saw to it that he sank into the complete anonymity required of very junior officers and trod warily when near his seniors whom he privately regarded as a bunch of old stiffs hide-bound by custom, embalmed in rank and governed by what he soon learned to call bullshit. His natural inclination, which he shared with others bound for fighters, was to go his own way and damn the consequences, but for the present at any rate he curbed it. How long this would last was another matter, but for the moment those warning words from Clare still rang in his ears. He not only liked and admired Clare but he also realised how much he had done for him by picking him up when he was down and out, and he was determined not to disappoint him.

And so he went on flying. But even after war was declared, since no shots were exchanged and no bombers tried to get through, peacetime practices still prevailed. White overalls with squadron badges for instructors were still *de rigueur*, etiquette in the mess and on the station was as formal as in pre-war times – no shop to be talked, silence amongst junior officers until spoken to, saluting and being saluted on every possible occasion.

None of it seemed to Kit to be a practical preparation for a shooting war. But they were at war, so why were they not being taught how to shoot? He itched to get on with things and his increasing friendship with Dai Evans did not help him to keep his ebullient nature under control. As Clare had suggested, he had made Brackley Place his base and was often there on free days or weekends, and Evans, too, was a frequent visitor. Evans had blossomed out into a wing-commander and had wangled his way to a training posting where he was making himself increasingly unpopular with certain of his seniors on account of his outspoken opinions. 'Most of them have persuaded themselves that the balloon will never go up,' he would snort over a pink gin. 'Hitler will cave in before Christmas; he's got no oil and his tanks are made of cardboard. And if he doesn't there'll never be another dog-fight: the bomber must get through. Did you ever hear such rubbish, Clare?'

'It seems from what young Kit tells us that they're still training for the Hendon Air Display,' Clare said. He too, was back in uniform, wearing the two-and-a-half stripes of a squadron leader, his old rank, the khaki RFC wings stitched over his left breast pocket above the DFC ribbon. 'It looks horribly as if we're giving the impression everywhere, to the French as well as the Huns, that we don't want to fight,' he said. 'Take racing, for instance, it's still going on just the same. That's no way in which to convince people we're serious. Ridden any more winners lately?' he looked quizzically at Kit.

Kit grinned. 'Just one,' he said. 'A chance ride Dick Harbison couldn't take.'

Racing indeed was continuing as if there was no such thing as a war on, the only difference being a sprinkling of uniforms in the enclosures. With the money saved from his allowance when he was at the Grange Kit had bought a third-hand MG and since most weekends were free he usually found occasion to drive to race-meetings and then back to Brackley Place to spend the night. Once at the meeting he would rendezvous with Dick and Carlow, share their fun and be helped by them to pick up the odd spare ride.

Dick was with a fighter squadron now, a crack one equipped with eight-gun Hurricanes, the latest thing in monoplane fighters. He could not always get away, and on his recommendation Kit had come in for one or two of his rides. And when he was away that left Carlow all to Kit.

Kit knew he was falling for her, knew he had fallen for her in that first moment when he had glimpsed her at Malloran Park. He knew, too, that she was Dick's girl and that as long as Dick was there his chance was hopeless. But this did not stop him longing for her company, and when Dick wasn't there she seemed happy enough with him. They shared the same interests, laughed at the same things and argued endlessly over the merits and demerits of the horses he and Dick rode. She enjoyed the fast and jouncy little car, too, and being whisked about in it from meeting to meeting, comparing it favourably, she said, with the big green Bentley Dick shared with two other officers in his squadron.

After a meeting at Taunton during that soft and balmy September, when their world was entering its death throes though they did not know it, they stopped for dinner at a road-house outside Exeter. Kit had ridden a young horse into a place in a Novice Chase, which was just what the owner wanted. When he had changed the owner had stood him two drinks in the bar and promised him the ride next time out. The horse had jumped like a stag and given Kit that feel which told him he should go on and do better. Altogether he was bubbling over with the simple pleasure of being alive, doing the things he most wanted to do and doing them well, when they sat down and the waiter handed him the menu. 'Will you have clear soup, the wing of a chicken, a pêche melba and, oh yes, a bottle of sweet champagne?' he said.

'I want a steak, underdone, sauté potatoes and crêpes suzette if they know how to make them. A bottle of light ale would be just the job. What the hell are you talking about?'

'That's what the old Earl told me I should order if I took a gel – that's how he said it, a gel – out to dinner. *Bon souper, bon gîte et le reste*, that's what he said.'

'Did he indeed? And what sort of a gel had he in mind?'

Suddenly Kit was afraid he had annoyed her as she gave him one of her direct looks from across the table, and he began to come down from the clouds. But his fears were groundless, for the next moment she burst out laughing. 'Bit out of date, isn't he?' she said. 'But he is an old dear. I don't know so much about Clare de Vaux, though. He gives me the creeps rather.'

Kit leapt to the defence of his friend and protector. 'What do you mean?' he said. 'I think he's a super chap.'

'I think he plays with people to cover something he's lost himself. Did you know he's had a bad arm too, ever since that crash in the last war? It's permanently weak or something and gives him hell at times. That's why he had to stop flying.'

'No. I didn't know that.'

'He keeps quiet about his injuries, I'll say that for him. But he's using Dick, and Dick knows it. And he's using you, too.'

197

'Me? What on earth for?'

'I'll tell you. Dick says there's been a sort of split in the RAF ever since it came into being. There's a bomber lobby and a fighter lobby, and the bomber barons have always been on top. They say any war will be a bomber's war. The fighter chaps have never accepted this. They hold that the way air fighting is being thought out is a bombers' way and it's all wrong. I don't understand one damn thing about it and it's like child's games to me. I'm only repeating what Dick tells me. Anyway de Vaux wants to find out first – hand from pilots in the squadrons just what is going on. That's why he got Dick back in so quickly and that's why, or one of the reasons anyway, that he pushed you in. Has he been questioning you about things in training?'

'Well, yes, he has a bit.'

'And that fire-eating friend of his, Dai Evans, too?'

'Yes, they both have, now I come to think of it.'

'And another thing,' Carlow went on, cutting her steak. 'With all that money and a title to come I think he should take more interest in the horses just for the old man's sake.'

'I don't think he's interested in the money or the title.'

'Isn't he? Who isn't? Don't be so naïve, Kit. Just because you've never been short of a bob or two in your life it doesn't mean everyone hasn't.'

'Short of a bob or two! My father cut me off when Angus pushed me out. I would have been stony broke only Clare picked me up and got me into the RAF. Surely you know that?'

'There are ways and ways of being broke, like being down to your last yacht. Come to think of it, haven't you got a title of sorts coming your way? He can't cut you out of that, can he? That'll be the day.'

Suddenly she realised she was treading on dangerous ground. She and Dick had discussed Kit's situation together more than once. 'I think Massiter knows he's not his son, he'd be a bigger bloody fool than he is if he doesn't,' Dick had said. 'And I think he hates the kid. He hated his father anyway, that's for sure. I've asked around a bit since we got to know young Kit. One of the stories is that Massiter was behind the burning of Raymond's house in the Troubles. It was the Black and Tans that did it and that's damned odd too. Mostly they left landowners alone. Massiter tried to make out that Raymond was mixed up with the Sinn Feiners.'

'Was he?'

'I shouldn't think so, but by all accounts he was a strange sort of chap who took his own line. He was a sort of an ace in the old RFC and a bloody good pilot in that war. Young Kit looks like following in his footsteps.'

She looked at the laughing boy on the other side of the table. Suddenly she felt intensely sorry for him, though she didn't quite know why. 'Are you a bloody good pilot?' she asked.

'I don't know about that but I love flying,' Kit said.

It was time to change the subject. 'Seen Mrs Meddler lately?' she asked him.

'No,' Kit said. 'I expect she's forgotten all about me.'

'I wouldn't bet on it. She's a sort of female elephant that way. She never forgets.'

As it happened, Carlow was proved right and he did meet Beatrice a few weeks later in Bond Street. He had been in Gieves buying shirts when he almost collided with her on the pavement. 'Master Who again as I live and dream,' she said. 'What, no wings? Don't tell me you've failed your flying? Been giving the Air Vice-Marshal his riding instructions, perhaps.'

'Neither,' Kit said. 'We can't put wings up until we've passed our advanced flying course. 'I'm on my way there now.'

'Are you indeed? It all sounds most important and exciting. Come along, I'll give you lunch. From what I hear about food in the mess you probably could do with a decent meal.' She hailed a taxi and told the driver to take them to Brook Street.

Like all Beatrice's rooms the upstairs first-floor drawing room into which she brought Kit wore an air of grace and elegance. In addition Beatrice had the ability to make her rooms comfortable. The gilded Louis Quinze chairs held fat cushions to ease their austerities. The Sèvres pieces and bibelots in the lighted alcoves round the walls had been chosen with care and taste. There was a Fragonard over the fireplace and a Monet faced it from the opposite wall. Drinks were laid out on a marble-topped Regency table in the window which looked out on to a little square of garden. 'Fix me a White Lady, will you,' she said. 'Oh, I don't suppose you know how. I'll do it myself. No, here's someone who will. Remember him?'

It was Dick Harbison who entered the room. He smiled at Kit, crossed to the drink table where he fiddled expertly with bottles, ice and a shaker. Once he had mixed the drinks he came over to Kit. He was wearing the one thick ring of a flying officer and was stationed, he told him, at Biggin Hill. 'Still enjoying your flying? Still want to come to fighters?' he asked.

'You bet.'

'Hullo, here's de Vaux. He should be able to help you get where you want. Wing-commander now. Personal assistant to one of the Air Staff. Stand to attention when you talk to him, and don't forget to call him sir.' The room was filling up. There were several senior officers of one or the other of the Services and some willowy young men not yet in uniform accompanied by smart-looking girls. Catching sight of Dick and Kit, Clare crossed to them.

'Glad to see you two,' he said. 'I'd like a word with you both later on. You'll be going north, Kit, I know, but there'll be plenty of time. Come to the Royal Air Force Club when this bash is over.'

'Now then, you boys in blue, mustn't talk shop.' Beatrice bustled up. 'Come and sit here.' She took Kit by the arm. 'We'll have a cosy little chat.' She sat on the Louis Quinze sofa and patted the cushion beside her. 'I met your father, Sir Andrew, the other day,' she said. 'He was at one of Chips Channon's dos. We had quite a talk, mostly about you. So you're to be the next baronet.'

'That'll be the day,' Kit said, remembering Carlow's words.

'You are a silly boy, you know. I tried to plead your case but it was little use I'm afraid. Sir Andrew strikes me as a most determined character. Why is he so *acharné* against you?' She looked directly at him, her baby blue eyes wide open and sympathetic. It was nice of her to try to help, Kit thought.

200

At the same time he suddenly realised that she was still a very attractive woman.

'Blessed if I know,' he said. 'But I think to be honest that Hugo, that's my brother, was always the favourite. He's, well he's a bit more like the Sir, that's what we call him, than I am. Hugo always wins; so does the Sir.'

'Perhaps if you get your wings he'll be proud of you and that will help. Isn't there a sort of flying tradition in the Bay where you come from? Wasn't there an ace in the last war, a man called Raymond, who hailed from there?' Again she looked innocently at him. 'Clare would know, Clare knows everybody. Clare,' she called to him, 'wasn't there a flying ace name of Raymond from Bellary Bay in the last war?'

God, the bitch, Clare thought. She's been doing her homework.

'We were in the same squadron,' he said quietly. 'He was one of my greatest friends.'

'There! You see! I knew I was right. So you're carrying on a sort of family tradition, aren't you?' She was gazing at Kit.

'I don't know about that,' Kit said. 'I never knew him. They were burnt out round about the time I was born.'

'When you were born – fancy!'

At that moment the door opened and a maid announced that luncheon was served. Beatrice rose from the sofa. 'Come and see me when you have those wings up,' she said. 'Keep in touch. You know how I like to help.'

There were no shortages for the rich in wartime then. Quail's eggs were followed by a sole, thin tender slices of veal perfectly cooked and *crêpes suzette*, the fashionable sweet of the day. It was all washed down by what Kit guessed was a superb hock; it tasted like nectar anyway, after which were circulated decanters of vintage port or brandy for those who preferred it. When they left the table Clare bore both Kit and Dick off to the RAF Club where Dai Evans, now a group captain with a brass hat, was waiting for them with tea and anchovy toast.

'Fired your guns yet?' Dai Evans asked Dick as he handed him his cup.

'Not since practice camp,' Dick answered. 'A hundred

201

rounds at a drogue. Some of the chaps haven't fired them at all.'

'What about camera guns?'

'Mostly they break down or the film is on the blink.'

'And what about you, young man?' Evans said, turning.

'They teach us to fly and they're bloody good at it,' Kit answered. 'So far, though, there's been nothing about fighting. I'm on my way to advanced flying school. Maybe I'll learn there.'

'Maybe,' Dai said. 'Can't you do anything about this, Clare? You got me my fourth ring after all.'

'The only reason I'm where I am,' Clare said, 'is that someone told my master the old boy was about to die, and he thought it would look well to have an Earl as his personal assistant. I've tried, but it's like banging one's head against a stone wall. None of the Air Staff has flown anything more modern than a Bristol fighter and precious few of them even flew that. Park is all right. He'll listen to you sometimes. But he's too damn busy and there are shortages everywhere – no Brownings, no .303 ammunition, no damn aircraft come to that, and no sense or urgency anywhere.'

The discussion ranged on until eventually Kit and Dick were released. 'Come to Hatchett's.' Dick said to Kit. 'I'm meeting Carlow there. We've something to tell you.'

When they had made their way down the stairs into the panelled bar, Dick ordered pints. He had seemed to Kit all day to be suffering from a sort of suppressed excitement. As soon as Carlow, looking as cool and elegant as ever, entered the bar he jumped to his feet and took her hand. Then Kit saw the diamond and sapphire engagement ring glowing on her third finger. 'We're going to be married,' Dick said. 'I've persuaded her at last.' Suddenly he no longer appeared the supremely self-confident leading GR or the dashing fighter pilot but rather a small boy who has gained his prize he had thought always to be beyond his grasp.

For his part Kit's stomach felt as if it had turned over and dropped out of him. So that was that. Whatever slim and unrealistic hope he had had was gone. He gulped at his drink and swallowed hastily. 'Well, congratulations,' he said. And then, knowing he must say something more if only to cover his confusion and dismay: 'Here's to you both and many of the happiest landings.' He stumbled over his words as he hesitated and groped for them but they noticed nothing. Oblivious to their surroundings they were too taken up looking at each other.

Hatchett's was then a sort of unofficial RAF club and a gathering place for junior officers. The news flew about the bar, and in a few minutes other pilots were about them, some of them slapping Dick on the back, others ordering more pints.

'So you've been at Mrs Meddler's,' Carlow said when the crowd had thinned. 'What's she up to now?'

'Meddling,' Dick answered with a quick look at Carlow, and hurried on to tell Kit they had taken a flat in Half Moon Street which they had got at a knock-down rent because of the exodus from the city of those who anticipated bombing. He must come and see them there, they both said, and there was a spare room available whenever he wanted a bed in London.

And then it was time for him to catch his train to the north. He was lucky enough to find a corner seat and almost immediately fell asleep. It had, after all, been quite a day.

CHAPTER XXVI

Kit went through his advanced flying course with very little trouble, save one or two brushes with his instructor with whom he did not always see eye to eye and, being Kit, said so. He had also received a rocket which he knew to be correct for starting to aerobat under the prescribed height. 'Carelessness and inattention,' the instructor had said. 'And if you're not bloody careful it'll become over-confidence. That's when you'll kill yourself. I don't give a damn if you do but that aircraft cost King George VI a hell of a lot of money and there aren't too many of them.'

'He's a bit crusty this morning,' Kit remarked to a fellow-pupil who was about to take over the aircraft.

This happened towards the end of the course. It was that afternoon that a Miles Master appeared in the circuit and came in to land. It touched down in a distinctly unorthodox manner, bounced twice and, after settling with a bump and a bang, taxied in towards the tarmac. Kit was not entirely surprised when he saw the figure of Dai Evans emerging from the cockpit and striding towards the flight office.

Group Captain Evans was, Kit guessed, on one of his periodic freelance visits of inspection and assessment of pilot quality for which his name was already something of a byword amongst the training establishments. He was a law unto himself, they said, and no respecter of persons. At the age of forty-five he had flown both Hurricanes and Spitfires and joined convoy patrols to gain operational experience. The damage to the undercarriages of these valuable aircraft on his return to base and landing had, however, been such that someone had finally had the courage to stop this particular enterprise. But no one had as yet put an end to his one-man crusade to make the RAF into a modern fighting force. Earlier in the course he had come down to give a lecture to prospective fighter pilots, the opening words of which were: 'Throw away those infernal operational manuals and listen to me – ' The repercussions of this lecture, which had been repeated elsewhere, had gone the rounds of the flying schools and had even penetrated to Fighter Command where certain senior officers had called for him to be silenced. But it was difficult to make an example of a man with a score of fifty enemy aircraft shot down in the last war, who sported a DSO, an MC and bar, a DFC and a Croix de Guerre, and who was, moreover, said to have friends in high places.

Spotting Kit, he walked over to him. 'Now then young feller,' he said. 'Not thrown out yet? Still want to be a fighter pilot?'

'More than anything else,' Kit said.

'That's the stuff. Get in close and clobber 'em, that's the thing. Balloon's going up any minute now, though no one believes it except myself. I'll see what I can do if it needs doing.'

Later, when discussing pupils' records with the chief instructor, he brought up Kit's name.

'One of the best I've had,' the chief instructor said. 'He can make an aircraft talk. But – '

'But what?'

'Like a lot of these chaps who are naturals he could be in grave danger of over-confidence. That's when you kill yourself, as you know. They think they've got it buttoned up and they haven't. Also he's headstrong and a bit free of his opinions.'

'Aren't we all? Anyway, you'll pass him for fighters?'

'Oh, yes. And I'll give him an above-average assessment. I might have made it exceptional but for what I've said.'

'Can he shoot?'

'I don't know. We don't teach shooting here. He'll have to pick that up on a squadron.'

'Christ! Where's he going?'

'I've had a word with the CO. We don't have the final say in postings, but we think he needs sitting on a bit. We're recommending him for 999 Squadron at Harbridge.'

'999 – that's Bare Arsed Barkley's station, isn't it?'

'That's right. Regimental as a button-stick, as we used to say. Now, what about a noggin?'

A week later Kit, new wings glowing above his left breast pocket, presented himself at Harbridge airfield in Lincolnshire and reported to his immediate superior, Squadron Leader Mostyn. Harbridge was a prewar airfield and the squadron leader was in his office in one of the permanent buildings. He was a large man with the build of the rugby forward he had once been, having played for the RAF. He had a face which was red all over, looking to Kit's rather apprehensive gaze like a highly polished ham.

Kit saluted and stood to attention. The squadron leader put down the pen with which he had been writing and stared coldly at him. 'I've read your file,' he said. 'You're assigned to B Flight. Flight Lieutenant Martin is your flight commander. Now listen to me carefully. On this station and in this squadron we regard newly-joined pilot officers as the lowest form of animal life both in the mess and in the air. You'll observe a proper standard of turn-out on the ground on all occasions. In the air obedience to instructions must be absolute. There'll be no split-arsing around – '

Another Angus Robarts, Kit thought. What have I done to deserve this? But the squadron commander was continuing. 'The station commander will address you and the other newly-joined officers in the billiards room after lunch. Get that?'

'Yes sir. Sir – I've never shot my guns. I was told to report this. Do we get any shooting practice?'

'You get it when I say so and when I'm satisfied with the reports on your flying. You talk too much. Now, get out.'

Group Captain "Bare Arse" Barkley was a tall, spare austere-looking man with a heavy moustache who had served with the Brigade of Guards in the last war before transferring to the RFC. He wore campaign medals below his wings but no decorations and had gained the name by which he was known throughout the Service by jumping from a balloon and leaving most of his trousers behind. He commanded two airfields, the fighter station where 999 was based and another adjacent to it, which housed Whitley heavy bombers. Barkley made no secret of the fact that both his interests and his preferences lay with the bombers, nor did he disguise his general feeling towards fighters. They were, he thought and said, an anachronism, and he had been known to refer to their pilots as pampered playboys. The fact that it was a fighter pilot in the last war who had witnessed his descent and had conferred on him his nickname did not increase his fondness for the breed.

There were three other newly-joined pilot officers who, along with Kit, sprang to attention when he entered the billiards room. One of them had a merry eye and fair hair grown longer than the conventional cut. Like Kit he had been allotted to B Flight and had introduced himself as Tony Menzies. 'Here we go,' he whispered to Kit. 'Sermon number one. I've heard all about it. Bare Arsed's balls they call it.'

Group Captain Barkley stared at them one by one as if searching for any irregularlity in dress, his gaze lingering for a moment on Menzies' hair. Then he began: 'I won't detain

206

you long – gentlemen,' he said with a faint but unmistakable hesitation on the last word. 'First I want to emphasise to you all that on this station I will not tolerate slackness of any sort. You are joining a fighter squadron. The air fighting in this war, if it comes at all, will be fighters against bombers. There will be no dog-fights. If any of you young men are nourishing ridiculous dreams of becoming aces and seeing your names in the papers as happened the last time, I advise you to forget them. The Air Ministry has set its face against personal scoring and the ace system which was invented by the French anyway. It is a valid tenet of modern war, gentlemen, that the bomber must get through. Therefore the air fighting will be more in the nature of a fleet action with you, like destroyers, carrying out concerted attacks on the enemy bomber fleet. Our bombers have power-operated turrets and can look after themselves. Fortunately for you the Germans have not. If you do sight them you will carry out formation attacks. These formation attacks are in your operational manuals. They must be studied and practised. On this station we go by the book. Our drill in the air will be carried out with the precision of the Brigade of Guards on the parade ground. I'll have no Prince Ruperting about or cavalry of the air nonsense here. Order, discipline, obedience, gentlemen, let these be your watchwords. I trust I have made myself clear. Any questions?' It was obvious from his attitude that he neither wanted nor expected questions, but the fair-haired Menzies was not to be put off and he spoke up.

'You say, sir,' he said. 'That there won't be any dog-fights. Why is that?'

'If you had learnt anything on that course you have just left you would know that the turning circle of the modern monoplane fighter combined with the positive G it sets up precludes anything of the sort. In any event, let me remind you we are fighting the Germans not the French. They have no bases near enough to allow their fighters to operate over this country.'

'What if they over-run Belgium, sir?' Kit, emboldened by Menzies' questions, asked.

'The Maginot line and the French Army will see that they don't. I repeat, gentlemen, this will be a bombers' war. Look

to your flying. And as to you – ' he glared at Menzies ' – see
that your hair is a regulation length before I meet you again.'
He turned and strode out of the room.

'Bloody old ass,' Menzies said to Kit. 'Regulation length!
What the hell's that?'

'Short back and sides, old boy,' Kit said. 'Let's go down
and have a look at these aircraft – if we're allowed to.'

999 Squadron was equipped with Hurricanes. Less glamorous
than the Spitfire, it was nevertheless a trusty war-horse and
a stable gun-platform. Down at dispersal Flight Lieutenant
Martin explained its cockpit layout and handling characteristics to Kit, and the following day, after giving him a grilling
on the ground to make sure he understood them, he sent him
off on his first flight in a front-line fighter. He found the
Hurricanes heavier on the controls than he had expected but
the acceleration and rate of climb were exhilerating after the
training aircraft, as were the sense of power and the feeling
of being able to take on anything given by the eight canvas-
covered gun ports in the wings. His time up, he made his
approach, came in over the fence and dropped down for a
three-point landing on the grass without encountering any
trouble or problems.

'That seems okay,' Flight Lieutenant Martin, who was
waiting for him when he taxied in, said without a smile. He
was a silent and uncommunicative man, as indeed were most
of the other pilots of 999, who gave the general impression of
being subdued and unwanted castaways, castaways moreover
ruled by the heavy and unforgiving hand of Squadron Leader
Tom Mostyn, their tribal chief.

But Martin's report on Kit's flying must have satisfied
Mostyn, for a few days later he was sent off to carry out firing
practice. This consisted of firing a few rounds at a ground
target and a few more at a towed drogue. It hardly fitted him
for fighting in the air but at least he had felt the aircraft pause
and judder under the discharge of the guns and had peered
through the reflector sight when aligning it on a target. That
having been done, battle practice under the squadron leader
began.

Day after day the new pilots and those not on readiness took off to form up in vics of three, climb up to fifteen thousand feet and there carry out 'fighting area' attacks. The sequence of each attack had to be memorised accurately from the handbook, so that when Mostyn's voice came over the crackling RT with its command, 'Fighting Area Attack Number – GO!' every pilot knew exactly what he had to do and what position he should take up in the complicated manoeuvres that followed. Mostyn appeared to have eyes in the back of his head and it was woe betide any pilot who lost his position, missed his turn or failed to take his correct place. On landing, this unfortunate would be subjected to one of Mostyn's renowned bawlings-out in front of his fellows as soon as he stepped from his aircraft. It did not make for a happy squadron.

'It's all balls,' Tony Menzies said to Kit over a pint in the local pub one evening after he had been at the receiving end of one of these tirades. By now they had both been passed as operational and were taking part in patrols and the occasional scramble after suspected enemy aircraft, all of which had so far proved to be false alarms. 'My brother's in Sailor Malan's squadron at Biggin Hill and he says he's chucked the rule book out of the window. They fly in pairs. That's what the Jerries do, too, apparently.'

'Do you know who I mean by Dai Evans?'

'Old "Get-in-close-and-clobber-'em"? Of course. Everyone knows him. He may be old and mad but my brother says he's got the right ideas.'

'He's a great friend of someone who is in the Air Ministry and she was very good to me when I got into a spot of trouble racing. He'd bust a gut if he knew what was happening here.'

'He'd be right, too,' Menzies said gloomily, burying his head in his drink. 'None of this squadron has ever seen an enemy aircraft, let alone fired his guns in anger. I wonder what will happen when we do.'

In the event he was to find out soon enough.

A few days later they were scrambled to intercept two enemy aircraft reported as Dorniers by the Observer Corps. They formed up in the usual vics of three, the squadron commander leading, and climbed out across the flat fenlands to their intercept course and height. Crossing the coast, they headed out to sea and then turned north as the controller gave Mostyn his instructions. The sky remained empty. The sea below was slate grey flecked with white. There were wisps of cloud about. Yet another interminable and fruitless scramble, Kit thought.

And then, suddenly, he saw them – two Dornier 1s, their pencil-like fuselages unmistakable, flying line abreast, ahead and a thousand feet below, making their way back to the Fatherland. A thrill of excitement ran across the nape of Kit's neck as he moved the firing button on the joystick from 'safe' to 'fire'. Here, at last, was real war. At the same instant the RT crackled in his ears. The squadron commander had seen them too. 'Engage starboard enemy aircraft,' came in his measured tones. 'Number 5 attack. Form line astern – GO!'

Behind him the vics of three began to sort themselves out into the required fighting formation. Oblivious of the stately pavane being enacted behind them, the Dorniers flew on.

We'll mess it up, Kit said to himself. In a minute they'll be out of range or in the cloud. Then the leading aircraft peeled off in an attacking dive followed by another and another at the prescribed intervals.

From his position towards the end of the line Kit could see the rear gunner of the unengaged Dornier pouring an accurate fire at the assailants of his fellow. With nothing to distract his aim he was scoring hits. One Hurricane broke away in a spin with a trail of smoke coming from his fuselage. All Dai Evans' teaching and talking flashed through Kit's mind. Here, beneath his very eyes, was a practical demonstration of the truth of what Evans had so often said. This stupid form of attack was going to get them into desperate trouble unless someone did something. With Kit to think was to act. To hell with this for a carry on, he said to himself, peeled off and dived on the unengaged Dornier.

It was too easy, a 'piece of cake' in later RAF slang. There was no opposition. The rear gunner, concentrating on protecting his companion, never saw him until it was too late and he could not swing his gun against the slipstream in time to bring it to bear.

Kit had the best gun-platform of the war underneath him. The Hurricane was rock steady in its dive. 'Get in close and clobber 'em' rang in his ears. He concentrated on the reflector sight as the Dornier's silhouette jumped into it and grew larger. Then he pressed the firing button and the guns chattered out. At that range he couldn't miss and he saw his tracer hosing along the Dornier's fuselage. Pieces flew from the port engine and flames began to lick across the cockpit cowling. Out of control, the Dornier dived in a long arc towards the sea, pieces breaking from it as it went. Following it down Kit saw it hit the surface with a tremendous splash and go under. He had scored! He pulled up and did a victory roll. Then he looked about him.

The sky was empty of aircraft. He was alone. The others had disappeared as had the second Dornier. He was by no means certain where he was, as he set course as best he could for home. After a few minutes he was relieved to pick up Norwich Cathedral, one of his landmarks, and soon the airfield was beneath him. When he taxied to dispersal the squadron commander was waiting for him with Martin and one or two others of the pilots standing around him. 'What the hell did you think you were doing?' Mostyn demanded.

'Shooting down a Dornier – sir,' Kit answered, pulling off his helmet.

'You heard my orders for a line attack on the starboard aircraft and you deliberately disobeyed them.'

'He was a sitting duck and I clobbered him,' Kit said. 'Who got the other?'

There was silence for a moment and then Tony Menzies who was with the little group of pilots, spoke up. 'We lost him,' he said. 'He got away into cloud. Your fellow got Teddy Franks before you nailed him. I can confirm Massiter's claim, sir. I saw the Dornier go in.'

Mostyn turned to stare at him. 'That's enough,' he barked. 'I didn't ask you to speak. Wait till you're spoken to. As for you – ' he addressed Kit again ' – you're on the mat before the CO tomorrow. Report to the station adjutant.' He walked away.

Next morning Kit presented himself at the office of the station commander's adjutant. He was a dug-out from the last war, wearing, like Clare, the khaki RFC wings with, Kit noticed, the purple and white ribbon of the MC beneath

them. Like most of the officers on that station he wore a
subdued air. Giving Kit a brief smile he rose from his desk,
went to a door behind him and knocked on it. 'Pilot Officer
Massiter, sir,' he said, and then, underneath his breath, to
Kit, 'Good luck.'

Kit snapped into his smartest salute and stood to attention.
'Cap off,' hissed the adjutant behind him. Snatching it from
his head Kit tucked it under his left arm and met the full
glare of the station commander's eyes from behind a broad
desk littered with paper.

'It has been reported to me,' Group Captain Barkley said,
'that you disobeyed orders, left formation and went off on a
sortie of your own. Have you anything to say?'

'I shot down a Dornier, sir. It's the squadron's first kill, I
believe. The other escaped.'

Barkley's eyes grew angrier and his cheeks redder above
the heavy moustache. Kit afterwards told Tony Menzies he
thought the old man might have a stroke and so get him off
the hook, but he didn't. 'I warned you when you joined
this station,' Barkley continued, biting out his words, 'that
discipline in the air is as important as on the ground and
that I would tolerate no Prince Ruperting about. You have
disregarded that warning. You strike me, Massiter, as being
the same type as some I knew in the last war who thought
they could win it by themselves and get their names in the
press doing it. I don't want you or anyone like you on my
station. You'll be granted seven days' leave pending posting.
I am also recording a reprimand against your name.
Understand?'

'Yes, sir. I must have been wrong, sir. I thought our job
was to destroy enemy aircraft. Pilot Officer Menzies saw
the Dornier go in. Do I get credit for one enemy aircraft
confirmed?'

The group captain looked down at his desk. On it was a
message from the Observer Corps verifying a Dornier down
in the sea off the coast. The bearings and times coincided
with the claim in Kit's combat report. A confirmation from
another pilot also engaged might just be disregarded. This
could not. 'That will be allowed,' Barkley said coldly and
then, because the boy standing before him seemed to him to

212

embody everything he disliked in fighter pilots, their impatience with authority, their arrogance and their casual contempt for the rest of the Service, he added: 'If you wish to continue in the RAF I suggest you learn to adapt yourself to Service discipline. As it is you're no use to anyone, least of all to me. I want you off the station by tonight. Leave your address with the adjutant.'

Outside Tony Menzies was waiting for him. 'My God!' he said when Kit had told him what had happened. 'Make the squadron's first kill and instead of getting a mention or a medal you're reprimanded and posted. What a squadron! What a bloody station! I wish they'd post me. It's my day off. Let's go and get sloshed.'

'I wonder where they'll post me,' Kit said gloomily as they sat over their pints in the local. 'Army co-operation more than likely. Flying Lysanders – Christ!'

'Look,' Menzies said. 'You told me you knew someone in the Air Ministry. I should get hold of him as soon as you can and tell him your side of the story. He may be able to do something. People who don't know the truth might think you've put up an immortal black like turning back when you shouldn't or something. It's all so bloody unfair, but your pal might help.'

'I shot down that Dornier, didn't I? They can't change that.'

'They can do almost anything if they want to,' Menzies said. 'My brother's a regular and that's what he says. That's why I think you should beat off to your friend in the Air Ministry as soon as you can. Let's have another of these.'

'And another and another and drink to the damnation of old Bare Arse and all old bastards like him.'

Meanwhile in his office Barkley was writing his report of the incident. There were some elements of fairness in him and Massiter *had* shot down that Dornier giving first blood to the fighter squadron. Even though he heartily disliked the whole lot of them and wished them off his station nevertheless some credit should be allowed for the kill unorthodox though it had been. He picked up his pen. *The destruction of the Dornier 1 has been confirmed by Pilot Officer Menzies*, he wrote. *And by the*

213

Observer Corps. I have also to add that Pilot Officer Massiter's flying assessments as confirmed by his squadron commander are above average. He is reported as being one of the best pilots in the squadron. He is, however, one of the most insubordinate.

CHAPTER XXVII

Later that afternoon Kit sat in the MG driving towards London. His head felt rather like a balloon from all the beer he had drunk at lunchtime but the fresh air whistling round his ears in the open car was rapidly driving the fumes away. He had given his address as Half Moon Street for he now had no other base. Save a few rooms in one wing occupied in rather a dazed fashion by the old Earl who could not understand why he was denied his simple pleasure of roaming its galleries and corridors, Brackley Place was shut up pending requisitioning for military use. The devoted Wilkins who had stayed to look after the old man sustained him with copious draughts of cold tea about whose taste and quality he still complained bitterly. Kit had had a letter from Wilkins enclosing a card from the Earl. He was failing fast, Wilkins said. The card, written in a spiky but surprisingly firm hand, ran:

Dear boy,
When this wretched war is over remember the only three rules worth observing in life. Never lay the odds, never travel entirely sober and never hunt south of the Thames.
                                                                    M.
P.S. The first is the most important.

Kit chuckled as he remembered the card now tucked into a breast pocket of his tunic as a sort of talisman. He was not likely to see the old man again. Between them their expectation of life was a short one. The Earl at eighty-nine was not likely to last much longer, and according to the statistics of the last war a fighter pilot's expected span was a maximum of three weeks – as Barkley had been accustomed to point out in no uncertain terms when fulminating in the mess on their conduct or lack of it. Kit had developed a fondness for the old man and it occurred to him that there might be something in what Carlow had said, that Clare was not caring for him as he should. But Clare was engrossed in his job and working the clock round in London. Tony Menzies was right; he would have to see Clare, though he rather dreaded the meeting for Clare might think he had let him down. On the other hand, hadn't he done just what Clare and Dai Evans had been preaching – got in close and clobbered one? But he had not seen Clare since that luncheon party at Beatrice's and it was possible that Clare might have become more conscious of good order and military discipline and of his rank and his coming title since rejoining the Service.

Certainly there was one who was very conscious of Kit's connection with the Marchesters and all it implied, and who had become much more interested in him as a result. That was his brother Hugo, now a subaltern in the 50th Lancers, Lord Nelson's Own. Hugo had noted Kit's success on one of Lord Marchester's horses and had been prompt in writing to congratulate him. He had made it his business thereafter to keep in touch and had written and telephoned Kit on the squadron. He had, in fact, telephoned that afternoon before Kit left, to say he would be in London on forty-eight hours' leave and could they meet. Kit, who knew very well that Hugo's eyes were fixed firmly on the main chance and that he was probably fishing for more information about whether he had kept up the Marchester connection, had somewhat reluctantly agreed to have a drink with him that evening in the Berkeley Buttery.

Parking the MG in Half Moon Street outside the flat, he let himself in with the key they had given him. The flat was empty, and after he had bathed and changed into his best uniform he scribbled a note telling of his arrival which he left propped on the mantelpiece and then walked along to the Berkeley.

The Berkeley Buttery at that time performed much the same function for junior officers in the Cavalry as did Hatchetts for the RAF. Kit had arrived early and had time for a quick look at the racing results in the *Evening Standard* before Hugo came in accompanied by another subaltern in his regiment. Both were resplendent in full-skirted cavalry tunics with slashed pockets, highly polished Sam Brownes without cross-belts as decreed by Lord Gort, and the dark blue trousers which it was the special privilege of the 50th Lancers to wear.

'Why the blue dungarees?' Kit said, after Hugo had introduced his companion as Charles Roughty.

Hugo assumed his most severe expression. 'As a member of the very junior Service I don't suppose you could be expected to know,' he said. 'But the great Lord Nelson never forgot the assistance given him at the siege of Calvi by a squadron of the 50th Lancers. He secured permission for the regiment to wear naval trousers as a mark of distinction for ever more.'

'In that case why haven't they got bell-bottoms?' Kit enquired. He rather enjoyed needling Hugo.

'He also,' Hugo continued, ignoring the question and the interruption, 'granted them the privilege of drinking the royal toast sitting down in accordance with naval custom.'

'Don't you believe a word of it,' put in his companion. 'He had to let them do it. They'd all drunk so much of his rum they were too tight to stand up!'

When Hugo had gone up to Oxford that autumn one of the first visitors to his rooms in Meadow Buildings had been Charles Roughty. 'Look here, Hugo,' he had said. 'We must do something about this damned war.'

'I know. But what can we do? Didn't I see somewhere that everyone now has to go through the ranks?'

'Ranks? No fear of that. I've had a word with my father. He wanted me to go to the Woodentops but I've talked him out of that, thank goodness. The colonel of the 50th Lancers is an old flame of my mother's. She's had him to tea and

216

spoken to him and he's put both our names on the Supplementary Reserve. That takes care of that. None of that nonsense about ranks for us.'

'What happens next?'

'We're supposed to have an interview before we're finally taken on. Only a formality. We'll drive over to Colchester next week.'

At Colchester they had been interviewed by a languid captain who informed them he was just off to play tennis. There was a racket under his arm and he was immaculately turned out in a double-breasted blue blazer with regimental buttons, spotless flannels and beneath them a pair of handmade buckskin tennis shoes. He had a silky moustache, very white teeth and was enveloped in an air of condescension. 'At the University, are you?' he said. 'Which one? Oh, yes, Oxford. Of course. How many horses have you brought up with you and who do you hunt with?' Apparently satisfied with their answers to these questions, he stared out of the window at the Alvis Speed Twenty which was drawn up outside waiting to convey him to his tennis party. 'By the way,' he went on, turning back to the room. 'School? Eton, I suppose. That's all right, then.' He reached for his racket and stood up.

'Are you still horsed, or is it all tanks now?' Charles Roughty asked him.

'Tanks,' the languid captain said. 'Tanks? Nasty smelly things. I've never been inside one and I intend to take damn good care I never am. Good day to you.'

Now here they both were, fully fledged cornets of horse and with about as much idea of modern warfare as their predecessors who had helped Nelson storm Calvi.

'I say,' Roughty went on, looking at Kit's wings. 'Fighter pilot, aren't you? Rather a lark, that. Shot down anything yet?'

'Well, actually yes,' Kit said. 'I got a Dornier yesterday.'

'Good Lord. How spiffing. This calls for a celebration. Champagne cocktails all round.'

No such plebeian drinks as pints for the 50th Lancers, Kit thought as he wondered if his pocket would stretch to the price of the round when his turn came.

217

'Did you indeed,' Hugo said. 'Quite a hero. He's a pal of old Marchester's too,' he said to Roughty. 'Rode a winner for him not so long ago. How is the old boy?'

'Shaky enough, I gather,' Kit said.

'Heard from the Sir recently?' Hugo then asked him.

'No,' Kit said. He didn't know how much Hugo knew of his banishment though he guessed that Hugo, being Hugo, had probably found out everything. He had no intention of revealing his more recent troubles with Barkley to his brother for he had no doubt that they would be instantly conveyed back to Dunlay, clothed in some decidedly spurious sympathy. All at once it came to him that he didn't really like Hugo very much.

'He's been here,' Hugo went on. 'At the Savoy, passing through on his way to look after one of his far-flung investments.'

'He wasn't in touch,' Kit said.

'My brother's the heir,' Hugo told Roughty smiling over his glass but Kit noticed that his eyes weren't smiling. 'Isn't he the lucky bastard?'

Was it, Kit wondered, his imagination or did Hugo put a strange emphasis on that last word? But Hugo was going on, 'Always provided, of course,' he said, so softly that Roughty could scarcely have heard the words but they carried to Kit as they were meant to, 'that he survives.' Once more he tilted his glass towards Kit with another of his knowing, mocking smiles.

Just then two chattering girls came in and joined them. 'Hugo, darling,' one of them greeted him rapturously. 'Champagne cocktails, how gorgeous. Did you see my picture in last week's *Tatler?*'

The four of them had a dinner date. There was nothing further for Kit here; these were not his circles and he had other things on his mind. He made his apologies, took his leave and escaped into blacked-out Piccadilly.

There was no one he knew in Hatchetts. It was the same in Shepherd's, another RAF haunt. Here he went into the telephone booth concealed in the sedan chair and rang the flat. There was no reply, so he ate a solitary dinner and, once more at a loose end, wondered what he would do to kill the evening. It was then that he recalled Beatrice and her invitation to visit her once he had his wings. Brook Street was just around the corner. He walked along to 14A and rang the bell.

A prim maid in uniform whom he remembered from the luncheon party answered the door. 'Madam is unavailable,' she said with a sniff as she let him in. 'I'll tell her you have called. Who shall I say?'

He gave her his name, and in a minute or two she returned. 'Madam is in her bath, and says will you kindly wait here,' she said and ushered him into the first floor drawing-room.

The black-out curtains were drawn but the lights gleamed behind the bibelots in the glass-fronted alcoves and over the pictures on the walls. The well-stocked drink tray was on the table in the window; *The Tatler*, *The Sketch* and *The Illustrated Sporting and Dramatic News* were neatly stacked on a sofa table. Kit wandered about, his feet sinking into the thick pile of the carpet. Here were comfort and luxury indeed, he thought, after the spartan discomforts of the mess under Barkley's rigid rule. He picked up *The Tatler* and leafed through its pages looking for the picture of Hugo's girl. There was – Lady Caroline Sturt at a smart society wedding. Hugo's girlfriends would, of course, be drawn only from the best people.

The door to the drawing room had been left ajar, as had another across the landing. From beyond this came faint sounds of splashing. Then a voice he recognised as Beatrice's called: 'Have you got those wings up yet, Master Who?'

'Yes. I'm a pilot at last.'

'Then tell Mullins to bring up a bottle of champagne. We must celebrate, mustn't we?'

'Er – how do I get hold of her?'

'Ring for her, you goose.'

There was a bell push beside the fireplace. When he had pressed it Mullins reappeared, accepted his request and departed. She was back very shortly, carrying a salver on which was a bottle of champagne in an ice-bucket. She put it down, looked at him disapprovingly and went out. She made as if to shut the door and then changed her mind, leaving it open.

'Has that fool Mullins brought up the fizz?' came Beatrice's voice again.

'It's here. In an ice bucket. All complete.'

'Well then, bring it in.'

Kit picked up the salver, crossed the landing and pushed the farther door open. He was in a very feminine bedroom. There were soft lights, a double bed with a pink eiderdown and a pink quilted headboard. White sheepskin rugs surrounded it. Beside a white bow-fronted dressing table picked out in gold and laden with gold-topped cosmetic bottles another door stood open. From beyond it came more sounds of splashing. 'What are you hanging about for?' Beatrice's voice came again. 'Come on in and bring the bottle.'

Kit picked up the salver and went through the door. Once inside he stopped in his tracks and the salver almost fell from his hands.

Beatrice was lying in a sunken bath. There was a rope of pearls round her neck. Her hands were arched lazily behind her head tautening a pair of perfect breasts. She smiled up at him.

'You – you said I could come and see you – ' Kit managed to stutter out.

'Well now, so I did. And now you see me, don't you, all of me?' Her tongue darted in and out of her lips in the way she had. 'Open the champagne. I like a glass in my bath.'

Kit's fingers were all thumbs as he fumbled with the wire. At last it was free. The cork flew out with a bang and the wine gushed into the glasses. 'That is *not* the way to open a bottle of champagne,' Beatrice said. 'Didn't your father's butler ever teach you?'

'Er, no, as a matter of fact he didn't,' Kit said, handing her the glass. All at once, ridiculously, he thought of Hugo. Hugo would know how to open a bottle of champagne. Hugo would handle this better. God, she hadn't a stitch on except those pearls. God, she did look smashing.

Beatrice sipped from the glass, looking over the rim at him and smiling a secretive, self-assured, mocking smile. Then she put the glass down, reached out an arm and twitched a huge, creamy bathtowel from its rail. In one fluid movement she was out of the bath and standing naked before him. The water glistened in little shiny globules on her skin. She flicked the towel towards him. 'Don't stand there gawping,' she said. 'Dry my back.' She turned and looked over her shoulder at him. Hesitatingly he advanced towards her. 'Hurry up, I won't break, you know,' she said.

A little later, wrapping the towel round her, she turned to face him. 'So, wings,' she said, running her fingers across them. 'New, gleaming, silver wings for Master Who to fly away, but where to, I wonder. Fighter pilot. Dear, dashing Master Who – and who'd have thought it. Shot down any Germans lately?'

'One. Yesterday.'

'Gracious. Battle for the warrior and woman for his ease. The warrior must claim his reward, mustn't he?' Her face was looking up at him; he could feel her breath on his lips, her hair brushed his cheek. Then skilled fingers were undoing the buttons of his tunic and, when it swung free, sliding it over his shoulders. One by one his clothes fell away from him.

He never quite knew how it happened but then they were together in the big bed and she was laughing, fondling him, stroking him and whispering to him. Things were happening to him that had never happened before. It was wonderful, a wildness and a delight.

Hours later he woke from a deep and satiated sleep. She was shaking him gently. 'Time to go now, Master Who,' she said softly in his ear.

'Master Who? Why do you always call me that?' he asked her sleepily.

'Ah, that's my secret, isn't it? Some day, Master Who, you'll know. Some day – '

London was asleep as Kit let himself out and walked slowly back to Half Moon Street. Once there he fell into bed and was asleep again in an instant. It was late when he woke, dressed and came into the living room of the flat.

Carlow was sitting in an armchair. A bottle of gin and a half-empty glass were on a table beside her. She was staring into space.

It was all so unlike her that Kit paused just inside the

221

door. She turned her head to look at him blankly, as if she was not seeing him.

'Is anything wrong?' he asked.

'Dick's gone.'

'Gone?'

'Gone for a burton, you silly bastard. Shot down. Disappeared. Missing, believed killed.'

Gradually, between sobs – 'You didn't know I had a heart, did you. Sometimes I wondered myself,' she said at one point. – the whole story came out. Dick had been promoted Flight Lieutenant and sent to take over a flight in one of the squadrons attached to the Advanced Air Striking Force covering the BEF in France. Though nothing was happening on the ground the air forces were in action probing each other's skills. His flight had engaged three Heinkels near the German-Luxembourg border. Dick had chased one of the Heinkels into cloud and neither had been seen again. The adjutant of his squadron had been back on leave. He had called last night to take her out to dinner and break the news before the bleak official intimation came.

'Missing. There's always a chance he's down somewhere safe,' Kit said, and knew as he said it that these were hollow words and little consolation.

'That's what they all say,' she said. 'But I've got a gut feeling. I know he's gone. Why did it have to happen to him? Remember how indestructible he was? Those awful falls he got racing, yet he always bounced back. He was such an alive man. And now he's gone. Damn this useless war. Damn. Damn. Do you want a drink? Get yourself a glass.'

Kit went to the kitchenette and fetched a glass. He didn't want a drink but he thought it better to keep her company. The level in the bottle was falling alarmingly.

'You were pretty late yourself last night,' she said when he returned. 'I didn't sleep much and I heard you come in. I saw the note you left. Where did you go? To one of Mrs M's soirées?'

Kit found himself blushing. 'Yes, well, sort of,' he said, hoping she would not notice his confusion. He need not have worried. Pouring herself another drink she was wrapped up in her grief. More to distract her than anything else, he said to her, 'Why does she always call me Master Who?'

Whether it was her own torment, the drink she had consumed, or impatience with the web of mystery Beatrice spun about everything that made Carlow say what she said next, she never knew. Later she rationalised it to herself by saying that he had to know some time and who better to tell him than someone he knew so well. 'Haven't you guessed?' she said. 'Christ, you are a silly bastard, like I said when you came in. That's what you are. You're not Massiter's son at all. You're a bastard and I'm a widow.' It was a brutal way of doing it and she knew it, but the words seemed to be ripped out of her as if, in hurting him, she was somehow solacing the wound of her own loss.

Kit sat for a moment, stunned. And yet, he told himself, subconsciously the knowledge had been growing on him. Now with Carlow's words, everything suddenly fell into place – his father's barely concealed dislike of him and open preference for Hugo, the hints and sidelong glances from Bob Ferris and the country people, his mother's protectiveness and Clare's interest in him from that very first moment at the Grange when he had profered him a drink and he had looked as if he had seen a ghost. Even Hugo's faint emphasis on the word 'bastard' last evening. Trust Hugo to have found out. 'Is this true?' he asked her, though in his heart he knew it was all too true, that he had been blind, that he should have guessed it long ago. Words he had once heard about unfaithfulness in marriage – 'the husband is always the last to know,' came into his mind. 'The bastard is always the last to know,' he told himself bitterly. He did not wait for her to answer but hurried on. 'Since you know so much, who is my father?' he said.

'Ask that bloody God Almighty Clare de Vaux. He knows everything. Why do you think he took you up and then got you in to the RAF? Him and his bloody passion for flying since he can't fly himself. He got Dick back in and now Dick's dead. He got you in and you'll be the next one to die. Oh, damn, what am I saying?' she hiccuped slightly. 'I'm not doing this very well, am I? I'm saying too much and too little. Where's that damn handkerchief?'

223

They stared bleakly at each other across the table, the bottle and the glasses. Then the shrilling of the telephone bell cut across the stillness. She sat on making no move to answer it. Kit picked up the receiver. It was Clare de Vaux phoning from the Air Ministry. 'I think you had better come and see me,' he said.

CHAPTER XXVIII

'Room Eighteen,' the porter on duty told Kit after his credentials and appointment had been checked. 'You're to go straight up.'

Kit took the lift, went along the corridor and knocked on the door of room eighteen. Inside Clare was sitting at a desk reading from a file. Kit came to attention and saluted. Clare nodded to a chair in front of the desk. 'Sit down,' he said. 'I knew Tubby Weston, your station adjutant, in the last show. I asked him to keep an eye on you so I know all about what happened. You shot down a Dornier, earned yourself a reprimand and are on leave pending posting. I ought to give you a rocket but I shan't. I know Barkley, too, or rather of him. But I'm beginning to wonder what's to be done with you.'

'Sir, before you go into that, may I ask you a question?'

'Certainly.'

'Who is my father?'

Clare leant back in his chair. 'So you've found out, have you,' he said. 'Perhaps it's just as well. It's a long story. These things are better discussed elsewhere than in these formal surroundings. We'll go out to lunch.' He stood up and reached for his hat.

A taxi took them to the Ritz where Clare led the way past the sandbags and downstairs to the Grill. Having ordered,

224

he watched the waiter pour the wine. Then he looked across the table at Kit. 'Your father,' he said, 'is a very fine man, though if he is still as he was when I knew him he would hate anyone saying anything like that about him. He was my closest friend in the last war. He shot down eighteen enemy aircraft and would have added to his score if he hadn't run into a patch of bad luck.'

'What is his name, what is my right name and where is he now?' Kit said doggedly. 'I think I have a right to be told.'

'Of course you have. His name is Stephen Raymond. He is or was a white hunter in Kenya. I imagine he is now serving in the Forces in one capacity or another.'

'What happened? Why did my mother marry Massiter?'

'As I've said, it's a long story and I don't know all of it. Your father was missing for months. He was posted as dead. Your mother came to believe he was dead. She married Massiter, I suppose, on some sort of rebound. Your father returned as it were from the dead and, you had better know this, he was court-martialled when he should not have been and was honourably acquitted. Then he went back to that place in Ireland where you all come from and seem to think there is nowhere like it – the Bay, isn't it called. They met again – ' Clare spread his hands leaving the rest unsaid.

'I should have been told and not left for everyone to make a fool of me.'

'Perhaps. That's not for me to say. I tried to help you. I felt I owed it to your father. It was better, I thought, to keep you away from Massiter, to try to give you a life of your own in the only way I could. Massiter, I think, never forgets or forgives.'

Kit felt as if he were a rudderless boat floating on an empty sea. He toyed with the stem of his wine glass trying to think. Then he stared down at the table cloth in silence. When his mind had cleared he knew beyond any doubt or hesitation what he had to do.

He must get away, right away, away from them all, from this man who sat across the table from him, from Hugo and his patronising airs, from Beatrice who would mock him still, from Sir Andrew Massiter, Bart., even from Carlow with whom he might now have had a chance at last.

'I'm waiting posting,' he said. 'Can you help? I want out of here as far away as I can go and as near to my father. And maybe see some real fighting. All we do is endless patrols over the coast and when you do engage the enemy you're on the mat. What about Kenya? That's where my father is, you say.'

Clare looked at the boy on the other side of the table with pity in his eyes. 'The South African Air Force has taken over Kenya,' he said. 'Our intelligence seems to think the stalemate on the western front will persist. There is certainly little sign of war here – ' Both their eyes roamed the room. Save for one or two senior officers in uniform the remainder were civilians eating and wining as if the Luftwaffe and Hitler's legions did not exist or were in truth equipped with paper aeroplanes and cardboard tanks. 'There are many in high places,' Clare murmured, 'who still favour a compromise peace and others who think we should be fighting the Russians. It is, indeed, as the Americans say, a phoney war. Perhaps you are right – '

'I want to start all over again,' Kit said. 'And I want to find my father – '

'The Desert Air Force then – ' Clare smiled suddenly. 'I'll see what I can do.'

When Clare said that he would see what he could do Kit knew from experience that it was as good as done. But there was something else. A posting abroad meant embarkation leave. Hugo had said that the Sir was away. The coast was clear. He could return to the Bay and see his mother and his friends there and look once more at the sea and the mountains and watch the changing colours of cloud and sky. But it was above all his mother whom he wanted, longed, to see again. He must tell her that he knew he wasn't the Sir's son, that it made no difference to what he felt for her, indeed it strengthened the bond between them and that he understood everything now.

'There'll be embarkation leave then,' he said. 'The Sir's away my brother said, looking after his money somewhere. I could go back to the Bay, for a day or two, see it once more before I go.'

Clare smiled again. 'You never forget it, do you, you people from there,' he said. 'Your father didn't either. I must go some day when this wretched war is over and see it for myself. Very well I'll have a warrant made out. You'll have to wear plain clothes but you know that. And when you find your father tell him we've met and that I haven't forgotten our old war.' He raised a hand and beckoned for the bill.

CHAPTER XXIX

A hacking jacket and grey flannel trousers sat oddly on Kit as he went through customs and emigration formalities and boarded the Rosslare steamer at Fishguard. There was no one he knew on the boat and he found an empty compartment in the little train that began to chug slowly across Southern Ireland. It was like emerging into a different world. If there had been few signs of wartime hustle in England there were none here. The walls of the compartment above his head bore daguerreotypes of Lisdoonvarna Spa and Parknasilla Hotel with Edwardian ladies and gentlemen grouped about them. In the tiny patchwork of green fields through which the train ambled on its leisurely way cattle grazed and hunters at grass threw up their lordly heads before galloping away, disturbed by the unaccustomed noise. The wayside stations, at every one of which the train stopped, were empty save for one elderly employee who gossiped with the guard while the few passengers were left to stare at the fading Paul Henry posters and broken chocolate vending machines.

A stillness enveloped the whole landscape. The thick, fleecy clouds scarcely moved against the pale sky. Always in the background, like a frieze, ran range upon range of purple mountains, Comeraghs, Galtees and Knockmealdowns, he remembered as he recited their names to himself. The only sign of human habitation was the occasional plume of smoke rising from some lonely farmstead. Accustomed as he had become to another over-populated island Kit could almost imagine he had gone back a century in time.

And he was in a fever of impatience. He tried to read a wartime paperback by a man called Hank Jansen which he had been told was hot stuff, but without success; he tried to sleep but sleep would not come. Eventually he played a game he had often done since childhood, imagining himself hunting across the country they passed through and picking the place in each fence where he would jump.

And then, at long last, the train heaved and chugged itself over the saddle between the hills that guarded the Bay. Immediately Kit was on his feet looking out of the window. The great sheet of water, shining in the evening sun and stretching away to the Atlantic between its ranges of gold and green and purple hills, lay before him. He drew a deep breath. The tang of turf smoke came through the window as he lowered it to reach for the brass handle and with it came the soft lilt of the country people's voices. He knew then how much he had missed it all and how glad he was to be back.

His mother was standing by the station entrance. 'Kit,' she cried as she saw him. 'Kit, how wonderful. We only just got your wire in time. Let me look at you. Have you got thin?'

'No, Mother,' Kit said laughing. 'We're not quite down to hard tack in England yet.'

They stood for a second or two after they had embraced, holding each other's arms. Their eyes met and something unspoken passed between them. In that instant both knew that what had been secret was now shared and would have to be acknowledged.

'Here's Larry,' his mother said, breaking the small moment of constraint. 'He'll take your case.'

'Glad to see ye, Master Kit,' Larry said extending his hand. 'Back again. Ye've been bombin' 'em, have ye?'

'No. Not yet,' Kit said smiling. 'And am I glad to be back, Larry. Gosh, it's good to see it all again.'

Outside was a smart dog-cart with a blood-weed between the shafts. Larry stowed his suitcase in the back and Kit climbed up beside his mother. 'Petrol shortage,' Babs said as she picked up the whip. 'We've gone back to the horse.'

228

'And where did you get this?' Kit nodded towards the blood-weed.

'A cast-off from Bob Ferris to save him from the knackers. There's no trade. You can't give bloodstock away. You'd buy something bred well enough to win the Derby for a tenner. This thing is my My Prince, believe it or not.'

The horse bent to his work at the touch of the whip and they trotted down the sleepy main street of Bellary. Instinctively as they left the little town Kit's eyes lifted to the bluff on which Bellary Court, the Raymonds' place, had once stood. The blackened ruin was all but obscured now by the summer foliage of the trees which had sprung up around it. But it reminded Kit of what he had come to do. 'How long have you got?' he heard his mother asking.

'Seven days. Five if you count the travelling,' he said. His eyes were still on the bluff as they turned along the shores of the Bay. 'That was the Raymonds' place, wasn't it?' he asked.

Beside him his mother sighed. 'Yes,' she said without lifting her eyes from the road. 'They were burnt out in the Troubles.'

Kit hesitated, and then, because he was never one to put off what had to be done, he said, 'Stephen Raymond was in the Flying Corps in the last war, wasn't he?'

'He was. He's in Kenya now. He left.'

'Mother, there's something I've got to talk to you about.'

Babs sighed again, still looking straight ahead. 'I guessed there would be,' she said. 'I think I knew it from the moment I saw you.' And then almost to herself, 'It had to come.'

'It's better that way,' Kit said gently, touching her arm. 'And don't worry, Mother. It makes no difference. It's all right.'

'I'm taking you to Knockbarton,' she said. 'Andrew is away but you can't come to Dunlay.'

'I don't think I want to much.'

'It would only cause terrible trouble when he found out. There's a room for you at home. We can talk there. Dads knows – well, everything.'

When they pulled up on the gravel sweep of Desmond Murtagh's house and went in through the open hall door they found Desmond out 'looking at a horse' and a maid brought them tea in the morning room.

Kit sat in the window seat and felt the warmth and friend-liness of the old place envelop him. It was all so unlike the stark gothic formalities of Dunlay. Behind him the lawn stretching down to the Bay; on the walls were sporting prints and racing pictures, most of them of Desmond in his heyday as a gentleman rider. Even the shabbiness of the faded chintzes enhanced the welcoming, lived-in air of it all. Babs, too, as she settled herself in her chair looked about her as if she had come home. She, after all, had been brought up here. She stared over her shoulder at the Bay. 'It's empty now,' she said. 'But last time there was a flotilla of destroyers here.'

'Something happened then, in that war, didn't it, Mother?' Kit said, and then the words came blurting out. 'Stephen Raymond is my father, isn't he?' There, it was in the open now, said, once and for all, never to be retracted.

Babs did not hesitate; she had had time to marshal her thoughts, to meet whatever he was going to say. 'So you know,' she said. 'Yes, he is. We grew up together. There was never anyone but Stephen for me. Before I tell you more I must know – do you hate me?'

'I'll never hate you. Surely you know that. Never, never. You've always been the sort of rock in my life. You stood between the Sir and me, I see that now. I'll always love you, Mums' – unconsciously he had gone back to the address of their childhood – 'whatever happens. But, Mums, why did you marry him?'

Babs took out her handkerchief and twisted it nervously between her fingers. 'It's a long and rather terrible story,' she said. 'Stephen's mother and elder sister were strong and domineering characters. They were envious of him, too, for they hated the thought that he'd get the place which they felt they would run far better. They bullied him unmercifully when he was growing up. I'm only telling this to you to try to explain things. I've always thought boys who are bullied by women when they are young become what they call nowa-days born losers. I never bullied, you, did I?'

'No, Mums, you helped us, both of us, all the time.'

'Then Stephen went to the war. He was in the Flying Corps until he was shot down and given up for lost. He was so unlucky, things never seemed to run right for him, even I came to believe it – '

'Look, Mums, if this is tearing you apart – '

'No. In a way it's a relief. I want you to know. All that time I was distracted with grief. Then Andrew came along. He thought, I suppose, that I'd add to his prestige, make sure of his position in the Bay. It's the one chink in his armour, perhaps, that longing for place and power. He had some sort of hold over Dads for some racing scandal. Dads was pretty wild when he was young, you know.' She gave a quiet smile and then went on. 'I didn't care what happened to me and Dads seemed to want it, so I married him. Then Stephen came back. Andrew was away. We became lovers. But I want you to know, Kit,' she said almost fiercely. 'You were conceived in happiness.'

'Why didn't you leave him?'

'Andrew? Wait. There's more you must know. After the Auxiliaries burnt Bellary Court – and it's an awful thing to say but I've always had a horror that Andrew found out about us and played a part in stirring things up against Stephen – anyway, afterwards Stephen disappeared for a while and then he was mixed up for a bit with Cosgrave and his lot. Everything went wrong for him. He was neither loyalist nor nationalist if you see what I mean. Some people here called him a traitor to his class. Then Cosgrave told him there was nothing further for him in this country with them. He went to Kenya.'

'And you stayed – '

'It was for you I stayed. Please understand, Kit. It was all so hopeless. I wanted you to have what we lost in that war and the Troubles – peace, security and a happy childhood. I thought I could make it for you here and I knew you loved the Bay. If I went with Stephen, Andrew would have found a way of ruining us all. And Stephen, I don't know, luck always seemed to run against him. I made the choice and I've had to live with it ever since. It seems in life if you try for the best you always end up with the worst.'

'But it's not the worst. You did give me happiness here. I thought at first I should have been told but I see now it was far better I shouldn't have learnt until now. Nothing has

231

changed between you and me, Mums. Nothing ever will. We belong to each other, and now we know it, that's all that matters – '

'Oh, my dearest Kit – ' she stretched out a hand to him and he went towards her.

The rest of the leave passed in a whirl. He rode out with Bob Ferris, examined the mares on Mikey O'Sullivan's stud in the company of their owner, who lectured him on the value of Ireland's neutrality though his final words rather contradicted what had gone before since he ended up by saying, 'Though I'm not tellin' ye I would mind havin' a crack at those nasty, murderin' Huns meself.' And he answered as best he could the questions Desmond plied him with on the merits and characteristics of the new eight-gun fighters.

'One forward firing Vickers, that's all we had on the old Brisfits,' Desmond said. 'Though we had a chap in the back cockpit with two Lewis. Heavy on the hand those old buses were too, they had the exact gliding angle of a brick. Ah, well, I wouldn't do much now with this wooden leg of mine. Now then, mustn't rattle on. No bore like an old war bore. What d'ye think of that four-year-old? Good mover, isn't he?'

And then, all too soon, he was back in the little train chugging once more towards reality.

There was one farewell he was determined to make and he had very little time to do it in. Because his day would be full seeing about his tropical kit and his movement order he rang the flat as soon as he got in. There was no reply and it was not until his third try later in the morning that he got through to her. Her voice was slurred when she answered and he feared she might have been at the bottle again. 'It's Kit,' he said.

'What do you want? I've been sleeping or at least I think I have.'

'Listen, Carlow,' he said. 'Have dinner with me tonight.'

'No. Why should I? I'm not much company these days anyway.'

'Balls. Come on, Carlow, remember those *crêpes suzette*.'

Suddenly she laughed. It was the same quick, lively, instantaneous laugh which had always entranced him. 'You might have something there,' she said. 'Where do they make them?' Her voice was clearing as if she were beginning to shake herself out of whatever black cloud of gin and grief and torment that had overtaken her.

'What about the Ritz?'

'Going it a bit, aren't you?'

'I've saved up. Besides, you see,' Kit paused awkwardly. 'We mightn't see each other – I mean, look, I am on sort of embarkation leave.'

'Oh, damn you, another one. Off to the wars. All right, Kit, you win. Where'll we meet?'

'I'll come and get you.'

He was a little afraid that she might have started on the gin again by the time he had changed back into uniform, but his fears were groundless. To all appearances she was the old Carlow, slim and smart with that go-to-hell look back in her eyes. She was wearing a print frock belted at the waist, the auburn hair had been brushed back and there was fresh scarlet lipstick on her mouth. 'Running repairs done and war paint on and all for you,' she said lightly as she took a cigarette and offered him one. As always the very sight of her, the way she looked and moved, made him catch his breath and it wasn't, he told himself, until you glanced again at her eyes that you saw the hurt behind them. 'Help yourself to a drink,' she went on. 'And get me one – a small one,' and she laughed.

He handed her the glass and their fingers touched. An electric thrill ran through him. She met his eyes and looked away. 'Let's get one thing straight at the outset,' she said. 'I'm not going to bed with you.'

'That wasn't what I'd planned,' he said quietly.

'Well if that's out of the way,' she stood up and smoothed down her skirt.

'No,' Kit said, meeting his challenges head on as was his custom. 'It's not quite out of the way since you've brought it up. There's something in it. Of course I want to sleep with you. I'm in love with you. I always have been since that first time I saw you at Malloran Park I think, and I always will be.'

233

Their eyes met again. 'Oh, Kit,' she said. 'You are a dear fool. It's all so hopeless with this bloody war. Why – oh, hell, I shall cry again in a minute. Not good for the image of a tough bitch of a lady rider, is it? I think it's time we went to get those *crêpes suzette*.'

Kit had reserved a table in the Grill and in due course the components of that fancy pudding were wheeled to them on a trolley attended by its acolytes. The flames were lit and spurted, curacao and brandy poured, the pancake spread and sizzled. She watched the whole ceremony, laughter in her eyes at its absurdity. '*Bon souper, bon gîte et le reste*,' she murmured. 'That's what the old man said, isn't it? Oh, Kit, I'm sorry I'm so mean to you.' She stretched out a hand and her long, cool fingers covered his. 'I'm a sort of one-man girl, I suppose, not like that slut Beatrice.' She looked at him mischievously and he dropped his eyes to his plate.

'Ah, ha,' she said. '*Touché* or I'm not mistaken. Did the old man teach you that piece of French too? And was *le reste* restful?'

'How is the old man?' Kit said, desperately trying to change the subject.

'Dead. Didn't you know? Fell off the perch a day or so back. It was in *The Times* and an obituary.'

'I don't read *The Times*. *Sporting Life* and Jane in the *Mirror* are more my mark. So Clare is now Lord Marchester.'

'A belted Earl. Why are Earls always belted?'

'Damned if I know. I wonder what'll happen to the horses.'

'He'll sell what's left of them and go out of racing with a happy smile, and Angus will have lost another good owner.'

'The stable is closed, someone told me, and Angus is back in the remounts.'

'Let's have another drink. This time I pay. Where are you bound for? Can't say, I suppose.'

'No. Careless talk and all that. I'll write or try to – if you'd like it.'

'Of course I'd like it. Didn't we say, the three of us, we'd always keep in touch? Oh damn, everything I do or say seems to bring him back. But I'm going to give up the flat. I'll try to get into the WAAF, if they'll have me. I can drive a car.'

'None better,' Kit said as the tables began to clear. 'So this is it, isn't it? It was fun with you and Dick – while it lasted.'

'You've been around a lot, haven't you, Kit, since that father of yours kicked you out.'

'He's not my father,' Kit said fiercely. 'You knew it. Everyone knew it but me. That's why I'm going to find the man who is.'

'We're all looking for something,' she said. 'And when we find it we lose it again or we wish our lives away or, oh, the hell with it.'

They left the table and walked in silence back to the flat. As they turned to their separate rooms, 'Perhaps it's better not to write,' she said quietly. 'Find someone else. Find 'em, fool 'em and forget 'em. Let that be your motto.'

'I've heard that before with all the ruder words.'

'So have I. But, Kit dear, don't be a one-girl man. You'll find 'em all right the way you look in that uniform and with those bloody wings on your chest. But, dear Kit, you must forget me.'

'I doubt if I ever can.'

'Well then, have a damn good try. And for Christ's sake, Kit – come back.' She kissed him and was gone.

He sailed from Liverpool the day Hitler's armoured forces crossed the Meuse and struck deep into France.

Part 4

STEPHEN 2

CHAPTER XXX

It was Job Hannaford who was on the other end of the telephone when Stephen went out to the box near the main entrance of the club. 'Stephen, lad,' he said. 'I've been looking for you. I'm at the Norfolk. Come on over.'

'Like old times, ain't it,' he said half an hour later as they sat in his cottage, a bottle of whisky between them on the table. Then he chuckled. 'It seems you were born to trouble, lad, as the sparks fly upwards.'

'Don't you start getting on to me, Job,' Stephen said. 'I've just knocked someone down in Muthaiga for a few remarks he made.'

'And who might that have been?'

'Gervase Winthrop.'

Job chuckled again. ' "A lusus naturae or a wrong 'un by nature", as Mr Jorrocks said, that's what our Mr Winthrop is. When you pick 'em you do pick 'em. Know what he's up to now? Flirting with fascism, believe it or not. Addressed a meeting about it the other day.'

'The devil he did. What did he say?'

'We and the Germans are one race and should never fight each other ever again. The Germans, too, know how to deal with uppity wogs. We'd be better with them than the French and a lot more of suchlike tommy rot. I fought the Huns the last time and so did you and I'll do it again if need be, though I don't think much of the shower that's running England now.'

'Does anyone listen to him?'

'Plenty, more's the pity. He still dines at Government

239

House. There's many will heed him, especially when he talks about putting the educated wogs like Kidogo up against a wall and shooting 'em. After it a whole lot were saying he should be dictator of Kenya and a good thing too.'

'I suppose it's a bit of a battle honour to have knocked a dictator down.'

'That fellow who spun the yarn about you to young Royle is mixed up with him.'

'Massiter? How come?'

'He's had a farm at Molo for years. One of his outlying investments, I suppose. There were a whole lot who bought up land in the twenties. Now he's turned it into a limited company and made Winthrop a director.'

'Covering his bets. That's his form all right. If Winthrop ever did get power or the Germans came in or Musso goes on the march he'd have Winthrop batting for him and his investment would be safe. He always likes to be on a hundred to nothing. But how did you know about Massiter and the yarn he spun young Royle, Job?'

Job looked hard at Stephen from under his bushy eyebrows. 'I've had a word with Bert Franklin and I've talked to Kamau and I believe him,' he said. 'It's only the bad 'uns like Winthrop and the gossipmongers who don't. But it's easier to perceive the wrong than to pursue the right as Mr Jorrocks says.'

'And mud sticks. But what's all this leading up to, Job?'

'I'll tell you, lad. My brother died a few years back and I'm getting old and lonely up there in the Loldaigas. And my stock is being poached and pilfered from the Reserves. I'm nearly too old and beat-up to go after the thieves myself. Besides they're come and gone in a minute, driving the stock into the Reserves, and once there I can't touch 'em. So I had the notion that if I bought an aeroplane we could find 'em either before or just after they'd started their mischief and frighten the lives out of them. There's a Moth for sale at Wilson Airfield. If I buy it will you fly it for me?'

'I haven't flown for, good God, twenty years.'

'They tell me it's like riding a bicycle. You never forget. Anyway, will you try it?'

'I suppose it wasn't old Jorrocks who said if one door shuts another opens. All right, Job, as I said to you on that first safari of ours, I'll give it a go.'

'Good lad. I'll ring them in the morning.'

'I hope I don't bust your bus. God, Job, it's good to see you again after all the phoneys I've been hanging around with recently.'

'And you, too lad. Now, fill up your glass and tell me just what did happen with that lily-livered cricketer you took out.'

Next day Stephen drove his Buick to Langata and pulled up before the airport buildings. Inside a stockily built man in a bush shirt was writing up a log book at a trestle table. 'I got some sort of a message about you,' he said without looking up. 'There's the aircraft on the tarmac. Take those.' He waved a hand at a helmet and goggles hanging on the wall. 'I'll be with you in a minute.'

Leaving him Stephen walked towards the Moth, pulling on the helmet as he went. Save for the headphones in the earflaps it was much the same as those he had worn during the war. The instruments in the cockpit did not seem to have changed either, he noticed as he peered in. The only addition which was new to him was the bubble mounted in a curved and calibrated tube which he took to be a rudimentary turn and bank indicator.

Standing beside the trim little machine, in many ways not unlike the fighters he had flown all those years ago, memories came crowding back. Shifting his gaze to look out across the grass airfield and the windsock hanging limply on its pole he thought of the men he had flown and fought with: of the incomparable Haynes, his first squadron commander and friend shot down by machine-gun fire from the ground; of the brutal Conway, his flight commander who had tried to get him killed and later by a quirk of fate had been killed himself as an Auxiliary that terrible night when his house at the Bay had been burnt; of Clare de Vaux with whom he had flown since the day at the school of aerial fighting at Ayr and who had later led the squadron.

'Right ho.' A brusque voice broke into his thoughts. 'Hop in and I'll give you a quick flip round to start with. That thing in front of you is a speaking tube. Plug your headphones into it and I'll tell you what's what as we go.'

There must have been a slip-up in communications at some level, Stephen realised. He opened his mouth to explain but the other was already climbing into the front cockpit and had his back towards him. Swinging himself up behind him Stephen settled himself into his seat. A mechanic arrived to help with the safety harness. He plugged the connection from his helmet into the Gosport tube and waited. The mechanic swung the prop and the engine burst into life. After running her up the pilot began to taxi across the grass.

As they climbed into the clear Kenya air Stephen saw the whole great cleft of the Rift Valley unfolding beneath him. At a thousand feet they went into a gentle turn. The instructor's patter was coming through the earphones but Stephen found it difficult to distinguish the words above the roar of the engine. In any event he was giving them only scant attention for he was feeling the controls and wondering whether the old semi-automatic skills and instant reactions would return. After a few minutes he was convinced they had not deserted him and that once more the aircraft could be a live thing underneath his hands. He reached out and unplugged the speaking tube. Then he began to send the Moth scurrying round the sky. As he banked over in a split-arse turn he had a glimpse of the instructor turning in his seat, mouthing something, presumably strong language, and then shaking his fists in the air. Grinning to himself, he took no notice. He could still fly!

Ten minutes later they landed. The instructor jumped down and strode over to where Stephen was pulling off his helmet. 'Just what the hell do you think you were playing at?' he demanded, his moustache bristling with fury. He paused as Stephen completed stripping the helmet from his head and stared at him intently. 'Good God!' he exclaimed. 'It's Raymond, isn't it? Raymond of 245 Squadron. And I asked you if you'd ever flown before! I was due to take a beginner up and the times must have got mixed. Remember me? Name of Spalding?'

'I'm sorry,' Stephen said, looking at him. 'It's been so long –'

'No, I don't suppose you would, now I come to think of it.

242

You were top scorer in the squadron then and I was one of the new men. I asked you what was wrong with my shooting and you told me to get close.'

'I think I remember now. There were some good times amongst the bad then, weren't there?'

'I was shot down a fortnight later. Spent the rest of the war in a prison camp. This deserves a celebration. Come and have a drink.'

They walked together across the tarmac. In his office Spalding produced a bottle and glasses and mixed pink gins. 'Cheerio,' he said.

'Cheerio,' Stephen answered. 'What do I do about a licence?'

'Licence? I'm the licensing authority round here. You can fly that thing any time and anywhere you like. Is there going to be a war?'

'Your guess is as good as mine. Some say this and some say that. If there is I suppose we'll be in it. And it'll be the Huns again like the last time.'

'But will it be the Huns? Whose side will we be on? I went to a meeting the other night addressed by that Happy Valley chap, Winthrop. Talked a lot of sense in a way. The Huns would be better than the bloody commies wouldn't they?'

'I don't think it's quite as simple as that. Nothing ever is. That's the one thing I've learnt in life.'

'Anyway ours is but to do or die I suppose. By the way, two things to watch when you're flying here. One's your altimeter setting. People tend to forget we're so high. And the other is down draughts. They can be the devil. That's what killed Finch-Hatton, or so they say. What about a refill?'

Job had arranged to meet Stephen at the Norfolk for lunch after his flight and he drove back to the city in a thoughtful mood. Wrapped up in himself and his own affairs, managing safaris, looking after clients and, when he wasn't, hunting alone in the sole company of Kamau, he had not until recently given any thought to what was happening in the world outside. But Mussolini's Ethiopian campaign followed by his clamour for Corsica, Nice and more room for empire had raised a small stir in the colony and he now was said to be

243

casting envious eyes over the border. If he wanted Nice and Corsica from the French, why not Kenya from the English? There had been jokes in the club about the castor oil treatment he dealt out to those who opposed him and who would be the first to receive it if he moved in. At least, though, they said, he would make the trains run on time. But – war. It had seemed inconceivable to Stephen that it should happen again after so short a time, but from what was being said it was not so inconceivable now, apparently. In his short life Stephen had been through one war and a bloody insurrection. He wanted no more of either. But what he was about to hear from Job seemed to bring the harsh reality of the present threat a step nearer.

Job was late keeping the appointment, which was unlike him, and when he did appear he was looking unwontedly serious. 'Sorry for keeping you hanging about,' he said. 'But you'll never guess where I've been.'

'No. Where? Drinking with Winthrop?'

'Not quite. The next best thing. I've just come from Government House.'

'Have you, by Jove. You're coming up in the world, Job.'

Job pulled up a chair and sat down. 'There's going to be a war, it seems,' he said. 'At least the Governor and his advisors think so. They're worried about the northern frontier and the Eyeties. There's nothing to stop them walking in if they want to.'

'Which they may well do. The White Highlands would make a nice trophy for Musso's bag.'

'That's it. But they'd have to cross the desert first. And that's where we come in.'

'We? Government House doesn't care much for me – as you well know.'

'They're changing their tune – a bit. The Governor isn't quite the stuffed shirt so many of us think. He served in the Flying Corps in the last show. Did you know that?'

'No. Never heard of him. What was he? A kiwi, a recording officer? An army co-operation chap?'

'I dunno.' Job gave one of his sudden grins. 'Who's being snobbish now? Just because you shot down eighteen Huns.

244

Anyway it seems after he heard you'd been in, he did some checking. Those eighteen Huns went a long way to set off what Massiter and Winthrop were saying about you. He's not exactly an admirer of yours yet and he still thinks Winthrop the hell of a fellow – a most amusing cove at a dinner party, don't you know. And they were at school together. But, as he went on to say, needs must when the devil drives.'

'That's one way of putting it. Come on, Job, what did he want?'

'When he heard I was getting an aeroplane it struck him as a good idea to tell the pilot to keep his eyes open for things that might be happening on the frontier or beyond. Tell him, he said, to record any troop movements or, more important, if they're building any airstrips. And if the worst comes to the worst and they do decide to walk in we should be able to spot them in time to give Government House some sort of warning.'

Stephen laughed. 'The devil is driving all right,' he said. 'Very well, I'll do it. But what happens if the Eyeties send up some of their modern fighters to investigate?'

'I mentioned that to HE and he said they hadn't got any. "Just tell that fellow Raymond to amble about keeping his eyes open," he said.'

'Nice and vague and he's all ready to disown us if anything does go wrong,' Stephen said. 'Still I suppose it adds a bit of spice to the thing. It'll be something like flying patrols again.'

'It's only a precaution really,' Job said. 'It's not likely you'll see anything of any interest.' He raised his hand and called for another pink gin.

CHAPTER XXXI

Job's house was set on the shelf of a hill looking out over a garden and trim grass lawns. It was built of logs knitted together and had been completed haphazard, piece by piece, room by room as his brother grew older and more prosperous. The last room to be built was a spacious living room; it had a polished cedarwood floor covered with rugs thrown down on it apparently haphazard. There was a great stone fireplace; beside it, cut out of the timbering, was a huge rectangular picture window that took up much of the wall space between it and a door leading to the dining room and the kitchen quarters. Standing at this window you looked out over the lawns and then away to the bulk of the Black Mountain and further still through the misty vastness to the border and beyond. Whenever he entered the room Stephen was drawn to this window. He felt he could stand there for hours gazing out across the lonely expanse, almost all of which was Job's land where his herds grazed and which it was his task to patrol. He was reminded of his father standing at the bow window of Bellary Court, staring down the Bay, watching its changing colours and moods and the sweep of sea and sky. But Bellary Court was a blackened ruin and he wondered now if he could ever go back. Set high on its bluff at the head of the Bay, its empty shell would be the first thing to strike the eye as one came by road over the saddle between the hills or by rail as one stepped on to the platform of the little station. Besides, he told himself, he had been away so long that even the fondest memories had faded. And this land of light and shade and great, aching, blue vast distances could also lay its hand on your heart. He stood, immobile, thinking, lost in memories, watching the shadows fall and night creep quickly up.

'Like it here, then?' Job's voice broke into his thoughts as he came into the room followed by a boy with a tray of sundowners.

'It's wonderful,' Stephen said simply. 'What a country this

246

is. Naivasha, Nakuru, the Lakes, the Molo Downs and now this – ' he gestured towards the window.

'Still longing for that Bay of yours, though, aren't you?'

'In a way, yes. But there's nothing for me there. I'm a member of a sort of lost legion. In fact I was just wondering if I'd ever go back.'

'A man should put down roots sometime, somewhere,' Job said as he poured himself a peg. 'And this is no bad place to do it. We called it Frisco Farm because when we first came out my brother and I owned a horse called San Francisco in partnership. We had a hell of a bet on him in race week when no one knew us and cleaned up at twenty to one. That gave him the money to start up here and me to set up the stable at Naivasha. We both worked like hell and now I'm here and I'm staying here. I'll fight to stay here if I have to. When a man stops fighting, when he thinks there's nothing left worth fighting for, he's finished.'

'I've had my share of fighting,' Stephen said with a grin. 'Still I'll fight for you, Job.'

'I reckon you would, Stephen lad. You know – ' Job suddenly pointed a stubby finger at him. 'When I first set eyes on you I said to myself he may look a bit ladylike so to speak but you mark my words, I said to myself, there's fire somewhere in that lad's belly.'

'Ladylike. I've never been called that before.'

Job coughed. 'It's not what you mean, exactly,' he said in an embarrassed way. 'It's just something I've noticed in the likes of you. You see it in the white hunters, the good 'uns that's to say. They're not thunderin' great rugger toughs with bulging biceps. They look as mild as milk, most of 'em, until the chips are down that is. Then it's what's underneath that counts. That's what I mean.'

'You may be right at that,' Stephen said, thinking of some of those he had flown with during the war.

'I'm getting old,' Job said. 'And it may come to fighting . yet. Have you given up those silly notions of handing over everything to the wogs?'

'I never had them. You got me wrong. All I tried to say was that I'd lost everything in one revolution and I didn't want to see you doing the same in another.'

247

'My brother made this farm and I helped him keep it. "Be it never so 'umble there's no place like 'ome", though I don't think Mr Jorrocks said that. You think I'm right not to want to give it away?'

Stephen looked about the long bright room, the logs burning in the fireplace, the battered, comfortable chintz-covered chairs. On the walls were racing pictures, and trophies of the guns. Racing cups, polished and burnished, stood on a chippendale table. There was a leopard-skin rug before the hearth. Suddenly he felt flow over him an air of belonging. He thought, too, of the hard-won acres outside the great window. 'I'd fight for it,' he said.

'That's more like it. Now then, what about these poachers? Not seen much of them, have you?'

'No. But you haven't lost any stock lately either.'

'Not so's you'd notice, that's true. So it's about time for another raid. You'll have a passenger tomorrow. I'm coming with you.'

They took off at first light into the clear pearly air that lay above the mists at the bottom of the escarpment. 'When we spot 'em, dive on 'em and then circle so as to show my chaps where they are and they can get after 'em,' had been Job's instructions.

It was bumpy as they climbed and the little aircraft jumped and bucked under them almost like an overfresh horse. Stephen smiled to himself as he stroked the stick to hold her straight. The old fascination of flying was coming back. It was almost as good as riding a race. Almost – but not quite. Nothing could really equal that, whatever Job and the old hunters might say. It came to him then with a little pang that he was in his late thirties, pushing forty if you cared to put it that way and that his racing days were over even if there had been an opportunity to renew them – which there wasn't. Had there been a son perhaps he could renew them through him, but – if. For the thousandth time he wondered where Kit was and what was happening to him. That brief message from Desmond Murtagh conveyed by Betty, and what Mikey had said of him, was all the news he had. He wondered about Betty, too, and how that marriage was making out. Then, enough of this harking back, he said to himself; he was doing too much of it. He turned his mind to the task in hand, and levelled off at a thousand feet.

It was Job who saw them first. His hand went up and then out into the slip-stream, pointing down and to the left. An inarticulate shout which Stephen took to be in the nature of a holloa to hounds came down the speaking tube followed by a torrent of words of which the only ones Stephen could clearly make out were, 'Those bloody d'Orobos.' Following Job's indication Stephen picked them up, a mass of moving dark specks some miles away ahead of them.

'All right, James Pigg,' he said into the mouthpiece. 'Here we go.' Then he tilted the wings, pushed the stick forward and dived.

The wind sang through the wires. All at once it seemed as if he was back twenty years, diving on a Hun. Instinctively he found himself feeling for the firing button and then laughed as the ground and the poachers swept up towards them. 'I hope the wings of this thing stay on,' he muttered as he eased back the stick. The d'Orobos were quite clear now, bang in his sights if he had had any. There were a considerable number of them driving the cattle. Some had twisted the beasts' tails into knots for better management and were controlling them from behind. Others had fanned out on either side, helping to manage the drive.

The tribesmen looked up startled as the great bird swooped down on them out of the clear air. Many dropped the tails of the cattle to stare upwards; others threw themselves flat on the ground. Most broke and ran. The cattle, freed from control, galloped in all directions about the plain. Stephen circled twice and then pursued the runners spreading them far and wide. It would take the poachers some time to reassemble themselves and collect the cattle if they ever did. By that time Job's people should have caught up with them. And then, as Job had said, 'God help them.'

Stephen was now very low. In front was a rocky knoll with a scattering of thorn trees at its base. He pulled the stick to clear it. The knoll had a top shaped like a saucer and, to his astonishment, Stephen saw that the saucer was occupied. There were two tents; outside them trestle tables had been set up, one at right angles to the other. At the nearest a man was sitting poring over what looked like a map. On the other was a bulky object Stephen thought he recognised. The man looked up, startled, at their sudden appearance and in the instant that they swept across the saucer Stephen recognised him. It was Gervase Winthrop who hastily ducked his head and then, getting to his feet, ran across to the object on the other table.

Pulling the Moth into a steep turn Stephen came back for another look. Winthrop was throwing a cover over the object on the table. Then he put his hand over his face and dived into the nearest tent. The map fluttered to the ground. Once more Stephen circled the little encampment but no one emerged from the tents and the cover remained on whatever the bulky object was that the man had been so anxious to hide.

'Did you see who that chap down there was?' he asked as they turned for home.

'It looked damn like Winthrop to me.'

'And what about what was on the other table?'

'Dunno about that, lad.'

'It looked damn like a wireless transmitting set to me.'

'We've got to tell the Governor,' were Stephen's first words when they landed.

'Tell him what, then?'

'That we caught Winthrop red-handed with a transmitting set out in the bush not all that far from the border.'

To his surprise Job did not fall in with his suggestion immediately in the way he had expected. 'Now, now,' he said. 'Don't be rushing your fences.'

'What do you mean?'

'Well now, are we certain it was Winthrop? I only caught a glimpse through those damn goggles and you didn't get much more, though your eyes are younger than mine. We'd look pretty foolish if he comes along and says he was in the Norfolk or Torrs with one of his lady friends.'

'It was Winthrop all right. I'll swear to it.'

'Even if it was him, was it a transmitter he had with him?'

250

Stephen hesitated. 'That's what it looked like to me,' he said after a pause.

'But you're not dead certain. It could have been something else. It could have been an innocent safari.'

'Winthrop's safaris are in other husbands' bedrooms.'

Job sighed. 'Now, you listen to me, lad. Winthrop's a pal of the Governor's. He may be doing the same job on the ground for him as you are in the air – keeping an eye on the Eyeties.'

'If he was he was acting damn suspicious when we bounced him.'

Job took no notice but went on: 'He might well have thought we were a wop plane. There are a hundred explanations, all of 'em innocent except one, and that's yours. And you've got to admit you're not exactly what they call in the law courts an unbiased witness. Another thing – '

'What other thing? Whose side are you on, Job?'

'Now you just take it steady, like. As I've said, Winthrop is an old pal of the Governor's. And he's from one of the old families of the colony. The Winthrops came to Gilgil before the war. That's one of the reasons he's been able to get away with the things he's done and why he's got a following despite all that Fascist nonsense of his. You're still not exactly a favourite son up at Government House. It's the old boy network. The Governor just won't believe you, and he'll accept any trumped-up story Winthrop cares to tell him – even if your guess is accurate. Incidentally, what in hell do you think he *was* doing?'

'Testing transmission distance to the Eyeties or actually transmitting. They'd be glad enough to know how thin we are on the ground and Winthrop would be in the way of knowing.'

'It's possible though I can hardly believe that with all his faults Winthrop could be a traitor as well. And if I can't then the Governor won't. Damn it all, I can almost hear him saying it.' Job began to imitate the Governor's precise way of speaking. 'The fellow was at school with me. I played in the eleven with him. It's just not credible.'

'You'll be telling me he's the Scarlet Pimpernel soon,' Stephen said sulkily. 'And I still think someone, if not the

251

Governor, should be told.' With that he stumped off to his room to change out of flying clothes. It was the nearest thing to an open disagreement they had ever had.

And Stephen could not get it out of his mind. It was true of course that he had his own reasons for disliking and distrusting Winthrop, and these could have played a part in his arriving at the deduction he had done but they were not the whole reason for it. Winthrop was an opportunist crook and he was mixed up with another, cleverer one in Andrew Massiter. Massiter would deal with anyone to save an investment. Stephen was pretty sure that he had dealt with the IRA to save his house back in the twenties. He was a great man now – baronet, Master of Foxhounds, member of the Turf Club, a senior steward even, for all Stephen knew, though he supposed his arch-enemy and rival Donal Westcott would do what he could to prevent that. All these honours were to Stephen's mind an empty sham. Massiter did not change his spots. The ruthless entrepreneur was still there alive and well beneath them.

During the next few days he mulled the whole thing over and over in his mind. He was sure he was right but as he cooled down he could see the strength of Job's arguments. As always he was the outsider looking in, the man with a brand on his back whose word would carry no weight against the closed ranks of those inside the palisade of the English upper class, whatever sort of shits they were. He knew he should do something, but he was totally at a loss as to what line of action he should take.

In this instance Job, for once, was unlikely to be of any help at all. He had already made his position clear; he didn't want to be mixed up in it. In fact Job had been noticably quieter and unlike his usual ebullient self ever since they had landed from that flight. Stephen thought, too, that he had seemed to be slowing up and becoming more careful in his movements, as if some spring of energy in him had dried up. At first he wondered if Job was annoyed with him over their difference concerning Winthrop, but that was so out of character that he dismissed it immediately. He then began to think that Job might be about to go down with an attack of malaria and watched closely for the symptoms which he knew

252

Job would fight to the last before succumbing. But it did not seem to be that either.

Two days later, over their drinks, Job asked Stephen to fly him to Nairobi after breakfast the next day, as he had some business to do which he did not specify. This in itself was unusual and Stephen now began actively to worry about his old friend. His anxiety was increased by the fact that Job did not, as was his custom, suggest a drink at the New Stanley or elsewhere before he went about his business, nor did he make an arrangement for lunching together. When Stephen dropped him in Delamere Avenue a glance in the rear mirror of the Buick showed him Job standing irresolute on the pavement before turning and walking slowly away, slightly stooped like a very old man.

Left at a loose end, Stephen drove to the club and parked opposite the main entrance. After the incident with Winthrop he was a little doubtful about his reception. He had thought it possible that he might be arraigned before the committee on the grounds of bringing the club into disrepute, but so far no call to present himself had come. Nor when he entered was he told that the secretary wished to see him. He considered it unlikely that Winthrop would have made a complaint, but there had been a witness, the chap who was reading in the alcove and whose name, Stephen finally remembered, was Jack Campion, who farmed near Nakuru.

Long afterwards he heard that the boy who had brought the message about the telephone had seen what had happened, and that there had been chatter among the servants which had come to the ears of the secretary. When Campion was next in the club a month or so later the secretary had interviewed him. Campion had said that he had taken little notice of what was going on, since he had found a photograph of an old girl friend in *The Tatler* and was engrossed in the report of her activies, but his impression was that Winthrop was a bit tight and had tripped over a bar stool. That had ended the matter so far as the club was concerned, though other versions of the affair, naturally enough, got about.

As it happened, the first person Stephen saw in the club was Winthrop. He was sitting in one of the chintz-covered chairs in the lounge talking to another man whose back was to Stephen. A mid-morning bottle of champagne stood on the table between them. Something made the other man turn and look up, and even after all these years Stephen recognised him immediately. The trim pointed imperial which gave the face its almost satanic cast, and those strange tawny eyes, were unmistakeable. It was Andrew Massiter. The eyes flickered over Stephen without betraying a hint of interest or recognition and then returned to his companion. So Massiter was still here and what the devil was *he* up to?

Stephen crossed to the desk to check for messages. As he did so another man brushed past him, paused to scan the room and then joined Massiter and Winthrop at their table. He sat down and called loudly for a third glass and another bottle of champagne. For which, Stephen said to himself, he most assuredly will not pay, for it was Toby Revere who was even then telling the boy to open the bottle and omitting to sign the chit.

A nice nest of robins indeed, Stephen said to himself and wondered once more what he should do about Winthrop. But he seemed openly to have Massiter behind him, and Massiter too was *persona grata* at Government House.

Still in the midst of conjecture as to his course of action, Stephen drove to the Norfolk. He had decided to lunch there so as to avoid having to meet any of the trio he had just seen. Once there several things happened which drove Winthrop, Massiter, Revere and all their works clean out of his mind.

Hardly had he entered when to his surprise the Asian clerk at the desk leant across and handed him a cablegram. 'For you, sah,' he said. 'Just arrived.'

Tearing it open Stephen read: *Arriving Mombasa ex-Orana Tuesday 12th stop Meet me Nairobi 13th if they haven't got you yet stop Set up safari just for one stop Love and lots of it Betty.*

Ordering himself a pink gin Stephen read the cablegram again. It raised all sorts of unanswered questions. 'Just for one' presumably meant she was alone. If so, where was Harvey and why was he not with her? Had the marriage broken down? There had been signs on the safari that it might be heading that way. Excitement at the thought of seeing her again, alone and unattached, gripped Stephen. He ordered

254

himself another large pink gin. Sipping it he began to work out times. The 13th was two days away. If the boat docked on time then she would travel overnight and be in Nairobi on the morning of the 14th. He could fly down to meet her. That would be a surprise for her. What fun it would be –

'Excuse me, sir,' a voice broke into his thoughts and he looked up to see a youngish man with a prim expression, wearing an immaculate lightweight suit and a collar and tie, standing beside him. 'Mr Raymond, isn't it?'

'Yes.'

'I'm from Johnson and McNab, solicitors. It's about Mr Hannaford. I'm afraid I have bad news to import, sir – '

Stephen's haze of pleasurable anticipation was suddenly shattered. 'What is it?' he said roughly. 'Out with it, man.'

'Well, sir, he was attending our office doing some business and he, well, he collapsed. It's believed he has had a heart attack. He is in the Maia Carbery Nursing Home.'

'How bad is he?'

'He was well enough to instruct us to find you and tell you what had happened. He used – er – some forcible language, saying we were making a great deal of fuss about some little indigestion.'

'That I can imagine. Can I see him?'

'I think, sir, you had better ascertain that from the hospital.'

When he rang, all the hospital would say was that Job was doing as well as could be expected and to call back the next day. Twenty-four hours later he received permission to see Job and he flew the Moth down to Nairobi.

'Don't stay too long with him,' the doctor warned. He was a round-faced, merry-eyed man from County Kerry whose voice still held traces of the tell-tale Kerry lilt. 'I know you,' he went on. 'You're Raymond the white hunter. From the Bay originally, aren't you?'

'That's right,' Stephen said. 'And you're a Kerryman, or I'm a Kikuyu.'

'That's right, too. Both of us exiles. Ever go back?'

'Never. We were burnt out, you know.'

'We missed that. Not grand enough, I suppose. Now about your friend. Frankly the medical profession knows damn all

255

about hearts but I don't think this attack was a bad one. More in the nature of a serious warning if you like. I gather it's in the family. His brother died from one. Tell him to slow down.'

'That won't be easy.'

'That's his decision. He'd better stay here for a couple of weeks or so anyway.'

Job was sitting in bed propped up by pillows when Stephen entered the room. He looked well enough but there was a greyish tinge underneath his tanned cheeks which Stephen did not like.'

'All a lot of bloody nonsense,' he exploded, in answer to Stephen's question. 'Touch of indigestion, that's all. I'd been feeling it a bit those last few days and meant to get some tablets for it and, damn, I forgot. Wouldn't be here if I hadn't. Good of you to come, lad. Now then, there's a bottle of whisky in that cupboard. Get it out.'

'Are you allowed it?'

'Of course I am. There's no medicine like it. And if John Jorrocks didn't say that he ought to have done.'

Stephen opened the cupboard and peered inside.

'What's the matter?' came from the bed. 'Can't you find it?'

'Not at the moment. It's hellish dark and smells of cheese,' Stephen said.

There was a cackle of laughter from behind him. 'You haven't forgotten your bible then,' Job said. 'Ah, you've got it. Now, pour and remember what the top of a glass is for.'

Hardly had Stephen put the bottle down when the door opened and a forbidding-looking nurse came in. 'What's that in your hand, Mr Hannaford?' she said, glaring at Stephen.

'Whisky, m'dear,' Job answered mildly.

'You know that's forbidden. A sip or two of water.'

'Never touch the stuff. As a friend of mine, a Mr John Jorrocks, d'you know him, says, it rots me shoes. Good luck m'dear – ' and he raised his glass.

'Oh, you're impossible. I'll speak to the matron – '

'You do that, m'dear, and I'll finish the bottle and then sign myself out. Speak to the doctor. He's an Irishman like

256

my friend here and knows what's good for me. *Aqua vita* they call it, speaking in Latin like Mr Jorrocks used to at times.'

'Quite incorrigible. Five more minutes.' She glared at Stephen and went out, shutting but not quite slamming the door behind her.

'There's something I want to say to you,' Stephen said when she had gone. 'And I'm not quite sure how to say it.'

'Say it anyway.'

'There's a girl – woman – I met on safari, Betty Lang, you may have heard me mention her. She's landing from the *Orana* tomorrow. Coming to see me, she says. It's a lot to ask, Job, but I know you'll like her. She's, well, she's quite something, and I want to bring her to the farm.'

'Of course you can, lad. It's about time we had a woman around the place again. And, anyway, who has a better right.'

'Better right – what's that mean, Job?'

'Before I got this damn thing I went to those legal sharks to put my affairs in order. I've made a new will, I've left you the farm and all that's in it or on it.'

'Job! But you can't – I never – '

'My brother was a bachelor like myself. At least I suppose I'm a bachelor of sorts. You have it and you enjoy it. You deserve a turn of luck, lad.'

'Job, I'm speechless. I can't think of words to thank you.'

'Don't say 'em. I know you well enough to know you mean 'em. Maybe it'll stop you hankering after that place in Ireland you lost.'

At that moment the door opened and the doctor came in, a stethoscope round his neck. 'Time's up,' he said to Stephen. 'And I hear I'm to issue a reprimand. No more whisky. Not for a few days anyway.'

The last words Stephen heard as he left were Job's from the bed: 'I thought you bloody Irish prescribed whisky for everything.'

CHAPTER XXXII

The next morning Stephen was at the station waiting for the Mombasa train. It was on time for once and pulled up puffing and wheezing after its long haul from the coast. Doors flew open and passengers poured out to throng towards friends or waiting cars. Stephen stood at the back searching for her in the crowd. When he picked up her slim figure his heart gave a little lurch as he recognised the easy grace of her movements and the well-remembered gesture of her hand to her hair. Almost at the same moment she caught sight of him and he saw her eyes light up. 'Stephen!' she said as she ran towards him. 'Dear Stephen. I knew you'd be here.' And she kissed him.

'That's nice,' Stephen said. 'And where have you been all my life or that bit of it you haven't been?'

'I'll tell you. I've lots to tell you. Come on, where'll I tell you?'

He took her to Torr's Hotel, and in the panelled, slightly shabby lounge, ordered Pimms. When the boy brought the brimming pint tankards she laughed as she reached out for hers. 'Goodness,' she said. 'But how I've missed it all. What is it about the place that gets you – the air or the altitude? Whatever it is it makes you want to keep on coming back.' Her eyes were dancing and she was bubbling with gaiety.

'You've forgotten one thing,' Stephen said.

'What's that?'

'The people.'

'You have a point, sir.' She looked mischievously at him. 'How's Kamau?'

'All right. He's still with me. He'll be all the better for seeing you. You were one of his favourite clients. You and Harvey.' Stephen hesitated. 'Where's Harvey?' he said then.

'Harvey's over the hills and far away.'

'Where? What?'

'He said there's going to be a war, a war for civilisation and we won't get into it. Too proud to fight, just like the last time. That means, he said, there'll be two yellow races in the

258

Eastern hemisphere – us and the Japs. His principles won't let him shoulder a gun but he said he had to do something. So he's high-tailed it to England where he'll get on to a mine-sweeper if he can, or if he can't he'll drive an ambulance. That's what he says, the poor silly sonofabitch.'

'I wouldn't call him that. It might be better if there were more like him. I don't know – '

'You should know. You made a man of him.'

'I didn't. He did it himself.'

'That's not what he thinks.' She raised her eyes to meet his. 'It didn't work out,' she said. 'That safari was a last try, I guess. And then having found himself he sort of lost himself again. It's that family of his and his cussed New England upbringing. One half of him is puritan and the other press on and damn the torpedoes. When they collide, that's when the stuff hits the fan. There are lots like him. I've seen them. It drives some of them to drink or drugs and it's driven him off to a war he doesn't want, without even a lance to tilt at windmills.'

'Will he make it?'

'Get into it, do you mean? Oh, yes, he'll make it. His family connections will see to that. Is there going to be a war?'

'Yes, and soon.'

'Too soon for us.'

'Too soon for all of us.' Stephen looked soberly about him. 'There'll be no safari, I'm afraid.'

'No safari. Oh, Stephen, and I'd hoped – '

'Never mind.' They finished their lunch and were standing up to go. 'I'm taking you somewhere better.'

'Somewhere better? Where?'

'To Shangri La,' Stephen said.

The Moth was on the tarmac, refuelled and ready, when Stephen turned into Wilson airport. 'That's our magic carpet,' he said, handing her a helmet. 'Put this on and pretend you're Amelia Earhart.'

'Where is this Shangri La?'

Stephen grinned. 'Somewhere in the wild blue yonder,' he said.

He saw her safely strapped in and swung into his own

cockpit. Then he ran the engine up, waved the chocks away and taxied out into the wind. In a moment they were climbing into the cloudless sky.

Over the Aberdares he put the Moth into a wide circle. 'Take a look about you,' he said into the Gosport tube. 'On your left is Kinangop and below and beyond it Naivasha where we used to train. Ahead and to the right, see it, that's the Mountain, Mount Kenya, Kilinyaa the Kikuyu call it, the White Mountain, because of its eternal snows. We're in luck, there's not a cloud about today. You can see it plain. Like it!'

'It's just magic.'

'Down below are the Aberdares. All this is the White Highlands. Take a good look at them. Magic, enchantment, call it what you like, but that's why the settlers, every man jack of them, will fight to keep them.'

'And you, will you fight too, Stephen?'

Stephen sighed. I have a stake in the country now, he thought. 'Me too,' he said as he levelled off and pointed the little aircraft north.

They flew over Naro Moru and Nanuki and then just for fun Stephen came down to follow the ten miles of unmetalled road that wound its way through Job's acres to Frisco Farm. They crossed the drift where once the Neru warriors had dipped their spears and then the cluster of farm buildings came into view. Picking up the windsock Stephen turned into wind and in a moment the wheels rumbled on the hard earth.

'Welcome to Shangri La,' he said as he jumped down. 'And look about you.'

The coarse grass of the lawns was trimmed and the terraces below the house were a riot of bougainvillaea; roses, arum lilies and frangipani too blazed in all their colours.

Betty stood, entranced, taking it all in and breathing the high, cool air. A faint breeze brought the scent of flowers across from the terraces. Below them, at the bottom of the escarpment, beyond the thorn trees, the herds grazed. 'Magic,' she repeated again. 'Pure magic. My, it is good to be back. You are fine for me, Stephen. And what part of heaven did this drop from?'

Stephen laughed. 'It's Job Hannaford's. We're sort of part-

260

ners. He's in hospital in Nairobi. Come on, I'll show you round.'

Everything delighted her, the gardens, the smiling boys – there was a joyous reunion with Kamau – the strange twisting corridors of the house which had been thrown together. When they came into the long living room for their drinks she caught sight of the big window and paused in front of it.

Beyond the Black Mountain the light was fading and the first pale whispers of dusk were creeping over the terraces. 'All Job's land,' Stephen said to her. 'Just about as far as you can see.'

'Magic,' she said again. 'Pure magic. It's been a magical day.'

Stephen looked at her as she stood, lips parted, staring out over the land that would sometime be his. 'If you like it,' he said. 'Then it's all been worthwhile.'

Later, waited on by soft-footed Meru boys, they dined off lamb killed on the farm and drank Bernkasteler Doktor, a case of which Job had given Stephen on his birthday. Back in the living room Stephen poured brandy into balloon glasses and they sat watching the flames leap in the roaring log fire. Mellowed by food and drink and the glowing warmth of the fire they talked together easily in the companionship of old acquaintance and the remembrance of once-shared dangers and delights. After a little Stephen found himself telling her of that last safari, of how Rolfe had run away leaving him to face the wounded buffalo and its consequences. 'What made it worse, of course,' he said, 'was that he was HE's nephew, and I was suspect at Government House right from the very beginning. The business of the fall in the Kenya Grand National years ago didn't help either. When you get into the black books of the powers that be you never come out of them – '

'You don't conform enough, Stephen. You're on the outside looking in. They never like that. You hear a different drummer. It makes two of us, I guess. Harvey's family never wanted me. I didn't jump when they cracked the whip, or at least if I did it wasn't in the right direction. I was the girl from outside. I was the unsettling influence. They couldn't know what was eating him. Only I knew that. They thought

I was the trouble, I was the one that was making him miserable. They were mad at me for taking him on that safari. But that's all about me. You haven't finished. What happened when you came out of hospital?'

'It was that swine Massiter who was staying at Government House who finally fouled things up. He spun a yarn about my court-martial during the war – '

'Massiter,' she said. 'That was the name you mentioned that night after the elephant hunt when you asked us to look out for news of the boy. Do you remember?'

Stephen was staring into the fire. 'Yes, I remember.'

'We never got to the Bay but I sent you that message from the nice man Desmond Murtagh. Chip off the old block, he said, and I was particularly to send you those words. I saw your face when Harvey asked you was he your godson. "Sort of" you said. He's no godson, is he, Stephen?'

'He's my son,' Stephen said. And then, slowly, he poured out the whole story to her. 'That's why Massiter wants to ruin me,' he said when he had finished.

'My poor Stephen. But look, there's more. Do you remember we stayed with that man, Westcott, in Tipperary and over the port he said there was something else about the burning of your house?'

'You wrote me about it.'

'Well, he asked us back for another day's hunting later on. Harvey couldn't get what he said about your house out of his mind and he tackled him about it. Westcott told him it was a long story, but everyone believed a man called Massiter was behind it. You were supposed to be having an affair with Massiter's wife and he set the Tans on to you. It was they, the Tans, I mean, who burnt your house, not the Sinn Feiners.'

'That's true enough, that part of it. Massiter – great God! I never thought even he would stoop to that. Do you suppose Westcott was telling the truth? He and Massiter have been at each other's throats for years. They're two of a kind. Money and power is all that interests them; and each wants to be top dog in Irish racing.'

'Harvey mentioned it to another man in the house party. This guy said something about there being a story to that effect. He changed the subject pretty quickly, Harvey said.

262

We found out people still don't care to talk much about those times. Harvey thought of writing to you, but then it was all so vague and it might only stir up more trouble. Now from what you told me about what he did with Rolfe and you – Stephen, why are you looking like that?'

Stephen's fingers were clenched round the brandy glass so tightly the white of his knuckles showed, and she feared the glass might shatter in his hand. His eyes were staring at the locked gun-racks on the opposite wall. 'If it is true,' he said, 'then I think I should kill Massiter.'

'Stephen, what have I done?'

'Nothing. I should have guessed. I always knew he was evil.'

'I've spoilt our day.'

'You couldn't spoil anything for me.'

They sat on in silence, staring into the leaping flames, each busy with their own thoughts. Then with that flowing grace of movement that was hers and which always captivated him she stood up. Her fingers brushed his cheek. 'Later, dear Stephen,' she said. 'Later – '

He gave himself another drink and then did his nightly rounds. When he came to her room the door was ajar. Gently he pushed it open. The moon was up and its light was pouring through the window, turning everything to silver. From somewhere near came the cough of a leopard, far away in the distance a jackal barked. She was lying facing him, a sheet thrown carelessly over her. Bending down he drew it back. Beneath it she was naked, her body glowing in the moonlight.

'You're even lovelier than I thought,' he said with a little gasp.

'It's been a long time,' she said as her arms went out to him. 'We've found each other at last.'

Two days later the crackling wireless told them: *'At 11.15 the Prime Minister made the announcement to the Nation and the Empire that a state of war exists between Great Britain and Germany as from 11 o'clock British summer time, today.'*

Part 5

KIT AND STEPHEN

CHAPTER XXXIII

On his arrival in Egypt Kit was informed that he would be
sent to a biplane refresher course to convert back on to Gloster
Gladiators with which the Desert Air Force was equipped.
He found them drawn up wing-tip to wing-tip looking for all
the world like pictures he had seen of squadrons on airfields
in France during the First World War. In fact the Gladiator
was the ultimate development of those biplane fighters of
World War I. It had neither the speed, the climb nor the
armament of the Hurricane but it was a delight to fly. Responsive, steady and aerobatic, it was far more manoeuvrable than
the modern monoplanes and could turn, as Kit told himself,
like a polo pony. Whether it had the performance required
to take on the Regia Aeronautica was another matter.

Kit had arrived a few days after 'the stab in the back',
Mussolini's declaration of war on the side of Germany. Intelligence as to Italian intentions in the Middle East was scanty
and no one at the time knew quite what was facing them in
the air. Rudimentary aircraft recognition charts of Italian
types thought to be in Libya had been rushed out and given
to pilots to study. There were lectures on survival if you were
shot down or force-landed in the desert, but apart from that,
as in the England he had left, there was at the base very little
sense of urgency and few signs of war. On days off in Cairo
there was cricket and tennis and polo for those who could
afford it. There was racing, too, at Heliopolis which Kit,
though he longed for a ride, could only enjoy as a spectator.
'Does anyone here realise there's a war on up the road,' a

pilot back from the desert remarked sourly to Kit as they watched a loser they had backed finish well down the field.

It did not take Kit long to convert to Gladiators, and soon his posting to a fighter squadron came through. A Lysander carrying mail and supplies flew him up to the desert airstrip. On leaving the aircraft he enquired the whereabouts of the squadron commander from a passing aircraftsman who indicated a tent set a little apart from the others. Opening the flat he went in and saluted.

Squadron Leader Bill Monro was sitting at a table smoking a pipe when Kit handed him his posting order and log-book. Taking the posting order he glanced at it and put it to one side. then he leafed through the pages of the log-book. 'Hurricanes – eh,' he said. 'And one Dornier confirmed. You're one ahead of any of us, then. And a reprimand. What's that for? Like to tell me about it? Take a pew.'

Keeping it as short as possible Kit recounted what had happened when he shot down the Dornier. When he had finished their eyes met. 'Never went much on those fighting area attacks myself,' Monro said. 'And in this squadron mistakes towards the enemy are ninety per cent certain to be overlooked.' He gave a sudden grin and stretched out a hand. 'Now then,' Monro went on. 'Let's see how you like the desert air.' He stood up and led the way to where the Gladiators were dispersed, shouting commands as he did so. But the commands were given with a smile and cheery wave of the hand, quite unlike Mostyn's snarling roar. They were obeyed with alacrity and there were answering smiles on the faces of the aircraftsmen as they ran to obey.

'Just come out, sir,' the corporal who had supervised strapping him in said to Kit. 'You're in luck, sir. This is the best squadron in the desert. You'll soon have those Eyeties out of the sky!'

Reaching up and sliding the canopy across his head Kit gave a sigh of satisfaction. At last, he felt, he had come to a well-led and happy squadron.

He took off alongside Monro and together they climbed to twelve thousand feet. Then the radio crackled in his ears. 'Right ho,' came Monro's voice. 'Let's try a dog-fight. Break – now!'

268

Kit had never been in a dog-fight, even a simulated one, before. All his battle training had been in those text-book attacks laid down in the operational manuals. But he had heard enough from Clare and Dai Evans to know that the first thing to do was to turn and turn tight and keep on turning. And he thought he could fly. And the Gladiator could turn on a sixpence. Immediately he flung her into the tightest turn he knew. Fine, he thought, these things are child's play after a Hurricane. Two wings. Dead easy. See how I can hold her! Not a trace of a slip!

But where was Monro? Still looking for him? Given up? Gone home? He craned his head around. And there was Monro, his nose almost touching Kit's tail. If this had been for real he'd have been dead ten times over. Desperately he tried to shake him off.

He turned, looped and spun, doing everything he knew and a bit more besides, and always there was Monro behind him, deadly, lethal and, if Kit didn't miss his guess, grinning all over his face.

'All right, level off. We'll come in now,' sounded in the earphones.

Monro was smiling as he waited for him on landing. 'Not bad,' he said. 'You need to tighten your turns a bit. Change from Hurricanes, aren't they, these old Glads? It's an old-fashioned form of fighting really.'

'We were told there'd never be another dog-fight,' Kit said. 'All we did in battle practice was to follow the book.'

'They're learning different now, back home,' Monro said slowly. 'And look. Don't get the idea that these Eyeties are ice-cream merchants who won't face us and can't fly. We've mixed it with them and some of them are bloody good. We haven't scored yet which just shows you. And those Fiat CRs of theirs are as good if not better than our old Glads, much as I love 'em. Now come along to the mess for a beer and I'll introduce you to the chaps.'

Most of the pilots were regulars who had been out since before the war. They crowded round Kit, asking for news from home, and when they heard he had been on Hurricanes they fired questions at him about its handling characteristics, its performance and its vices, if any. 'When the hell are we going to get them here,' one said. 'The Glad is a bloody marvellous aircraft but it's had its day.'

It was a verdict Kit was to find borne out in the days to come as he piled up flying hours, for the limitations of the Gladiators in modern war soon became obvious. They had hardly the speed to catch the Savoia bombers they were supposed to shoot down and, once caught, their armament of four Browning machine guns carried insufficient hitting power to destroy them in a conventional attack. The Fiat CRs which supported and escorted the bombers had much the same performance as the Gladiators and could usually be seen off, but the Italians had a seemingly endless supply of them. The Gladiators were all the Desert Air Force had, and there were all too few of them.

The conditions under which they lived, too, were the next best thing to intolerable. Flies plagued them, tormenting their eyes and ears and mouths, the sun blazed down and scorched them, but the worst plague of all was the sand. It permeated their nostrils, their teeth and their clothes; it was in their bedding when they slept or tried to, and in their boots when they woke up. It formed a surface dressing to the bully beef which they gobbled off tin plates between patrols and it flavoured their drinks when they came back – if they came back. Even their nights were broken, for the Savoias came over whenever weather permitted and plastered the airfield. No sooner had sleep come than they tumbled cursing from their beds into slit trenches and then came to breakfast red-eyed with fatigue to take off once more into the blistering desert sun.

As the weeks went on strain on muscle, physique and nerve began to take their toll. Along with the wear and tear on body and mind, desert sores came to add to their hardships. Kit had little time to think about anything but survival but when he did he pondered on the odds against his ever reaching Kenya, now so tantalisingly close, to search for and find his father. That search was, he told himself, all that there was left to him now, coupled with a determination to prove himself, here in the desert, as a person in his own right, no longer just one of those rich Massiter boys, which was the false flag under which he had sailed for too long.

But the strains were telling on him as on everyone. Had it not been for Monro, morale would have sagged. Kit had often heard it said that a squadron was as good as its commander and in Monro he saw living proof of this. He flew as often as any of them and was in the thick of every action. It was he who scored their first victory, bringing down a Savoia near the airfield from which they were able to salvage the white cross from its tail fin to decorate the mess tent. 'They say it's a cross between the black cross and the double cross,' Monro proclaimed as they celebrated as best they could in lukewarm beer laced with sand. It was the prelude to more victories and Monro's personal score started to pile up, though he took no heed of it, for his only interests were the squadron and the well-being of his pilots. Unruffled, unshakeable, he was the prop and stay upon whom all of them leant. Kit, watching him, could only marvel at his ability to put in so many flying hours, cope with the paperwork, the demands of senior officers, the heat, the sand and the flies, and yet remain cheerful and unruffled. Always, too, he was ready to discuss tactics and accept suggestions. It was he who devised the best method of attacking a Savoia. 'Come up from below and behind and aim for the engine,' he said. 'It's the only way our four guns can cripple them.' And when Kit put forward the idea of flying in pairs instead of the rigid vic formation, after an initial period of experiment he adopted it. The squadron, Kit knew, would have fallen to pieces without him.

Gradually, too, Kit's own score mounted. Soon he had six stencilled fasces on the side of his cockpit each denoting a certain kill. He didn't care much for them, thinking they smacked of line shooting but the ground crew liked them and he had not objected when they put them there.

Casualties, sickness, postings and promotions in the natural course of events thinned the ranks of those who had been with the squadron when Kit joined. Because he survived and many of the familiar faces fell away, he and Monro were thrown more and more together. Monro liked Kit's company on the ground and his flying and shooting in the air. When he flew on operations, as often as not he took Kit along as his wing man. Some weeks later when one of the old hands who was leading A Flight went missing, Monro said to him:

271

'You'd better take over. I'll put you up for another ring. You've earned it. Beginning to get the hang of these old Glads at last, aren't you?' He slapped him on the back and led the way to the mess tent.

Shortly after his promotion had come through Kit sat wrestling a letter to his mother. Up to now his letters had been a hasty scribble telling her as much as the censor would allow of his adventures and movements, keeping it light-hearted for home consumption. But strain and fatigue and the desert were all telling on him and he had the feeling that his luck was running out. He wanted Babs to know that he understood her feelings, that he understood and loved her the more for it and that he was presently searching as best he could to find his father. The letter was to be put with his effects and only forwarded if he failed to come back. It was not an easy one to write. He tore up three drafts and was not entirely satisfied when at length he finished the fourth, but it was the best he could do and he was determined somehow to get his feelings down on paper. Having addressed and sealed it, he picked it up and walked to Monro's tent. It should have been given to the adjutant, he supposed, but the adjutant was away, he didn't care for him much and anyway he wanted Monro to have it.

The squadron commander was sitting behind a table staring distastefully at a pile of paper. 'Bumph,' he said. 'Always bumph. What can I do for you, Kit?'

'Would you look after this if I go down?' Kit said, handing him the envelope.

'Shouldn't think that's very likely,' Monro said, taking it. 'We seem to have got the measure of them – ' The shrilling of the field telephone interrupted him and he stretched out a hand to the receiver. When he had listened in silence he nodded. 'I see,' he said. 'I'll tell the chaps.' He replaced the receiver and, with his hand still on it, remained motionless for a moment, looking unwontedly serious. 'That was HQ,' he said. 'Intelligence thinks that the Eyeties have sent over two squadrons of Macchis for escort duty. They'll be stepping up their bombing. We'll have to watch out.'

'Macchis!' Kit echoed the word. 'Now that's not very nice, is it.' It was, in fact, what they had all, at the back of their minds, feared and dreaded. The Macchi was the most modern Italian fighter; a match for the Hurricane, it could out-climb, out-dive and generally out-fly their ageing Gladiators. Kit then put into words the universal cry of the desert pilot: 'When the hell are we going to get Hurricanes?'

'There's one somewhere about, I believe. The AOC is switching it around to try to convince the Eyeties they're everywhere.'

'Some hope.'

'A bottle of whisky came up with the rations. We'd better have a drink.' Monro went over to the wooden press, opened it and took out a bottle and two tin mugs. Pouring generous measures he handed one to Kit. Sand, as usual, had got into it from somewhere, discolouring it and making it gritty to the mouth. 'Bloody sand,' Monro said as he sipped. 'It even beats the seal on the bottles.'

He picked up the envelope and glanced at the address. 'Dunlay Castle, County Kilderry,' he read aloud, and then: 'Has it ever occurred to you,' he said quietly, 'that even if we come through, it'll never be the same for anyone, but especially for the likes of you? You'll never have it so good again. You were one of the privileged few. How many servants had you?'

'I don't know. I never counted them. Fifteen or something, I suppose. Anyway I don't want it or them. My brother Hugo can have them.'

'Ever been to Hartlepool?' Monro asked him.

'No. Can't say I have. Why Hartlepool?'

'It's the last station before hell,' Monro said. 'It's where I was brought up.' He twirled the whisky in his mug, looking down at it as if to read something there before he sighed, glanced up and went on. 'My father was an engineer employed by one of the big firms. He was lucky to have a job and spent his days in dread of losing it. We lived in a terraced house – a bit different from your castle. There was one maid and my mother did all the cooking. They scrimped and saved in order to send me to a public school. In the holidays there was nothing to spare for pocket money for me. I couldn't even go to the flicks. All I could do was to sit and stare at the street. There weren't any spare time jobs to try to make a few bob. There weren't any jobs at all. My father found you could live on your pay in the Air Force. He sweated his guts out to try to get me into Cranwell. I didn't know there was a life beyond that ghastly house and that awful street where the three of us lived like prisoners until I got there. I owe everything to the RAF. I want to give it something back if I can.'

'You make me feel a bit of a shit,' Kit said.

'I didn't mean to. I think that ghastly upbringing I had, the struggle of parents to give their children what they hadn't got will go after this war. And that's another thing about the RAF. We're a new service and it's not like the Army where you've got to produce your family tree or your bank balance before you get into a decent regiment. With us no one gives a damn. It's not what you do but what you are that counts.'

'I wish I knew just what I was,' Kit said, almost bitterly for him, and then, as Monro refreshed their drinks, because of Monro's confidences to him, because of the whisky they were drinking and because of the thoughts of danger on the morrow, he suddenly found himself telling Monro everything. It all came out, his being cut off by Massiter, and Clare's taking him in, his discovery through Carlow that he was not Massiter's son and Clare's telling him his real father was a white hunter in Kenya; and that that was the reason he had wangled a posting to the desert so as to have at least a chance of finding him and establishing his real identity. 'So you see,' he ended. 'I'm not quite what you took me for. I feel as if I were in a sort of limbo, though that may be a bloody silly thing to say. All I know is that the only thing I want is to find my father and discover what sort of chap he is. You see, I'll say this for the Sir, he brought us up in a sort of security – more or less, we had everything we wanted, my brother and I, and when I found nothing of it was real it knocked me endways. Am I talking rot?'

Monro gave his sudden smile. 'I'm hardly in a position to judge, am I,' he said. 'But my guess is not. Anyway, here's something that may help.' He picked up a sheet of paper from the table beside him and read from it. It was a commendation to the whole squadron as the longest serving fighter squadron in the desert, and for their sterling work in the face

274

of vastly superior numbers. 'And there's something more,' he added. 'Both Flight Commanders get DFCs. Congratulations.'

'A gong. Good Lord. I'd almost forgotten about gongs. But what about you, Bill? You're the one who – '

Monro handed the sheet of paper to him in silence. Then, 'They've gone and given me a DSO,' he said.

Kit had a headache when he woke next morning and the desert tea at breakfast tasted worse than usual. He didn't have time to have the DFC ribbon stitched to his bush jacket before first patrol, in which he was to lead the squadron: Monro had been called to HQ.

Instead of improving, his hangover had, if anything, worsened – a sure sign of tiredness – and his desert sores were giving him hell every time he shifted his position and the harness rubbed them. He kept repeating to himself that at least he had got a decoration. Now it remained to find his father and establish his identity.

They had been told to watch for Savoias operating out of Sidi Barrani and to engage if they found them. It was getting towards the end of the patrol and weariness was overwhelming him. So far they had seen nothing. Rousing himself he glanced at his petrol gauge for they were operating near the extremity of their range. Very soon it would be time to return. He turned his head to sweep the sky once more. And then, by God, there they were! Six of them, in formation, three thousand feet below. Remembering the warning of Macchis, Kit stiffened in his seat to look above and beyond the bombers. Hell's delight! They were there too, stubby little brutes looking a bit like Gladiators with one wing, masses of them, stacked up in tiers behind the Savoias.

'Blue leader,' he said into the microphone. 'See those Macchis at six o'clock.'

'Okay. I've got the bastards.'

'Stay up and cover us. I'm taking red section down on the bombers.'

'Message received and understood.'

Kit knew just what he had to do. He had to get in and hit and get out fast. His other section couldn't hope to keep those

275

Macchis busy for long. Their performance was too damn good and there were too many of them. And for him to have a hope of getting even one of the Savoias he had to place himself just right. 'Come up from below and behind and come up fast,' were Monro's fighting instructions. There was cloud about, too. He had to catch them before they could escape into it. He put one wing down, pushed the stick forward and dived.

The wind screamed through the wires as the Gladiator went down. It was as steep a dive as he had ever done. She was all but vertical. She'll either break up or I'll black out, Kit thought as he took the firing button off safe.

Neither thing happened. He had judged it just right. He came up behind the leading bomber with its port engine slap in his sights. Pressing the button he saw his bullets strike and smoke start to gush out across its wing. Then he was up and over.

At the same instant bullets ripped into his Gladiator. Christ, the Macchis! They were everywhere. Blue section hadn't had a hope of holding them. Two of the buggers were on his tail shooting hell out of him. A red hot iron lashed across his thigh. And he was still on his zoom. And these buggers could out-climb a rising lift, let alone a clapped-out Gladiator. Desperately he kicked on the rudder and rolled off the top. I can do that faster than you, anyway, damn you, he thought. There was the cloud, thank God. He took a chance and dived for it. Another burst raked him and then the murky grey wetness enfolded him. He was safe for the moment at least.

The compass was spinning, the engine sounded rough, every needle was chasing its tail round its dial, the controls were limp and there was an ominous clanking sound coming from underneath.

He eased her back on to a level keel and the instruments steadied. After a few minutes he burst out into brilliant sunshine and, looking around for danger, found the sky empty.

Twisting and turning his head as he went lest he should be bounced from behind, Kit set course as best he could for the base. He wasn't at all sure how long the controls would continue to answer and the creaking and clanging from underneath was getting worse. Below him was the desert, bleak, arid and unfriendly. He had heard too many survivors' stories to welcome the thought of finding himself on its floor even if he could walk away from the landing, which he very much doubted with the aircraft in its present condition. Nothing stirred on its surface and the sky remained empty.

Creaking and groaning, its airspeed dropping and its engine rough, the sturdy old Gladiator still flew on. The miles slid slowly by. His desert sores were hurting like hell, the sun was scorching through the canopy, blood was seeping down his leg. At least his compass appeared to be working. He hoped he had got his navigation right. The next thing to be thought about was how to get her down when he reached the airstrip. Something was badly adrift underneath, that was abundantly clear. The trouble was he didn't know what or how much. If he'd been in a Hurricane with its retractable undercart his instruments would with luck have told him if one or the other of his oleo legs had jammed up or down from which he could plan his approach and a belly landing if necessary. But that wouldn't happen in a Gladiator with its fixed undercarriage. He couldn't hope for directions from the ground either, for his radio had been shot to bits. It looked like all he could do was to bring her in as softly as possible – and pray.

And here was the airstrip. Bang on. That was something anyway. Gingerly he put the Gladiator into its approach. The noises from below were getting worse. Concentrate now, he told himself as you've never concentrated before – happy landings here I come!

He was over the edge of the airstrip, almost floating in. One good thing about the old Glad, she didn't stall easily. A touch on the throttle brought her nose up. The ground was very near and the airspeed was dropping fast. He eased back the stick. She was touching. She should be down – now. She was.

There was a crash and a crunch as the right oleo leg hit the ground and collapsed. Then everything happened very quickly. The right wing went in, scraped the ground for an instant before collapsing in a cloud of dust bringing the upper one with it. The Gladiator spun to its right like a top and then stood on its nose. Kit was thrown forward. There were rending and smashing noises. The whole aircraft was falling into bits on top of him. Something hit his head an almighty smack and he blacked out.

Kit was in hospital for a week recovering from concussion and having the gash on his thigh and the desert sores dressed. He was restless, longing all the time to get back. Despite the dangers and discomforts of the desert, the squadron under Monro's leadership had been a happy place for him. Returning to it, there was a sense of homecoming which he had never before experienced.

When the week was up he discharged himself by the simple process of walking out, hitched a lift in a Wellington going up the desert, another in a Humber staff car which a visiting American journalist had somehow purloined and eventually arrived at the airstrip. The first person he met was Monro. 'What the dickens are you doing here?' Monro asked him.

'Reporting back – sir,' Kit said.

'Well, you're not, you know. While you've been away things have been happening. We're being pulled out of the line. I've put you in for a rest and a change. You've seven days' leave and a posting as an instructor.'

'An instructor? Hell, Bill, you can't do this to me. Is this a joke?'

'Not so far as I know. We can talk later. But you'd better cut along and put on your best bib and tucker if you have one. We're having a visitor.'

'Who's that?'

'The AOC is about to descend on us to tell us what splendid chaps we are before we pull out.'

Hardly had Kit changed when the convoy of Humber staff cars and attendant vehicles, with the AOC's pennant flying from the first, swept on to the airstrip.

The AOC, a flamboyant character with a line of first World War ribbons across his chest, leapt from his seat to a flurry of salutes and began to walk down the line of officers, pausing for a word here and there. Kit's eyes swept over the entourage, past the AOC and the staff and then, to his astonishment, lighted on a figure at the tail of the procession. He blinked and looked again to make sure he was not seeing things. But there was no mistaking the cap set at a rakish angle, the patch of scar tissue below the left eye or, for that matter, the khaki RFC wings still worn instead of the standard RAF issue in open defiance of repeated Air Ministry orders. It was Clare de Vaux, or Clare, Earl of Marchester, as he now was. He smiled as he came abreast of Kit. 'Didn't expect me, did you?' he said. 'I'll have a word with you later on. You've done quite well, I hear.'

After the little ceremony was over and the AOC was proceeding to the mess tent to refresh himself with pink gin or what passed for it, Clare sauntered over to where Kit was standing. 'Come along,' he said. 'I've been given the use of the CO's tent while he entertains the great man. Where is it?'

Kit led the way, and once inside Clare threw his hat on the table, ran his hand through his thinning hair and gestured Kit to one of the canvas chairs. 'Congratulations on your DFC,' he said, and then: 'I suppose you're wondering what I'm doing here?'

'I am, a bit,' Kit said.

'I had a brush with a bomber baron, so I decided that a period of absence might do me very well. A tour in the sun, I thought. I knew the AOC from the last show. He was a flight commander in my squadron for a little while. So here I am.'

Kit knew from experience Clare's ability to pull strings on behalf of others; now, apparently, he had pulled them for himself. 'It's wonderful to see you again, sir,' he said. 'What's the news from home?'

'What news of the Bay, you mean, don't you? Isn't that the first thing you people from there always ask? Well then, I have something to tell you. I've been there.'

'What?' Kit said in astonishment. 'You mean you've actually been to the Bay?'

'That's what I said. When I was at a loose end, waiting confirmation of my posting, I'd heard so much about it from Stephen Raymond and you I decided to see it for myself. I changed my clothes and went across. It's all you said – peaceful, lonely, lovely. I can understand now the hold it has on your hearts.'

'Did you meet anyone – my mother?' Kit asked eagerly.

'I met her and we talked,' Clare said quietly.

'How was she?'

'She doesn't think very much of me,' Clare said. 'She blames me for your being caught up in the war, especially for your being in the RAF. She has a hatred of flying and all things concerned with it, and I can understand why – now. But – we talked and talked again and I think it safe to say we came to an understanding?'

'And Hugo and the Sir?' Kit asked. 'What of them? Were they there?'

'Your brother is ADC to a Corps Commander in Scotland,' Clare answered. 'I don't think your mother has any grave anxieties about him, for the moment at any rate. "A born survivor – like his father," was how she referred to him. Sir Andrew Massiter himself was away. Once she knew that I knew who you were she spoke quite freely to me. She has made up her mind to see it out. She will never leave the Bay – or Massiter for that matter. Her fears are all for you and what he may try to do to you or to your father. She feels that by staying on she may somehow be able to temper the wind of his vindictiveness.'

'I don't give a damn about him any more.'

'Nor for anyone much else, I fancy. The fighter pilot's credo. But your mother cares for you. That's why she is doing what she feels she must.'

'I didn't mean I don't care for her. Of course I do. More than anything in the world. Poor Mums. Nothing ever really went right for her after what happened in the Troubles.'

'When you get older you'll see that peace has its casualties as well as war.'

Kit suddenly wondered if he was thinking of his lost wife and child. Then he saw him sigh and stare out through the open tent flap to where the Gladiators were dispersed, perhaps thinking back to the days when he was young himself, as Kit was now. 'If the luck runs out or runs against you – ' he said, half to himself. Then he shrugged his shoulders as if putting a memory behind him. 'Well now,' he said. 'Enough of that. I have another piece of news for you about your friends. Young Harbison is back.'

'Dick! I always thought he'd turn up. How'd he manage it?'

'He was shot down over Luxembourg, walked across France and the Pyrenees and got out through Portugal.'

'That's wonderful news, sir. God, I'm glad. We had good times together.'

There was someone else, too, Kit thought, who would be glad. His mind went back to that last night of his leave and the dinner he had had with Carlow. Well, it put an end to whatever slight hopes he might have had in that direction, but he had to admit that time and separation and the war were all wearing them thin anyway. He was beginning to forget, the enchantment was fading. And in some strange way, the severing of this bond, such as it was, made him more than ever determined to find his father.

'He was back in the flat in Half Moon Street with that girl of his, he married her didn't he, waiting posting, when I left,' Clare went on. 'He'll get a squadron. I spoke to someone about him.'

Kit smiled. There it was again, the easy assumption of privilege and power that came from generations of having the one and wielding the other. Unthinking and unreflective though Kit was, because he had been born to a different culture and because he had talked to his fellows like Bill Monro in and out of the mess and had mixed with all sorts and conditions of men, even to him came the speculation of how long it would last once this war was over.

No such doubts, for the moment, at any rate, appeared to assail Clare. He sat in an easy patrician pose, one hand lying on the table before him, the other reaching in his pocket for his slim gold cigarette case. 'Before I left the Bay,' he said, 'I told your mother why you had applied to come out here. She gave me this – ' Along with the cigarette case he took an envelope from his pocket and slid it across the table to Kit.

Picking it up Kit recognised his mother's handwriting. It was addressed to 'Captain Stephen Raymond, MC'.

'She said,' Clare went on, 'that she knew you would find him and she wanted you to give it to him from your own hand and from hers. Now, you're due a rest, I believe.'

'Yes,' Kit said. 'And I'm to be sent off as a bloody

instructor, God knows where. Can you do anything about that, sir?'

'I already have,' Clare said mildly. 'I've had a word.'

Kit looked across the table at him. 'Where are you pushing me off to?' he asked.

There was a faint smile on Clare's lips. 'Nairobi,' he said. 'I thought that posting might suit you. Good luck, Kit.' And he held out his hand.

CHAPTER XXXIV

It took Kit only a few days to find his feet in Kenya and about a week to decide that instructing bored him. The flies, the sand, the heat and all the other discomforts of the desert were quickly forgotten as the days passed. The itch for activity came back and he longed to return to the squadron and to action. When a South African pilot called Castries with whom he had become friendly suggested he should accompany him on a 'milk run' to Marsabit with petrol and supplies, saying they could fly low and see some game on the way, it appeared an excellent change of alleviating the dreary routine he was settling into. He had a day off due and agreed to go.

His enquiries as to Stephen's whereabouts had not made much progress, for most of those with whom he worked were newcomers like himself and had no acquaintance with the colony or its personalities. As a serving officer he was, however, an honorary member of the Muthaiga Club. It was there that he learnt that Toby Revere was employed in some capacity on the Massiter farm. Thinking he might learn something from him, he enquired his whereabouts when he went to the club to dine with Castries the night before the Marsabit run. He found him, as usual, propping up the bar and drinking someone else's champagne. But he was friendly enough once he learnt Kit's name, for he had taken the trouble to find out that Kit, black sheep of the family though he might be, was the next baronet, and he answered his questions as best he could. Since Toby's journey through life had also taught him never to neglect an opportunity of gleaning information, however trivial, that might be useful later on, he also tried to pump Kit on his reasons for wanting to find Stephen.

'Lonely sort of feller,' he said. 'Out in the bush now with some tracker, chasin' wops. Relation of yours?'

'Sort of,' Kit said. 'Do you know where he is based?'

'Lives up in the Loldaigas with old Job Hannaford on his farm there. Got a gorgeous American popsie with him too. These damn white hunters get all the best pickings.'

'The Loldaigas, where's that? I'm flying to Marsabit tomorrow.'

'Well, you're in the general direction anyway. Couple of hundred miles one way or the other. Not much if you say it quickly. Frisco Farm, Hannaford calls his place.'

'Thanks.' Kit went back to his friend, vaguely wondering what the gorgeous American popsie would be like. Stephen seemed to have carved out a niche for himself in this strange country where, from what little he had seen of it, the old inhabitants appeared to live like medieval barons. For the first time he began to think about what his reception would be if and when he met his real father. Would he be wanted at all or would he be rejected by him too?

They were loading the old Vickers Valencia under the pilot's watchful eye when Kit arrived at the airfield the following morning. Standing a little to one side and also watching the loading was another officer with wings on his tunic. He was wearing full webbing equipment with revolver and ammunition pouch and carrying a map case. Following Kit's gaze Castries drew him to one side. 'Take a good look at that chap,' he said. 'He's been shot down over the border, wounded and shot up. Had to walk back and had the devil of a time generally. He's got a bit of a shake on, if you ask me.'

'What's he doing here?' Kit asked.

'He's coming with us. They're mounting some sort of a do from Marsabit. There's to be a fighter escort. Hurricanes.

And one of the pilots has gone down with dysentry. He's the replacement.'

Watching him Kit saw that the other pilot had a compulsive and apparently uncontrollable twitch in his upper lip which he tried to conceal by sweeping his hand across it as if brushing aside a fly. One of the pockets of his tunic bulged with what looked suspiciously like a flask.

'Hurricane pilot – hmm,' Kit said.

'They're thin on the ground. No one else available apparently. That's why we've got him. Keep an eye on him as we go, will you. Hullo, looks as though we're off. I'll sign for this stuff and then we'll get weaving.'

Kit climbed in beside him and they trundled out to take off. Even by the flying standards of the day it was slow progress. Their ground speed was about eighty miles per hour which gave them plenty of time for watching what was taking place below them. Herds of oryx, zebra and gazelle galloped away across the bush frightened by the clatter of the great strange bird banging and roaring across the sky. Kit's attention was divided between watching the game and the spare pilot. His guess about the flask had been correct. Twice he caught him surreptitiously pushing it back into his pocket and then taking out a khaki handkerchief to wipe his lips. The next time he turned in his seat he was horrified to see that he had taken the .38 Webley from its holster and was spinning the chamber as if he were about to play Russian roulette.

'Bloody old cow, this thing,' Castries was saying beside him. 'Damned if I know why the old country has to fight every war with what it used in the last one or precious nearly. The things they built to bomb Berlin the last time were faster than this. Know what they call her? Pregnant Polly – Christ, what was that?'

Kit had opened his mouth to warn him when the shot rang out. Almost immediately he saw the revolver come up again. There was another report and a bullet tore through the fuselage six inches from Castries' head. 'Jesus wept!' Castries exclaimed, turning in his seat. 'What the hell is going on?'

'The mad bastard's got a gun,' Kit said.

'I told you to keep an eye on him, didn't I? Go and get it

off him and damn quick. We've a full load of petrol on board this bloody old crate.'

Kit stood up and left his seat. He looked to where the spare pilot was sitting with his back to the fuselage. He didn't care much for what he had to do. It meant walking pretty well the length of the aircraft and there was no knowing what action the lunatic with the gun was going to take next. As he took a step forward the aircraft hit a bump. He lost his balance for a moment and then went slipping and sliding down towards the muzzle of the gun which looked about the size of a small cannon. 'Missed,' the man said, raising the gun towards his own head. 'I'll not miss this time.'

Almost falling as he was, Kit grabbed for the gun. His fingers met empty air.

'Want it? Here, then, take it,' the man said suddenly. 'It's no bloody good, is it?' And he dropped it to the floor between them. He put his head in his hands and fell into uncontrollable weeping. Heaving a sigh of relief Kit picked it up and returned to the cockpit.

'Got it?' Castries asked him.

'Yes, with a bit of luck,' Kit said.

'We'll go down and dump him,' Castries said, swinging the Valencia round in a wide arc.

'I wouldn't do that,' Kit said. 'The poor bugger seems quiet enough now. Once is enough to walk home. Anyway take a look at the ground. If we pile up here landing with all that petrol on board we've had it.'

'Maybe you've got something there.' Castries pulled out of the turn and levelled off at fifty feet. As the ground slid beneath them Kit could see it was littered with boulders and tree stumps. It was, as well, criss-crossed with ridges formed by age-old lava deposits. 'I don't like going on with that mad bugger behind,' Castries said and circled again to try to find a clear strip on which to land. But none appeared. At length he gave up and climbed to crusing height. 'It's not on,' he said. 'And now we're going to get a rocket for being late. Go back and hold the gun on him. Tell him you'll shoot him if he moves.'

Forty anxious minutes later they picked up the landing strip north of Marsabit and began their approach.

A South African major was waiting for them when they taxied in. 'You're damn late,' he greeted them. 'And we need that petrol.' He nodded to where the two Blenheims and a pair of Hurricanes were drawn up. 'What the devil is going on?' He looked angrily at the little group of three who had left the aircraft and were standing by it, Kit with the revolver in his hand. The spare pilot was a little apart from the other two, mumbling to himself, his hand still brushing away the imaginary fly.

'I want this officer put under arrest,' Castries said, indicating him and then quickly told what had happened.

'Very well,' the major, whose name was de Graz, said. Then, surprisingly he added, 'Poor devil,' as he watched him led away. 'But what the hell am I to do now? The raid has to go in. Those are my orders. We're late getting off and I have to provide an escort. Where the hell am I to get a second Hurricane pilot?'

'Here,' Kit said quietly.

De Graz swung on him. 'Who the hell are you and what the blazes are you doing here?' he said.

'I came up for the run,' Kit said. 'But I flew Hurricanes on operations in England.'

'Did you, by God. Got your log-book? No, I suppose not. Come in here.'

A ramshackle wooden structure had been hastily run up to serve as a squadron office, briefing room and operations room combined. Once inside and alone with de Graz Kit was subjected to a verbal gruelling to ascertain his experience and qualifications. At length, satisfied, de Graz sat back in his chair. 'Very well,' he said. 'I'll take a chance. If anything goes wrong there'll be two courts-martial instead of one off this airfield. It should be all right. No one but us knows the raid is going in and we've lost enough time as it is.' He pulled a map towards him, opened it and spread it out. 'The fort at Mega,' he said, placing his finger on it. 'That's the target.'

Fifteen minutes later Kit was airborne and revelling once again in the feeling of power transmitted by the Merlin engine in front of him. Whatever you had to say about Gladiators, he told himself, and some of the old hands said it, they were relics of the past. Here, where he was sitting, was the real thing.

In front and below him the two Blenheims rose and fell slightly in the thin air. Throttled back to cover them Kit and his companion kept their station, their noses pointed north. There was a map strapped to Kit's right thigh but he had very little notion where they were going. 'Keep close up and I'll get you there and back,' the other pilot had said. 'I could do it blindfolded. Hang up your socks and I'll smell my way in.'

Kit looked to his right. The other pilot met his gaze and raised his thumb. After checking his instruments Kit returned the gesture and then relaxed in the cockpit. De Graz had told them it was improbable they would meet any opposition save ground-fire which was unlikely to be nearly enough to bother them. The escort was as much to keep the Blenheim pilots happy and to show the flag as anything else. The steady beat of the engine went on. Far below, mile after mile, the desert slid back. Kit yawned. What with the banging about in the old Valencia, the heat on the ground and now this progress through the cool clear upper air, he was beginning to feel sleepy. There was nothing to worry about; this was just another milk run. But it was good to feel a Hurricane under his hands again. He yawned once more and then shook himself. They had been flying for about half an hour and must be nearing their objective. He blinked and peered out through the windshield. Was that the fort, far away near the limit of sight in that cluster of hills?

At that moment his earphones crackled followed by a shout: 'Bandits! Coming down! Break! For Christ's sake *break*!' It was his fellow pilot's voice and it was almost too late.

Something sliced across the nose of Kit's Hurricane making for the Blenheims. It was a low wing monoplane. He caught a glimpse of a red and white striped tail with the crest of the Regia Aeronautica on the fin. Macchis again! Where the hell had they come from? God, the sky was full of them. There was another on his tail. Milk run – where are you?! They'd been bounced, and well and truly bounced at that. Tracer was flashing past, missing him by inches. He slammed the Hurricane into the tightest turn he knew. 'I can turn inside you, you bastards,' he muttered. 'Take that!' A Macchi had jumped into his sights and he sent a burst into him. The Macchi fell away into a spin but he had no time to see what happened to him. There were two more coming down on him for a beam attack and another was on his tail. They were all around him, and turn as he would he could not shake them off. A burst tore into the cockpit smashing the instruments. Bullets slammed into his engine. The engine coughed twice; the airscrew spun lazily, its blades sprang into sight from its arc and it stopped.

'Time I was getting out,' Kit said to himself. Miraculously the Macchis seemed for the moment to have disappeared or to have left him to concentrate on the bombers. Far below he had a glimpse of a Blenheim going down pouring black smoke and the other surrounded by Macchis like a cloud of hornets. A bang on the quick release freed his harness. Muttering a prayer that it had not jammed, his fingers groped to free the canopy. He pulled and it slid sweetly back. Then he jumped.

CHAPTER XXXV

Immediately he had heard the declaration of war Stephen offered his services to the armed forces in Kenya. At first however, there seemed little urgency. The war was far away and Italy, the likely enemy, a non-combatant. The Germans, too, so the wiseacres said, would soon be beaten if the war in the west ever became a reality. The social whirl, amongst those who lived it, went on unabated.

Job came back to the farm, flown up by Stephen in the Moth. He looked frail and now had a stick to help him get about, though he swore continually at the necessity for it. He fell for Betty and became her slave and even talked of reviving his brother's pack of hounds for Stephen and her to occupy themselves hunting jackal. The District Commissioner came to lunch and told Stephen, unofficially, to continue his watch on the border with the Moth but on no account to cross it.

He flew out every day sometimes taking Betty with him, looking over the stock and keeping an eye out as best he could for movement beyond the border. He had a sling fitted in the cockpit to take the Winchester in case they were forced down in unfriendly territory, but it wasn't needed. Nothing happened. Mussolini's legions were still sleeping. Once he landed near the knoll where he had, as he thought, seen Winthrop and his wireless set, and taking the Winchester had climbed up it. The saucer shaped depression at the top was empty and held no traces of recent occupation. Whoever it was had had his warning and had not returned. The matter remained much in Stephen's mind and loomed even larger after he had run into Toby Revere one evening at the Muthaiga.

The club was filling up. New faces were appearing as the military slowly filtered in. 'Veldt' coloured uniforms many of them with wings on their tunics began to appear more and more as South African personnel flew up from the south to take over the air defence of the colony and to look for new airstrips in the north and east. The older members of the club tended to hold themselves aloof from these newcomers and to group together. So it was that Stephen, rather to his surprise, found himself hailed by Revere who was sitting alone turning over the pages of an illustrated magazine and looking at some South African officers with the sort of gaze usually reserved for intruders into a hitherto unoccupied railway carriage. 'Rough lot of buggers, really, aren't they?' he said to Stephen. 'Still, better than Aussies. Thank God we haven't got them. Straight from the trees, they are. What brings you here?'

Stephen, in fact, had been summoned by HQ to be told that he had been commissioned into the King's African Rifles as an intelligence officer, that the Moth was to be grounded and that he was to take himself off to the Ethiopian border or thereabouts and spend his days sitting on a hill with a pair of binoculars observing and noting any movement across the border which he was again specifically enjoined not to cross on any account. He was also to give what assistance he could if called upon by the SAAF in advising on locations for landing grounds and advanced airstrips from which raids could when necessary be made into Italian territory. Something, he thought, must be stirring in official minds. He did not see fit to inform them that his DC and his Italian opposite number were close friends and regularly dined together and that they were far more likely to get accurate information from him than from any Stephen could glean in the bush. It meant leaving the farm, too, and he would have to work out something with Job and Betty about running it. Altogether he was not in one of his better frames of mind when he dropped into a chair beside Revere; 'I'm supposed to be putting on uniform again,' he said.

'Rather you than me,' Revere said with one of his wicked grins. Someone once said to Stephen that Revere was such a shit that you almost had to admire him and latterly Stephen had come, if not to like him, at least to find him good company if taken in small doses. He was amusing when he wanted to be and there was no doubting his charm for either sex when he cared to exert it. He could scarcely have lived for so long on his wits without possessing it, Stephen reflected as he called for the boy and told him to bring a bottle of champagne.

" 'The nuisance of the tropics is the sheer necessity of fizz",' Revere quoted as he sipped. 'Wasn't it Finch-Hatton who composed those deathless lines? All too true. The thing is, it's a necessity anywhere, I've found – provided someone else pays for it, of course!' He gave another of his wolfish grins.

Stephen was staying in the club, as he had to get himself uniforms the next day, and half an hour later he found himself dining with Revere. It was a way Revere had. 'No one else here of any consequence,' he said. Then over a second bottle, he grew talkative. 'Musso's coming in,' he said. 'No doubt about that, and damn soon too. I happen to know.' Here he gave a portentous wink. 'Think he'll walk in here? You ought to know. You know the country better than most.'

'They say he's put backbone into his troops,' Stephen said. 'I don't know. They didn't do much in the last show except cut and run. And there's a hell of a desert to cross.'

'The fascist business must have something,' Revere went

on. 'Take old Gervase now. It's really got hold of him. First time in his life he's got a cause if you know what I mean. Different man now from the feller I used to know. Don't see eye to eye you two, exactly, I know, but I'm a bit worried about him, I don't mind telling you.'

'Why would that be?' Stephen asked quietly.

'He's become great chums with that Italian count fellow up at Meru who plays around with wireless and things and who'll be interned the minute Musso does come in or I miss my guess. And I'll tell you another thing – ' Revere leant confidentially across the table and dropped his voice almost to a whisper. 'He's taken to disappearing into the blue. Why's he doing that? He never went on safari before. I'm left to run the farm. How the hell do I know how to run a farm? Only way I know is to kick wogs' bottoms. It's that fellow Massiter's farm. I suppose he knows what's going on. I don't know how much old Ger is telling him.'

Probably more than you think, Stephen said to himself. Aloud he said: 'Doesn't Massiter keep in touch?'

'He keeps in touch all right. Lots of letters. I'm not supposed to open them if Ger's away. D'you know Massiter? You do, I suppose, since you both come from Ireland. Frightening sort of feller, I've always thought. Has to be one jump ahead. Two sons of his are serving. One's in the 50th Lancers, the other in the RAF. He's just been posted to Egypt, so Massiter told Ger.'

Stephen sat up. 'You wouldn't know which one is in the RAF?' he said.

'No, old boy, I wouldn't. He's the unsatisfactory one, I heard Ger say. Massiter hardly ever mentions him. Got into trouble somewhere and Massiter booted him out. Only told Ger about his being in Egypt in case Ger ran into him. Now, how about a glass of port?'

Three days later Mussolini declared war on the side of the Axis, and Stephen was despatched on his border watch which he was to share with Ronnie Baines, another of Hayes and Franklin's white hunters who had also been commissioned as an intelligence officer. In addition to their own observations they were instructed to talk to the tribesmen who were

291

constantly coming and going across the border to try to find
from them any news of Italian forces concentrating for a move
south; and sometimes to fly with South African pilots on
their patrols to help them identify landmarks and search out
emergency landing strips.

Already the South Africans were raiding into Ethiopia and
beyond. What effect these forays had was to Stephen's mind
extremely doubtful but at least they were showing that here
on the northern border the old lion was not entirely toothless.
Any deterrent, however slight, to the Italian legions, to their
morale and their high command, must be of value, for
Stephen knew better than most how feeble Kenya's defences
were. In fact at this time they were all but non-existent. The
KAR had fought a gallant holding action at Moyale and
were patrolling and skirmishing south of it but if the Italians
crossed the desert and mounted a determined push there was
nothing to stop them, as far as Stephen could see, from
overrunning the colony.

All this knowledge brought further worries with it, for there
were Job and Betty and the farm to be thought of, and the
farm lay directly in the path of any invader. Plans had been
drawn up that, in the event of an invasion, the white
community should collect in Nanyuki and, since the Italian
aircraft would almost certainly machine gun the roads, they
should then trek together across country to Naivasha. Later
perhaps they could return to evacuate the stock.

Job truculently and firmly refused to contemplate leaving
the farm. 'If I don't stay here alive I'll stay here dead, which
I damn nearly am anyway,' he declared. In this Betty backed
him up, adding that the Italians would never dare to molest
an American citizen and that she would remain on to protect
both him and the farm under the banner of the stars and
stripes.

Winthrop's forays into the bush as revealed by Toby Revere
were also constantly in Stephen's mind. He fruitlessly combed
the area for any sign of him, and when he interrogated
tribesmen to ascertain if they had observed a strange white
man, possibly with bearers and burdened with wireless equipment, their answers revealed nothing of value. Finally he

came to the conclusion that Winthrop was either lying low or else had removed himself to another part of the country.

The Italian count mentioned by Revere had left and gone no one knew where the day before Mussolini entered the war. When a detachment arrived to bring him into internment they found signs of hasty departure and the house empty of human occupation. Amongst the personal possessions left behind nothing more sinister was discovered than a comprehensive collection of pornographic literature.

Then Stephen's area of operations was switched to the Somali border. This meant covering his beloved Tana river country, but even there it was soul-destroying work. Nothing at all happened, and the days dragged on occupied only by sitting staring into nothingness or slugging through the heat to trace the origin of some ill-defined rumour of troop movements by questioning tribesmen who were either surly and uncommunicative or else given to flights of fancy. Always, too, there was the worry about the farm with which he was then out of touch. It came therefore as a welcome relief when a message came telling him to take ten days' leave.

A pilot who was returning from one of the advanced airstrips near the Somali border on an early flight agreed to take Stephen back to Nairobi. Having collected his car he called in at the club on his way north. The club was a sort of posting house. Messages, even movement orders, were sometimes left there. Nothing was on the board for him nor had the porter anything but, early though it was, he saw Toby Revere sitting at a table in the lounge with a half-bottle of champagne in front of him. 'Hullo there,' Revere hailed him.

Stephen was about to leave with a perfunctory greeting when Revere's next words stopped him in his tracks. 'Young RAF feller in here last night looking for you,' he said.

Stephen crossed the lounge towards him. 'Hair of the dog,' Revere went on, indicating the bottle. 'New feller just come out threw a party last night. Name of Delves Broughton. Remember him? Owned a few bloody slow horses at home. Got a new young wife.'

'Who was this young chap in the RAF who was asking for me?' Stephen said to him.

'Massiter's his name. Remember I told you there were two sons, one of them in the RAF? Well, it's that chap. Done his tour of the desert and posted here as an instructor. Found I was running his father's farm – old Ger's off in the blue again. Asked for me and wanted particularly to find out about you. Told him you were somewhere in the bush watchin' for wops.'

Kit, Stephen thought, it must be Kit. His pulse quickened. 'Where is he now?' he asked.

'Damned if I know. He'd an SAAF feller with him. They were to fly up to Marsabit on some do today. Know what he wanted you for?'

'Oh, yes,' Stephen said. 'I think I know what he wanted me for.'

He was almost running when he reached the car. It started immediately and he drove like fury over the bumpy roads back to the farm. Every mile seemed like ten and he fumed with impatience, his thoughts running back twenty years to that long, languorous, tropical summer when the Bay had been torn apart by strife and Kit had been begotten, and then jumping forward to wonder and ponder on what he would be like now and how soon he could get to Marsabit and find him. Bouncing in and out of pot-holes and wrestling the car through the red mud left by recent rains, at last he drew up on the sweep in front of the farm. Switching off the engine he jumped down. Betty had heard the car approaching and was standing in the doorway, waiting.

'Stephen,' she said. 'It's you. Back again and safe. Aren't we pleased to see you – Job will – ' And then, seeing the look on his face, 'Stephen, what's happened?'

'It's Kit,' he said. 'I've found him. He's at Marsabit in the RAF. Tell them to get out the Moth. I'm flying up.'

'Can you? You're grounded surely, or the Moth is.'

'Be damned to that. It'll fly and I'm flying.' He went into the house. Job was sitting in one of the armchairs in the long living room. To Stephen's eyes, not having seen him for a long period, he now looked old and somehow shrunken.

'I heard what you were saying outside,' he said. 'Betty told me about the boy Kit. So you've found him. Good luck, lad.'

'I'm flying up in the Moth.'

'Better take that with you,' Job nodded towards the gun-rack. 'Wouldn't do to come down without it in the Reserve amongst those d'Orobo you've fixed for poaching once or twice. No knowing what they'd do to you in the way of uncomfortable things.' Job gave one of his throaty chuckles. 'What would Mr Jorrocks say – '

Stephen noticed that *Handley Cross*, unopened, was lying on the table beside him together with a bottle of whisky. Rushing though he was, he resolved to humour his old friend, and in an odd way, looking at the book, he found himself wishing to discover what the *sortes Surteesianae*, as Kipling had called them, would bring forth. Things had recently taken a turn for the better. He had found peace and contentment on the farm and with Betty in the loving companionship she brought with her. Was this run of luck going to continue, he wondered, or would fate with that piece of lead piping strike again? He gestured towards the book. 'Open it, put your finger on the sentence and we'll see,' he said.

Reaching for his glasses Job picked up the book and allowed it to fall open. He stabbed a stubby finger at the page and then peered at the text. " 'Treasonous, treacherous rogues, exclaimed Pretifat, I'll hand you over to the law officers of the Crown",' he read out as he closed the book. 'Now what the devil help is that?' he said.

'Not much,' Stephen said. 'Old Jorrocks J. has let us down for once.' He crossed to the gun-rack and took down the Winchester. 'It's been a long time since you gave me this, Job,' he said.

'Our first safari, your first lion. I'm not likely to forget. Aye, it's been a long time like you say, lad, and time, as I'm finding out, waits for no man. I'll see you off.' He poured himself three fingers of whisky and swallowed them at a gulp. Then he groped for the stick on the floor beside him, and with much cursing and groaning, began to heave himself out of the chair. 'No, don't help me, dammit,' he said as Stephen moved towards him. 'I'll stand on me own feet like I always did.' But as he came upright, breathing heavily and leaning on his stick, he staggered and caught hold of Stephen's arm to steady himself. 'Seedy and rocky like an old beaten-up bull buff,' he said then, his breath coming in gasps. The grey tinge was back in his cheeks. He looked up at Stephen and their eyes met. 'I won't last much longer,' he said. 'Now remember, lad, everything here and all that's in it is going to be yours, and that lass seems to want to share it, too.' He gave a throaty chuckle. 'No accounting for taste. What was it John Jorrocks said – nothing so peculiar than scent 'cept a woman!' Together they walked slowly out into the sunlight where the Moth was waiting on the grass airstrip.

At the edge of the grass Job paused. 'This is far as I go,' he said, panting with the effort of even covering that short distance. 'Go on, lad, and good luck to you.'

Betty was standing by the aircraft. She looked quickly at Job and then back to Stephen. 'He couldn't come any further,' Stephen said to her. 'He hardly made it even to there. How bad is he?'

'Oh, Stephen, it's so sad. The doctor says he could go any minute. He only gives him weeks, perhaps days. This altitude, too, isn't doing him any good, but of course he won't dream of leaving. It's his heart. It's just worn out, the doctor says.'

'Who is it? Old Wauchope from Nyeri?'

'Yes.'

'He should know. He looked after his brother before him.' Stephen hesitated. 'I wonder. When it happens, should you stay?'

'Of course I should. And I can, and I must and I will. Kamau and I can hold the fort. It's pretty well what we've been doing for the past three weeks anyway, isn't it, Kamau?'

Suddenly Kamau was standing beside her, giving his familiar toothless grin. 'We hold fort, b'wana,' he said, repeatng Betty's words after her. 'Still carrying own gun, b'wana – ' He grinned even more widely as he looked at the Winchester in Stephen's hands.

'Very well, then, you old reprobate,' Stephen said, slapping him on the back. 'Mind you take good care of her and b'wana Hannaford too.' He leant over and slid the Winchester into its sling.

'Good luck, Stephen dear,' she said to him. 'I hope you find him. I know you will. Job has told me what he's done for us. And don't forget, I'll be here waiting – always.' And then she raised her lips to be kissed.

Stephen ran the engine up and found no trace of missing

296

or hesitation. He raised his hand, waved to the boys to pull away the chocks and taxied out. Then he turned into the wind and took off. As he climbed, a glance over the side showed him the diminishing figures of Job and Betty standing by the windsock waving goodbye.

At least, he told himself as the Moth flew steadily on, Job's final words had made sure that the place was safe for him and Betty when this bloody war was over, if it ever was. And Betty had said she would wait for him, and what Betty said she meant.

When he landed at Marsabit the airstrip was deserted. De Graz came out of the makeshift office as he taxied up to it and cut the engine. 'And who the hell may you be?' he demanded truculently. 'Landing a civil aircraft on a military airfield without permission. Damn lucky you weren't shot down.' Then, taking in the RFC wings on Stephen's tunic with the MC ribbon beneath them, his tone modified. 'From Nairobi, are you,' he said. 'Special delivery, or something?'

'Not quite,' Stephen answered. 'It's a private matter. I was told I'd find an RAF officer here. Name of Massiter.'

'Oh.' De Graz hesitated and then said, 'Come inside, will you.'

In the hut he waved Stephen to one of the wooden chairs and, placing himself behind the table, picked up a pencil. After fiddling with this for a moment or two he said, 'Look here, it's all highly irregular but this chap, Massiter, came up with the stores Valencia. We had a raid on and I had a Hurricane pilot down with dysentry. The replacement that was sent, well, he went off his head. Massiter told me he'd flown Hurricanes on operations and, well, the long and the short of it is I let him go in the sick chap's place. They're overdue. I wish to hell – ' He stared out of the window.

At that moment the door opened and a corporal put his head in. 'I think I hear something, sir,' he said.

Both Stephen and de Graz pushed back their chairs and ran outside. The whole personnel of the airstrip was gathered in a group, shading their eyes and looking north. The sound of an aircraft engine came faintly to them and then grew louder. A speck appeared in the sky and swiftly materialised into a low-wing monoplane – a Hurricane. Stephen drew his breath. Kit – at last!

The Hurricane circled the field and came in for a bumpy landing. The engine sounded rough and as it approached them they could see the scorched and blackened gun-ports and the bullet holes that studded the fuselage. The pilot climbed down and walked slowly towards them, his shoulders humped in a posture of weariness and dejection.

With a sick feeling of disappointment and fear Stephen saw the veldt coloured uniform and realised it could not be Kit.

'What happened?' de Graz demanded. 'Where are the others?'

The pilot slumped down on a bench. 'Gone. Shot down. Busted,' he said.

'What do you mean? What happened, man?' de Graz repeated.

'We were bounced. Macchis. They were waiting for us, above us in the sun. We hadn't a chance.'

'The Blenheims?'

'Both down. One of them in flames.'

'And Massiter?'

'I think he got out. I'm not sure. I was too bloody busy.'

'Did you get any of them?'

'I got one and a probable. I think Massiter got one. It was all so quick. They were waiting for us. We were sitting ducks. How the hell did they know – '

'Come inside,' de Graz said.

They went through the door of the hut and Stephen followed them, a sick feeling at the pit of his stomach. To be so near and to have him snatched away – that man round the corner with the piece of lead piping was working hard to make up for lost time. But the pilot chap had said he might have got out. There was just a chance –

The pilot was telling de Graz his story in more detail and as best he could. De Graz got out his maps and together they studied them, trying to pin-point the place where Kit had gone down if, in fact, he had got out. The pilot was, as was to be expected, very vague. He freely admitted that it could have been almost anywhere in a huge area of sand and scrub

298

and waste. 'Bounced,' he said again. 'Bounced. I can't understand it – '

'They must have bloody good listening posts all along the border,' de Graz said. 'But if they have, our intelligence have never reported or pin-pointed them. You'd think, too, our patrols could have picked them up – '

'Even if they have them I don't see how they had time,' the pilot went on stubbornly. 'They were there, sitting in the sun, I tell you, up above and ready and waiting for us.'

Listening posts! Suddenly everything clicked into a conviction in Stephen's mind. It was Winthrop. He'd gone into the blue again; Revere had said so. And Winthrop had a wireless transmitting set. Stephen was even more sure now that it was he whom he had surprised that day with Job, and that he had been right all along. A transmitting set in a place that could overlook the airfield so that the operator could tell when a raid was taking off would get the message through in time for the Eyeties to prepare an ambush. Winthrop! Mr Surtees and Mr Jorrocks had been right after all. A treacherous and traitorous rogue was about, and it was now Stephen's business to hand him over to the forces of the Crown. Winthrop was back in his old haunts and operating somewhere near, he was sure of it. And Winthrop might have just been responsible for the killing of Kit. Stephen's lips tightened at the thought. He would hunt him down and find him if it took the rest of his life. He went outside and looked about him.

To the north stretched a sandy waste studded with thorn trees. Beyond and lying directly in the path of any aircraft making for the border were two low, craggy hills with a rocky valley between them. Either would serve as an admirable observation post from which to keep the airstrip under surveillance. It was from them that the course of the raid had been plotted, Stephen felt certain. After studying them for a few minutes he went back into the hut.

'The pilot said he was bounced,' he told de Graz. 'And he couldn't make out why. You mentioned listening posts. That isn't really on and your chap didn't think so either. For my money there's someone in those hills to the north with a wireless. I'm going to take the Moth and find him.'

299

'Just a minute,' de Graz said. 'What are you doing here, in any case?'

'I'm an intelligence officer attached to HQ. Ring Nairobi if you like and confirm it. My name's Raymond. As I told you I came here on a private errand, but I've had my suspicions about someone operating in this area for some time. Now, from what your chap told us, I'm sure of it.'

'What do you intend to do?'

'I think I can spot him from the air. If so I'll land and nail him down before he cuts off. I suggest you take any men you can spare and follow in a truck. Go to that cleft between the hills.' Stephen went to the door and pointed. 'When you get there fire a shot. If I have him I'll answer it. Then you can come and collect him.'

'You seem very sure of yourself. Why do you think you can handle him alone? There may be more than one.'

'I made my living as a white hunter for ten years. Once you've hunted buffalo men come easy.'

De Graz looked at the grim set of his features. 'White hunter, eh,' he said. 'Very well. Carry on. Sure you don't want anyone in the front cockpit of that Moth?'

'He'd only be in the way. I'll manage alone, I'm used to it,' Stephen said, and went out to the aircraft.

It did not take long to cover the miles between the airstrip and the hills. Not wishing to give the appearance of a search lest he might flush his bird Stephen kept as high as he dared but as he went his eyes probed the crannies and gulleys of the broken hills.

At first it did not look as if it was going to be as simple as he had thought, for trees and thick vegetation grew where desert met rock. Shrubs and scrub growing upwards from the foothills too, afforded plenty of concealment.

Then he had a stroke of luck. There was a sudden flash of light from one of the spurs which he recognised instantly for what it was. Someone was using field glasses to pick him up and plot his course. In doing so, the glasses had caught the glare of the sun and reflected it. He held the Moth level and took a quick look over the side of the cockpit. He had to locate the source of the flash but at the same time if the glasses were powerful enough to define him clearly, which they probably were, he must not betray his interest to the watcher below. The flash was repeated as he looked down and after that it was easy enough. It came from a shelf screened by trees and situated on the outermost spur of the eastern hill. He flew on and then swung round in a wide circle losing height all the time. Soon he was behind and below the hills, well out of sight of the watcher on the shelf. He cut the engine and glided down to land on the hard, packed earth.

Once on the ground he reached into the cockpit and slid the Winchester from its sling. Working the action to put a round into the breech, he looked about him. He had landed behind the western hill. In front of him was the little valley; beyond it was the eastern hill with its shoulder running out into the desert. The ground at the immediate base of both hills was littered with boulders, old tree stumps and the odd camel skull. Picking his way through these, he crossed the valley and began to skirt the base of the farther hill. Whoever was on that shelf, he reckoned, and he was sure in his own mind that it was Winthrop, must have needed a path of some sort to get his equipment up and he searched the outcrops to find where it commenced.

It was only a matter of minutes before he came upon it. Narrow and twisting, beginning from between two boulders and roughly concealed behind a screen of scrub it led upwards towards the ledge. Noiselessly, without disturbing stone or twig, treading as he had been taught and learnt from his years in the bush, he made his way along it. Because he was alert to anything on the path which might convey a warning of his approach and because his eyes after all those years of experience were attuned to detecting signs of threat or danger, he spotted the warning device almost immediately. It was a trip wire laid across the path six inches from the ground and barely discernible against its dusty background. Stepping over it Stephen gave a grim smile. Here was confirmation if he wanted it that whoever was on the shelf was up to no good. His senses made sharper still and hitching the Winchester so that it was instantly ready, he went silently on.

The path ended a foot or two above the shelf. He could

301

look down on it and command the whole scene and, doing so, he found that all his guesses had been correct.

A transmitting set stood on a trestle table erected towards the edge of the shelf. In front of it was a camp chair. Another camp chair was beside a smaller table on which was a map, a bottle of whisky and a glass. At the back, in the hillside itself was the dark opening of a cave or recess before which a camouflaged curtain hung. In the centre a figure stood, looking upwards, field-glasses to his eyes, sweeping the sky. It was Gervase Winthrop.

After a few moments Winthrop put down the glasses, letting them hang by the strap round his neck, and turned slowly round. As if instinctively feeling the presence of another being on the shelf, he raised his head and their eyes met.

To Stephen's surprise Winthrop held his gaze without flinching and without betraying discomfiture or, for that matter, any emotion at all. 'Ah, Raymond,' he said. 'D'you know, somehow I thought it might be you in that Moth. Ever since Toby told me you were up to your antics in the bush I had a feeling we might meet. And just what are you doing here?'

'Looking for you,' Stephen said. 'And I've found you, caught red-handed you might say, communicating with the enemy.'

Winthrop strolled over to the camp chair beside the wireless and sat down. Taking a slim gold cigarette case from the top of his safari jacket, he opened it. 'Care for a cigarette?' he said. 'No. And just what makes you think that was what I was doing?'

'The raid from Marsabit was bounced. They lost all but one aircraft. The Eyeties had previous information. From you – from here – '

Winthrop sat back in his chair, crossed his legs and blew a series of smoke rings before saying contemptuously, 'Who's going to believe you – a renegade Irishman, discredited in all he's done, who ran away from a buffalo and left his client to face it. Your word against mine. You'll never prove it.'

Stephen's fingers tightened round the stock of the Winchester. 'Won't I though,' he said. 'The wavelength the set's on will show it all to the follow-up party that's on its way. They've only got to home in and get an answer and that's it. Hadn't thought of that, had you? And take your hand away from that table.' Stephen's voice sharpened to a bark. 'Or I'll blow it off.'

Winthrop hastily pulled back the fingers that were creeping towards the dial.

'Perhaps I should do that anyway,' Stephen went on through clenched teeth. 'Perhaps I should shoot you and save others the trouble.'

'Oh, but you won't do that, you know. You're far too decent a chap for that, which is a kind way of saying that you haven't got the guts. All right, assume you're correct in what you say. You're acting the fool bringing me in. If you've any sense the way things are going you'll come in with us. You can just say it was all a mistake, that I'm helping you on an intelligence mission. As it is you're playing on the wrong side.'

'What the devil do you mean?'

'England's finished, done in, done with. We've had the hell of an innings but it's over. We can't win. Look at it sensibly. Our only chance was the Yanks and they're not coming in. Their chap in London, Kennedy, has told Roosevelt we're beat. I know this. I have it on damn good authority. They won't move. And the Eyeties can walk in here whenever they like. It's only a question of time and not much time at that – '

'I didn't come here for a lecture on politics.'

'You're going to get one just the same.' Winthrop drew coolly on his cigarette and looked at him. He showed neither fear nor apprehension, instead he appeared to exude confidence that he knew what he was doing and that he was right. Stephen had the strange feeling that the initiative in this encounter was passing away from him.

'The newer nations,' Winthrop continued, 'the dictator-ships, the fascists, they're going to rule the world, you mark my words, Raymond. And there are a hell of a lot of better people in England, too, politicians and cabinet ministers for that matter who think the same way, let me tell you. It's only ambitious warmongers like Churchill and Eden who want this war to go on. It's Russia we should be fighting – if we should be fighting at all.'

'Who's been filling you up with this rubbish?'

'Never mind. And it isn't rubbish. There are plenty of people round Churchill pressing him to make a separate peace and save what he can from the wreck. Some of their names might surprise you. And as for us, we'd be a damn sight better off under Musso. At least he'd keep the wogs in order.'

'And you'd be drinking castor oil instead of champagne in the Muthaiga if you put a foot out of line. You're mad, Winthrop.'

Winthrop leant forward, and it was then that Stephen could see the fanaticism in his eyes. 'Mad, am I?' he said. 'You and those like you will find out pretty quickly how sane I am. Anyway you're Irish. What the hell are you fighting for? England's peril is Ireland's opportunity – ever heard that? If you haven't others have. You should be with us, not against us.'

With the mention of Ireland a light began to dawn on Stephen. 'It's Massiter that's behind you, isn't it?' he said. 'That's where you're getting your information from. He's using you, you know, like he uses everyone. As it happens, I have a private score to settle with Massiter.'

'You'll never do it. He's safe in neutral Ireland whatever happens. He has money and power and friends in high places. He always wins. And what are you? A failed white hunter. He had a hand in that too. The authorities are only using you because they're short of experienced men in the bush. And even if this patrol of yours takes me in, what can they do to me?'

'Execute you, I imagine. That's what they do to traitors, isn't it?'

'Nonsense. The most they'll do is intern me, and it's only a few weeks before Musso walks in and then I'll be on top and you and your like, unless you learn sense in a hurry, had better look out. Execute me? Execute a white man for communicating with the enemy? They'd never do it and lose face with the wogs at this juncture in time, and well you know it. You're on a hiding to nothing, Raymond.'

'Then as I said, maybe I'd better do the job myself.'

'Don't be melodramatic. Shoot me, indeed. That's cold-blooded murder. You couldn't get away with it even if you had the guts.'

'I might have a special reason.'

'And what might that be?'

'There were two Hurricanes escorting the Blenheims on that raid. One was shot down. It's not known if the pilot is alive or dead.'

'What does it matter? One pilot more or less? There's a war on.'

'It matters to me.'

'And how, pray?'

'He was my son.'

Their eyes met. Reading in Stephen's the menace that was there, the killing anger that was building up and beginning to burn like a fire in his brain, for the first time Winthrop faltered. He ran his tongue across his lips. 'I didn't know – how could I?' he said. Even then the remains of his defiance stayed with him and he faced Stephen squarely. 'But you wouldn't dare – ' he said, though his voice shook as he said it.

At that moment a shot sounded from below. In reply the Winchester in Stephen's hands seemed to go off almost involuntarily, but the shot went where he wanted it, close enough for Winthrop to feel the wind of its passing. 'The next one goes through your head,' Stephen said as he stared into Winthrop's appalled eyes. 'Unless you do as I say. Think I wouldn't? You may have killed my son, you and Massiter between you, you bastards. You'd be shot while trying to escape. Heard of that before? No one is going to query it with the evidence round here.'

Winthrop swallowed. He put his hand to his head. The nearness of that bullet's passing, together with the look in Stephen's eyes, had broken him at last. 'What do you want me to do? What can I do?' he said.

'Two things. First there's a map on that table. My guess is that you've kept the line open all the time and you've a pretty good idea where they were bounced. Go and plot it on the map. By my reckoning we've about ten minutes before the patrol gets here. Get moving.'

Winthrop got to his feet and crossed to the table. Taking

a protractor and dividers he worked silently for a few minutes. Then he threw down the pencil. 'It's the best I can do,' he said.

Glancing at the map Stephen saw that it more or less confirmed what the pilot had indicated. It would be a help in the search but not much more. 'I said there were two things,' he said.

'What's the other? For Christ's sake, Raymond, what are you going to make me do?'

'Take that pad of paper there and write on it: 'Sir Andrew Massiter of Dunlay Castle, Bellary, County Kilderry, Ireland, financed me in my dealings with the Italians and paid for the wireless equipment I used this day to betray a raid on Mega by two Blenheims and two Hurricanes to the enemy, resulting in the loss of three aircraft." Date it and sign it.'

'It's under duress. No one will believe it.'

'There's about five minutes now before the patrol gets here. You can either meet them or eternity.'

Winthrop looked into the muzzle of the Winchester. It pointed straight at his heart. He picked up the pen and wrote hastily. 'Not worth the paper it's written on,' he said venomously to Stephen as he tore off the sheet and handed it to him.

'It'll do me,' Stephen said, folding the sheet and putting it in his pocket. 'Just in time too, almost a dead heat; a short head perhaps or a neck might be more appropriate,' he added as de Graz, a big World War I Webley in his hand, stepped on to the shelf. 'Here's your man,' he said to the South African. 'I wouldn't treat him too gently if I were you.'

CHAPTER XXXVI

When Kit found himself falling into space he had a moment of panic that he would fail to find the handle of the ripcord. As he sought for it he seemed to be rushing towards earth at a frightening speed. Then his grasping fingers touched it and he wrenched it free. The canopy blossomed out above him and stopped his descent with a jerk. Floating down, he had time to wonder what his landing would be like and what he would do when he got there. As it happened the last plunge of the parachute brought him into a clump of stones and boulders and he came down in an awkward stumbling heap with one of his ankles buckled under him.

Banging his hand on the parachute release, he stood up, and instantly a stab of pain shot through his ankle and leg. With one hand he steadied himself against a boulder and began to haul in the silk. That done, he sat down and felt his ankle. Already it was beginning to swell and when he took off his shoe and sock he found the whole area round it red and sore to the touch. He managed with some difficulty to get the sock and shoe back on again and then looked about him.

All around him stretched a vast, sandy waste. Here and there were the inevitable thorn trees and irregular patches of scrub. On the far horizon to what he guessed to be the north was the range of hills where the fortress of Mega lay and in the opposite direction to the south other hills smouldered in the purple haze of heat. The map had been torn from his thigh in his descent so he had no idea where he was. From the sun and his recollection of the course they had taken, if he was right in placing the Mega hills to the north, he could make a rough guess at the points of the compass and that was all.

From his quick glance at the map before they had set out he had a vague recollection that there was a road somewhere leading towards Marsabit. If he could reach that he might find help. But where and in what direction it lay he had no means of telling. There was only the desert, vast, empty,

307

desolate with no sign of life on it as it lay under the burning heat. He had no water, no rations, no weapons. The Italians, too, would almost certainly be searching for him. And his ankle in the state it was did not hold out much hope for a hundred-mile walk through hostile country.

After a little while the sun began rapidly to sink and then the quick short dusk came on, bringing with it the chill of night. Shivering, he decided to wait until morning before trying to formulate some plan of action. It wasn't the greatest of places to bed down but it would have to do. Things might be worse. He could have broken an arm or leg. Something would turn up. Pulling the parachute silk towards him and wrapping himself in it as best he could, he tried to compose himself for sleep.

He spent a restless night. The desert may have appeared empty by day; it came alive after dark. As soon as night fell and the brilliant stars emerged, a throbbing sense of life came with them to surround the little knoll. Nearby there were stirrings and rattlings as things slithered over stones; once or twice there was a larger disturbance as a denizen of the wild went by. At intervals came the horrid high cackle of the hyena and in the distance was a muffled roar which, although Kit did not know it, told of a desert lion on the prowl. Despite the cushion of the parachute silk the stones made a hard mattress, his ankle throbbed and burned when it touched anything. His sleep such as it was was haunted by nightmares through which passed Andrew Massiter, his eyes alight with hatred, Dai Evans shouting 'clobber 'em' before in some strange way turning into Beatrice jeering him for being a bastard, and a shadowy figure who presented himself as his real father.

When he woke he was shivering and the sun was coming up. Soon it was a red glaring ball burning down on him and scorching him. There was no shelter from it to be had amongst the stones of the knoll which rapidly became too hot to touch. It was obvious he could no longer stay there but had to find shade of some sort, where he could at least try to think out what he should do next. Looking around he saw that about a hundred yards away was a patch of scrub with a few thorn trees growing about it. That should, he thought, provide some

308

shelter from the sun and perhaps he could rig the parachute silk into a sort of tent. Dragging it behind him he picked his way through the stones and hobbled towards the scrub. He was attempting to throw the silk over a lower branch of the tree when he heard the sound of an aircraft engine.

At first he thought it must be an Italian searching for him and looked about for a hiding place. Then the realisation came that the sound was from the south, hardly the direction frm which an enemy plane would approach. Leaving his shelter and shading his eyes he searched the sky. Soon the aircraft became quite clear. It was a light aircraft flying very low. It was some distance away to the east but as it appeared Kit recognised it as a Moth. So far as he could see, too, it had civilian markings. What on earth was it doing here? At all events the Italians, so far as he knew, had no Moths, so it must be friendly whatever it was. With hope rising within him he advanced further into the open, raised his arms and shouted. The Moth flew on. Either its occupant didn't see him or else it was on some other errand. It turned away to the east.

Kit continued to watch its progress. Whatever its object was it did appear to be searching for something. It flew a leg to the east, turned south and then west again. It looked like a square search but so far as he was concerned there was little hope to be derived from it, for the area it covered was away from, not towards, him. He shouted and waved but to no avail. The Moth turned again, the drone of its engine faded and it disappeared.

Kit went back to the shade. At last despair was beginning to stare him in the face. He had to accept that there was no chance with his ankle in the state it was of walking to safety or walking anywhere for that matter. He sat down, tried to think things out and as he did so hope began to come back. There was no doubt that the Moth had given the appearance of making a systematic search. That being so, might it not return? If it did surely its new area of cover would be towards him. He put aside the idea that it might choose to make its search even further away and instead concentrated on finding a way of attracting the pilot's attention, for even if it did come over him he might be missed. He was only a speck in this burning wilderness.

Then inspiration came. The parachute – that would serve as a marker signal. Picking up a piece of wood lying at the foot of the tree and using it as a crutch he began to pull the silk into the open. Once there he spread it and fetched stones to secure it at each corner. With any luck it should stand out clearly against the drab background of the desert soil.

The effort exhausted him and he went back to the shade to rest. An hour passed and there was no sign of the Moth returning. Despite the scorching heat he felt he had to do something. Taking his stick he hobbled over to the knoll and clambered up it. It was possible, he told himself, that he might catch a glimpse of the Moth in the clear air before he heard it. But the sky to the south was empty. Turning to the north he saw something that made his heart sink. A small cloud of dust was rising from the direction of the Mega escarpment. He stared at it again and began to make out dark specks in the dust. They were moving. That could only mean one thing. It was an Italian motorised patrol on its way and it could only be looking for him.

CHAPTER XXXVII

At first light that morning Stephen and de Graz had pored over their maps. 'He's there or thereabouts, if he's anywhere,' de Graz said looking at the marked maps and comparing them. 'But you know as well as I do – better, I imagine – '

'Like a needle in a haystack,' Stephen completed the phrase for him. 'Of course you're right. But there's a chance he is there and alive, and I must take it.'

'If you meet Eyetie fighters,' de Graz said doubtfully. 'Macchis – '

'I won't now we've got Winthrop and there's no one to give me away. Besides I'll be too low and too slow for them. I'll turn inside them if I have to. I've done it before. They won't get me.'

'I hope you're right. There's nothing here I can send with you. The other Hurricane is unserviceable. Shot to bits. It's a miracle he got back at all.'

They walked together to where the Moth was pegged down. 'Will they hang Winthrop?' de Graz asked abruptly as they reached it.

'I doubt it,' Stephen said. 'Much as I hate to say it, a lot of what he told me is true. He knows too many people at the top, knows their secrets for all I know, knows where the bodies are buried as we used to say in Ireland. And again, like he said, this is no time for hanging a white man. Pushed off quietly into comfortable internment that's my guess. Odd thing is, I believe the fellow is doing it out of conviction. He thinks what he's doing is right.'

'Funny sort of war, isn't it? Think Musso's going to walk in here?'

'Winthrop says he is. If it's the case he's taken a hell of a time to make up his mind.'

'If we could get a few more Hurricanes we could give him a bit of a welcome in the air, but I'd say we're mighty thin on the ground.'

'I think Winthrop's wrong. From what little I've been able to get out of the tribesmen who wander around, the Eyeties are too snug in their forts and garrisons up there. They don't want to face the desert.'

'Here's to hoping then. Good luck. Watch your fuel.'

Stephen took off into the speckled sky of dawn and set his course for the border and beyond. His first search proved fruitless and as he turned for home to refuel he began to realise the enormity of the task he had set himself. The vastness of the desert was more apparent from the air than anywhere and how, he began to ask himself, could he possibly spot one figure on its arid wastes other than by pure chance? Nevertheless he determined to persist as long as daylight lasted.

'Any luck?' de Graz asked him as he taxied in.

311

Stephen shook his head. 'None so far,' he said. 'Nothing but that damn desert.'

'Come and have some coffee while they fill her up.'

As they drank Stephen looked again at the maps. He ruled off the area he had covered and shaded it. Then again, he told himself, that might not mean anything, for if Kit was down and wandering about he could well enter it again later on. That possibility could entail his having to go back and cover it once more before nightfall. In the meantime he measured off another square to the west of where he had just come from, set his course and took off again.

He flew low, as low as he dared, and swept the terrain with his eyes. Nothing came up to catch his attention. The desert was as empty as before. And then, just as he began the western leg of his search he saw it. There was a patch of something down on the desert floor, something white against the brown, something that did not fit in with the pattern of the rest.

Banking over, he swung round to investigate. Yes, by God, it was a sheet of material laid out almost like a signal. It *was* a signal. As he drew closer he could see the stones securing it at each corner. And there beside it was a figure waving – he had found him!

Kit heard the aircraft a few minutes after he had picked up the dust of the Italian patrol. He watched it come into view and fly past him on its first leg without deviating towards him. Missed again, he said to himself bitterly. If only when it made its turn, as it surely would, it turned the way he wanted it to. Scrambling down from the knoll once more he shouted and waved his arms. And then with relief surging within him he saw the wings tilt and the pilot begin to turn in his direction. In a moment there was no doubt he had seen something and was coming in to investigate. The Moth came down almost to nought feet and swept over him. As it passed he saw the pilot raise a hand in a signal that he had seen him.

The little aircraft rose and came round again as the pilot made a run over the desert floor to ascertain what part was clear of obstruction to a landing. Coming in on a gentle glide,

312

losing what height he had, holding her almost on the edge of a stall the pilot brought her down and she only ran a few yards before coming to a halt. Whoever he is he knows what he's about, Kit commented to himself as he saw the pilot beckoning to him.

His attention had all been on the aircraft. Suddenly he remembered the Italian patrol and, looking beyond the edge of the knoll, he saw it approaching in the middle distance. In the clear desert air he could make out quite distinctly an armoured car and a lorry bristling with troops bouncing and bumping towards him. They were near enough to be menacing too. He shouted a warning and began to run towards the Moth. He hadn't taken five paces when his ankle gave way and he fell face foremost into the dust.

As he attempted to get to his feet he saw the pilot heave himself from the cockpit, look about him and then run to where he lay. At the same time the machine gun on the armoured car opened up. The range was long and the gunner was not making good shooting but one or two were near enough to be uncomfortable. They struck the rocks and their richochets sent them shrieking into the sky.

Kit was trying to climb to his feet when Stephen reached him. Bending over him, Stephen took in the wings on his chest and the DFC ribbon beneath them with a little throb of pride which was intensified when he saw the wry grin on his son's face. This was the boy he had been told about, unbeatable, undefeated. 'Can you walk?' he said.

''Fraid not. It's my bloody ankle.'

'Put your arm round my shoulders. We'll make it in a three-legged race. And be quick about it. Those ruddy Eyeties are getting too damn close.'

Together they hopped and hobbled the remaining distance between them and the Moth. By this time the riflemen on the lorry had joined in and bullets were kicking up the dust about them.

'It's a good job those wops can't shoot,' Kit said, panting, as he reached for the edge of the cockpit. 'What's happened to that machine gun?'

'Jammed I expect. They can't maintain their weapons. Hop in and look smart about it.'

'Buggered if I can with this ankle.'

'You've ridden. Put up your leg and I'll throw you up.'

'The old horse. Good for him. He never lets you down, does he?' Kit did as he was told and the next second he was bundled into the cockpit.

Stephen had wound the seat belt over the stick to hold her steady when he ran to Kit. Now he reached in to undo it. His fingers fumbled for it had caught somehow and would not come free. The shooting was wild but the range was closing and if they got that machine gun going again things would become really nasty. Stephen swore. He hadn't come so far to be put into the bag by a bunch of Eyeties. And they were getting closer. A bullet hit the engine cowling and spanged off into space.

'What's going on? Won't this bloody thing fly? I never did think much of civilian aircraft,' he heard a voice behind him say.

'Shut up and keep your head down,' Stephen snapped.

At last the belt came free and he dropped into his seat. They were facing the patrol and would have to take off directly over it but there was nothing else for it. He banged the throttle forward. The engine coughed once and burst into full life. But the armoured car was now bearing down on them. And it looked as if they had cleared the machine-gun stoppage. The gunner was traversing his turret towards them. A burst came from it and sand spurted up around their wheels. But the tail of the Moth was coming up and the ground speed was mounting. The armoured car was slap in front of them and the gunner was trying frantically to elevate his gun.

'Too late, chum,' Stephen said as he yanked back the stick and they cleared the turret by inches.

'What ho, she motors! She even flies!' Stephen heard the boy behind him shout, and as they gained flying speed he made derisive finger gestures at the Italians below. Then they were out of range of the stray shots that followed them and setting course for Marsabit.

Presently the airstrip came into view and Stephen brought the Moth in, taxied towards the hut and cut his switches. He threw off his harness and swung himself from his seat. As his feet touched the ground he found that Kit was standing beside

314

him. 'I daresay you don't know who I am,' he said. 'My name's Raymond.'

'Oh, but I do, or I've guessed,' Kit said. 'I've come all this way to find you. I rather think by rights that should be my name too!'

Stephen threw back his head and laughed aloud. 'You're an irrepressible young devil, aren't you?' he said. It occurred to him it was the first time he had really laughed for weeks, if not months. 'Well, that's the way it should be at your age. Let's see if de Graz has any whisky in that hut of his.'

De Graz was walking towards them relief at Kit's safe return written large across his features.

'I've brought him back alive,' Stephen said.

'So I see and a good thing too,' de Graz said soberly. 'Thanks. You may have just about saved my chips when the court of enquiry comes up. Now then, young feller. Let's get together over your combat report.'

Inside the hut he produced a bottle of whisky and the usual battered enamel mugs. As they drank Kit reached into his pocket and took out the letter he had been given. 'I was told to hand you this,' he said to Stephen. 'It's from my mother.'

Stephen stood looking at it for a moment, recognising the once familiar writing on the envelope. 'How did you come by this?' he said.

'Clare de Vaux gave it me. He guessed we'd find each other somehow.'

'Clare? You know him – '

'He's been the best friend to me anyone could ever have had. He said he owed it to you.'

'Clare,' Stephen said again. 'He didn't forget then after all these years. He's an Earl now, I suppose.'

'The old man died just before I came out.'

De Graz stared from one to the other, noting the resemblance. 'You two seem pretty well acquainted,' he said.

'It was that private errand I mentioned to you,' Stephen told him. 'Let's just say we're close relatives.'

De Graz looked down at the sheet of paper on the table before him, noticing the difference in their names. He coughed. 'Well, er, let's get on with this combat report,' he said.

Stephen opened the letter. The sentences that meant everything to him were brief enough. 'When you get this,' he read, 'it will mean that Kit will have found you. It's too long ago and too much has happened for me to try to reclaim him. For the same reasons I can't leave here. I must come to terms with the years that are left as best I can. At least I have the Bay and all that means to me. If you should ever come back – but I must put that thought away from me. There is this terrible war to be won. I hope you will find someone good and kind to look after you. You deserve what luck you can have, darling Stephen, and at least we have our memories from that time when we were young – and now you have Kit. And it means everything to me that you have found each other.'

Stephen's eyes misted as he folded the letter and replaced it in its envelope. He felt nothing but sadness for Babs, but that was what she had chosen, after all, before their lives had drifted so hopelessly apart. He looked at the tousled head of the boy bending over the combat report. He remembered Betty waiting for him at the farm. Thoughts of the man with the piece of lead piping waiting round the corner began to fade.

The fates had relented. For once he could look to the future, not the past. His eyes found the boy again. Kit raised his head, met his glance and grinned. Stephen lifted his mug. 'Maybe,' he breathed, 'I've come lucky at last.'